Dear Reader:

The thinking behind the *Tony Hillerman's Frontier* series which this Ken Englade novel introduces is that truth is not only stranger than fiction but also often more exciting. The traditional "western" gave us gripping tales of gunslingers, cattle barons, clean-cut heroes, fierce Indian horsemen collecting scalps, and the U.S. cavalry racing to the rescue. But, with some notable exceptions, it concerned a frontier as mythic and romantic as Camelot.

Thanks to the work of historians, we now know that what was happening on the western frontier was far more complex than the myths, and far more interesting to today's reader. In the middle years of the 19th century the rules determining who owned that "sea of grass" and the mountains which surround it were being formed. The horse was revolutionizing Indian cultures. Tribes were jostling with tribes over hunting grounds, the Spanish frontier was collapsing, and the new Americans were trickling westward looking for their fortune, their freedom or simply for adventure.

Ken Englade is best known for books focused on notable criminal trials. In this series he taps a lifelong fascination with the history of the American frontier to give us novels of this era as it really was. I hope you will enjoy this as I have and look for future titles in the series, coming soon from HarperPaperbacks.

Sincerely,

*Tony Hillerman*

## BOOKS BY KEN ENGLADE

*Hoffa*

TONY HILLERMAN'S FRONTIER
*People of the Plains*
*The Tribes\**
*The Soldiers\**

NONFICTION
*To Hatred Turned*
*Blood Sister*
*Beyond Reason*
*Murder in Boston*
*Cellar of Horror*
*Deadly Lessons*
*A Family Business*

\*coming soon

# TONY HILLERMAN'S
## ~ FRONTIER ~

# PEOPLE
# *of* THE
# PLAINS

## Ken Englade

**HarperPaperbacks**
*A Division of HarperCollinsPublishers*

This is a work of fiction. The characters, incidents, and dialogues are products of the author's imagination and are not to be construed as real. Any resemblance to actual events or persons, living or dead, is entirely coincidental.

HarperPaperbacks   *A Division of* HarperCollins*Publishers*
10 East 53rd Street, New York, N.Y. 10022

Copyright © 1996 by HarperCollins*Publishers*
All rights reserved. No part of this book may be used or reproduced in any manner whatsoever without written permission of the publisher, except in the case of brief quotations embodied in critical articles and reviews. For information address HarperCollins*Publishers*,
10 East 53rd Street, New York, N.Y. 10022.

Cover illustration by Steven Assel

First printing: March 1996

Printed in the United States of America

HarperPaperbacks and colophon are trademarks of HarperCollins*Publishers*

❖ 10 9 8 7 6 5 4 3 2 1

*For Heidi Jo, the vamp of McCook, NE*

# PEOPLE
*of* THE
# PLAINS

~*~ *1* ~*~

The eight men who made up the council of the Wazhazha band of the Sichangu oyati, the people the white men called the Brulé Sioux, sat cross-legged in the greening grass, luxuriating in the welcome sunshine.

"Truly, this is a magnificent day," commented Scalptaker, the oldest member of the group, "a day as pleasant as any during the Moon When the Strawberries Are Ripe."

"And, as far as I'm concerned, it's not a bit too soon," added Badger. "The winter was a brutal one but *Wi* has finally smiled upon us."

In recognition of the unseasonably fine weather, each of the men, even Fire-in-the-Hills, who had been suffering from a respiratory ailment for months, had shed his stained, smelly buckskin shirt, willingly exposing his winter-tender skin to the new season. Firing up a pipe, they circulated it lazily around their circle, telling each other how good it felt to bask in the springtime sun.

"Listen!" Fire-in-the-Hills said suddenly, cupping a hand behind an ear and cocking his head.

"What is it?" Jagged Blade asked curiously. The second brawniest member of the band, smaller only than Roaring Thunder who stood six feet six inches tall, Jagged Blade was one of the band's best hunters and a fearless warrior who cracked enemy skulls with impunity. But he was not an exceptionally fast thinker and suffered as the butt of countless pranks, all of which he accepted without rancor.

"You mean you don't hear it?" Fire-in-the-Hills asked in sham disbelief.

"No," Jagged Blade replied, tilting his head and furrowing his brow in concentration.

"You really can't hear it? You mean these old ears are sharper than yours?"

Jagged Blade leaned forward, listening intently. But the only sound he could hear, outside the background noise of the camp, was the wind sighing softly through the still-bare trees.

"I don't hear a thing," Jagged Blade confessed in embarrassment.

Fire-in-the-Hills cocked his head and stared into the nearby forest. "I think," he began, struggling to suppress a grin. "I think it's . . . yes, *that's* what it is!"

"*What!*" Jagged Blade demanded, his muscles tensing as if in anticipation of an enemy attack.

"It's winter telling us good-bye," Fire-in-the-Hills replied, simultaneously emitting a long, deep rumble, a magnified but remarkably accurate representation of a death rattle. Although he was considered one of the wisest men in the band when it came to serious decision-making, Fire-in-the-Hills also served as the group's humorist and satirist. During the long winter nights, he entertained the Wazhazhas with dramatic tales of ancient valor, inventive one-man skits, and remarkably accurate animal imitations. His favorites, which he repeated at every opportunity, included the tortured, plaintive cry of a rutting elk and the explosive sound of a buffalo breaking wind.

Jagged Blade looked puzzled at first, then flashed an disconcerted grin. "You caught me again," he mumbled, staring at the ground between his crossed legs.

The members of the group guffawed, especially Fire-in-the-Hills, who laughed so hard he lost his breath. "That was winter's final song," he managed to gasp in between wet, hacking coughs that unintentionally but ironically resembled the noise made by a wounded elk whose lungs were filling with blood.

Roaring Thunder looked at his friend with concern. "Would you like me to get you some water?" he asked solicitously. Despite his great bulk and fearsome name, Roaring Thunder was one of the most tenderhearted of all the Wazhazhas, a born worrier who watched over members of the band like an anxious mother.

"Thank you, but no," said Fire-in-the-Hills, recovering. But his coughing spell had triggered a chill, another reminder that his illness had not completely left him. Removing his buffalo robe from his knees, he flipped it over his bare shoulders and pulled it tight. Seeing that everyone was watching, he tried to make light of his frailty. Reaching down, he yanked a handful of hair from the robe and tossed it into the air. "I think this old skin has seen too many winters," he said. "It is so old it's losing hair faster than a huge-bellied *isan hanska*." Extending a skinny arm, he patted Roaring Thunder on the shoulder. "If you really want to get something for me," he said kindly, "get me a new robe."

"*All* of us could use new robes," added Scalptaker, packing the pipe with a fresh load of their favorite mixture, a carefully measured blend of *shongsasha* and precious white man's tobacco. Lighting it with a brand extracted from the small fire burning in the center of the circle, he took a deep puff and passed it to his left.

Accepting the pipe, Conquering Bear lifted it high, making sure all the council members had a chance to admire anew the instrument he had obtained in a trade with a Cheyenne two and a half years earlier during the gathering of the tribes at the council that resulted in the Treaty of the Long Meadows, the pact called the Treaty of Fort Laramie by the white men. "I think I did well," he said proudly.

Fire-in-the-Hills rolled his eyes, having heard Conquering Bear boast about his accomplishment throughout the last two winters. He was ready to fire back an acid remark when Buffalo Heart, anticipating trouble, cut him off. "It is, indeed, a handsome pipe," Buffalo Heart agreed.

One of the younger warriors, Buffalo Heart was more of a politician than a fighter and it was his ambition to follow Conquering Bear into a position of prominence on the council. As a result, he was overly protective of the older man and was not above using shameless flattery to make Conquering Bear look favorably upon him. "Look at that graceful stem and that intricately carved bowl," he gushed. "You must have spent a lot of time polishing it this winter because it shines so beautifully."

Conquering Bear beamed. "It was such a good bargain, too," he said. "All I gave the Sihiyena in return was an old hunting pouch."

"Yes," Fire-in-the-Hills replied sarcastically, speaking quickly before Buffalo Heart could interject his fawning comments, "you drive a tough bargain. But isn't that to be expected from the Chief of All the Lakotas?"

In addition to his self-imposed duty as top entertainer, Fire-in-the-Hills also took it upon himself to serve as the band's main ego deflator and Conquering Bear was one of his favorite targets. In his view,

Conquering Bear had become much too pompous ever since he was designated the official signer for the tribe on the Long Meadows treaty.

Conquering Bear, aware of what Fire-in-the-Hills was trying to do, spun angrily on his adversary. "Careful," he warned. "You're treading on dangerous ground! You may have escaped the lung sickness but you might still have to reckon with me."

Fire-in-the-Hills grinned, delighted that his dart had hit. "Forgive me," he said in mock apology. "We've been confined to our lodges for too long."

That just made Conquering Bear angrier. "You know that title was forced upon me by the *isan hanska*," he said indignantly. "I didn't want it; I tried to refuse it."

"Obviously, you didn't try hard enough," countered Fire-in-the-Hills.

A one-time accomplished hunter who had allowed his lean frame to become pudgy and soft, Conquering Bear glared at the younger man. "As even someone of your limited intelligence is aware," he said hotly, "it is not our custom to have a single chief, to rely upon one man to make all the decisions. I'm not the Chief of All the Lakotas; I'm only one council member in one band. I can't speak for all the Wazhazhas, much less all the Brulés, and certainly not for the other tribes that compose the Lakotas: the Oglalas, the Miniconjou, the Itazichola, the Ohinupa, the Hunkpapa, and the Sihasapa. It is the delusion of the *isan hanska* to believe that I can. That just proves how foolish the white men are."

"Listen to you," interjected Blizzard, a sharp-faced, quick-tempered brave with more than two dozen coups to his credit. "Both of you. You sound like women arguing over a buffalo tongue."

Fire-in-the-Hills shrugged. He had made his point and it was too beautiful a day to waste any more of it arguing with someone as stubborn and self-important as Conquering Bear.

For a long time, no one said anything, remaining content, it seemed, to soak up the sun, smoke the pipe, and revel in the feeling of liberation from winter's stranglehold. A thin cloud of smoke from the campfire hovered over the group like a giant halo before dissipating in a gentle breeze that swept down the snowcapped mountains at their backs. Although it was little more than a zephyr, they all recognized it as a precursor to the normal springtime wind that would reach tree-bending force by late afternoon and threaten to blow away anything not tied down.

A hundred yards away a half-dozen naked boys scampered noisily along the shore of the creek, each of them carrying a miniature bow and a handful of small, blunt-ended arrows. They carefully skirted the shaded banks, which remained covered in snow, and stayed well away from the water, which was now mostly ice-free but still cold enough to instantly numb the limbs of anyone so foolish as to attempt an early-season dip. Laughing and squealing, playing some impromptu game, the boys bounded with energy accumulated during the long, dark months they had been confined to their cozy but insufferably confining hide-walled tipis. This was their first chance to break free of their mothers' watchful gaze and they seemed as determined to enjoy it as the men sitting in the council circle.

Hearing their carefree laughter, Badger, who had watched the Conquering Bear/Fire-in-the-Hills debate disinterestedly, looked up. A compact, athletic man in his late twenties, he was known for his good humor, his zest for combat, and his extraordinary skill with a bow. In the period before the lull in intertribal warfare that resulted from the Treaty of Fort Laramie, Badger had led a number of highly successful war parties against the Brulés' traditional enemies, the Crow and Pawnee, and had accumulated considerable honors. But much of his spirit had gone out of him the previous autumn when his only son had died, a victim of cholera that had been brought to the Sichangu by the white emigrants on their westward trek. Hearing the boys' laughter had reminded Badger of his loss. Broken Antler would be with them, he thought, smiling wistfully, but for the Sickness. Because he was distracted by his thoughts, he only half-heard Blizzard impatiently demand that the council get down to business.

"It is time we talked of serious matters," Blizzard intoned, tapping Badger on the knee for emphasis.

"And what is that?" asked Badger, tearing his attention away from the boys.

"Scalptaker said it earlier," Blizzard replied. "We need new robes. We also need fresh meat. In short, what we need is a hunt. We should begin a search for the buffalo before they lose their winter coats."

Blizzard's statement was met with silence.

"We all know it isn't that simple," Buffalo Heart finally said. "There is much more to be considered than a hunt."

"This past winter had been especially hard on the horse herd," said Badger. "Many of the animals died in the storms that never seemed to cease."

"Before we can even consider a hunt, we have to devise a way to replace the lost horses," said Roaring Thunder.

"Are you *all* old women?" Blizzard asked contemptuously. "Do I have to jab you with my lance to awaken you to the fact that we need to make some decisions?"

"What do *you* propose?" Fire-in-the-Hills asked, staring intently at Blizzard, all joviality gone from his voice.

If Fire-in-the-Hills was the group's comedian, Blizzard was his polar opposite. A humorless, unsmiling man given quickly to anger, he was nevertheless an unquestionably brave warrior. The tale was still told around the campfires of how, three winters before, he had sneaked into the lodge of a Pawnee he believed had killed his brother during an earlier raid. While everyone in the lodge slept, Blizzard crawled to where the man was snoring on his stack of buffalo robes, slit his throat with a fine, sharp knife he had taken off a dead fur trader, and then slipped out again as quietly as he had entered. Blizzard was well-named because his heart was as cold as a February storm; he showed no mercy toward anyone who crossed him, no matter if the victim was one of the Sichangu's sworn enemies, the Crow or the Pawnee, or one of his own people.

"What I suggest is very simple," Blizzard snapped, unflinchingly meeting Fire-in-the-Hills's gaze. When he moved, smooth muscles rippled along his back and shoulders, making a huge, raised scar on the upper left side of his chest, a reminder of a hand-to-hand combat with a Pawnee whom he subsequently eviscerated, ripple like a caterpillar wriggling along a cotton-wood trunk. "As Conquering Bear said, even you might be able to understand it. We must have new horses and there's only one reasonable place to get them: the same place we have always gotten them—from the Kangi."

"The Crows *do* have good horses," Fire-in-the-Hills acknowledged. "Almost as good as those of the scat-eating Padani who left you with that souvenir. It's too bad their warriors aren't as good with their knives as they are at training horses," he added, wanting to show Blizzard that he was not intimidated.

"But neither the Padani nor the Kangi would be will-ing to trade with us," said Jagged Blade.

Blizzard shot him a scornful glance. "Don't be an idiot! Who said anything about trade? I suggest we steal them. It is the Kangi's destiny that they breed good horses and train them well. It is ours that we go and take them."

"And *you*," Scalptaker interjected. "Would you so easily disregard the promises we made at the Long Meadows?"

"Yes," echoed Fire-in-the-Hills. "Would you be willing to break the terms of the treaty?"

"The treaty is a farce," Blizzard spat. "It is nothing but an attempt by the white man to keep us from showing how strong we are. The *isan hanska* were very clever. They tricked us into going along with an agreement that forbids us from making war with the Kangi and the Padani. They may as well demand that we stop breathing. It is our nature that we make war with our sworn enemies, and no piece of white man's paper is going to stop us."

"He's right," added Buffalo Heart. "Just because the *isan hanska* feels we should embrace the Kangi like brothers doesn't mean that is what we have to do. I remember what they did to my uncle. He fell bravely in battle, but they humiliated us all by mutilating him. They skinned him, hacked off his limbs, and took turns tasting his blood. I hope I'll have the chance to do the same to one of them and I don't want the white man to tell me that I can't. Blizzard is right; we are not pawns of the *isan hanska*."

"Why should we spend so much time considering a horse cutting against the Kangi," said Jagged Blade. "The *isan hanska* themselves are even easier targets, plodding along in their clumsy wagons with their pale, soft-skinned women and squalling children."

"I agree!" Badger added forcefully, causing the others to stare at him in surprise. "The treaty also prohibits us from attacking the whites moving through our territory, but it is the whites who brought us the illness that killed my son. That is something I will never be able to forgive."

"Everyone has lost relatives in the diseases that have afflicted us since the coming of the white man," Scalptaker argued. "But that is part of the nature of our existence. Change always comes, and with it sometimes undesirable results."

"We're talking about two different things," said Buffalo Heart. "The issue is not whether we should move against the white man but whether we should organize a horse raid against the Kangi."

"For now," Conquering Bear said, joining the discussion, "we should abide by our agreement to leave the white man's caravans alone. It behooves us to avoid open hostility until we see how powerful the white warriors prove to be. Besides, who among us would give up the presents that come every year?"

"The presents!" Blizzard barked contemptuously. "The annuity! It is just a bribe. The whole treaty is of no more substance than smoke and the annuity is a bone the white men have tossed us to try to get us to do their bidding."

Scalptaker cleared his throat, signalling he was about to speak. The other members of the group turned to him respectfully, honoring his position as elder. "You are forgetting one thing," he said softly.

"And what is that?" Blizzard asked sardonically.

"What is important," the aging warrior explained patiently, as if lecturing a child, "is that we gave our word to live by the terms of the treaty, whether we now agree with the treaty or not. If we would go against our word just because we need a few horses, what does that mean for us in any future dealings with the white man?"

"That is nonsense!" barked Blizzard. "It is time that all of you recognized that the *isan hanska* are our enemies as much as the Padani and the Kangi. They fight us in a different way. Rather than meet us face-to-face, as warriors, they send among us people infected with poisons that strike us with a horribleness such as we have never known. Last year there was the red-spot sickness that caused terrible sores to erupt on our bodies, making even brave warriors scream and whimper. Have you forgotten Man-with-Many-Coups and how he was in such agony that he shoved an arrow down his throat to end his misery?"

"That's true," added Jagged Blade. "They eradicate the beaver and frighten away the antelope, the elk, and the bear. Every year it becomes harder to find the buffalo because the *isan hanska* kill them for pleasure and drive them farther and farther to the west, forcing us to go into Kangi territory."

"What do the white men do to keep their part of the bargain?" asked Blizzard. "Last summer the soldiers at Fort Laramie killed three of our Miniconjou brothers for no reason at all. The white men talk grandly about peace but they have been the first to bloody the ground."

"The Miniconjous were not exactly blameless," Fire-in-the-Hills retorted. "It was a Miniconjou who fired first at the soldiers."

"If that is the case . . ." Blizzard began.

"Enough!" exclaimed Scalptaker. "Quit bickering like children. Let us all talk reasonably, like the wise men and brave warriors we are supposed to be. Our immediate responsibility is not to decide how to deal with the white man but whether we should raid the Kangi horse herd. Undeniably, we need horses. So what happens if we don't have a horse-lifting? Without adequate horses we would be particularly vulnerable if *they* decide to send a war party against *us*. Let us discuss, in a measured manner, not only the feasibility of sending out a horse-stealing party but the feasibility of *not* sending one out. If we intend to be around for another winter we have to come to agreement on what to do this spring."

Roaring Thunder reached for the bags of *shongsasha* and tobacco and began refilling the pipe, which had been forgotten in the discussion and set aside to grow cold. "Scalptaker is wise," he said quietly. "Let us consider."

Summer Rain struck with rattlesnake-like swiftness. Leaning slightly forward from her kneeling position, she plunged her index finger and thumb into the spot she had cleared in Badger's thick, midnight-dark hair, deftly seizing the tiny white louse that was scrambling frantically to escape among the tightly packed roots. As she expertly cracked the parasite with her right thumbnail, she was already parting a new patch with her left, searching for yet another potential victim. Her efficiency had been gained from years of experience. Delousing was a skill that Brulé women began learning almost as soon as they were old enough to walk, so her task was no longer one that required total concentration. She could search for vermin with her fingers and let her mind wander down other, more important paths.

Flicking her gaze from her husband's scalp to his face, visible only in profile as he lay prone on a beaver skin, she could see that he was almost asleep, lulled into semiconsciousness by the familiar, soothing process. Now, she thought, rocking back on her haunches, is as good a time as any to bring it up.

After the council meeting, at which it had been decided to send a warrior party to the Crow camp along the Yellowstone River, a hard trek to the northwest, Badger and Summer Rain had wandered into the forest, where they rested in a small thicket to savor the early afternoon sun.

"Ata," Summer Rain whispered softly, using the word that meant "father," which was how Brulé women respectfully addressed their husbands.

Badger's left eyelid flickered but did not open.

"Ata," she repeated, speaking louder.

"Ummmm," Badger mumbled, still not opening his eye.

"I hesitate to disturb you, Father," she said respectfully, "but there is something we need to discuss. Are you awake?"

"I am *now*," Badger replied in forced irritation. It wasn't a good idea to let a woman, even one's wife, become too demanding.

"Maybe this is a bad time," Summer Rain said coyly.

Badger rolled over on his back, exposing a hairless, well-muscled chest.

"All right, Ina," he said, letting her know by his tone and the use of the word that meant "mother" that he was not truly angry. "I'm awake. What is it you want to talk about? But," he added, smiling, "what's so important that you would rouse your husband when he's trying to get a little much-needed rest before going out to risk his life against the Crow?"

Summer Rain suppressed a smile. She knew her husband was no more worried about the potential dangers of the forthcoming horse-lifting than he was about the return of winter.

"I was thinking," she said solemnly, "about Broken Antler."

Badger sobered at the mention of his dead son's name. "I think about him too," he said. "Sometimes I imagine I can still hear his laughter. It's hard to believe he's dead."

"I find it hard to accept, too," Summer Rain agreed. "But life has to go on. We need to put his death behind us."

Badger looked at her closely. "We've talked about this before," he said. "We agreed that we wouldn't dwell on it. Why are you bringing it up?"

Summer Rain paused. "I think it's time we called a *waki cagapi*," she said, watching carefully for his reaction.

"A feast to release his spirit?" Badger asked in surprise. "You don't think it might be a little premature?"

"No," Summer Rain replied slowly. "It's been more than six months. It's time we put away our grief."

"And you think this is a propitious time?"

"Well," Summer Rain said, smiling slightly, "I didn't mean tomorrow."

"When?" he asked, sounding more abrupt than he intended.

Summer Rain paused. "I'm not sure," she said. "Perhaps next month, maybe even the month after."

Badger's mind was racing, he was thinking of all the preparations that would need to be made: the recovery from the spirit-keeper of the bundle that contained a lock of Broken Antler's hair . . . the notification that would have to go out to the military societies . . . the pipe that would have to be sent to Scalptaker, who would be sought as the master of ceremonies . . . the spirit posts that would have to be cut with a knife purified by the smoke of a sweetgrass fire. . . . and the food that would need to be collected for the feast.

"It will take some time to do all this," Badger pointed out. "In fact, we really should wait until after the hunt so we know we'll have enough meat."

"As always," she said, "you are right. But we need to start planning it. We won't be the only ones involved. Some new parents will want to take advantage of the ceremony to announce the names they have given their children. Others will want to use the opportunity to sponsor a ritual ear-piercing."

Badger grunted. "It gets very complicated, doesn't it?"

Summer Rain laughed. "Only if you're a man. It's the woman who does the work. I'll begin making preparations while you're gone. Then we can formally announce the ceremony. The more I think about it, the more I think that a good time would be in the Moon When the Chokecherries Are Red."

Badger nodded. "That sounds reasonable. Two and a half months isn't too long to plan ahead for something like that."

For awhile, neither of them said anything; the issue was settled: The ceremony would be scheduled for July.

"There's one other thing," Summer Rain said tentatively, glancing sideways at Badger.

"Ummmm," he said distractedly. With talk of the *waki cagapi* completed, he had turned his mind to the preparations he would have to make for a more immediate event: the horse raid. He and a dozen others, including Blizzard, Jagged Blade, and Roaring Thunder, along with his younger brother, Running Antelope, and two other budding warriors, young Wazhazha men anxious to collect their first scalps or count their first coup, would depart on foot in two days, carrying only their weapons, extra moccasins, and enough food to last them on the sustained march. There would be no time to stop to hunt; once they got into Crow territory their lives were potentially at risk since any Crow they might run across would automatically assume that the Sichangu were interlopers. Once they crossed the boundary there would be no cooking fires and no loitering. They would have to move rapidly, strike quickly, and escape as swiftly as possible back to their own territory because the Crow would be in hot pursuit.

"You aren't listening to me," Summer Rain said somewhat crossly.

Badger blinked. "Of course I am, Ina" he said. "I *always* listen to you."

"You weren't listening to me then."

"I was," he protested. "What did you say?"

Summer Rain laughed. "See. I knew you weren't listening."

"Well, what did you *say*? I can't be expected to remember everything."

"I said," she said quietly, blushing slightly, "that it is also time we thought about having another child."

"Oh ho!" Badger laughed. "That isn't what you said; that is only what you *wanted* to say."

"What difference does it make if I actually said it," Summer Rain replied. "I was *thinking* it."

"But I'm no mind reader," Badger said. "If you want me to respond, you have to get my attention."

"All right," Summer Rain said determinedly, "I'll get your attention! Will this help?" she asked slyly, reaching behind her and pulling her buckskin dress over her head in a single, effortless gesture.

Badger glanced appreciatively at his wife, his eyes lingering on her upturned breasts topped with nipples the size and color of freshly roasted hickory nuts. Slowly his gaze slid down her body, moving past her slim waist, her stomach as flat as it was before she became pregnant with Broken Antler, to her firm thighs. Over the last few months he had been too preoccupied with thoughts about Broken Antler and the boy's lingering, pitiful death to give much thought to sex. But spring had truly arrived and his sap, as well as that of the trees in the surrounding forest, was beginning to rise. For the first time since he could remember, he felt desire surge through his body.

Summer Rain eyed him carefully, watching in satisfaction as his leather breeches trembled and rose. "I would say," she whispered, "that I still know how to make my husband listen."

"And *act* as well," he replied in a voice half an octave

deeper than normal. His right arm snaked out, grabbing Summer Rain's thin wrist. Without perceptible effort, he tugged, using the strength in his shoulders to pull her forward.

Summer Rain squealed in delight, throwing her naked body on top of his so she could feel his erect member hard against her stomach.

From his position on his back, Badger could see that her nipples had tightened and shriveled, looking, he thought, as delectable as dried blueberries.

"If you expect to plant another son," Summer Rain exclaimed, her breath coming in rapid pants, "you had first better get rid of these." Slipping her strong fingers into the waistband of his trousers, she pulled them downward until they were below his knees.

When he leaned forward to slip them over his feet, she swiveled to the side and rose to her knees. Placing her hands on his bent back, she pushed hard, sending him sprawling off the buffalo robe on which he had been reclining.

"You have my place," she said, laughing at the startled expression on his face. While he struggled to regain his balance, she stretched on the robe, spreading her legs slightly and holding out her arms.

"Come, my husband," she breathed, "let's make a strong new warrior-to-be."


The group of boys who earlier had been playing along the creek was returning to the camp from their day-long adventure deep into the forest. When they were almost to the collection of tipis, which were lined along the creek in an orderly semicircle, one of them stopped abruptly.

"Did you hear that?" Prairie Dog asked.

Pausing in midstride, the oldest of the group, a youth

of about nine, raised his hand, bringing the small party
to a halt. "You're right," Bear's Ear said excitedly.
"There *is* something moving in there."

Six pairs of ears strained to identify the sounds, muf-
fled and made indistinct by the noise of the creek, which
was flowing full with snow-melt. Earlier, they had been
playing "raider," a game in which they pretended to be
braves on a war party. With their imaginations running
full tilt, they interpreted the indistinct noise to be a band
of clumsy *toka* sneaking up on their tipis.

"They're looking for scalps!" Bear's Ear said. "They
want to catch the camp at a moment when everyone is
relaxed."

"Let's run give a warning," White Wolf, one of the
younger members of the group, said nervously, his face
pale with fright.

"No!" Bear's Ear said sharply.

"Why not?" asked Thunderstorm, apparently siding
with White Dog.

"If we could stop them ourselves, we could gain
much honor," Bear's Ear argued.

His suggestion was met with silence.

"What could we, six young boys, do to stop a raiding
party?" Thunderstorm asked.

"We could jump one of them and take his weapons
and use them against the others," Bear's Ear proposed.

"I don't know . . ." Prairie Dog said indecisively.

"At least," Bear's Ear urged, "let's scout them out.
Then we can report exactly how many *toka* are sneaking
up on us."

The boys looked at each other. That made sense.
They didn't actually have to *fight* with the raiding party.
All they had to do was creep close enough to determine
its strength. That would still bring them much honor;
they all would be heroes.

Seeing that he had won them over, Bear's Ear

notched a blunted arrow, readying his half-sized bow. Raising a finger to his lips, he cautioned silence. Dropping into a crouch, he began moving silently into the forest in the direction of the noise. Carefully, one by one, the other boys fell into line behind him.

After five minutes of quiet movement, they could see sunlight ahead, indicating a clearing. The closer they got, the more audible the sound became.

"For *toka*, they're making an awful lot of noise," White Wolf whispered. The reward for his observation was a warning glare from Bear's Ear.

As they approached the clearing, the underbrush grew thinner, allowing them to sneak to the very edge of the opening. When they peaked through the leaves, they saw not a group of fiercely painted enemy warriors but Badger and Summer Rain cavorting on a buffalo skin robe.

Immediately recognizing the activity for what it was, Bear's Ear turned away in disgust. "Ughhh," he said, making a face. "Let's get out of here."

The others reversed their courses and were starting to slink away as well, all except for Red Elk, the youngest member of the group, a boy of about six. "So *that's* how it's done," he exclaimed, his mouth open in amazement.

Bear's Ear did not bother to answer; he simply grabbed the younger boy's arm and jerked him forcefully away.

Secretary of War Jefferson Davis marched straight to his liquor cabinet and poured himself a stiff shot of French brandy, the better to calm the pangs of indigestion set into motion by his lunch with General Hawkins.

A supercilious two-star in Operations and Planning who was still mad at Davis for cutting his budget when the secretary had been a senator from Mississippi, Hawkins had ruined the Excelsior's normally superb lamb chops with his ranting about Manifest Destiny and the need to "exterminate the filthy red savages" who were "impeding Westward expansion."

There's just so much of that shit a man can take, Davis said to himself, tipping the half-full snifter. The golden liquid slid down his throat and settled warmly in his stomach, instantly brightening his mood. Sighing contentedly and wetly smacking his lips, Davis erased Hawkins from his thoughts as easily as he shed his claw hammer coat, which he tossed nonchalantly across a nearby Queen Anne chair. Loosening his tie and kicking off his handsome, handmade calfskin boots, Davis gathered a stack of reports that had just arrived from the Department of the Army and stretched out on the horsehair couch that ran along the far wall of his inner office. With the paperwork perfectly balanced on his ample paunch, Davis began to read. Within minutes his eyes grew heavy and slowly closed. He was snoring quietly when Captain Hayward V. Browning, his pedantic, Boston-bred aide-de-camp, rapped twice on the heavy oak door.

"Sir!" Browning barked in the parade-ground bellow he obviously thought necessary to protect his soldierly image.

Davis opened one eye and focused it on Browning, sighting over the dead-white toe that protruded through a gaping hole in the sock on his right foot. "What is it, captain?" he asked crossly, irritated at having his siesta interrupted. Davis harbored a secret suspicion that Browning's assignment to his office somehow had been engineered by Hawkins.

"You dropped your reports, sir," Browning said archly, pointing to the papers that had slipped off Davis's stomach and fallen to the floor.

"Oh," Davis said in mild surprise, working himself upright. "Damned interesting reading, too," he added. "After-action reports about last summer's Indian killings at Fort Laramie. Did you read them?"

"No, sir."

"You should," Davis said. "They're damned interesting. Goes to show how the Army can really fuck up a situation, especially one that involves the Indians."

At the mention of possible Army misconduct, Browning recoiled as if he had been struck.

"When is the Army going to learn it can't run roughshod over the Lakotas? They're proud people and it's *their* land. We should act like grateful guests, not like their masters. They're not a bunch of nigrahs."

"No, sir, they're not," Browning answered dutifully, in actuality totally indifferent to what happened to a group he considered nothing less than simpleminded barbarians.

"I don't understand why the Army doesn't listen to people with frontier experience before they formulate Indian policy. Did I ever tell you that *I* served on the frontier, back in my Army days?"

Browning rolled his eyes. "Yes, sir. You've told me. Several times."

Davis glared at him. "What did you want?" he asked icily, making a mental note to see what he could do about getting a new aide-de-camp.

"Senator Fontenot is here to see you, sir," Browning said stiffly.

Davis's eyebrows shot up. "Emile?" he said in surprise. "Did he say what he wanted?"

"No, sir. But," he added, wrinkling his nose, "he did *not* have an appointment."

"An appointment? For Christ's sake, captain, Emile is an old friend as well as a powerful senator. He doesn't *need* an appointment. Do I have anything on my calendar this afternoon?"

"No, sir."

"Then send the senator in."

"Yes, sir," Browning said, turning away.

The aide was almost out the door when Davis had an afterthought. "Wait, captain," he said. "Give me a minute to get my boots back on."

"Yes, sir."

"One other thing, captain."

"Yes, sir?"

"Take that ramrod out of your ass."

Browning reddened. "Yes, sir."

"Hey, Emile," Davis cried happily when the senator, a tall, rail-thin man with snow-white hair and deep circles under his eyes, walked in. "Damn, it's good to see you."

"It's good to see you, too, Jefferson," Fontenot said, warmly clasping the war secretary's proffered hand. "It's been a long time. Too damn long. But you know how it is when Congress is in session."

"All *too* well." Jefferson grinned.

"*That's* right," Fontenot said, slapping himself on the forehead. "For some reason I keep forgetting that. I must be getting senile."

"If that's the case," Davis replied easily, "I hope I get as senile as you."

Fontenot smiled. "Ever the politician, Jefferson. One of these days I swear you're going to be president."

Davis laughed. "In a pig's ass. I wouldn't be able to stand the bureaucracy. And the country, much less Washington, would never be able to stand *me*. That's one of the problems with being an old Army officer; we tend to say what we think rather than what everyone else wants to hear. God," he added apologetically, "my manners are deserting me. Have a seat. How about a cigar? A glass of brandy? It's very good stuff. French. Straight off the boat. I have a few kegs sent over every year."

"I'll pass on the cigar," Fontenot said, "but I never turn down a glass of good French brandy."

Davis grinned. "That's the old Emile I know. Sit down. I'll pour."

Since Davis had not bothered to don his coat, Fontenot felt at liberty to remove his as well. When Davis returned with the brandy, they clicked glasses and toasted each other's health. For several minutes, they sat in silence, sipping their drinks and enjoying each other's company. "What *do* you think?" Fontenot finally said.

"Excuse me?" Davis said, puzzled.

"*Think*," Fontenot repeated. "You said earlier that you say what you think."

"Oh." Davis laughed. "I'm always happy to share my thoughts. Did you have any particular subject in mind?"

"How about the national situation?" Fontenot asked. "Does it look different from a cabinet member's office than it does from a senator's?"

Davis's face fell. "No, Emile," he said grimly, "I'm afraid it doesn't. I can feel the tension growing by the day. It's almost palpable. There are strong minds on both sides of the slavery issue and, mark my words, there's not going to be any compromise."

"I think you're right," Fontenot said solemnly. "I don't see any solution either. As much as I hate it, I see war coming. And it's going to be a very bad war, one that will make that little fracas with Mexico look like a picnic on the Potomac. It's going to be North versus South and it's going to be very, *very* bloody."

"Yes," Davis agreed. "And long, too. This one, when it comes, isn't going to be settled in a few weeks or months. Things have been festering too long; there's way too much hatred."

"Amen," said Fontenot. "The only good news is I don't see it happening any time soon. Maybe if we're lucky we won't be around to see it at all."

Davis smiled slightly. "To hell with that, Emile. I don't know about you, but I intend to be around for quite a while yet. I'm certainly not anxious for another war, the Mexican conflict cured me of that, but I don't think I'm going to be dead and buried before it comes. If I were a betting man, I'd say three years. Five at the most."

Fontenot shook himself like a dog climbing out of a lake. "I don't want to think about it," he said, downing the brandy that remained in his glass. "Not yet. Not right now."

"Well, look on the bright side, my friend. When it does come you'll be too old to fight. And you don't have any sons. Elizabeth, God rest her soul, blessed you only with a daughter."

Fontenot stared at the floor and looked so glum that Davis worried he had said something to send him into a depression. Maybe the remark about his late wife . . .

"Can I have another thimbleful of that brandy?" Fontenot said, straightening.

"Sure," Davis said, relieved. "Then maybe you'll tell me why you're here. I don't think you took time out of your busy day to talk about the problems between the North and the South. You know that situation as well as I do."

"No," Fontenot said with a tight smile. "I should have known you'd see through that. I'd like to talk to you about a personal matter."

"Personal?" Davis said in surprise, pouring a healthy dollop into Fontenot's snifter. "What the hell? Do you want to borrow money?"

"I wish it were that simple." Fontenot laughed. "No, this is much more serious. It has to do with Marie."

"Your *daughter*? What could possibly be the problem there? Ever since Elizabeth died you've done a wonderful job of raising her. You've . . . "

"No," Fontenot interrupted. "I didn't put that exactly right. It deals only *indirectly* with Marie."

Davis looked puzzled. "I don't understand."

"Of course you don't, Jefferson. How could you? Let me explain."

"Please do. And while you're doing it are you sure you won't have a smoke?"

Fontenot shrugged. "Why the hell not."

Davis reached for a delicately carved teakwood box

that rested on the table at his elbow. Removing the lid, he extended it to his guest. Fontenot took one of the cigars, bit the end off and looked around for some place to spit it.

"There," said Davis, pointing with his chin at a brass spittoon sitting on the floor at the end of the couch.

Taking a cigar for himself, Davis chomped off the end, hawked it into the spittoon, and produced a match from a waistcoat pocket. Striking it with a thumbnail, he lit Fontenot's cigar, then his own.

Settling back, he nodded. "Okay, my friend. Shoot. Tell me about the *indirect* problem with Marie and what I can do about it."

"The problem," Fontenot began slowly, "is Brevet Second Lieutenant Jean Francois Xavier Benoit the third."

Davis bolted upright. "Jean Benoit?" he asked in surprise. "The Jean Benoit from New Orleans? The son of your best friend . . . "

"Yep . . . "

"The one who's working now in the Army Department?"

"That's the one."

"If he's violating Marie . . . "

"Hold on, Jefferson," Fontenot said. "before you get too excited, let me tell you what *I* think."

"Okay," Davis said, leaning back. "Tell me."

"*I* think," Fontenot said uncomfortably, "that it's the other way around. I think Marie is seducing him."

"*What*?" Davis said, popping forward again.

"Well, Jefferson," Fontenot said calmly, "when you stop and think about it, it shouldn't be too surprising. Times are changing; women have different ideas now than they did when we were young. They . . . "

"That's no excuse," Davis said. "I'll see to it that young scamp . . . "

"No, no, no," Fontenot said, signalling his friend to calm down. "That's not the point."

"Well, what *is* the point? If Benoit is having an affair with Marie . . . "

"I'm *sure* he is," Fontenot said, "but I don't think it's all his fault."

"Well, that's mighty damn understanding of you, Emile. If it were my Jane . . . "

"But it *isn't* your Jane," Fontenot interrupted. "You see, I figure this is a lot my fault."

"*Your* fault? How could it be your fault?"

"I didn't see to it that Marie got the proper upbringing. After Elizabeth died I had no interest in remarrying . . . "

"That's understandable . . . "

". . . and I couldn't bring myself to send her to the convent. That's what I should have done. Let the nuns at the Ursulines Academy teach her right from wrong. But she didn't want to go and I didn't want her to go. She was all I had left and I couldn't stand being separated from her. So I took the coward's way out, the selfish old man's way. I tried to do it myself. And I botched it. Right now all she sees is Jean Benoit; he's her ticket out of the Fontenot household. Out of Washington, actually. And I don't want that to happen."

For what seemed a long time neither man said anything. Finally, Davis broke the silence. "Well, old friend, what do you want me to do?"

Fontenot paused. "I think I have a solution," he said. "Or at least a plan. Marie is a good girl. She's beautiful. She's intelligent . . . "

"True enough . . . "

"She would make some man a very good wife."

"*Some* man," Davis said. "But not Jean Benoit."

"Right," Fontenot nodded. "*Not* Jean Benoit. Neither of them knows it, but they're not really in love. Not," he said quickly, "that *love* really has anything to do with it . . . "

"I understand," Davis said quietly.

"What I'm trying to say is, they're just not made for each other. If they got married, it would be a disaster. He's a *soldier*, for God's sake. His father may be one of the best maritime attorneys in New Orleans, in the entire South for that matter, but t-Jean — that's what he's called at home — t-Jean wanted to go to West Point. Holy Jesus, *I* got him the appointment! So in a way, I'm responsible for him too."

"I see," Davis said slowly.

"You do?" Fontenot said, surprised.

"I *think* so. What you're trying to say is that you feel a tremendous obligation to both of them, Marie and Benoit. Even though you love them individually, you don't love them enough to see them get married. Or maybe I should say that you love them too much to see them marry each other."

"That's right," Fontenot said, bobbing his head. "It wouldn't be good for either one. It . . . "

"So you need to find a way to separate them," Davis interrupted. "And that's where I come in?"

"You're a damn smart man, Jefferson. For someone from Mississippi, that is."

Davis grinned. "Spare me the flattery you old swamp rat. Okay," he continued, "I think I can arrange it. One advantage of being Secretary of War is having some influence with the Army. Where do you want him posted?"

Fontenot's face sagged. "Just like that?" he said. "It scares me to think how much power I have over people's lives."

"Me, too," Davis agreed. "But I try not to let it keep me awake at night. I assume you want him someplace far away, someplace where it would be almost impossible for Marie to join him?"

"That would be nice," Fontenot said. "But I don't want to ruin his career. I think too much of his father. Of him, too, actually. He's a fine young man. He's . . . "

"I get the idea, Emile. You want him *absent* and you want him *distant*, but you want him to have a chance to carve his own niche. Is that it?"

"Precisely," Fontenot said, looking more relaxed than at any time since he walked in. "Do you want to tell me what you have in mind? Or do I want to know?"

"Yes," Davis said solemnly. "I think you need to know. It *is* your idea."

"I knew you were going to say that," Fontenot said. "I guess I'm not going to get off the hook after all."

"No, you're not, Emile. Every man has to be responsible for his own actions. That's one thing the Army taught me."

"Okay," Fontenot said with resignation. "What do you have in mind?"

"Fort Laramie," Davis replied quickly.

"*Fort Laramie?* You mean way the hell out there in Nebraska territory? Good God, man, that's the end of the earth . . . "

". . . almost."

". . . That's Injun country."

". . . You're right."

". . . A man could get *killed* out there."

". . . He could."

". . . For Christ's sake, he could get *scalped*."

". . . There's a chance of that, too."

"Jesus, Jefferson," Fontenot said, blanching, "I don't know . . . "

"Oh, come on, Emile," Davis said firmly. "Knock off the shit. You come in here and ask me to help you get your daughter's lover, the guy who's screwing your darling Marie, transferred someplace where he can't be sticking his hands up her dress and I agree to help. And then you start having second thoughts."

"But, God, Jefferson, *Fort Laramie* . . . "

"Look, Emile," Davis said gently, placing his hand on his friend's shoulder. "It isn't *that* bad. Benoit, after all, *is* a soldier. No one promised him life was going to be beautiful. And Fort Laramie, contrary to what you might think, is not the *worst* place I could send him. It sure as hell ain't Washington and it sure as hell ain't New Orleans, but it's probably a lot more civilized than you think. Besides, if you want to look at it this way, it probably will be *good* for him. If he's serious about the Army . . . "

"Oh, I think he is. That's one reason I came to you. I can't see Marie married to a soldier. I know her too well."

"If he's serious about the Army," Davis repeated patiently, "this could even be good for his career. He'll have the chance to develop some leadership qualities. Nobody out there is going to powder his butt for him. You see this?" Davis said, reaching for the stack of papers he had been reading when Browning interrupted him.

"Yes. But what . . . "

"These are action reports," Davis said. "About an incident between the Army and a bunch of Miniconjou Sioux, a branch of the Lakotas. Best I can figure from these papers, some brave who wanted to make a name for himself took a wild shot at one of the soldiers. Didn't hit him, of course. It would be a miracle if any one of them could hit anything at all with those antique weapons they have. Anyway, the fort commander, who apparently isn't too bright, sent a group of soldiers led by some dumbass lieutenant into the camp to arrest the Indian. Naturally, the Indian refused to surrender. Hell, we don't have any right to go into an Indian camp and arrest *anyone*. Anyway, the Miniconjou refused to go peacefully, probably figuring if he did they were going to stand him up against the wall and shoot him. Somebody, probably that same glory-seeking brave, fired a round or two. Again, no one got hit but the lieutenant panicked and ordered his men to open fire. Three Miniconjou were killed and three more wounded. The point is, the Army had no business being in that camp in the first place, and certainly shouldn't have opened fire. It could all have been settled by a nice talk around the campfire."

"I don't remember hearing about that," said Fontenot.

"It hasn't been publicized a lot," Davis replied. "At least not yet. But it will. The Army is going to try to make it sound as if it were the Indians' fault. They'll want to use the incident to stir up anti-Indian feeling in Congress. Believe me, you *are* going to hear about it."

"So what are you trying to say?" Fontenot asked, suspecting that Davis had not yet gotten to his real reason for passing on that information.

"That dumbass lieutenant who was leading the contingent that killed the Indians is now a captain," Davis said. He paused, then added: "And he's now the commanding officer at Fort Laramie."

"Oh *ho*," Fontenot said. "And you want to send Benoit out there to serve under him."

"Yep," Davis replied. "And I'll tell you why. That dumbass didn't get any smarter because they pinned captain's bars on his shoulders. He's still a dumbass and before too long he's going to do something really stupid. And then his ass is going to be gone. Maybe then the Army will send in a commanding officer who knows what he's doing. What I'm trying to say is, Fort Laramie is going to be a place of opportunity. And if Benoit is any kind of soldier at all . . . "

"He is," Fontenot interjected. "I can sense it."

". . . then that is a good place for him to be."

"Maybe you're right," Fontenot grudgingly agreed.

"I think I am. Plus, there's one other thing."

"What's that?"

"We may actually be *saving* his life, not putting it in jeopardy. Remember what we were talking about earlier?"

"The coming war?"

"Yes," Davis replied. "I'm as convinced as you that there's going to be a war between the North and the South, and it's going to be a real dog-eat-dog affair. If Benoit is on the frontier he may stand a chance of staying out of it."

"I never thought of it that way," Fontenot said.

"Try to," Davis said. "It will help you sleep. I wish I were twenty years younger. I'd *want* to go to Fort Laramie. I think it will make Benoit or break him. In fact," he said with a tight smile, "come to think of it, I may even arrange to have Captain Browning go with him."

"Your aide-de-camp?" Fontenot asked in surprise. "Why?"

Davis laughed. "Forget it, Emile. That's a joke. I wouldn't do that to Fort Laramie."


"Oh, Phi," Marie Fontenot said, throwing open the door of the neat brick townhouse she shared with her father. "I thought you'd *never* get here."

"I hurried as fast as I could," Jean Benoit replied, grinning broadly. "You know your time isn't always your own when you're an aide to an aide to General Hawkins, the grand poo-bah in Operations and Planning."

"'The Hawk' knows my father," Marie cooed. "Why didn't you just tell him you had to leave early so you could hurry out to Georgetown to make love to the senator's daughter? Judging from the looks he's given me at some of the receptions he would like to be in your shoes."

"Marie!" Benoit said in alarm. Looking over her shoulder, he was relieved when he didn't see the maid hovering in the background. "You're going to have to be more careful about what you say."

"I sent Beatrice on an errand." Marie laughed, "and Andrew's taking the coach to pick up daddy. There's no one here but me. And now you, of course. Besides, I just *love* it when you get that look on your face. For such a big, brave Army lieutenant you surely get shocked awfully easy."

"It's *brevet* lieutenant, Marie. I'm not even a real lieutenant yet."

"Brevet, schmevet. It's all the same thing. You're a graduate of the U.S. Military Academy, you're in the Army, and everybody *calls* you lieutenant, so that's the same thing as *being* a lieutenant."

"No it *isn't*. A lieutenant is a real officer; a brevet lieutenant is next to nothing, lower even than a plebe at the Point. At least that's what everyone in General Hawkins's office keeps telling me."

"Oh, hush," Marie said, placing a long, slim index finger on Benoit's lips. "We don't have time to talk about Army Department. Daddy will be home in an hour and," she said, smiling, "I want to keep you busy until then."

Grabbing his hand, she dragged him across the small foyer and into her father's library, a secure nook lined from floor to ceiling with books, half of them in English and half of them in French, as befitted the senior senator from Louisiana.

"Why do we always have to do it in here?" Benoit complained mildly. "It makes me feel like such a traitor. Your father and mine are best friends. Your father got me the appointment to West Point . . . "

"And *I'm* your sister Marion's best friend," Marie broke in. "So what? That has nothing to do with you and me." Slowly she started working on his tunic, undoing the brass buttons one at a time. "Why do they *put* so many buttons on these things?" she asked, her breathing getting heavier.

"Why don't we just once make love in a bed?" Benoit asked, helping her with the buttons.

"Oh, wouldn't that be nice!" she exclaimed. "But not until we're married. Can you imagine what Beatrice would say if she found your stains on my sheets?"

"It's a good thing she can't see *my* sheets." Benoit laughed. "All the wet dreams you've caused me to have would drive her up the wall."

"Oh, Phi," she said, mocking him. "You're so romantic."

"Romantic, hell," he said, bending over and grabbing the hem of her dress. "This isn't romance; this is pure sex. And you like it as much as I do." Straightening up, he lifted her skirt above her waist, catching his breath when he saw that she was wearing nothing underneath. "I must be the luckiest guy in the world," he groaned, "finding the only blonde in all of Louisiana."

"Oh, it isn't luck, Phi," she said, hurriedly unfastening his trousers. "It's fate. You found a blonde and I found a man with the most beautiful *la verge* a girl could ask for." Leaning down, she took it in her hand and gently kissed it. "I just love it to death," she gushed.

Benoit shuddered. "We'd better get over to the sofa pretty quick," he said, "or it's going to be all over."

"To hell with the sofa," said Marie, sliding to the floor and pulling him on top of her. "There's nothing wrong with right here. But hurry. I want it as badly as you."

Forty-five minutes later, they were sitting in the parlor, delicately sipping imported British tea and nervously awaiting the arrival of Marie's father.

"Do I still look flushed?" Marie asked anxiously, patting her hair.

"I don't know." Benoit winked. "Hike up your dress again and I'll tell you."

"Oh, *Phi*," she said in mock annoyance, "you're so *terrible*."

"I wish you wouldn't do that," he said earnestly.

"Do what?" she said, puzzled. "Make love to you?"

"No, no," Benoit said emphatically. "Call me 'Phi.'"

Marie giggled. "But I've called you that for years and years. Your sister calls you 'Phi.' *Everybody* calls you 'Phi.'"

"No, they don't," Benoit said. "People from New Orleans call me 't-Jean' — Little Jean, Jean Junior. People here call me 'John.' Except that bastard Hawkins. All he ever calls me is 'Ben-oit.' He can't even pronounce my name. I've tried and tried to tell him that it's Ben-WAH."

"You want me to sympathize with you?" Marie chuckled. "Try 'Fontenot.'"

"Anyway," Benoit said, trying to get back to his original point. "I don't like being called 'Phi' or 'Phideaux.' How would you like being referred to as a dog?"

"My, aren't we sensitive." Marie laughed. "I didn't invent the nickname. Your sister did. Because you used to follow her around like a little puppy."

"For God's sake, Marie . . ." he began, stiffening at the sound of a door slamming.

"Hello," a deep voice called from the foyer. "Marie, are you here? I'm home."

"Daddy," Marie whispered.

"Ah, there you are," Fontenot said, bustling into the room.

"Good evening, senator," Benoit said, jumping to attention.

"*Bon jour*, t-Jean," Fontenot said warmly, clasping Benoit's hand. "*Comment ça va?*"

"Very well, sir," Benoit said stiffly.

"*Hello*, Marie," Fontenot said pointedly. "Aren't you speaking to your father?"

"Oh, Daddy." She blushed. "I'm sorry, I was just thinking how tired you looked." Running to his side she gave him a hug and pecked him on both cheeks. "Is that better?"

"Much." Fontenot smiled, sinking into his favorite chair. "I am tired. It's been a long day. But it's been productive, too. Want me to tell you about it?"

"Well . . . ," Marie said hesitantly.

"That wasn't meant to be a question, *chere* I have something to tell you. You and t-Jean both. For God's sake," Fontenot said, noticing that Benoit was still standing. "Will you *please* sit down. You don't have to pull that West Point routine with me; I've known you since you were a baby."

"Sorry, sir," Benoit said, coloring. "Sometimes I forget."

Carefully sitting as far as he could from Marie, he threw his shoulders back and turned to Fontenot.

The senator leaned forward. "As both of you know, I'm not one to beat around the bush."

Oh my God, thought Marie, he's found out.

"You may not realize it," Fontenot said uncomfortably, "but I've discovered that the two of you may be more than . . . well . . . er . . . friends."

*Merde*, thought Marie.

"Oh, shit," Benoit mumbled under his breath.

"Daddy," Marie began . . .

"Senator," Benoit fumbled . . .

Despite the seriousness of the situation, it was all

Fontenot could do to keep from laughing. "Just a second," he said. "Before either of you say anything, let me finish."

"Yes, Daddy," said Marie.

"Yes, sir," said Benoit.

"Would the two of you, for God's sake, *stop* it and let me say what I have to say? As I was *trying* to say," Fontenot continued gruffly, "I *suspect* that there is some sort of . . . uh . . . liaison going on between you two . . ." When they did not contradict him, he continued. "And I *suspect* that you're going to tell me that you're going to want to get married."

Marie and Benoit stared straight ahead. Neither spoke.

"Hmmm," Fontenot said. "I guess I *am* right. Anyway, I don't think that's a good idea."

"But Daddy . . . "

"But Senator . . . "

Fontenot waved them to silence. "Be quiet! I'm not through. I not only don't think it's a good idea, I'm steadfastly against it. In fact, I forbid it."

Benoit opened his mouth. Fontenot raised his hand. Benoit remained silent.

"I have my reasons for adopting this position," Fontenot continued, "and I have an idea what you're thinking. You're figuring that I don't know what I'm talking about and that I couldn't do anything about it anyway. You're both over twenty-one and you can, you think, do what you want. *Well, you can't.* It's as simple as that. Marie is still living here at home, presently otherwise unemployed. T-Jean is, thank God, in the Army. And I happen to have a few connections with the Army. You may hate me for it now, but you might thank me for it later. Even if you don't, it's done. I've arranged for t-Jean to be posted out of Washington."

Turning to Benoit, he looked deep into his eyes,

noticing, for the first time in the twenty-plus years that he'd known him, that they were blue. He'd always assumed they would be brown, like most Cajuns'. "T-Jean," he said gently, "I don't blame you for *whatever's* happened. It takes two to have an affair. I've always thought of you as a son and I will *continue* to think of you that way. Believe it or not, it's because of my affection for both of you . . . because I love you both . . . I've arranged for your transfer to Fort Laramie. You leave next week."

Finished with his speech, he leaned back in the chair and studied the two of them, the young blonde woman who was every bit as beautiful as her mother had been, and the dark-haired, slim young man who looked remarkably like *his* mother, except for the color of his eyes. Where in hell did the blue come from, Fontenot wondered. When he walked in Fontenot looked tired; now he looked haggard. "I've had *my* say," he said quietly. "Now is there anything you want to say?"

*"Sacre merde!"* cried Marie.

*"Fort Laramie!"* exclaimed Benoit.

## ~~3~~

While the weather had been warm when they left the
Wazhazha camp, the Moon When the Ducks Return
began showing its true colors on the second day of
the journey. Without warning, a cold, stiff wind
swept in from the northwest and hit them squarely
in the face, peppering them with snow and sleet. The
storm lasted for almost two days. Although Spotted
Bear and Lame Elk petitioned Blizzard to call a temporary halt so the group could take shelter in one of
the dozens of shallow caves that were everywhere
along their route, Blizzard refused, contending that
the storm would help conceal their presence should
the Crow be anticipating a springtime raid and have
scouts combing the southern edge of their territory.
"Most likely, though," Blizzard said, "they are hud-
dled around a fire in their lodges, like fat, old
squaws become complacent in their false sense of
security."

After the storm blew on to the east, the weather

remained cold and crisp, which presented an additional hardship since the group had left the camp travelling lightly, carrying only robes, subsistence rations, and extra moccasins. They had planned to hunt along the way, at least until they got into Crow territory, but the storm drove all the game to shelter and Blizzard had to implement rationing. As a result, the men were not only cold but hungry, grumbling as they hunkered in the knee-deep snow at the end of the day, eating rock-hard buffalo jerky and pemmican at a fireless camp.

In the way of arms, each man carried a knife, a bow and a quiver of arrows, plus whatever other implements fit his style of warfare. Several carried tomahawks, but only Lame Elk and Charging Buffalo brought along their unwieldy smooth-bore muskets. As a rule, rifles were considered too cumbersome to worry with on a horse raid, an operation where stealth, quickness, and maneuverability were more important than firepower. But a Brulé raiding party was a highly individualistic group and its members typically hauled along whatever weapons they felt most comfortable with. Roaring Thunder had his favorite lance, which was more of a good luck charm than an instrument he might be able to use with effectiveness in a skirmish where fighting, if it occurred, would be at close quarters. Badger had his shield, a disk about two feet in diameter, made of buffalo hide stretched across a wooden frame. It was covered with an outer layer of buckskin and decorated with painted figures, including a bear and several dragonflies, picked because they represented special traits he wanted to embody: the bear because of its ferociousness and the dragonfly because of its elusiveness. And Blizzard, who boasted a dozen ragged scars to testify to his fondness for hand-to-hand combat, carried his treasured war club, a fierce looking instrument about two-and-a-half feet long, painted red and black, his "power" colors. The head of the club was a carved ball about five inches in diameter, out of which protruded a five-inch-long metal spike. On the back of the weapon, Blizzard had carved the image of a weasel, his personal totem chosen as a symbol of deadly efficiency.

Blizzard, Badger, Jagged Blade, and Roaring Thunder, the most experienced warriors among the group, also carried their own medicine bundles, small packets filled with items of special personal significance. Badger's contained a handful of brightly colored pebbles he had collected along a river bank deep in the Black Hills; Blizzard's included a crow's skull that had once belonged to a celebrated shaman; Jagged Blade's, a small piece of lightning-singed mountain oak, a remnant from a tree that had saved his life by offering itself as a more favorable target during a fierce thunderstorm, and Roaring Thunder's held an intricately carved buffalo rib that he had taken from a Pawnee whose throat he had slit one fine autumn afternoon.

Roaring Thunder, the group's most skilled scout, roamed as much as several miles ahead of the group to make sure there was not an ambush around the next bend or over the next hill. It was reputed that Roaring Thunder could spend five minutes examining a barely decipherable footprint and be able to tell not only which direction its maker was going, how long ago he had passed that way, and whether he had been walking or running, but also his height, weight, approximate age, whether he was heavily armed, what he had eaten that morning, and when he last had sex with his wife.

At the head of the main body, which travelled in single file at intervals of five or six yards, was Blizzard, the *blotahunka*. As group leader, he was responsible for

setting the pace of the march. He decided when and
where the group would camp at night and when they
would stop to rest. He did not, however, even if he was
the *blotahunka*, have absolute authority over the other
members of the group. Each man who had decided to
come along was an independent agent to the extent
that he could make his own choices and was free to
turn back whenever he wished without facing disgrace
or censure.

Nevertheless, to preserve order, Blizzard mandated
the order of march, grouping the men according to
their experience and abilities as warriors. Following
behind him was Badger, the next most experienced
fighter. In theory, if the group was attacked, the assault
likely would come from either the front or the rear of
the column and that's where the most able fighters
were grouped. In order, behind Badger, were Otter,
Spotted Bear, and Lame Elk. Then the three weakest
links in the chain: Storm Cloud, White Crane, and
Running Antelope, three boys in their mid-teens each
of whom was participating in his first horse raid.
Although they also were armed they were not expected
to play a major role in any fighting that occurred. For
them, the raid was an initiation into warriorhood and
their main duties were to learn what they could and
assist the others.

Behind the three youths were Strong Bow, Charging
Buffalo, and Jagged Blade, three other experienced
braves. As Roaring Thunder roamed well in front of the
group, Jagged Blade stayed a respectable distance
behind to make sure no enemy was sneaking up on
them.

For more than a week, the group of twelve had
been travelling northwest from the Wazhazha winter
campground, getting ever closer to Kangi territory. On
the ninth night, just as a half moon peeked over a

nearby heavily forested mountain, Blizzard called a halt.

"Roaring Thunder says we're getting closer to the Crow camps," he explained tersely. "I don't want to stumble across one of their hunting parties and have them sound an alarm. We're going to stop now and sleep until the moon is high, then push on for the rest of the night. Tomorrow, we'll rest during the day and travel only after dark. Disperse into the heavy timber and sleep for four hours. Then we'll resume."

"That's fine with me," White Crane whispered. "I'm glad for the chance to rest. My feet are killing me."

"Mine, too," Running Antelope replied. "I've gone through two pairs of moccasins already. Let's go find a place away from the others where can have some privacy."

"Wait for me," cried Storm Cloud, running to join them.

The youths, left on their own and virtually ignored since they were not yet part of the warrior fraternity, moved up the slope seeking shelter. Fifteen minutes later they found a good-sized clearing in the ground-cover, apparently a favorite bedding spot for an elk who had decided to move higher into the mountains with the arrival of spring.

Within minutes, the boys had made themselves comfortable. Knowing they should stretch out to grab a few hours of precious rest, they couldn't resist the opportunity to discuss their adventure.

"Here," Running Antelope said quietly, proffering a small buckskin bag he had carried since leaving the camp. "Have something to eat."

White Crane took the bag and opened it. "Ugh," he mumbled in distaste. "Is that all you have?"

"And what's the matter with dried grasshoppers?" Running Antelope asked, suppressing a smile.

"I guess you'd rather have some hot dog-stew?" added Storm Cloud. "Or maybe some nice bloody liver from a freshly killed buffalo?"

"As a matter of fact," White Crane replied, starting to salivate at the thought of two of his favorite meals, "I would. *But*," he added, "I think I'd settle for anything but grasshoppers. Don't you have any pemmican left?"

"We finished it this morning," said Running Antelope.

"This is no time to be picky," said Storm Cloud, helping himself from the bag. "This is a horse raid. A *man*," he added, stressing the word, "has to understand that he can't always have what he wants."

"I know that," White Crane replied peevishly, "but I'd rather eat my robe, hair and all."

"As long as you don't eat *my* robe," Running Antelope joked. "I don't want to find out which can kill me quicker: freezing or starvation. Maybe you'd rather go hungry," he added, dipping eagerly into the bag, "but I like grasshoppers."

"You'd better eat some," Storm Cloud told White Crane. "You're going to need all the strength you can get. Two days from now we won't even have them."

"In two days we should be at the Crow camp," White Crane said. "And by then I'll be too excited to be hungry."

Running Antelope shrugged and resumed chewing.

"Can't you do that more quietly?" White Crane asked. "The Crow can probably hear you all the way to their camp."

Running Antelope, deep in thought, ignored the comment. Pushing the bag aside, he belched heartily. "Are you scared?" he asked abruptly.

White Crane looked surprised. "Scared?" he said, ready to reply that fear was the last thought in his mind.

But knowing his friend would quickly recognize the lie, he responded more judiciously. "A little," he said, still fudging on the truth.

"Not me," Storm Cloud bragged. "I welcome the opportunity to meet a Crow face-to-face and count my first coup."

"You just think a golden eagle feather would impress Mountain Pine," said White Crane, looking for a way to get back at his friend for challenging his manhood.

"I'll admit it," said Running Antelope. "I'm frightened. For two years now I've been looking forward to this day so bad I thought it would never get here. Now that it has, what I really want to do is go back home."

"Don't talk like that!" Storm Cloud hissed. "Blizzard may hear you and think we're all cowards."

"There's nothing cowardly about being afraid," Running Antelope argued. "Don't you think Blizzard ever feels frightened?"

"No!" White Crane and Storm Cloud replied in unison. "Blizzard is not afraid of *anything*."

"I don't believe that," Running Antelope said. "He's only human and all humans have fear of something."

"Well," conceded Storm Cloud, "he may be afraid of something but it sure isn't the Crow."

"You want to know something?" Running Antelope said, leaning forward and lowering his voice. "I don't think Blizzard cares how many men get killed as long as it enhances his reputation as a warrior."

"Don't talk like that!" White Crane admonished. "If Blizzard heard you, he'd kill you in a minute and we'd be having *your* liver for dinner."

Running Antelope grinned. "All I meant was I think he's a natural born killer. To him, that probably would be a compliment."

"He's not a killer," said White Crane. "He's a warrior. There's a difference."

"I think you're wrong," said Running Antelope. "He's the coldest person I've ever seen. Truly, he is well named. It's as if nothing at all touches him. Not anything. Not ever."

"Maybe that's what it takes to be the best warrior in the Wazhazhas," said Storm Cloud.

"I wonder if we'll ever be like that?" White Crane ventured.

"Sure we will," replied Storm Cloud. "Once we've been on a couple of horse raids and war parties we'll be just as fearless and ruthless as Blizzard."

"Maybe *you* will," Running Antelope said after a pause. "But I don't think I could ever get like Blizzard."

"Like him or not, you have to admit he's brave and he acts decisively."

"I'll agree to that," Running Antelope replied. "But I just can't adjust to how unfeeling he can be. Roaring Thunder is a brave warrior, too, but he's also generous with others. Blizzard never brings food to the meeting lodge."

"That's just the way he is," said White Crane. "He lives to fight. That's why he's the best warrior among all the Brulés."

"If that's what it takes," Running Antelope said soberly, "I don't think it's in my future."

"If we don't get some sleep," Storm Cloud added lightheartedly, looking at the darkening sky, "I don't think we're going to *have* any future. We'll probably pass out from exhaustion and get left behind."

"I bet I'm asleep before either of you." Running Antelope grinned, stretching out in the tightly packed underbrush.

"Then you'd better hurry," laughed White Crane, reclining next to his friend.

"Sleeping has never been my problem," added Storm Cloud. "I can be dreaming before you can adjust your robe."

For several moments the youths were silent, then White Crane whispered: "Running Antelope? Are you asleep?"

"Almost," came the drowsy reply. "Why?"

"It just occurred to me, how are we going to know when to wake up?"

"Jagged Blade will rouse us," he responded, yawning.

"I *know* that, but how is *he* going to know when it's time?"

Running Antelope chuckled. "You mean nobody has explained that to you?"

"No," White Crane replied, puzzled.

"My brother, Badger, told me how it's done," said Running Antelope. "In situations like this, one man is designated to awaken everyone else."

"Does he stay awake the whole time? Is that how he knows when it's time to move?"

"No," Running Antelope replied. "He needs sleep like everyone else. But before he goes to sleep he drinks a lot of water. Lots and lots of water. Then within a couple of hours he has to get up to relieve himself. So he knows it's time."

"Oh," White Crane said quietly. "That sounds simple enough. I wonder why I didn't think of it?"

When Running Antelope didn't reply, White Crane lifted his head to see if he had heard. Both Running Antelope and Storm Cloud were snoring softly.


From just before midnight until the first hint of dawn in the eastern sky, the group moved silently through the forest, up one hill and down another, deliberately avoiding the valleys because they knew if they were going to

be detected it would more likely be along the trails that
followed the low ground. With the stars still clearly visible, Blizzard called a brief rest.

"We'll go one more hour," he whispered once the
men had gathered around him, "then we'll shelter until
nightfall."

Weary to the bone, exhausted from a full night of
quick-time walking over rugged terrain with only four
hours of sleep, the men plodded along like zombies,
paying little attention to the ground underneath their
feet. As the group snaked along a steeply inclined section of the trail, flanked on one side by a steep drop into
a boulder-filled arroyo, Storm Cloud stepped on a loose
rock and lost his footing. With a brief cry of surprise, he
slipped off the narrow path and tumbled head over
heels down the cliff.

Running Antelope, who was next in line behind
Storm Cloud, was about to run down the cliff to see how
badly his friend was hurt when Blizzard froze him with
a sharp command.

"Wait!" he barked. "Stay exactly where you are.
Every one of you. Don't anybody move."

"What?" Running Antelope asked, confused, not sure
whether to see to his friend or obey Blizzard.

"I said not to move," Blizzard whispered, who suddenly materialized at Running Antelope's elbow.
Gripping the youth's arm tightly, Blizzard repeated his
order to remain motionless. "Storm Cloud made a lot of
noise falling down that cliff. We have to know if any
unfriendly ears heard it."

Blizzard waved his arm and the men melted into the
shadows, readying their weapons and waiting to see if
they had been discovered.

Running Antelope shifted impatiently, biting his lip.
He could hear Storm Cloud moaning softly fifty yards
below.

"He's hurt," Running Antelope whispered to Blizzard.

"He'll have to suffer a little, " Blizzard replied. "I don't want to risk everyone being killed."

"But he would help you," Running Antelope argued.

Blizzard glared at him. "Be quiet and do as I tell you," he snapped. "We'll go to his aid as soon as we know it's safe."

For what seemed a long, long time, the men remained totally motionless. Gradually, as the sky got lighter, their forms were more distinct. Finally, with one last look around, Blizzard grunted and motioned the group forward. "I guess we've been lucky," he said, sliding down the rocky slope.

By the time Running Antelope reached Storm Cloud's side, Blizzard was already there, running his hands quickly over Storm Cloud's arms and legs.

"Where does it hurt?" Blizzard asked when his quick examination showed only superficial cuts and scratches.

"All over. Especially my back," Storm Cloud replied, his eyes wide with fright. "I feel numb, too, like I've been asleep in one position for too long."

"Can you sit up?"

Storm Cloud struggled but his body would not respond. "No," he whispered.

Blizzard reached out and grabbed Storm Cloud's arm, lifting it off the ground. "Does that hurt?"

"Yes." Storm Cloud grimaced. "It feels like it's on fire."

Blizzard frowned, still holding Storm Cloud's arm. "Can you move your fingers?" he asked softly.

Storm Cloud's face clouded in concentration but his fingers remained limp. "No," he said in a high-pitched tone verging on panic.

Blizzard grunted and stared at the youth.

"What is it?" asked Badger, who just arrived at the boy's side.

"Storm Cloud has broken his back," Blizzard replied.

When he heard those words, tears began forming in Storm Cloud's eyes.

"Does this mean I'm going to die?" he asked, his voice on the edge of panic. "I don't want to die," he said. "Not on my first horse raid. Not before I've seen my first enemy."

"Are you sure his back is broken?" asked Badger, who had joined the small group clustered around Storm Cloud. "Maybe he's just stunned by the fall."

"I'm sure," Blizzard said. "I've seen it before. He's paralyzed."

"What can we do?" Badger asked.

"Nothing. We can't move him; we can't carry him with us." Turning to look upward, where the sun's rays were just appearing on the top of the mountain behind them, he added: "And we have to make a decision because we can't stay here in the daylight or the Crow will find us. Then all of us will be killed."

"So what choice does that leave us?" Badger asked.

"Only one," Blizzard replied soberly.

At first, Badger was not sure what he meant. When it dawned on him, the shock registered in his eyes. "Are you suggesting we kill him?" Badger whispered, hoping that Storm Cloud would not hear.

"Not you, me," Blizzard replied. "It's my responsibility as *blotahunka*."

"There must be some other way," Badger said, gazing sadly at Storm Cloud, who had heard the conversation despite Badger's concern and had started weeping audibly. Tears rolled down his cheeks and his narrow chest jumped in shallow heaves.

"Just leave me," Storm Cloud begged. "Leave me

with some water and then come back on your return. Maybe by then I'll be better."

Ignoring him, Blizzard looked at Badger. "There is no other way," he said with finality.

Seemingly feeling he owed the injured youth some explanation, Blizzard leaned forward until his mouth was near Storm Cloud's ear. "Your back is broken, young warrior. You aren't going to get any better. Now you have to be brave and accept death like a friend. You will be a hero among the Wazhazha. Your name will be spoken in deference."

"I don't want to be a hero," Storm Cloud whined. "I don't want to die. Please," he pleaded. "Please leave me. I'll get better. I know I will."

"I'll stay with him," Running Antelope volunteered.

"I will too," added White Crane.

"To what end?" Blizzard asked. "Then all of you would be as good as dead."

"Like Storm Cloud said," Running Antelope continued. "We'll wait for you to come back after the raid. Then we can make a travois and take Storm Cloud back to his lodge."

Blizzard slowly shook his head. "We can't leave you."

"Why not?" Running Antelope asked.

"Yes, why not?" Storm Cloud echoed.

"What if the Crow found you?"

"I wouldn't say anything? I promise," Storm Cloud said.

"Neither would I," added Running Antelope.

"Or me," echoed White Crane.

Blizzard looked at them contemptuously. "Three boys, one of them paralyzed. Children who have never been in battle. Do you think you could hold off a single old Crow? They would capture you and make you talk, make you reveal where the rest of us have gone."

"We wouldn't do that," Running Antelope persisted.

"Don't talk foolish," Blizzard said harshly. "They would have you singing like magpies quicker than you believe possible. You've never seen a victim of Crow torture. Quicker than you could soil your leggings, you would be *begging* them to let you talk."

Running Antelope and White Crane exchanged tortured glances. In their hearts, they knew Blizzard was correct.

"I would never tell," Storm Cloud insisted. "I would never . . . "

Blizzard reached out and put his hand over Storm Cloud's mouth, cutting off the sentence. Looking directly into the boy's eyes, Blizzard spoke softly. "Be brave, Storm Cloud. It will all be over in a moment and your soul will soar with the eagles." Using his thumb and forefinger, Blizzard squeezed the youth's nostrils closed.

Storm Cloud's eyes grew wide and he stared fixedly at Blizzard. Blizzard returned the look, watching until the youth's eyes rolled back in his head and his chest quit moving.

Removing his hand slowly, ready to clamp it back if Storm Cloud showed any sign of renewed life, Blizzard turned to his two friends. "You carry his body. Find a place where he will be securely hidden and safe from predators."

As the two youths struggled up the slope with the body of their friend between them, Badger turned to Blizzard. "We need to talk about this," he said angrily. "You acted too quickly. You didn't consult anyone."

"I did what I had to do," Blizzard replied dismissively. "Talking about it wasn't going to change the situation."

"You mean you really plan to go ahead with the raid?" Badger asked in surprise.

"Of course," Blizzard said, glaring at his fellow warrior. "What would be gained by abandoning our plan now? It won't help Storm Cloud. Nothing is going to help Storm Cloud. He was as good as dead as soon as he lost his footing and fell over the edge."

"We still need to talk about it," Badger insisted stubbornly.

"Talk," Blizzard responded, his temper growing short. "You talk more than an old woman. Are you," he asked, hurling one of the Sioux's cruelest insults, "a warrior or a squaw?"

Badger reached for his knife, anger flashing in his eyes.

Blizzard tightened his grip on his war club and swung it back, ready to strike if Badger drew his weapon.

"Wait!" said a voice from behind him. Roaring Thunder sprang forward and seized Badger in a tight bear hug. "Blizzard has a point," he rasped into Badger's ear. "Storm Cloud is dead. There's nothing we can do about it and fighting among ourselves isn't going to bring him back."

Badger continued to glare at Blizzard, then his muscles slowly relaxed. "You're right, Roaring Thunder." Dropping his hand, he urged his friend to let him go. "I won't attack Blizzard no matter how much I would like to." Sagging to the ground, looking exhausted, he nodded sadly. "You also right about Storm Cloud. Nothing will help him now. But," he added, lifting his head defiantly, "we still need to discuss what we are going to do next."

"Then we'll discuss it later," Blizzard said, having lost interest in the argument. "If we sit around jabbering in the bright sunlight we'll almost certainly be found by the Crow. And then we'll all join Storm Cloud, except his death will have been much easier. All of you," he said, looking around the group, "find shelter and wait until nightfall."

Dejectedly, the men slipped among the trees, knowing any further argument at that point would be futile.

A hundred yards away, Running Antelope and White Crane panted heavily with the effort of carrying Storm Cloud's body up the steep embankment. Gingerly laying it on the ground, they spread out and searched until they found a small cave. Returning for Storm Cloud, they lifted him again and carried him to the opening in the rocky wall. After laying his body inside, they sealed the entrance with boulders.

"Will you remember the spot?" White Crane asked nervously. "So we can find him later."

Running Antelope nodded. "I'll never forget it," he said emphatically. "Not as long as I live."

That afternoon, as if it were proof of Blizzard's prescience, the group watched silently from deep in the trees as a party of four Crow passed below them, following almost the same path they had taken the previous night. Along with the Kangi, one of whom was mounted on a magnificent black gelding with white stockings on his forelegs and a white blaze, were two pack animals heavily laden with fresh meat. Running Antelope's mouth watered as he watched the pack horse disappear behind a bend in the trail.

"I'd just as soon we forget the horses and get the meat," he said quietly to White Crane, who smiled in reply.

"What for?" White Crane replied. "You have plenty of dried grasshoppers left."

"The presence of those pack horses proves we're near the Crow camp," Blizzard pointed out later. "From now on we have to be especially vigilant."

Again, he proved correct. As the men were gathering for the night march that would take them to the outskirts of the Crow camp, Roaring Thunder returned from his daily scouting expedition.

"I have good news," he said breathlessly.

"Tell us," Blizzard ordered, signalling to the men to gather round.

"The Crow camp is just over the second ridge," Roaring Thunder reported. "About fifty lodges strung along a small river."

"Any indication they know we're here?" Blizzard asked.

"None that I could see. Everything looks peaceful enough. And there's even better news."

"What's that?" asked Badger.

"There are not that many warriors around, maybe two-thirds of what I would expect. I figure they're off hunting. It must have been a rough winter for the Crow to send so many hunters out so early."

"And how about the horse herd?" Blizzard asked. "Did you find it as well?"

"Yes," Roaring Thunder said excitedly. It's south of the camp in a narrow valley surrounded on both sides by steep cliffs."

"How many horses?"

"I counted sixty-five but there probably are more since the better ones are bound to be tethered inside the camp itself where the owners can keep an eye on them."

"How far to the camp?" Badger asked.

The scout shrugged. "Half a day's journey. No more."

"Good," Blizzard replied, parting his lips in a grimace that was as close as he ever came to smiling. "We'll start as soon as it gets fully dark. We'll travel slowly so we won't make any extra noise and get into position above the camp before sunrise tomorrow. Then we'll spend a day looking over the area carefully before making our move. I want to make sure I know what we're getting into."

He had turned, intending to gather up his robe and his weapons, when one of the men coughed nervously.

"What is it, Lame Elk?" Blizzard asked agitatedly. "Do you have something to say?"

"I—I do," Lame Elk stuttered. "I have been talking with Spotted Bear and Otter. We think you should reconsider the plan to grab the Crow horses."

"Oh?" Blizzard said, his lip curling upward. "And why is that?"

"Spotted Bear had a dream . . . "

"A dream?"

"A dream. A vision. Whatever you want to call it. During his sleep this afternoon his totem, the wolf, appeared." Lame Elk paused, waiting to see what Blizzard's reaction would be.

Although Blizzard was a fearless warrior, unafraid of any man he had ever met, he knew better than to scoff at another's claim to have contact with the supernatural. If he had no belief in such things, he would not have brought along his personal medicine bundle, whose power he relied upon to bring him safely through the forthcoming period of danger.

"And what did the wolf tell him?" Blizzard asked, not unkindly.

Emboldened by Blizzard's response, Lame Elk added: "The wolf said what had happened to Storm Cloud was a bad thing. It was an omen, a sign that we should abandon the plans for the raid before it is too late."

"Is that all?" asked Blizzard.

"No," Lame Elk said. "The wolf said if we persist there will be bloodshed among the Wazhazha. That no good will come of this venture and by continuing we will be bringing much misery upon our people."

"Did the wolf say when this might occur?"

"No," Lame Elk replied. "The wolf said only that Storm Cloud's death cast a shadow over us all. That we need to purify ourselves before meeting our enemies."

Blizzard dropped into a squat and rocked back on his haunches. While the others stared at him expectantly, he appeared deep in thought. Finally, he spoke. "Have you discussed this with the others?" he asked.

Lame Elk nodded.

"Do any of them feel the same way as you and Spotted Bear?"

"Only Otter," Lame Elk said, glancing at a tall, thin warrior standing near the left end of the semicircle that had formed behind Blizzard.

"So you, Spotted Bear and Otter think we should return immediately and go into the sweat lodge?"

Again, Lame Elk nodded.

Blizzard sprang to his feet and spun around to face the group. "Does anyone else agree with that?" he asked loudly. "Do any of you want to join those three?"

When no one spoke up, Blizzard turned and walked up to Lame Elk. "Brother," he said, speaking slowly and distinctly. "I cannot tell you what to believe and I will not try to command you to go against your principles. As for myself, I think Spotted Bear misinterpreted what the wolf was trying to tell him. No one here, least of all me, is happy about Storm Cloud's accident. If I could undo it, I would. It was unfortunate, but I don't think it was prophetic. Accidents happen, and that should have no bearing upon the actions of the rest of us."

He paused, glancing around to see if anyone was going to contradict him. When no one jumped into the conversation, he continued.

"I propose this. If the three of you feel that strongly about Spotted Bear's vision, I suggest you turn back. We are strong enough to continue without you. I think you are wrong, but I am not going to use my authority as *blotahunka* to try to make you change your minds. The decision is yours."

"In that case," Lame Elk said hurriedly, looking relieved, "we will leave."

Blizzard nodded in agreement. "Is there anyone else?" he asked, searching the faces of the others. Although none would meet his gaze, no one else seemed ready to join the three.

"How about you, Badger?" Blizzard challenged. "You said this morning that you thought we should consider calling off the raid."

"I've had time to think about it," Badger said, walking to within arm's reach of Blizzard. "At first I thought continuing with the raid was a bad idea. But after reflection, I believe we should go ahead. Storm Cloud's death was unfortunate but it has nothing to do with the raid. We've come this far and I don't think we should turn back now."

Blizzard grunted, knowing that was the closest Badger would come to apologizing about his apparent threat toward his authority.

"Then let us go forward," Blizzard said, shouldering his war club. "But one more thing?" he said, stopping in midstride.

"Yes," Lame Elk said expectantly. "What is it?"

"Make a travois," Blizzard ordered, "and take Storm Cloud's body back with you."

"Very well," said Lame Elk, unsheathing his knife, which he would need to trim pine branches for the makeshift frame. "Storm Cloud's family will be grateful."

"What about us?" Running Antelope whispered to

White Crane as the group began moving down the trail the Crow had followed earlier in the day. "Storm Cloud was *our* friend. Shouldn't we have some say in the matter?"

White Crane put a warning finger to his lips. "Shhhhh," he murmured. "This isn't the time to call attention to ourselves."

Running Antelope rolled his eyes. "Some warrior you're going to make," he mumbled, falling into his place at the end of the line.

—4—

Dobbs knew he was in trouble as soon as he walked
through the door. He could see by the look on the general's face that the old warhorse had not called him in
for a friendly chat, such as those they often had during
the Mexican campaign when Briggs, then a colonel, had
shared a bottle of mescal with his unit's most skilled
surgeon. No, Dobbs told himself in the seconds it took
him to cross the large room to Briggs's desk, his heels
clicking on the bare heart-o'-pine floor, *this* is serious.
But, he asked himself, how in hell did he find out?

Stopping in front of Briggs's desk, he threw back his
narrow shoulders and whipped off the snappiest salute
he could manage. "First Lieutenant Jason Caldwell
Dobbs reporting as ordered, sir."

General Jebediah Briggs eyed him coldly. Since he
was not a hidebound spit-and-polish man, he found it
surprisingly easy to ignore Dobbs's sloppy military
comportment. What passed for precision among Army
physicians, he knew, was far from the same as that

required of infantry troops. Still, Briggs paused before returning the salute, holding the stare, making sure that Dobbs knew this was not a social summons.

It was not an easy thing to do, Briggs knew, holding himself in judgment over a man whose friendship had been cemented with blood from the battlefield. That period in Mexico had been remarkable, the general reflected briefly, a time when all they had to do was fight and eat and sleep. More fighting, actually, than eating and sleeping but that was what war was all about. Thank God for war, he told himself yet again, a phrase he repeated so often he wouldn't be surprised if someone didn't have it engraved on his tombstone. The prospect of war was what made the peacetime Army bearable for him and other professional soldiers, men who endured the empty, endlessly boring years so they could come alive again when other men were suffering and dying around them.

Briggs ran his eyes down Dobbs, mentally ticking off the violations of garrison regulations: Unpressed trousers . . . tarnished buttons . . . stains on his tunic, either food or blood from the hospital . . . scuffed boots. Jesus, Briggs realized, this man is a walking demerit. But he is also one hell of a surgeon. And that forgave a lot, especially on the battlefield where a good sawbones might not only save your life, but keep you intact. For a soldier, there were many worse things than getting killed in battle. The thought of coming home without an arm or a leg or both sent chills down even the bravest man's spine. Dying a heroic death was one thing; living a life as a cast-aside cripple was quite another. Given his choice, Briggs himself would take death any time. But that was a fighting man's decision and physicians were not fighting men, not like the cavalry, the artillery, or the infantry. Still, they *were* soldiers and they were not exempt from the incurable disease that struck a number

of those who had seen battle: the sudden realization that
they *liked* war.

As certainly as men who used their weapons, surgeons must also become addicted to the excitement.
They had to, Briggs told himself. How could they not be
as susceptible as the infantrymen to the feeling of exhila-
ration that overcame them when their lives were in danger? The general knew well what it was like to feel the
blood pounding through his veins, the energy surging,
the feeling that every sense was sharpened to the
utmost. Sex was a poor substitute for battle, Briggs felt.
A man could always go out and find a woman, even if
he had to pay for the experience. But a good fight was
hard to come by. The roar and flash of cannon, the whiz
of deadly shot, the screams of men and horses. The feeling of elation that came afterwards; the realization that
you were alive while many of those around you were
dead; the fleeting certainty that you were one of God's
chosen; the perception, even if it was false, that you
were invincible. Those were things that could not be so
easily replaced.

Briggs had seen it many times in others; had even
experienced it himself to an almost frightening degree.
And he knew there was no cure; once the war-bug bit, it
was a lifetime fixation. Men came back from the war
and they felt totally lost without the daily stimulation
that battle provided. They went into bars and picked
fights with the biggest and meanest men they could
find. They sought out dangerous occupations. Or they
drank themselves to death, ending their lives in a gutter
covered with vomit and horseshit. And then there were
those like Dobbs. He missed the war all right, Briggs
was sure of that. But he was far too smart for barroom
brawls or alcoholism. Dobbs's escape, Briggs had heard
from very good sources, was laudanum, that mind-
numbing tincture of opium that was even easier to

obtain than booze. Every pharmacy from Maine to Florida would be happy to supply the drug on demand.

Briggs had to admit that he had been surprised when he heard about how rapidly Dobbs had gone downhill. He had seen the surgeon at his best: as a sleep-deprived, ministering angel hovering over a wounded man, debating whether he should take off his leg or his arm or if he should try to save the shattered limb and still prevent an even worse fate: dreaded gangrene. In his day, Dobbs had made life and death decisions as facilely as most men try to decide what kind of rotgut they're going to order. And most of the time he had been right. He saved my nephew's life, Briggs reminded himself. Jess had left the battlefield without most of his right leg, but he had nevertheless gone home to Janet and the kids and he wasn't planted in some peon's corn patch, his remains eventually seeping into Jose's tortillas. Jess's leg had been in terrible shape, even an old veteran like Briggs had to admit that it looked as bad as any leg wound he had ever seen. But Dobbs had dived in and cleaned it up and took off just enough, just as much as he absolutely had to. Jess may have to serve as a pissing post for most of the neighborhood curs for the rest of his life, but it probably was better than rotting in the maggoty soil in May-he-co. Now Dobbs needed help and Briggs felt it was his duty to do what he could to try to save him, not only because he owed him a favor because of Jess, but because he owed an even bigger favor to the Army. Dobbs had been a damn good soldier once and he would be again. Probably. Maybe. In any case, Briggs was going to try. The country may be at peace now, he told himself, but that was only transitory. Even though the politicians were afraid to admit it, this country was heading toward civil war as sure as healthy soldiers shit solid turds. And judging by what he'd seen since he came to Washington it wasn't going to be that long. He

could *smell* war on the horizon. It may take a little time
to get here, he thought, but by God, it's coming, as the
private said to the whore. And when that time came, he
wanted to be back in the forefront, him *and* Dobbs. Him
doing the best he could to kill the other sons of bitches,
Dobbs doing the best he could to patch up the detritus
of Briggs's efforts.

If Briggs had been a surgeon instead of an infantry-
man, he would use the same tactics that Dobbs had
adopted. He'd examine a wound and decide what was
the best thing he could do to save the man's life. If it
meant chopping off the hand he used to wipe his ass,
that was the way it had to be. The man would learn how
to use the other one. And that was what he had to do
with Dobbs. If Dobbs was "wounded" by laudanum,
what Briggs had to do was cut out the injured part. In
this case, it wasn't so easy. In the settled part of the
country, laudanum was everywhere. What Briggs had
to do, he felt, was put Dobbs someplace where he
couldn't get it. Then he would have to learn to live without it. If he couldn't, that was the way it went. But
Briggs felt he had to try to rehabilitate his friend. The
next problem was to find a place for the surgeon where
he wouldn't have ready access to the drug. And what
place, Briggs reckoned, would be better for than the
frontier?

After the Mexican War, the United States Army had
slipped into a terrible state. The flow of money had been
cut off. The manpower stream had been cut off. The real
soldier's balls had been cut off. The only place on the
whole goddamned continent where this did not totally
apply was in the West, where there was still some fighting going on, where a soldier and a surgeon could still
exercise their trades. Sitting in a Washington hospital
delivering babies for officers' wives and helping old soldiers through a bout of pneumonia was not proper duty

for a battlefield surgeon. Dobbs deserved better than that. There were many, Briggs knew, who would shrink at the thought of being posted to the frontier, but the general was sure that Dobbs was not one of them. Sure, the frontier was tough duty. The pay was miserably low and the weather was atrocious, either too hot or too cold or too windy or all three. The troops that an officer was required to lead and depend on were, for the most part, social misfits, criminals, shady characters escaping from troubled pasts, or newly arrived immigrants who barely spoke English. There were no women in the Western forts and damned few amenities. Housing was inadequate, the food was abominable, recreational facilities nil. Unless, of course, one looked upon the opportunity to gallop across open, untamed, unmapped, desolate, unfriendly land as an enjoyable pastime. If that was the case, the Western soldier was having the time of his life. There was, fortunately for those honed by the experience of war, the added fillip of being killed and scalped—or being captured, tortured and scalped—by a naked savage. He could also be shot by one of his own, one of the thousands of soldiers who deserted the Army for any number of reasons, principal among them currently being to try their luck in the West Coast gold fields. The officer who escaped either of these fates was likely to fall victim to disease: smallpox, cholera, influenza, or a hundred other lesser known but equally life-threatening maladies hovering in the frontier background like a well-trained waiter, anticipating that sooner rather than later he would be called to the forefront. But that's what made it so *exciting*; made a military career worthwhile.

All told, Briggs was convinced, the frontier was *the* place to be for a man who had fought the chilibellies, come away victorious, and needed a new interest in life. In short, it was just the place for Lieutenant Jason Dobbs, even if Dobbs did not yet know it.

Clearing his throat, the general greeted the surgeon for the first time since the two of them had returned to the United States. "Dobbs," Briggs said, in what for him amounted to gruff bonhomie, "you look like shit."

The physician rocked back on his heels, momentarily taken by surprise. When he realized that the general was trying to be friendly in his heavy-handed way, he allowed himself a tiny smile. "It's nice to know you've missed me, sir. It's good to see you too."

The general's horsebrush-sized moustache quivered, an indication that he too was smiling. "What do you know about the frontier?" he asked, quickly changing the subject.

Dobbs shrugged. "No much, sir. About what you would expect for a transplant from New Hampshire. The farthest west I've ever been is New Orleans. I hear it's a bitch though, a place where it's a common occurrence for men to lose fingers and toes to frostbite, *while they're in quarters*. In the summer the sun can fry your brain if you go outside without a hat. And just about any time of year the wind blows hard enough to take the enamel off your teeth if you don't have the good sense to keep your mouth closed. And that's only the weather. You want to know what I hear about the Indians?"

Briggs shook his head. "Nope. I've heard it all myself. What do you know about the state of medicine along the Platte?"

"The Platte?" Dobbs asked in surprise. "The so-called river they say is too thin to plow and too thick to drink? The river that's the source of water that has to be chewed?"

"That's the one," Briggs said, ignoring the surgeon's attempt at humor.

Dobbs shrugged. "Nothing specific, sir. I would imagine, though, it's god-awful primitive. I would guess that disease is as big a problem as the savages. I remember reading the newspaper stories about outbreaks of smallpox and cholera among the emigrants and Indians alike. Dysentery is probably pretty common. Not to mention the odd arrow wound and tomahawk slice."

"I think that's just scratching the surface," Briggs commented.

Dobbs looked curiously at the general. "May I presume enough upon our former acquaintance, sir, to ask why you're asking?" he asked cautiously

Briggs's face reddened. "Goddamnit, Dobbs!" he roared. "It's because I'm a general and you're a lieutenant. That's why I'm fuckin' asking."

Dobbs, who had seen the general explode before, was unfazed. He knew he'd get around to telling him before too long. "My apologies, sir. I spoke out of turn."

"You're goddamned right you did, Dobbs. But it *might* have something to do with the fact that I understand that you've let yourself go to hell."

"Sir?" Dobbs asked, raising an eyebrow.

"Don't play games with me, Dobbs. I understand that you've become more of a liability than an asset. That you show up for surgery so damn intoxicated that you're likely to amputate your own fuckin' finger."

"I don't drink, sir. Maybe an occasional beer."

"I'm not talkin' about alcohol and you goddamn well know it."

Shit! Dobbs told himself. He has spies everywhere. "I don't know how to answer that, sir."

"It wasn't a fuckin' question, Dobbs. It was a statement of fact. You know me well enough to be certain that I won't put up with any crap. I won't tolerate an incompetent in my command. And that's what you're on the verge of becoming, a fuckin' incompetent."

Dobbs felt as though he'd swallowed a cannonball. He's right, he thought. I've known it for months now; I just didn't want to admit it. Well, to hell with him. It's my problem, not his. What's he going to do? Exile me to the Platte?

"Are you going to answer me, Dobbs?" Briggs barked. "Or are you just going to stand there like a dumb fuckin' messican who can't speak English?"

Dobbs braced, puffing out his skinny chest. "I have nothing to say, sir."

"You're fuckin' right about that, soldier. But *I* do. I'm tellin' you, as you stand here now, you're a fuckin' disgrace to the uniform. I put up with a lot of things from my men. I don't mind 'em whorin', or gettin' drunk on Saturday night, or fightin' in the streets. All that's part of soldierin'. But I also expect 'em to do their jobs. I won't suffer a man who doesn't pull his own weight."

"Yes, sir," Dobbs said, staring into the distance, unable to meet the general's eye.

"And that's what you've become, Dobbs. Fuckin' useless. So far, as well as I can tell, no one has died yet because you've taken a sudden likin' to laudanum. But I'm not going to take the chance that it might not happen tomorrow. You understand what I'm sayin'?"

"Yes, sir," Dobbs answered softly.

"As of right now, Dobbs, you're suspended from duty. I don't want you to go near the hospital except to pack your bags."

"Pack my bags, sir?"

"You heard me. Pack your bags and report to the quartermaster to draw your equipment."

"Equipment?"

"Yes." Briggs sighed. "The equipment. The material you'll need to set up a hospital at Fort Laramie, you damned idiot. Do I have to spell out everythin' for you?"

"No, sir."

"See Captain O'Malley. He'll fill you in on the details."

"Yes, sir," Dobbs replied uncertainly. "Is that all, sir?"

Briggs studied him carefully before replying. "No, it's not all," the general replied, not unkindly. "I hate to see a man ruin his life because of an addiction." He paused. "And I hear that's what your problem is, Jace. I'm not goin' to try to tell you what to do. You're a grown man and you're smarter than most. You're . . . no, you *were* . . . the best surgeon I've ever seen. I don't want to see you toss that talent into the latrine. The day is going to come not too far from now when your talents are goin' to be needed again. What I want is to see you get hold of yourself. I've seen some men who just couldn't beat an addiction. I've seen some put a pistol to their heads because they didn't want to try. I expect more from you than that, Jace. The frontier is heatin' up. Trouble's brewin' with the Indians. The War Department is buildin' up the forces in the West, tryin' to prevent problems before they really get started. Reinforcements are goin' to be sent to Fort Laramie and they're goin' to need a good doctor. I want you to go out there and open a hospital and pull yourself together. You think you can do that, soldier?"

Dobbs looked at the floor. "I don't know, sir."

"Well, let me put it this way," Briggs said. "I think you're worth tryin' to rescue. That's why I'm sendin' you out there. This is your first and your last chance. If I hear that you've messed up out there I'm goin' to be mighty pissed off."

"I understand, sir."

"No, you don't, Dobbs," Briggs said slowly and clearly. "In the long run, what you do with your life is your business. If you want to resign your commission and spend the rest of your life in a cloud that's up to you. But you have to do it *now*. If you go to Fort Laramie

and men start dyin' because of *your* problem, I'm not
going to take it lightly. I have a long reach. If men suffer
and die because of your incompetence, I can arrange it
so you become an unfortunate casualty of 'an Indian
attack.' Now, do I make myself clear?"

Dobbs raised his head and stared into Briggs's eyes.
"Perfectly, sir."

There was no doubt about it this time, Briggs actually
allowed himself a small, tight smile. "Dismissed!" he
bellowed. And, more congenially, "Good luck, Jace.
Don't fuck up."

Alone in the small third-floor room he shared with
another lieutenant off the south ell of the officers' quarters, Dobbs tossed himself on his cot and reviewed his
meeting with General Briggs.

Goddamnit, he thought, I'm really in the shit now.
Briggs has given me the ultimate ultimatum: straighten
up or my ass is *dead*. Not just professionally, really, actually, physically *dead*. So what's it going to be, as if I had
a choice? I've been in the Army for almost ten years; it's
been my life. I regret like hell—and I will until the day I
die—that I wasn't home when Colleen came down with
the yellow fever. I should have been there to help her; at
least been available to hold her hand when she died. But
I wasn't, I was in Mexico fighting a war. That's part of
being a soldier. It was much tougher on Patrick and
Mary Margaret than it was on me. But kids are resilient;
they're doing fine with Sean and Agnes, growing up to
be real fine adults. Patrick says he wants to be an Army
doctor, like his old man. I hope not; his life will be a lot
easier if he sticks to politics, like his uncle. Mary
Margaret's still too young to have any idea about the
future. But what the hell does any nine-year-old know?
She'll get married and have a half dozen kids of her

own; never leave New England. But what's wrong with
that? Even if I resigned my commission, I sure as hell
couldn't pick up my old life. What if I showed up in
Boston and said I wanted my kids back? Jeez, Sean
would probably shoot me. As far as the kids are concerned, Sean and Agnes are their parents.

Sitting up, Dobbs swung his legs off the cot and
stared across the room. Through the narrow window he
could see the top of the oak tree that grew in the narrow
plot between the building and the brick sidewalk.
Leaves were popping out all along the branches. Spring
is here, he thought; time for change.

Walking stiffly to the battered desk that served as his
work area and table, he lowered himself into the familiar rickety straight-backed chair. Reaching down, his
hand easily found the broken handle that marked the
second drawer. Automatically, he pulled hard, knowing
without thinking about it that this is the drawer that
always sticks in damp weather. Yanking to overcome
the resistance of moisture-swollen wood, he was surprised when the drawer popped open, almost shooting
out of the framework, sending his .44 caliber Walker
Colt revolver slamming against the drawer's front
panel. Dobbs half smiled. No round in the chamber, he
thought. Otherwise, I may have lost a thumb.
Deliberately, he picked up the six-shooter and turned it
over in his hands, feeling its heavy bulk. For several
minutes he stared at it, wondering how long it had been
since he fired it. Although he had carried the weapon all
through the Mexican campaign, he had never used it.
Running his hand slowly along the barrel, as carefully
as a man might caress a woman's thigh, he realized he
had not cleaned and oiled the pistol in months. Already
spots of rust were beginning to emerge, ugly reddish-
brown patches that looked like the first signs of pox. The
mental connection triggered another thought. Have to

do that, the clinical part of his mind said; make sure I take along some smallpox vaccine. God knows it will come in handy.

Placing the pistol on the edge of the desk, he slid open another drawer. Reaching inside, he closed his hand around a quart bottle, two-thirds full of a dark liquid. He removed the cork and had the bottle halfway to his lips before he realized what he was doing.

Goddamnit! he thought, now is as good a time as any to break the laudanum habit. If I don't, it's sure as hell going to kill me. Angrily, he threw the cork across the room, watching as it bounced off the wall and skidded under his cot. Clamping his jaw in determination, Dobbs pushed back from the desk, stood, and strode to the window, the bottle in his hand. Sticking his head out to make sure there was no one underneath, he turned the bottle upside down and watched as the liquid fell in a long, dark stream, splashing slightly when it hit the still-brown grass below.

Returning to the desk, he opened the long drawer that ran across its front and extracted a sheaf of blank paper and a quill pen. He was busy scribbling away thirty minutes later when the lieutenant who shared the room returned from his shift at the hospital.

"What're you doing?" Schaeffer asked, plopping on his cot and bending to unlace his boots.

"Making a list," Dobbs replied, writing away.

"God, that feels good," Schaeffer said, removing his right boot and dropping it unceremoniously on the bare plank floor. "What kind of list?"

"Ummmmm," Dobbs answered distractedly.

Schaeffer removed his remaining boot and let it fall alongside its mate. "Ahhhhh," he sighed. "That's almost better than sex. Like the old joke about the recruit who asks the veteran, 'What's the first thing you do when you go home on leave?' And the veteran answers, 'I ain't gonna tell you that, but the second thing is I take off my goddamn boots.'"

Smiling, Schaeffer looked up, expecting Dobbs to react with a laugh. "What's the matter? Don't you think I'm funny?"

Receiving no response, he rose and padded across the room. Peering over Dobbs's shoulder, he struggled to read the surgeon's writing. "What the hell *is* that?" he asked curiously.

"I told you," Dobbs said, mildly aggravated. "It's a list."

"Looks like medical supplies to me," Schaeffer commented.

"It is," Dobbs said. "These are things I'm going to need at Fort Laramie."

"Fort Laramie!" Schaeffer said in surprise. "What the hell is this about Fort Laramie?"

"It's my new duty station." Dobbs smiled. "Aren't you going to congratulate me?"

"*You're* going to Fort Laramie?"

Dobbs grinned. "Yep."

"Christ on a crutch. When?"

"Next week. I'm going to run up to New England, see my kids, then come back here to rendezvous with another officer. Then we go to Missouri and join up with a wagon train heading for Oregon."

"But why?"

"Because Briggs says so."

"Briggs? You've been to see the general?"

"This morning."

"And just like that he said, 'Lieutenant Dobbs, I think a change of scenery would be good for you so I'm going to arrange for you to take a new job at Fort Fucking Laramie.'"

"That's pretty close."

Schaeffer returned to his cot, swinging his feet up and stretching out. Carefully he plumped his pillow and gently laid down his head. "You must have really pissed somebody off."

"On the contrary," Dobbs replied. "Briggs is doing me a favor."

"A favor, huh," Schaeffer snorted. "I hope he never does *me* any favors."

"No," said Dobbs. "It's okay. For the first time since I've been back from Mexico I feel like I'm going to be able to do what I've been trained to do. Do some real soldiering."

Schaeffer stared at him solemnly for several seconds, then smiled. "You poor, dumb fucker. But at least there's one bright point."

"What's that?" Dobbs asked, pen poised.

"I mean," Schaeffer said, "since most of your hair is gone anyway at least you won't have to worry about getting scalped."

> 13 May 54
> Washington

*Dear Mamman and Papa,*

*By the time you receive this, I shall already be en-route to my new post. I know this will come as something of a shock to you, but that is the way the Army seems to operate. No one tells you anything until the last minute, and then all of a sudden, it's "pack up and move out."*

*Actually, the reason for this unexpected development is more than a little complicated, a tale that probably is best left for when we can next get together over a steaming bowl of mamman's etouffee, the very thought of which makes my mouth water. You don't know how much I miss your cooking, mother dearest, as well as you yourself. That is not to say that I don't miss Papa, Marion, and Theophile as well, but they don't cook as well as you.*

*As I said, this may surprise you, but your older son is on his way to an adventure in the West. Specifically, I have been assigned to Fort Laramie, a place of which you probably have heard because of the treaty that was negotiated there in '51. It is, to describe it briefly, a major stop on the Overland Trail that runs from Kansas to Oregon and California. Superbly situated along the North Platte River, it serves as a major stopping place for the emigrants as they approach the Rocky Mountains. At least that is what I have been told. Before you know it, though, I'll be able to give you my own firsthand description.*

*I am quite optimistic about this turn of events. As you know, one of the reasons I wanted to attend the Academy and go into the Army was the opportunity it afforded to see new places and experience new things. Washington has been delightful, but almost a year here has cured me of any desire I may have harbored to "settle in" in the nation's capital. There are just too many politicians around here to suit my taste. From the talk around the Department, especially from other soldiers who have been there, I have quite a change to look forward to. They all say that the West is like nothing I have ever experienced before. I can easily believe that.*

*I know you probably will worry that I somehow will be in physical danger. Please don't do that. Those same soldiers who have served in the West tell me that is not the case. They say the savages are under control and when they make the occasional minor indiscretion they are promptly and suitably dealt with. They well know the consequences of violating the rules that we have set down. As a result, they have become very obedient and*

*peaceable, despite anything you may have read in the*
*penny press. The West, while not yet totally civilized by*
*the standards to which you are accustomed, is neverthe-*
*less very safe, at least as safe as Washington if not more*
*so. These days it is almost impossible to go anywhere in*
*the capital without feeling threatened by brigands,*
*whose number seems to be increasing daily.*

*I will close this quickly because I still have many*
*last-minute details to take care of, but I will write you*
*soon about my wonderful adventure. You will be*
*pleased to know that mail service to Fort Laramie is*
*regular and quite dependable; packets arrive at least*
*monthly. Give everyone a kiss for me and know that*
*you are always in my heart.*

*Your Loving Son,*
*t-Jean*

## 5

Running Antelope and White Crane lay on their stomachs, each peeking around an end of a large boulder. Beneath them was the narrow meadow that Roaring Thunder had described in his report, a bright green patch with steep rock walls on two sides, split by a stream that ran full with snow-melt. Scattered throughout the meadow, as best they could see in the rapidly fading light, were at least half a hundred Crow horses, nibbling hungrily at the abundant grass.

Slowly the two boys inched backward until they were totally behind the boulder. Levering themselves upright, they sat with their backs to the large rock and faced up the slope into the pines that grew in profusion along the top of the ridge. Speaking in a barely audible voice, in case there was a Crow horse-watcher nearby that they were unable to see, Running Antelope leaned close to his friend. "I didn't see that black gelding," he said, "the one with the white blaze."

"I didn't either," replied White Crane. "His owner must have him picketed next to his lodge."

"Just our luck," Running Antelope said in disgust. "I haven't been able to think about anything else since I first saw that horse."

"Me either," admitted White Crane. "He would be a real prize."

"Can you imagine how we would be greeted if we brought an animal like that back from our first horse raid? He'd make a great gift."

"You'd give him to Red Leaf, wouldn't you?" White Crane said with a smile. "You're trying to impress Porcupine."

Running Antelope flushed, causing White Crane's smile to broaden into a grin. "You look like the sunset," he said jovially. "I must have hit a sore spot."

"Who said anything about Porcupine?" Running Antelope asked defensively.

"You don't have to. I know you have your eye on her. The whole village knows you're interested in her."

"So what if I am?" Running Antelope bristled. "Does that become everyone's business?"

"It becomes my business," White Crane said soothingly, "because we're like brothers and I care what happens to you. If you want that gelding to give to Red Leaf because you think it might help your case with Porcupine, I'll help you. That's what brothers are for."

"You'd really do that?" Running Antelope asked, touched by the show of affection.

"Of course I would," White Crane said. "And I'd expect you to help me when the time comes."

"It's a promise," Running Antelope said, clasping White Crane by the shoulders. "You help me now and I'll help you later."

"Agreed," White Crane said, returning the embrace.

With that issue settled, Running Antelope changed

the subject. "If you were Blizzard," he ventured, "what would you do now?"

White Crane's response was immediate: "I'd attack at dawn."

Running Antelope nodded. "I would too. But one thing bothers me."

"What's that?"

"I worry that Lame Elk, Spotted Bear, and Otter may not have made it safely out of Kangi territory. What if they were captured and revealed our presence?"

White Crane shrugged. "I don't think that's the case. Everything looks too normal down there," he said, pointing with his chin toward the meadow.

"You don't think it might be a trap?"

"Well," White Crane said philosophically, "I guess we'll find out tomorrow."


When they got back to their camp they found the others sitting cross-legged on the ground, animatedly discussing plans for the next day. There was no fire because they were much too close to the Crow village, though one would have been more than welcome. A fresh, cold wind had whipped in from the north, causing the men to burrow deeper into their robes. As Running Antelope and White Crane walked up to the group, several heads turned, but none of the men offered greetings. Seating themselves behind their elders, as was expected of two neophytes on their first horse raid, the youths listened intently to the debate.

In an excess of caution, even though Strong Bow and Jagged Blade had been posted as sentries, the men leaned inward toward each other and strained to keep their voices low.

"Are you sure about the coming storm?" Badger asked Roaring Thunder.

"Absolutely," Roaring Thunder replied with finality. "The wind is already up. Can't you feel it?"

"But how can you be so certain it's a major storm?" Charging Buffalo asked. "Not even my old bones have given me a clue."

"I just know," said Roaring Thunder. "I can *smell* it. By the time the moon is up, the storm will be upon us. I suspect it probably will blow for at least two days."

"Are you certain enough for us to count on it?" Blizzard asked. It was not a serious challenge to Roaring Thunder's ability to foretell the weather. The same instincts that made Roaring Thunder a superior scout and a superb hunter made him sensitive to nuances in nature that slipped by others, even those as accustomed to living attuned to their surroundings as the Wazhazha. If Roaring Thunder said there was going to be a storm, there was going to be a storm.

"The question is," said Badger, "does that mean we need to delay our plans?"

Roaring Thunder knew the query was not directed at him but at Blizzard. The men were silent as they all looked at the *blotahunka*. He did not hesitate.

"Certainly not," Blizzard said vigorously. "A storm is to our advantage. At this time of year and at this elevation, it will be accompanied by much snow, which will not only make it nearly impossible for the Crow to see us clearly during the raid, but they won't be able to track us very well either. *Wakan Tanka* could not have been more generous."

"Don't be too quick to say that," cautioned Charging Buffalo. "Remember Spotted Bear's vision?"

Blizzard looked at him scornfully. "As I said at the time, I think he misinterpreted what the wolf was trying to tell him."

"That hasn't been proved yet," Charging Buffalo persisted.

"No, it hasn't," Blizzard said icily. "But it will. I'm confident we have the blessing of *Wakan Tanka*. And if we are successful I will make a special offering once we get back to our camp."

His confident tone effectively silenced the group and for several moments none of them spoke.

"Very well," Badger said at last, "let us work out a plan of attack."

For the next half hour, as White Crane and Running Antelope looked on, the men argued quietly about the best strategy. Finally, Blizzard picked up a stick and began drawing in the dust. "Here is what we are going to do," he said.

Looking up, he motioned to Running Antelope and White Crane. "Come here, you two, and see what I am about to draw. The plan involves you."

After making a deep scratch which he said was the creek running through the meadow, Blizzard began poking holes into the ground. "These are horses," he explained. At the right-hand side of the drawing, the south side, he drew a wiggly line. "This is a trail through the canyon that Jagged Blade found earlier. I originally planned to use it as the escape route, but now that we know we will be aided by a storm, we can take a more daring approach. Jagged Blade tells me the entrance to the trail is blocked by several logs, which the Crow have placed as a gate to keep their horses from roaming. We're going to leave that in place." He marked the barrier by two straight lines in the dirt.

"Here," he said, making an x on the east side of the line representing the creek, "is White Crane. And here," he said, making an identical mark on the opposite side of the stream, "is Running Antelope. When I give the signal, you will start yelling and waving your robes, driving the horses this way," he said, pointing north, "toward the Crow village. The rest of us will be stationed at spots along each side of the meadow. Once the horses start running our way, we will fall in with them and we will all drive the herd directly through the encampment. Since we know the Crow are not completely stupid and keep their best horses near their lodges, we can easily cut the tethers in the confusion and scoop those animals up, along with the ones from the meadow. With luck and sufficient help from *Wakan Tanka* we will be able to grab just about every horse the Crow own."

"And then what?" asked Badger, rubbing his chin thoughtfully.

"Then," Blizzard replied, "we drive the herd to the west, along the river, going through the much broader entrance to the valley that the Crows normally use."

"What happens when we're out of the valley?" asked Strong Bow.

"Then we head due north . . ." Blizzard began.

"Due north?" asked Charging Buffalo. "That's the opposite direction that we want to go."

Blizzard nodded. "Exactly! If the storm makes the visibility as bad as Roaring Thunder predicts, the Crow won't be able to get a good look at us. If we head north, they may think we're Blackfeet heading directly for our own camp."

"That's clever," agreed Badger.

"By the time the snow has covered our tracks," Blizzard continued, "we can swing back to the southeast and head for home."

"Do we fight?" Badger asked.

Although he had anticipated the question, Blizzard had not been sure how he was going to respond. Acting on experience gained in some two score battles and skirmishes with various enemies, Blizzard couched his reply with uncharacteristic delicacy.

"Yes and no," he said.

"What?" Charging Buffalo exploded. "How . . . "

". . . What I mean," Blizzard said, cutting him off, "is we fight while we're still in the Crow village, but once we have cleared the valley we simply show them our backs. If fortune is with us, they will not have recognized us as Wazhazhas. Once they have gathered themselves we don't want them to know who we are. It will be to our distinct advantage if we can convince them we're Blackfeet."

Charging Buffalo broke into a huge grin. "What a great idea," he enthused. "We get the Crow horses, we get to kill some of those wretched excuses for humans, and we get to start a new war between the Crow and Blackfeet as well. What more could one ask?"

"Don't get too excited yet," Badger cautioned. "In situations like this, even the best laid plans sometimes fall apart."

"What we have to remember above all," Blizzard said seriously, "is that we have to stick together. What with the swirling snow, the screaming, the noise of the horses, it will be awfully easy to get separated. Once we get the animals moving up the valley, we're committed. If someone gets left behind we won't be able to go back and get him."

Turning to White Crane and Running Antelope, he repeated his instructions about staying together. "You don't know how confusing it can be under circumstances like this," he warned. "When you come up the meadow with the horses, I want you," he said, pointing at Running Antelope, "to find your brother and stay at his side at all times. "You," he said, indicating White Crane, "will find me and become my shadow. Don't either of you," he said emphatically, "go off on your own *for any reason*. Do you understand?"

"Yes, Blizzard," said White Crane.

"Yes, *blotahunka*," echoed Running Antelope.

Blizzard continued to stare at them for several minutes, as if trying, by the force of his glare, to burn his instructions into their brains.

"If you listen to me and do what I tell you," he added, "you will learn much from this experience and the next time we go on a raid you will be comfortable in your knowledge of what is going to transpire. If you *don't* listen to me you could end up like Storm Cloud, only worse. The Crow are experts at dragging out a captive's death."

Running Antelope swallowed hard. "We understand," he said softly. "You won't have any worries because of us."

"Good," Blizzard replied. "Then it is settled."

Dismissing the two youths, he turned back to the circle of men. Reaching under his robe, he produced an ornately beaded elk-hide bag that contained the Wazhazhas' war pipe. As group leader, he also carried the title of pipe holder. Carefully removing the instrument, which was painted red and decorated with feathers that also had been dipped in red dye, the colors that represented war, he packed it with *shongsasha*. But before lighting it, he made a brief speech about bravery, comradeship, and tribal unity. Then, as the freshening wind whistled around the group, he lifted the pipe and offered it to the Four Winds, the Earth, and the Sky. Bringing the stem to his lips, he took a deep puff and passed it to Charging Buffalo, who went through the same ritual. Gradually, the pipe went around the circle and came back to Blizzard.

"We have prepared well," he said. "My heart tells me we will be successful tomorrow, capturing many horses and bringing much honor to ourselves and the Wazhazhas. Go now and sleep well. We have an eventful day before us."

"He didn't have to do that," White Crane said in annoyance once he and Running Antelope were alone.

"Do what?" Running Antelope asked, puzzled.

"Call attention to us like that. Treat us like children. We can fight just as well as anyone else. We're not five-year-olds."

"Don't be angry," Running Antelope cautioned. "He has a point. We've never been on a raid before. Badger told me it's mass confusion, what with the dust and the noise and horses running every which way, not to mention the fact that the Crow are going to be trying to kill us. I don't care for the insinuation either, but I can understand his reasoning."

"You're being too kind to him. Have you already forgotten what he did to Storm Cloud? Do you think he cares about what happens to us?"

"I'm not stupid enough to think he has our interests at heart," Running Antelope shot back, "give me more credit than that. But I do think he's worried about his own reputation. We've already lost Storm Cloud and three others have turned back. If he hopes to lead another raiding party, he has to make this raid a success. We *have* to come back with a lot of horses or Blizzard will be in disgrace. And if that happens because of us, what do you think he's going to do then?"

White Crane swallowed hard. "I hadn't thought of it that way, but you're right. If the raid isn't successful and it's our fault, Blizzard will find a way of getting us. I'd be willing to bet my bow on that."

"So would I," Running Antelope agreed.

Although both boys knew they would sleep little that night, they went through the motions of preparing for rest, scooping out a comfortable spot on the forest floor and arranging their robes. As they lay on their backs staring at the stars as they ducked in and out of puffy clouds that were travelling fast across the sky, blown by the stiff north wind, it was White Crane who broke the silence.

"Isn't it strange?" he asked.

"What's that?"

"Before we left our camp we were certain that at last our dreams of becoming warriors were going to come true. Remember how we dreamed about counting coup and maybe even lifting a scalp?"

"Yes," replied Running Antelope. "So what's strange about that?"

"The weird thing is," White Crane continued, ignoring the interruption, "that Storm Cloud, who was just as full of hope of distinguishing himself as you and I, is already dead and we haven't yet seen a Crow. We never, even in our wildest dreams, considered a possibility like that."

Running Antelope grunted.

"But then," White Crane went on, "we get here on the outskirts of the Crow camp and we discover that the Crow isn't our only enemy. We also have to watch out for Blizzard, who we thought would be on our side. If we don't perform to his satisfaction we can count ourselves on his enemy list. It doesn't seem fair."

"It isn't," Running Antelope agreed. "But there's nothing we can do about it. We just have to make sure we stick to him like the hide on a buffalo. We can't give him any reason to find fault."

"Agreed," said White Crane. "I just hope that someday I'm in a position to do something to revenge Storm Cloud. Maybe one day I'll be able to go face-to-face with the mighty Blizzard."

Running Antelope looked at his friend in surprise. "You're talking like a child now. We've entered a different world and we have to start acting like men. Put aside those thoughts of revenge, they will only keep you from concentrating on what we have to do tomorrow."

Unexpectedly, White Crane chuckled softly. "You're right," he said. "But thinking of killing Blizzard keeps me from being frightened about the coming encounter with the Crow. He's a known quantity; the Crow are not."

Running Antelope laughed with his friend. "Go to sleep," he chided him. "We'll need all the strength we can get tomorrow."

A full ninety minutes before dawn, Jagged Blade crawled to where Running Antelope and White Crane were sleeping and roughly shook them awake. "Come," he said brusquely, "we are preparing for the raid."

When they stumbled still half asleep to the spot where the men had gathered, White Crane and Running Antelope looked about them in mild surprise. Even though snow was falling heavily, just as Roaring Thunder had forecast, the older members of the raiding party were ignoring the weather in their dedication to last-minute detail. Although the youths had not noticed it before, each of the men had brought along a small bag containing his favorite battle garments.

Roaring Thunder was wiggling into a shirt made from exquisitely tanned elk hide. A fringe ran down each sleeve and around the neck hung strings of human hair, parts of scalps he had collected during his illustrious career as a warrior. Once he had donned his shirt, he turned his attention to his lance, which he began decorating with other items pulled from his personal kit: otter skins and eagle feathers.

Badger removed the buckskin cover from his shield and, carefully setting it aside, began sharpening his knife with a stone he had brought with him for that purpose.

Jagged Blade had produced his buckskin war leggings, which were rich with symbolism. On the right leg were painted two red hands, which meant that he had killed two adversaries in hand-to-hand combat. Below the hands was a black cross—a symbol for having rescued a friend during a fight. On the left leg were a series of vertical stripes, six black ones for the number of coups with which he had been accredited, and two red ones, that indicated he had twice been wounded in battle.

Charging Buffalo had wrapped his quilled armbands, which he believed brought him good luck, over his biceps, while Strong Bow adjusted his handsomely carved bone breastplate over his neck.

Blizzard, the most decorated of all the warriors, had slipped on shirt and leggings profusely decorated with red and black vertical stripes and four red hands. Around his waist was a small rope and miniature moccasin that signified he had captured more than ten horses during his career.

In their hair, the men wore a variety of feathers: a single golden eagle feather worn upright indicated the wearer had counted a first coup, that he had been the first to touch an enemy in battle. Among the Brulé it was considered more of an honor to have touched an adversary than to shoot him from afar with an arrow or a rifle because getting close enough for personal contact took more courage. A man who counted second coup wore an eagle feather tilted to the left, while one entitled to a third coup wore the feather horizontally. Those with fourth or fifth coups wore vertical buzzard feathers. Roaring Thunder, the Wazhazhas' best tracker, also wore three black feathers ripped down the center with the tip remaining: symbols of successful scouting expeditions.

Standing off to the side, Blizzard limbered up by repeatedly swinging his heavy war club, while Charging Buffalo gave a final inspection to his most prized possession, a .50 caliber Hawken that he had taken from an uncooperative fur trader six years earlier, having split the man's head open with his tomahawk after the unwise Canadian refused to surrender his weapon in exchange for Charging Buffalo's proffered stack of beaver pelts. As unsuitable as the rifle was for a horse raid—it had a thirty-six-inch barrel and weighed eleven pounds—Charging Buffalo would as soon have stayed in camp as go on a raid without his Plains rifle.

The main weapon of choice among the group, however was the bow, a custom-made instrument fashioned from fire-hardened ash and trimmed to an individual's height and build: The length coincided with the distance between the ground and the owner's waist, and its thickness was determined by the user's arm strength.

As White Crane and Running Antelope watched in awe, all the men, even the rifle-toting Charging Buffalo, attached fresh bow strings fashioned from a unique sinew found just below a buffalo's shoulder. First they hooked the loop at one end of the string into a notch at one end of the bow, then flexed the instrument to its desired tautness before tying the sinew string to the other end. While inexperienced *isan hanska* scoffed at the Sioux's primitive weapons, those white men who had been in battle against the Brulé knew that a good warrior could loose more than twenty arrows a minute under battle conditions, and at close range they hit with amazing accuracy and power.

Once the men were dressed for war and their weapons readied, they painted their faces, each using a pattern and color determined by what he believed was pleasing to his own supernatural guardian. Jagged Blade, Badger, and Charging Buffalo also dipped into their pouches and removed small bags of their own special medicine, a powder, which they first offered to the gods, then rubbed around their eyes and noses before putting a dab in their mouths.

Once they were totally ready, they turned to
Blizzard, the *blotahunka*, who delivered a final, ritualized
chant.

With the wind-blown snow swirling around him,
Blizzard threw open his arms and sang, not too loudly
for fear of alerting the Crow, a traditional Brulé song
warning his enemies that he was going to get their
horses.

Without a glance in the direction of Running
Antelope and White Crane, the men sprinted swiftly
down the slope to assume their positions around the
Crow horse herd. Looking at each other in mild bewil-
derment, the youths realized if they didn't hurry the
raid would start without them.

Everything he had been told about the confusion of battle, Running Antelope quickly discovered, had been a
vast understatement. Fighting to maintain his seat on
the roan mare he had climbed aboard at the beginning
of the raid, the youth unhappily discovered that he was
totally disoriented. All around him were Crow tipis,
blurred and indistinct in the blowing snow and the
cloud of dust created by the tromping of almost a hundred panic-stricken horses. Adding to the lack of visibility was the smoke from the Crow campfires and the
eerie light coming from several tipis which had been set
ablaze after they were toppled by Jagged Blade and
Blizzard, aware that the more confusion they could
cause the better.

The noise was deafening, much greater than anything
he or White Crane had anticipated. There was the
pounding of the horses' hooves, the battle cries of both
the Wazhazha and the Crow, the screams of the women
and young children, the panicked cries from the horses,
and the loud explosions of Crow rifles being fired. The

noise seemed to clamp around his head like a tightly bound strip of wet rawhide and created a pain that made his stomach churn. Involuntarily, he retched down the front of his robe and into the mane of the horse he was desperately trying to control.

As if all that were not enough, Running Antelope's senses were further assailed by a variety of smells, many of them noxious. There was the smell of wood smoke, the stench of burning buffalo hide from the blazing tipis, the odor of fear among the horses and, most of all, the scent of blood.

When the Crows fired indiscriminately into the attackers, many of their bullets hit the plunging horses rather than the Wazhazha raiders and their blood flew through the air like water from a basket. Running Antelope himself was soaked, not only with his own vomit but the blood of a horse next to him which had been hit in the throat by a Crow musket ball. Another horse nearby had been downed by an arrow from Badger, who had been aiming at a Crow brave when the horse vaulted into his path. The screaming horse was being trampled by other animals who were trying to escape in panic.

Prior to the raid, Running Antelope had agonized over the thought of how he might be paralyzed by fear and disgrace himself before the warriors. But once the battle was joined, he felt the fear lift from him like a puff of smoke from a rifle barrel. Instead of being paralyzed, he found himself possessed of a surge of superhuman energy. In his mind, a single word repeated itself again and again: survive!

"Be calm! Be calm!" he whispered into the mare's ear, trying to convince the animal to peacefully accept his unexpected presence. Slowly, despite the confusion around him, the mare settled down and responded to Running Antelope's knee pressure, turning first right and then left as Running Antelope struggled to get his bearings. Despite the pre-raid admonitions from Blizzard, Running Antelope had lost sight of his brother and had given up trying to find him. Then, through the smoke and blowing snow, Running Antelope spotted a familiar figure.

"White Crane!" he yelled as loudly as he could. "White Crane!"

Hearing his friend, White Crane turned the pinto he had appropriated, a smaller horse that he apparently had more success in controlling than Running Antelope was having with his larger mare, and gestured wildly.

"Come with me!" he screamed. "Over this way."

Maneuvering through the confusion, Running Antelope fought his way to White Crane's side.

"Are you all right?" he yelled.

"Of course I'm all right. But come, I have something to show you."

White Crane dodged around two tipis and yanked the pinto to an abrupt halt. Pointing excitedly, he yelled at Running Antelope. "Look!" he screamed. "The black gelding."

Running Antelope's eyes widened in elation. Twenty yards away was the horse he had first seen on the day that Storm Cloud died, and he was even more magnificent up close than he had appeared from a distance. Rather than panicking like the other animals, the large gelding stood more or less in place, stomping impatiently at its tether, a sight that told Running Antelope that the horse was not only beautiful but well trained and experienced in battle.

Forgetting every warning that Blizzard had given him, Running Antelope turned to White Crane. "I'm going to get him," he yelled, slipping off the back of the mare he had been riding. As he sprinted closer to the black, his knife already out to cut the tether, a fierce-looking Crow emerged from the tipi behind the horse.

Raising his rifle to his shoulder, the warrior took aim at Running Antelope, a target he could hardly miss considering his proximity.

"Running Antelope!" White Crane screamed, digging his heels into the sides of his pinto and urging him forward.

Hearing his friend's cry, Running Antelope looked up and saw the Crow warrior with the rifle pointing directly at him. The sudden realization that his life might very possibly be over brought Running Antelope to a sudden stop. Staring at the rifleman, he froze in place, making himself an even easier target.

Before the Crow could fire, however, White Crane quickly closed the gap. It was this sudden spurt that saved Running Antelope's life.

Out of the corner of his eye, the Crow saw White Crane approaching on the pinto. An experienced fighter, he knew better than to swivel to face the new challenge, not when he already had an enemy in his sights. But the sudden appearance of another enemy was enough to distract him and cause his rifle barrel to waver slightly. When he pulled the trigger, his sight was no longer on Running Antelope's chest. Instead of striking the youth directly in the heart, as the Crow had intended, his ball hit Running Antelope's right thigh, just above the knee.

The impact of the ball spun Running Antelope in a clockwise direction and threw him violently to the ground. Flipping immediately onto his back, he looked up to see the Crow, whose mouth was open in a full-throated battle cry, dashing toward him with his knife drawn, apparently intending to finish the job by eviscerating Running Antelope.

The Crow was three yards away when Charging Buffalo rounded a nearby tipi, his rifle at the ready.

Without pausing his horse, Charging Buffalo continued toward Running Antelope and the Crow at a full gallop, heading straight for the enemy. Using his horse to knock the Crow to the ground, Charging Buffalo whirled and brought the animal to a full stop. Lifting his rifle, he took careful aim at the Crow, who was struggling to regain his feet, and pulled the trigger.

Running Antelope heard a tremendous roar and watched in awe as the Crow's head disappeared in a cloud of bright red mist, having been struck at close range by a ball that measured a half inch in diameter and was capable of stopping an attacking grizzly. Running Antelope's last thought before he lost consciousness was, "Too bad Charging Buffalo had to blow his head off; now he won't be able to collect the scalp."

The next thing Running Antelope knew was waking up by a campfire, acutely aware of the aroma of freshly roasted meat. Instantly, he was ravenously hungry. Driven by his desire for food, he attempted to rise, only to be brought up sharply by a horrible pain that enveloped his entire right side. Suddenly, he remembered the raid, the Crow, and being shot in the leg.

Almost as soon as the memory came back, White Crane materialized above him. "Lie still," White Crane said. "You're not yet in condition to do much of anything."

Gently propping his friend against a nearby tree, White Crane brought him a portion of hot venison. "Eat slowly," he cautioned. "Your stomach has been empty for three days and if you try to eat too quickly you'll only lose it all."

While Running Antelope nibbled at the meat, the first hot food he had in almost two weeks, White Crane brought him up to date on the raid.

"Your wound was bad," he explained, "but your brother knew how to bind it to stop the bleeding. His treatment saved your life."

"No," Running Antelope corrected. "It was you who saved my life. If you had not charged, the Crow would not have been distracted and he would have killed me for certain."

"If you insist on thanking someone," said Badger, who had arrived to check on his brother's condition, "give thanks to Charging Buffalo because he is the one who killed the Crow."

"Where is he?" asked Running Antelope. "I want to express my gratitude."

"Unfortunately," Badger said, "you'll have to thank his wife. Charging Buffalo took an arrow through the throat shortly after he killed your Crow. He died almost as quickly."

When he heard that, Running Antelope thought he was going to vomit again. "Charging Buffalo is dead?" he asked in surprise.

"Yes," interjected White Crane. "And so is Strong Bow. He fell off his horse and was tomahawked to death by two Crow before Blizzard could arrive and kill them both with his war club."

"Anyone else?" asked Running Antelope, his face the color of the snow that remained in the shade of the nearby trees.

"Jagged Blade has a bad knife wound in his side," Badger said, "but he will live. Your friend, White Crane, has a slight wound on his left forearm that he is too modest to tell you about, and Blizzard took an arrow through his calf. But he was very lucky; it hit no bones and he is already walking again, although a little stiffly."

Running Antelope did some quick calculation. "Two dead and four wounded, including me. Out of eight warriors, that's not very good news."

Badger shrugged. "It could have been a lot worse. Apparently, during the night many of the Crow warriors who had been off on a hunt returned, so there were many more braves in the camp than we had figured going in."

"Is there any good news?" Running Antelope asked dejectedly.

"Yes," White Crane answered brightly. "We captured more than three score horses, some of them really prize animals. Blizzard got three scalps, Roaring Thunder, two, and I got my first coup. It was against a Crow youth no older than I. I killed him with a single knife thrust between his ribs."

Running Antelope stared at the ground and did not answer.

"And there's one other thing, too," White Crane said happily, saving his best news for last.

Running Antelope looked at him without speaking.

"We got the black gelding," White Crane said enthusiastically. "At least you did."

"No, I didn't," Running Antelope said. "I was going to cut his tether when the Crow shot me. I never got there."

"That doesn't matter," said White Crane. "You were almost there and would have been successful if the Crow bullet had not stopped you. In any case, the gelding is now a part of the herd and as far as anyone is concerned, he is your prize."

"I can't accept him," Running Antelope said. "You know that."

"Of course you can," White Crane insisted. "He's your horse because he undoubtedly would have been if your plan had not been interrupted."

"But . . ." Running Antelope began.

"There will be no more talk about it," White Crane said gruffly. "The gelding is yours. You can keep him yourself or you can give him to Red Leaf. The choice is yours."

He paused, then added with a smile, "However, if he were mine, I'd give him to Red Leaf. Horses come and go but maidens like Porcupine don't come along every day."

Three days later, travelling much faster on horseback than they had on foot, the Wazhazhas were within a half day's ride of their own camp. The feint to the north had proved successful since the Crows went galloping off toward the Blackfoot lodges and had offered no further threat to the fleeing raiders.

As customary, Blizzard sent a man—Badger—forward to notify the camp of their return. Stopping on a ridge a few miles from the Wazhazha lodges, Badger dismounted and signalled to the camp. Slowly, he waved two robes, which signified that the party had lost two men in their skirmish with the Crow. For that reason, when the entire group arrived the next day, it was not a joyous greeting. More significance was given to the mourning ceremony than to the raiders' otherwise successful mission. Even though Blizzard, Roaring Thunder, and White Crane rode in with their faces blackened, symbolizing they had returned with scalps, the victory dance that could have lasted for a week or more was cancelled. Instead, the families of Charging Buffalo and Strong Bow went into the forest to collect wood to build burial scaffolds and Running Antelope was deposited at the tipi of the band's most respected medicine man to receive professional treatment for his wound. The news was bad: Running Antelope would be able to walk with an exaggerated limp but he would never run again. So he would never be tempted to denigrate the significance of

what had happened to him that day in the Crow
camp, he formally changed his name from Running
Antelope to Crooked Leg and seemed to evolve
overnight from a happy-go-lucky youth to a somber,
melancholy adult.

*~6~*

Jean Benoit was about two deep breaths from being asleep, submerged contentedly in the double-thick feather mattress that was a point of pride for the owner of the Palace Hotel, when he felt the hand slide gently along his ribs, pause to tenderly massage his stomach, and then slip slowly lower.

"Again?" he asked, suppressing a grin.

"Only if you think you're up to it," Ellen Harrison replied, working magic with her fingers.

"I swear," Benoit whispered, "you're the most insatiable woman I've ever known."

"Only for you, my love," she said teasingly. "You awake passions in me that I never knew existed."

"Is that so?" Benoit replied good-naturedly, not believing a word of what she was telling him. Rolling on his side, he pulled her closer to him and began caressing her back, letting his hand move down to one of her perfectly formed buttocks. Among her other attributes, Ellen's skin was smooth and flawless as carved marble, and it was the same bleached-bone white hue as well.

It's a good thing she has such a wonderful body, Benoit thought, because, in all honesty, she was rather homely. Her face was long, coming to a sharp point at the chin, and her nose was a trifle too broad. What saved her from being downright ugly, Benoit reckoned, were her eyes, which, even though they were too close together, were a remarkable, startling green. Next to her shape and her satiny skin, they were her best feature.

When Benoit and First Lieutenant Jason Dobbs rode into the rough frontier town a week earlier after a hard, hurried trip from Washington, anxious to make sure they did not miss the next wagon train west, the young officer was unsure exactly what to expect. It would not be like New Orleans, he knew. Or upstate New York. Or Washington. But the last thing he imagined he would find was a woman like Ellen Harrison.

Once Dobbs and Benoit discovered that their great rush was for naught, that the next westward-bound caravan did not depart for almost two weeks, they began looking around for ways to amuse themselves until it was time to depart. It was while he was wandering down one of the town's side streets, looking for some place to buy shaving soap, which he figured might be hard to get at Fort Laramie, that Benoit stumbled upon the Harrison family store. He may have passed it by since a quick glance inside showed shelves overflowing with odds and ends and a profusion of customers, the type of place that he normally avoided. But then he noticed sign posted in the window adjacent to the front door. In inch-tall, neat, black letters it read:

**GENERAL STORE**
EVERYTHING YOU NEED FOR THE TRAIL
Tobacco, Raisins, Flour and Spice;
Sugar, Butter, Eggs and Rice.
Sausage, Salt Pork, Knuckles of Pigs,
Biscuits, Crackers and Jars of Figs.
Molasses, Corn Meal, Honey and Bread;
Balls of Yarn, Spools of Thread.
Parasols, Hats, Boots and Slickers;
Shoes, Socks, Corsets and Knickers.
Tubs, and Buckets, Kettles and Pails,
Wrenches, Hatchets, Hammers and Nails.
Rifles, Pistols, plenty of Ammo;
Dynamite, Caps and vials of Nitro.
Knives, Razors, Saws, and Axes,
Harrison's has it or we pay your Taxes.

Whoever composed that, Benoit thought with a smile, has to have a good sense of humor. As an admirer of anyone who could face life with a laugh, he wandered inside, intending to buy his soap, congratulate the author, and meander on down to the Aces High Saloon, where he was told there was always a moderate-stake poker game in progress and the beer didn't taste like buffalo piss. Not that he had ever actually tried any buffalo piss, he reminded himself, but some of the frontier "pilsner," he had heard, was so bad that bison urine would be an improvement.

Striding up to the counter he waited impatiently while a beefy, red-headed man with thick muttonchop whiskers wrapped a parcel for a florid, broad-faced woman in a gingham dress.

"That salve will be invaluable once you get on the road for Oregon, Mrs. Finnegan," the man said. "You have to use it morning and evening because the western sun is like nothing you've ever seen before. If you don't take care of your skin, it will get as dry and brittle as the buffalo hide the Injuns use on their tipis."

"It can't be *that* bad," the woman said skeptically.

"Oh, indeed it can," the man cautioned. "Just you wait. When the sun beats down and the wind blows and there ain't a tree as far as the eye can see, nothing but mile after mile of sizzling, burning prairie, you'll think you're in Hell's back forty, that's for sure, pardon the expression."

"If it's that bad," the woman said, hefting the parcel. "You think this is going to be enough?"

"That's a good point, Mrs. Finnegan. If it was me, I'd take about twice that much. As you can see, I'm a redhead and my skin can't much stand the sun. Being Irish yourself, I suspect you're just as sensitive to the elements, the likes o' which they've never seen in County Cork. It's a good thing I'm inside all day because if I had to travel where you're going, and I didn't have no lotion to rub on my skin twice a day, I wouldn't be nothing but a small pile of fried pork rind by the time I got there."

"In that case, maybe I'd better double that order, providing you got enough in stock, that is."

The man grinned, showing a mouthful of yellow teeth. "It just happens that I think I can accommodate you," he said. "Wait here and I'll go check in the back room."

Benoit, his patience taxed to the limit, turned on his heel, intending to find his soap somewhere else, when he practically tripped over the woman who had come up behind him.

"Don't be in such a hurry to leave, lieutenant," she said in a deep, rich voice. "My father isn't the only one who works here. What can I get for you?"

Benoit found himself staring at a woman in her early twenties, petite but shapely, not pretty but

merry-looking with a lilt in her voice and an attractive
way of cocking her head when she talked. Her hair was
the same color as her father's, but she wore it bound
tight in a bun, and when she smiled Benoit noticed happily that she apparently had inherited her mother's
teeth.

"You must be the one who composed the advertise-
ment," he said, jerking his head toward the door.

She looked puzzled, not comprehending at first what
he meant. "Oh!" she exclaimed when it dawned upon
her. "The sign!" Blushing—attractively, Benoit
thought—she smiled again. "Yes," she admitted, "I have
to take the blame for that."

"Blame isn't the word I would have used," Benoit
said. "I thought it was extremely clever."

"Well, you know how it is," she said, waving her
hand. "We don't have much else to do out here on the
frontier except sit around and try to be creative."

At first, Benoit wasn't sure if she was being serious or
sarcastic. When he realized she was pulling his leg, he
chuckled. "I can't imagine it's much of a strain for you,"
he said. "Being creative, that is."

"You'd be surprised," she shot back, "how little
chance we frontier women get to exercise our brains.
The dream of my life is to get out of this hellhole and
move to New York. Tell me, lieutenant, since you look
like a man of breeding and discernment, is the city as
exciting as they say?"

"I haven't spent enough time in New York to answer
that one way or the other," he said, "but my home is
New Orleans and I can tell you it is quite an exciting
place."

"Oh, my god," she enthused, pretending to swoon.
"New Orleans! If there's any place that sounds more
attractive to me than New York, it has to be New
Orleans. I would just *love* to hear all about it." Eyeing

Benoit carefully, she added, "Tell me, lieutenant, do you read?"

"Why, yes, of course," he said, somewhat surprised. "In school . . . "

"No," she said, cutting him off. "I don't mean *can* you read. I mean *do* you read. Are you a lover of literature? A connoisseur of contemporary letters?"

"Oh, that." Benoit sighed. "Sure. I mean, yes. I like books. I try to keep up."

"Have you brought any with you?" she asked anxiously.

Looking at her somewhat strangely, Benoit replied that he had, indeed, brought a few with him since he figured they might be good companions at the isolated post where he was headed.

"Are they new ones?" she asked excitedly. "What are the titles?"

"Let me think," Benoit said, rubbing his chin. "I've brought Longfellow's *Evangeline* because it reminds me of home, and Stowe's *Uncle Tom's Cabin* because it deals with a subject near and dear to the heart of all Southerners . . . "

"Oh, don't get political on me," she chided. "What else?"

"When you're travelling by horseback," he said, "you can't exactly tote a lot with you. Most of my books are in my kit, which will catch up with me later."

"Well, didn't you bring anything to read along the way?"

"As a matter of fact," Benoit said, smiling brightly, "I have a brand new one by that New England hermit, Henry David Thoreau . . . "

"You mean *Walden*," she interrupted. "I read a review of it in a New York newspaper that one of the emigrants left behind, but there aren't any copies yet in Independence. Do you think . . . "

"It would be my pleasure to share it with you," Benoit interjected quickly. "You name the time and the place."

Ellen Harrison paused. "Tomorrow," she said enthusiastically. "I'll make us a picnic. I know a beautiful, quiet spot . . . "

"Tomorrow it is," Benoit said gleefully, happy with the way things were turning out. "In the meantime, I need some shaving soap."

Ellen Harrison blushed again. "Of course," she said. "I forgot you came in here to buy something. Come with me. We have several brands you can choose from."

That was on Monday. On Tuesday, they picnicked in a shady grove along the turgid Kaw River, east of its junction with the broader Missouri, spending three hours reading excerpts from Thoreau and discussing his message. On Wednesday they took a long horseback ride. With his copy of *Evangeline* propped on the pommel of his saddle, Benoit read aloud as they ambled through the forest, spontaneously translating portions of the classic love poem into French as he went along. Seemingly inflamed by Longfellow's purple prose, Ellen allowed herself to be seduced, although Benoit would later wonder exactly who did the debauching. At the time, though, he was profoundly grateful for the interlude, not only because he had wanted to make love to her since the first time he saw her, but because his voice was getting raspy from all the unaccustomed oratory.

On Thursday, she slipped up the back stairs to his third-floor room at the Palace Hotel and they fell hungrily into his bed, a performance they repeated on Friday, Saturday, and the following Monday. Sunday was a day for forced abstinence because Ellen had to accompany her family to a day-long series of services at a particularly demanding local branch of the Methodist Church. By Tuesday, a week after their first time alone together, the trysts had fallen into a pattern. Ellen told her father she was spending the midday hours performing one social obligation or another, ranging from visiting a sick friend to helping organize the lessons at the new Independence school. Then she would hurry to his room, where they spent the time in pursuits more physical than social or intellectual. After some ninety minutes of testing the hotel room bed, Ellen would slip back into her clothes and return to her father's store, glowing and smiling.

John Harrison, a hard-working storekeeper and a good provider but otherwise rather dense, never suspected his daughter was having an affair. Rather, two days later when Ellen was restocking some yard goods in the rear of the store, a section where her father could not see her, she overheard him telling a customer how proud he was of his daughter's newfound community awareness.

Ten days after the liaison began, it ended as abruptly as it had started.

"I have to leave tomorrow," Benoit blurted one forenoon, panting and sweating from an especially strenuous but highly inventive maneuver that Ellen had proposed.

"Damnit, Jean," she said angrily. "You didn't have to tell me like that."

"What do you mean?" he said. "I thought you appreciated honesty."

"Honesty is one thing; stupidity is another. Don't you know *anything* about women?"

"No," he said quietly. "I'm woefully ignorant about women. Women in general, that is. I do know a lot about you and I have to admit this has been a wonderful . . . "

"Oh, Jean," Ellen purred, forgetting her anger. "Tell me later. First, there is something I just thought of that might be fun . . . "

A half hour later, Benoit sprawled exhausted across the bed, too tired even to cover himself with the soggy sheet. Ellen leaned forward and whispered in his ear, "A penny for your thoughts."

"Thoughts?" he said, smiling thinly. "I don't have enough energy left to think."

"I have to confess I don't either," she said. "You've flat worn me out."

"That goes double for me," he said, weakly caressing her back. "I'm going to miss you."

"Me, too," she mumbled.

"I wish I could take you with me, but . . . "

Ellen sprang up, jumping as if she had been prodded with a hot poker.

"Take me with you!" she said explosively. "Don't be a damned fool."

Benoit furrowed his brow, perplexed. "I don't understand . . . "

"You have to understand this," she said, swinging her feet to the floor. "I wouldn't go to Fort Laramie for a million dollars. I wouldn't go if you promised to crown me queen. I wouldn't go if . . . "

"But . . . "

"No buts, perhaps or maybes. Independence is bad enough, a goddamned jerkwater town in the middle of nowhere. Fort Laramie, from what I hear and can imagine, is even worse, the virtual anus of civilization as we know it."

"It can't be that bad . . . " Benoit began.

Ellen stopped buttoning her dress, looked at her lover and smiled, not unkindly. "Tell me that in six months," she said softly. "Write me a letter and explain to me in detail exactly what I'm missing by not being a part of the great American experience to tame the West."

Benoit tried to rise, but she waved him back.

"Don't get up. I can find my way out. Take care of yourself out there. Don't let the Indians cut off your hair. Or," she smiled and glanced pointedly at his crotch, "anything else."

Blowing him a kiss, she hurried out the door. Benoit could hear her as she walked quickly down the hall. Then there was the sound of a door squeaking on its hinges and footsteps moving down the stairs. Soon, he couldn't hear them any more, only the noise of the wind moving through the elm tree that grew outside. Benoit clasped his hands behind his head and stared at the ceiling. Slowly a smile began to form on his lips. Gradually it grew wider. Uttering a sigh of profound relief, he closed his eyes. Ain't life wonderful, he thought just before he fell asleep.

The next morning, shortly after daybreak, Benoit and Dobbs rode out to the site where the wagons were gathering for the journey to Oregon. Since the animals needed grazing land and the emigrants had to have space to pitch their camps, the gathering spot was several miles southwest of the town of Independence.

What they found when they arrived at the campsite was apparent mass confusion. Wagons were pulled off on the side of the road, still muddy and deeply rutted as a result of the spring rains and the heavy traffic, and their owners were clustered around their vehicles, frantically packing and repacking the high-axeled conveyances that would be their only homes for the next five months. Fires were burning beside many of the wagons as the womenfolk prepared breakfast, typically a nourishing meal since the journeyers would need all the energy they could get to power them through their strenuous days. Once the train got moving, breakfast would take on an increasing importance, surpassed only by the midday meal. Supper, the last meal of the day, was usually a light repast because on most days the emigrants kept going as long as there was enough light to see the trail.

As they rode closer, thanks to a light northerly breeze, Benoit and Dobbs could smell the coffee and the bacon.

"That makes me damned hungry," Dobbs commented as they drew closer to their first campfire.

"Me, too," agreed Benoit. "It sure smells a hell of a lot better than our hardtack and jerky. I'm glad you had the foresight to lay on some supplies and have them shipped to the wagonmaster."

"Yeah," said Dobbs. "It was right hospitable of him to agree to carry our victuals."

"Speaking of the wagonmaster," Benoit added, "we need to look him up and see what our duties are going to be on the trip. According to our orders, we're more or less under his command."

Benoit broke off from Dobbs and rode fifty paces to the east to ask directions to Alf Stuart's wagon. Ten minutes later he returned. In his handkerchief were two hot biscuits, courtesy of an emigrant family.

"Here you go," he said, handing one to Dobbs. "Buttered and everything. These people seem right friendly; this might not be such a bad trip after all."

Dobbs grinned thinly. "My experience with large groups on the move tells me not to judge too quickly. People tend to get short tempered when the going gets difficult. I think you'd be wise to withhold your opinion for a few days yet."

Benoit nodded but did not reply. Jesus, he thought, what a spoilsport.

Twenty minutes later, they reined up at Stuart's wagon. While disorientation seemed to be the norm elsewhere in the camp, the atmosphere around the wagonmaster's site radiated calm and serenity; the eye in the hurricane, thought Benoit, who had seen more than his share of tropical storms.

"Hidy," Stuart said, glancing up as the two officers dismounted and dropped their reins. Being Army mounts, the horses were trained to remain in place, in contrast to Stuart's horses tethered in a nearby copse of oaks, their forelegs bound together with just enough rope to let them hobble about.

"Was beginning to wonder if you boys was goin' to make it," drawled Stuart, a burly, deeply-tanned man with a large belly, a full head of thick gray hair, and a flowing beard stained dark around the mouth by tobacco juice. When he smiled, deep wrinkles formed a spiderweb around his deep blue eyes, which twinkled like a teenager's. As long as you look at his eyes, Dobbs thought, everything's okay. Unfortunately, Stuart's smile also revealed a double row of crooked, stained teeth with large gaps, indicative of a lifetime of neglect and a tendency to revel in barroom brawls.

"Come up and sit," he said warmly, reaching for two extra tin cups. As he poured steaming coffee as thick as quicksand and as dark as coal, Stuart outlined the technical aspects of the trip.

"This is my twentieth crossing," he explained. "Been doing it regular since '43 when I seen there was going to be a demand for skills like mine. Before that I was a trapper but the beaver petered out and I had to find a new line of work. That's when I seen the future. It weren't easy to begin with, I tell you. That first year a thousand emigrants made the trip and me and the others had our work cut out for us. We didn't know where all the springs was, and the shortcuts, and the places where we could always find a deer or antelope to give us some fresh meat. I tell you, boys, I damn near starved myself on those first two trips. Then me and the other wagonmasters got together in the winter when we couldn't do nothin' noway and started comparin' notes. Not that we told *all* our secrets, but some things we shared because it was good for ever'body.

"That first year, I thought a thousand emigrants was a hell of a lot. But I larned better'n that in '49. Now *that* was a year. After that lucky sumbitch found gold at Sutter's Creek, more than fifty-five thousand people pushed across. You believe that? *Fifty-five thousand.* Dumb fuckers couldn't wait to get out West and strike it rich."

"Did they? asked Benoit. "Strike it rich, I mean."

"Sheeet," Stuart said, spitting a stream of tobacco juice into the fire, where it sizzled and popped. "Some of 'em did, I reckon. Most of 'em didn't. A lot of 'em never even had the chance. In '49, using what figures I compiled and those from othern like me, five thousand never got across. Got laid low by Asiatic cholera. Right mean shit that was."

"You can say that again," said Dobbs. "I've seen what it can do to an Army regiment."

Stuart nodded, agitated by the interruption. It wasn't often he got the chance to expound on his own abilities and when the opportunity arose he didn't like being sidetracked. Giving Dobbs a stern look, he continued:

"Disease and Injuns ain't the only hazards, though. Weather can be a real bitch. In '47 a bunch of dumb emigrants tried to take a shortcut through the Wasatch Mountains in California. Got snowed in, all eighty-seven of 'em. When rescuers finally found 'em the next spring, only forty-five were still alive and they stayed that way because they et their friends, their work animals, their pets, even their fuckin' boots. Cannibalism ain't just in Africa, boys. It's a real popular activity on the Plains."

"Are we going to have weather problems?" Dobbs asked.

Stuart looked at him like a teacher looks at a backward first grader. "You can bet your ass on that, soljer. Rain like you never seed before. Hail that'll rip a wagon cover to shreds quicker'n you can take a piss. Wind that'll blow your skinny ass back to Virginny or wherever the hell you're from. Sun that'll boil your brains if you ain't got the god-given sense to wear a hat. Mud up to your knees and dust that'll suffocate a mule. The only thang you prob'ly ain't goin' to see is snow since you ain't goin' but to Fort Laramie. The real mountains don't start 'til you get west o' thar."

"Snow?" Benoit asked in surprise. "You going to be on the trail that long?"

Stuart grinned; it was not a pretty sight. "Sonny," he said condescendingly, "it's two thousand miles, give or take, to whar these folks is going. If we make fifteen miles a day we're doing damn good. A lot of days, we ain't going to make that, not when you consider down time for busted wagons, floods, the need to hunt fresh game, and whatever else might come up. It's a long fuckin' trip, no matter how you figure it. I recollect one trip in '51, thought we was never goin' to get thar 'cause most of the folks was highly religious and they refused to trek on the Sabbath. Said it was agin' God or some such shit. I tried to tell 'em that might be good back in Ohio but come September in the mountains, they might be ass deep in snow. God wasn't likely goin' to postpone a blizzard because those assholes been keeping the Sabbath. But what I said didn't make no nevamind to them; one day a week they just laid up. Hardheaded as a bunch of goddamned mules. We barely made it through that time. Maybe God was listenin' to them because the fall storms was two weeks late. Otherwise, winter woulda caught our asses just like it did that group with

the Donner brothers. I ain't anxious to repeat an experience like that. That's why I've gotten tougher with these
folks. When I say we're trekking today, by God we're
trekking today. If they want to sit on their asses and sing
hymns and listen to some pissant try to tell 'em what hell
is like, I'd just as soon ride on. They know that before we
get started so I don't expect any shit along the way."

"What's the makeup of the current group?" Dobbs
asked, anxious to change the subject.

Stuart looked blank. "How's that?"

"What kind of people are on this trip? Nationalities?
Occupations? Age groups?"

"Oh," Stuart said, looking askance at the surgeon.
"Lots of feriners this time. Some krauts, some dagos,
and lots of goddamned Irish. Being of Scot descent
myself, I ain't real happy with the Irish. Would rather
have niggers if it comes right down to it. They ain't as
stubborn."

Dobbs cringed visibly when Stuart used the deroga-
tory terms for people of different races and nationalities.
But Benoit, who came from a different background, took
it in stride. Not that he agreed with Stuart's prejudices,
he just wasn't shocked by then.

"How many people, all told?"

Stuart shrugged. "Persackly twenty-seven wagons,
not countin' mine, o' course. I ain't sure exactly how
many people, but figure at least two adults per wagon,
plus a few more relatives, brothers or ol' mamas mostly.
Some of them ain't gonna make it but try tellin' Junior
that. God knows how many kids. With the Irish, 'specially, you never can tell. They'll probably be droppin'
babies from here to Oregon."

Dobbs looked a little surprised. Pregnant women
were a factor he hadn't considered. There weren't many
of those on an Army trek.

"When are we going to get started?" Benoit asked.

"First thang tomorrow," Stuart replied.

"Why not today?"

Stuart shook his head. "I need one more day to try to convince these greenhorns they're carryin' too much shit. Ain't gonna be successful, o' course, but I wanta try. Cuts down on my problems later."

"What do you mean *too much shit*?" asked Dobbs.

Stuart looked around, then pointed to a wagon about thirty yards away. "Looka thar," he said. "Them people are loaded down with stuff they'll never be able to get to Oregon. Them wooden boxes prob'ly hold granma's dishes. They'll be tossed out in three days. I'd be willin' to bet if I were to go over thar and start goin' through their goods I'd find all kinds of useless crap from fire tongs to sewin' machines. Time they cross their first rainswole creek, they'll be leavin' that shit on the banks. An' food! You wouldn't believe what some of these folks'll bring. Had one train where a man drug along three cases o' champagne and two boxes of canned oysters. Champagne and oysters, for shit's sake. Can you believe that? I'da loved to have been there when the savages got aholda *that*."

"Do they have any idea what they *should* be packing?" asked Dobbs.

"'Course they do," Stuart replied testily. "Gave 'em all a list. Had it printed up and everythang. Tells 'em persackly what to carry." Reaching behind him, he dug in his saddlebags and produced a wrinkled sheet of paper, which he handed to Dobbs.

Benoit leaned over Dobbs's shoulder and read what the wagonmaster recommended as a minimum. Under the heading of "essentials" Stuart suggested:

### COOKING UTENSILS

1 barrel of flour
100 lbs. bacon/pork

Enough fresh beef to be driven on the hoof to
    make up parts of the ration
25 lbs. sugar
25 lbs. coffee
25 lbs salt
Baking soda or yeast powders for making bread
1 small keg molasses
25 lbs. dried apples or apricots

"Apples or apricots?" Dobbs asked, raising an eye-brow.

"You a doctor or not?" Stuart asked.

"I am," Dobbs replied icily.

"Ain't you never seen scurvy?"

Dobbs's face reddened. "Guess I wasn't thinking too well."

"What about weapons?" Benoit asked.

"Turn the paper over," Stuart said with a tight smile.

On the back, under the heading "Optional Material" was:

### PERSONAL FIREARM(S)

25 lbs. gunpowder
Sufficient lead to make shot
2 knives
Whiskey

"Whiskey? Dobbs asked.

Stuart smiled. "Good for snakebite."

"You mean weapons aren't considered essentials?" asked Benoit.

Stuart shrugged. "These are city folk. Or farmers. They ain't outdoorsmen. Some of 'em don't even know how to load and shoot a rifle. I ain't anxious to have a bunch of greenhorns walkin' around with weapons they don't know how to use."

"Didn't you say you planned to spend some time hunting?" asked Dobbs.

"Sure did," Stuart replied. "But the huntin' is for them that knows how. And they know enough to bring their rifles."

"But how about as defense against Indians?" said Benoit.

"Sonny," Stuart drawled. "You been readin' too many dime novels. Injuns ain't goin' to be a real problem, least as far as attackin' goes. They keep to their territory, we keep to ours. The biggest problem from Injuns, less'n someone stirs them up, is from the goddamned beggars. They're drawn to the trains like flies to shit. Always lurkin' around, askin' for handouts. They purely love biscuits and coffee and they'll drive you goddamned crazy 'til you give 'em some. Didn't get attacked even once my last trip. The Injuns was too busy huntin' buffler to mess around with us."

"Well," Dobbs asked, tiring of the wagonmaster's opinionated monologue, "where do we fit in?"

"Beats shit outta me," Stuart replied. "All I know is I was contacted by an Army officer from Fort Leavenworth and he said I should expect to have two soljers along on the trip. Way he explained it was your commanding officer or whoever figured since you was goin' to be responsible for protectin' trains like this 'un once you got to Fort Laramie, you should at least know what kinda problems we have to contend with. Guess you might come in handy on the off chance we run into some hostiles, but I figure that ain't gonna be likely."

"I guess we could always offer our services if you need some help with discipline," suggested Benoit.

Stuart's look was a mixture of contempt and incredulity. "Sonny," he snarled, "if I need discipline I'll administer it myself. And if by some chance I need some help I got muleskinners who'd take your ass apart in about two seconds flat. You just sit back and relax and try to larn sumthin'. 'Less you got a problem I don't want to see your ass 'til we get to Fort Kearny. Do I make myself clear?"

"You sure do," Benoit said, his face so red that Dobbs feared for a minute that he might suffer a stroke. "We'll keep out of your way."

Again, Stuart smiled broadly. "That's good," he said. "That's the way I like it."

## 7

Benoit welcomed the trail. For one thing, it gave him and Dobbs the chance to get to know each other, a luxury that had been denied them on their hurried trip from Washington when all they were interested in was making time. From before sunup until after sunset all they had done was ride, and when they finally stopped for the day both were too tired for conversation. Similarly, they had not been together much in Independence, thanks mainly to Benoit's romantic diversion. But riding along at a comparatively leisurely pace with the wagons afforded them the opportunity to build a friendship, a circumstance that both surprised and pleased each of them, considering their different backgrounds and interests.

Dobbs was a pencil-thin, six-foot–two New Englander with a long chin and pointed nose, close-set, sky-blue eyes, wispy, rapidly disappearing blond hair, and long, reedlike fingers. The eldest son of a wealthy landowner in western New Hampshire, he grew up in a

town named after his grandfather. Intense even as a
youth, Dobbs concentrated on his books and graduated
cum laude from Harvard medical school. Soon afterward he married the daughter of a locally prominent
physician, but surprised everyone who knew him by
choosing the Army over a comfortable future as the
inheritor of his father-in-law's prosperous practice. A
social and political liberal, Dobbs deeply disapproved of
slavery and states' rights, two of the top issues of the
day, and absolutely detested the government's Indian
policy, which he felt was driven by greed and expedi-
ency and was completely devoid of empathy for the
bronzed, noble men who roamed the West.

Benoit's contrast to Dobbs, both physical and intellectual, was considerable. At six feet he was a little
shorter, but he was a natural athlete who sat a horse as
easily as a Lakota warrior. He also was an expert
fencer and a much better than average shot with a
handgun, two skills that youths of his class in New
Orleans began developing at an early age in deference
to the time-honored tradition of dueling that prevailed
in the city. From the time he was barely in his teens,
Benoit also showed an extraordinary interest in the
opposite sex, a proclivity that led to a dispute with
another youth while he was home on vacation after his
second year at the academy. The other blueblood, a
hot-tempered Creole named Francois Lasseigne,
became convinced that Benoit was trying to steal the
affections of his fiancee, a dark-haired young beauty
and an audacious flirt. Although the accusation was
only partly true, Benoit felt duty bound to defend her
honor when Lasseigne accused her of being a slut.
When Benoit vociferously objected, Lasseigne slapped
him across the cheek with his new calfskin gloves and
challenged him to decide the matter according to local
custom.

Two day later, Benoit and Lasseigne met face-to-face under a drooping oak tree along Bayou St. John, a traditional place to settle such controversies. Lasseigne, anxious to draw first blood, fired first and his ball zinged by Benoit's left ear. Benoit, slower on the trigger, proved only slightly more deadly. His ball tore through the meaty part of Lasseigne's inner right thigh and exited without striking bone, making Lasseigne eternally grateful that he escaped with both his honor and his sexual apparatus intact.

The first son and middle child of a well-to-do maritime lawyer, a man who emigrated to Louisiana from the Alsace-Lorraine region of France in 1816, and a Paris-born would-be opera singer, Benoit early on developed a political philosophy that in some ways was not too unlike Dobbs's. Basically a social liberal by current American standards since the influences on his life were strongly European, Benoit nevertheless understood, in a way that Dobbs never would, how slavery was part of the thread that was woven throughout the fabric of the South's agrarian society. His family was as far removed from the institution of slavery as Dobbs's, yet he grew up surrounded by the system and was able to see how dependent Southerners were upon the practice. Although he personally viewed slavery as an odious practice he also saw it as one of the foundations of the prevailing financial structure. He felt certain that attempts to eradicate it without replacing it with a viable alternative—which seemed to be the goal of the Northern abolitionists—seemed certain to lead to disaster.

Where Benoit and Dobbs really differed, however, was on the issue of states' rights. Dobbs was an uncompromising defender of the concept of a strong federal government, a dedicated believer in the idea

that the country could prosper only under a powerful
central organization rooted in Washington. Benoit, on
the other hand, felt that a central government's role
should be restricted to an organizational one and decisions that dealt with everyday governmental operations should be left to the individual units, the states.
In Dobbs's view, the country was like a human body
and Washington was its heart and brain. It was his
conviction that the individual parts, the states, were
like arms and legs that would be unable to function
without direction from Washington. Benoit, on the
other hand, had a different vision. In his mind's eye,
the country was simply an overlarge assembly whose
members might come together for a common cause but
that did not mean they were abandoning their preroga-
tives to retain their rights to act individually and inde-
pendently.

These markedly different philosophies on the role
of government would simultaneously fuel and
threaten their friendship for all the time they were to
know each other. They were, however, issues that
would not come out until later. In the early days of
their relationship their talk mainly was about their
immediate surroundings and the sense of wonder-
ment each was experiencing as a new world began to
open up.

"Do you think," Benoit ventured late on the afternoon of the second day as they ambled alongside the
line of wagons, trying to keep on the windward side to
avoid the dust that rose in a huge cloud along the line of
march, "that these people have any idea of what they're
letting themselves in for?"

"It is kind of hard to imagine, isn't it?" replied
Dobbs. "Look," he said, waving his arm to encompass
the trekkers, "everything they own is in those little
boxes with wheels. Back where I come from people are

buried in vaults that have more space than those Prairie Schooners."

"That's true." Benoit chuckled wryly. "These people sold their farms and their businesses. They left friends, lovers, and relatives behind to go off on foot across two thousand miles of strange country searching for God knows what. I may have been able to understand it better when Oregon was giving away free land to settlers, but that offer expired a year and a half ago. What's drawing them out there now?"

"Gold?" Dobbs posited. "Virgin land even it isn't free anymore? Explicit freedom? The opportunity to get in on something from the beginning? Who knows. I guess there are as many different reasons as there are emigrants."

For awhile they rode in silence, each lost in his own thoughts. Then Benoit turned to Dobbs and spoke in a quiet voice, not anxious to share his worries with a potential eavesdropper. "In your professional opinion," he began, slightly stressing the word "professional," "how many of them you figure are never going to make it?"

"Good question," Dobbs said, considering his reply. "It's really hard to tell since there are so many variables. If these people were troopers on the march, it wouldn't be as difficult to predict."

"How so?"

"Well," Dobbs replied, also in a quieter tone, "troopers for the most part are relatively healthy adult males. You would have to accept as a given that they are at least somewhat inured to hardship and are in better than average physical condition. But look around at this group. You have infants . . . you have toddlers . . . you have teenagers . . . you have adults . . . and you have a surprising number of elderly. With the exception of the young adults, all of those age groups are susceptible in varying degrees to disease, fatigue, and the rigors of dehydration as well as a diminished food supply. A serious malady like cholera could—and has—wreak havoc on similar groups in the past. Just a wave of dysentery could be devastating, especially to the very young and the very old. Plus, you have pregnant women and people already ravaged by ailments."

"You do?" Benoit asked in mild surprise. "Some already sick?"

"You bet," said Dobbs. "I saw one guy this morning, couldn't have been more than thirty or so, coughing up blood. If he isn't in the late stages of consumption already I'm going to be the next Senator from Massachusetts."

"That bad, huh?"

Dobbs nodded. "And possibly worse. I've only been figuring the dangers they face from the elements and disease. I have *no* idea how to calculate the probabilities of an armed attack or how these civilians, as opposed to a unit of trained troops, would react."

Benoit looked at him sharply. "You mean you don't believe the wagonmaster when he talks about how peaceable the Indians have become?"

Dobbs laughed bitterly. "Not for a single goddamn minute," he said emphatically. "I don't know who Stuart thought he was talking to but he has to know *we* know he's full of shit. The Indians haven't even started to rebel yet. If the tribes are so tranquil how come the Army is sending reinforcements westward and is building even more forts?"

"Maybe it's just an excess of caution," Benoit suggested.

Dobbs smiled. "'Excess of caution' my fat Aunt Fannie's big butt. Big trouble is coming to the West. In my opinion, which may not be worth much in the long run, things are going to get a lot worse before they get better. But I think the Army knows that. Congress probably knows it. Shit, even *I* know it, and I'm not the most politically astute surgeon that ever wore a uniform. Most of all, even Alf Stuart knows it. Did you get a glimpse inside his wagon the other day when we were having coffee?"

"No. What did I miss?"

"Probably just the greatest collection of weaponry between Forts Leavenworth and Kearny. That man has enough armament in his Conestoga to fight a small war. If those poor bastards at the Alamo had been blessed with a comparable amount of firepower, the Mexican War would have been over before it got started."

"That's interesting," Benoit commented.

"What's more," continued Dobbs, "did you notice his reference to being anxious to keep this train moving, saying he didn't intend to surrender to demands by the trekkers to observe the Sabbath?"

"Sure," said Benoit. "He wants to get across the Rockies before the snow starts flying."

"That's what he *says*," Dobbs confided. "I suspect it's because he's nervous about what might happen with the Indians. I think he wants to get the hell across the Plains because he figures if he's moving fast enough the Indians won't have as much time to get organized for an attack."

"By God," agreed Benoit. "You may be right. I didn't pick up on that. I guess my naivete is peeking through."

"No." Dobbs laughed. "You just aren't old enough to be as cynical as I am. I didn't use to be this way either—distrustful of just about everyone—before I went to Mexico. Before my wife died."

"Your wife?" Benoit asked in surprise. "She died while you were off on campaign?"

Dobbs nodded. "Shouldn't have mentioned it," he said sharply. "I'm really not ready to talk about it yet."

Benoit looked at him curiously. "I can understand that . . ." he began.

"Besides," Dobbs interrupted. "We don't have time for a big philosophical discussion. Stuart," he added, pointing to the front of the train, "must have decided to call it a day. He's bringing the group into a circle."

"Okay," Benoit said, making a mental note to himself to dance around the subject of Dobbs's widowerhood.


The days spent on his trip from Washington to New England to visit Patrick and Mary Margaret had been much harder on Dobbs than he had anticipated. Withdrawal from laudanum had brought on more severe rigors than he had expected, including fatigue and debilitating chills. But by the time he rendezvoused with Benoit for the trip west, the worst had passed. Although there still were times he craved a nip—and there probably always would be—he held the temptation at bay by throwing himself into other activities.

At first, during the headlong dash from Washington, he had not had time to get restless. But the plodding pace of the wagon train proved hard on his psyche; within a few days he began resenting the snail-like crawl across the prairie. By then, the journey had fallen into a fairly predictable, monotonous pattern. Every day was pretty much the same: Rise at dawn . . . eat a substantial breakfast . . . hitch up the teams . . . and start out. Around noon, the wagons came to a halt so the trekkers could prepare their main meal, after which they normally took a long break. This gave them a chance to catch up on routine chores such as shoeing the animals, making minor repairs to the wagons, patching the canvas, or just enjoying a long nap. The march resumed around three and continued until dusk, when the wagons were driven into a circle for the night. After the stock was taken care of, the men in the group usually gathered together for a few pulls from someone's whiskey jug while the women visited among themselves. Bedtime was early since there was no sleeping-in the next day. As long as the weather was nice, the men mostly stretched out on the prairie, under the stars, while the women and girls slept in the wagons. A few had brought along tents, which seemed to Benoit to be a very sensible solution.

Risking the hazard of being labelled antisocial, Dobbs mostly eschewed the male end-of-the-day gatherings. Since he wasn't anxious to replace one bad habit with another, and since the talk usually revolved around farms, crops, draft animals, and families—none of which particularly interested him—he began seeking solitude. Nestled comfortably next to a small campfire, with a tin cup of freshly made coffee at his elbow, Dobbs would pull out his writing implements and set to work on his new project: a surgeon's diary of conditions in the West.

Using a leatherbound journal he had the foresight to buy before leaving Independence, Dobbs seemed totally content spending thirty minutes to an hour recording events of the westward trip as they unfolded before him.

Virtually every night he went through the same routine, making himself comfortable and digging his writing paraphernalia out of his saddlebags. Before recording his thoughts for that day, he looked quickly over his earlier entries, marveling how, in ink on paper, they reflected his overall impression of a certain sameness to the days.

*June 28, 1854. A thunderstorm struck last night with a ferocity not often seen in my part of the country. Fierce wind that blew over two wagons, followed by a lightning storm the likes of which I have never seen. Flash upon flash ripped through the night, easily visible far in the distance because the trees are thinning and it is possible to see for miles in almost every direction. A large cottonwood near the O'Brien wagon was hit. It erupted into a ball of flame. Sparks burned holes in canvas but because of wet condition did not spread. Luck of the Irish. No serious damage.*

*June 30, 1854. Muddy start today because of last night's storm. As a result, the going was slow. Made only nine miles instead of usual twelve or thirteen. Hamilton's ox threw a shoe. Never before seen an ox shoed. Quite a job. Lot harder to handle than a horse. In the end, legs had to be tied so new shoe could be affixed.*

*July 3, 1854. Camped along the Big Blue River. Good grass for stock and plenty of fuel available. Am told this will change drastically once we get closer to Kearny and beyond. Alf Stuart says not to be lulled by picnic-like atmosphere that has prevailed so far; that hard, long days are coming. Have yet to make a major river crossing, which reputedly can be quite dangerous.*

While he was bored with the day-to-day routine, Dobbs was under no illusions about the enormity of the task he would be facing once he got to Fort Laramie. From what he had been told there were some 150 officers and men at the post, all members of the 6th Infantry, and more reinforcements were expected before winter. The men had been without a surgeon since the post was opened several years ago so he was, in effect, breaking new ground. There was no hospital as such and he knew that one of his first tasks would be to set up his surgery using the material that was being shipped in on the first available supply train from Fort Leavenworth. What he was unsure of was how much he would be able to contribute to the well-being of the troopers. What he expected to find were the usual problems dealing with disease and privation. Cholera remained a constant threat, like a grizzly in hibernation. Dysentery was a constant problem, and venereal disease could be troublesome indeed since men deprived of female companionship were liable to bed down with anyone who came along regardless of the possible threat of disease, disregarding the fact that anyone who contacted syphilis was doomed to a slow, terrible death since there was no known cure. Typhoid also loomed in the background, as did typhus, tetanus, tuberculosis, and influenza. While smallpox was always a threat, he had taken the precaution of ordering a large supply of vaccine and he was determined to make sure that every breathing, walking human being he could force or coerce into it was going to be inoculated.

Looming as an even larger problem than disease, he felt, was trauma. Surgery, he knew better than anyone within hundreds of miles, was still a very rough science, little improved upon in hundreds of years. A Boston dentist that Dobbs had met a decade earlier, William T. G. Morton, had amply demonstrated back in 1846 that a sulfuric ether he had concocted could be used as an anaesthetic. Dobbs remembered that Morton had, in fact, removed a tumor from the neck of a patient during an operation at the Massachusetts General Hospital after using it earlier to extract an ulcerated tooth from one of his own patients. But the compound was far from perfected and certainly was not yet even close to being readily available. The only things Dobbs could rely on to anesthetize a patient would be laudanum and whiskey, neither of which were particularly effective. If one of his troopers needed an amputation the procedure Dobbs would follow would be no different than what he had used in the recent war: Give the patient something to clamp down on, saw like hell, and be ready to cauterize. Then pray that infection did not set in.

As Dobbs hunched over his journal, musing about these problems, he was distracted by a man running through the camp, apparently headed in his direction. When he got closer, Dobbs saw that it was the hefty muleskinner called Bull, one of Alf Stuart's regular crew.

"Dr. Dobbs," he panted, coming to a halt and gripping his side, which throbbed from the unaccustomed sprint.

"Take it easy, man," Dobbs cautioned. "Don't work yourself into a heart attack. Breathe slowly and deeply, then when you can talk tell me why you're trying to ruin my period of contemplation."

"Mr. Stuart . . . sent . . . me," he man huffed.

"I figured that much," Dobbs replied. "I didn't reckon you'd come running after me because you're overly fond of me and anxious to share my company."

Despite his discomfort, the man shot Dobbs a dirty look. "Don't . . . give me . . . any shit . . . Doc . . . "

"Sorry," Dobbs apologized. "Seems my biggest problem is controlling my tongue. Now *why* did you track me down?"

"It's Jim Emerson's ma, the old lady, Sara . . . "

"Sara Emerson?" Dobbs asked, puzzled. "I don't believe . . . "

"You probably don't know her," Bull interjected.

"But that ain't important. She's some fuckin' sick and Mr. Stuart wants you to take a look."

"Oh!?" Dobbs responded with interest, feeling stale since he hadn't seen a patient in almost a month. "Why didn't you say so? Don't stand there gawking, man, lead the way."

Sara Emerson, Dobbs discovered, was indeed gravely ill. By the time he arrived, the old lady's skin was whiter than paper and her skin was cold and clammy. Lying on a makeshift bed in the back of her son's wagon, Sara Emerson's breathing was in short, rapid bursts and her pulse was racing. Her son and his wife hovered over her, wringing their hands.

"Tell me what happened," Dobbs asked, looking worried. "When did she first get ill?"

"She started upchucking before we stopped for dinner," her son explained. "An' it ain't got any better. Thrown up everything but her toenails and I wouldn't be surprised what that's next."

"Is that all? Just nausea?"

"No. She took to trembling as well. Thought she was going to shake to pieces, I did."

Wiping the old woman's head with a cool, damp cloth—the only treatment he could administer until he had a better handle on the problem—Dobbs began quizzing her family about what she had eaten and when. What he finally learned was that Sara Emerson possessed a lifelong yearning for fresh cow's milk, a desire that apparently was not shared by her son and daughter-in-law. That morning, as usual, she had milked the family cow which her son had decided to bring along expressly to help satisfy his mother's craving, and had eagerly downed a pint of the fluid, as she had almost every day as long as Jim Emerson could remember.

"Did you drink any of the milk?" Dobbs asked carefully.

Jim Emerson looked at him in mild surprise. "Hell, no," he said swiftly. "I can't stand the goddamn stuff."

"How about your wife?"

"I feel the same way," Doreen Emerson replied.

Dobbs gnawed his lower lip, afraid of what the answer to his next question was going to be.

"Where did you leave the cow last night?"

"We turned her out to graze, like we usually do," Emerson replied. "Along the creek bottom."

It was the response that Dobbs did not want to hear.

"I think she's suffering from tremetol poisoning," Dobbs said gently. "It happens when someone drinks milk from a cow that's been grazing on the snakeroot plant, rayless goldenrod, or a handful of other plants."

"Well, what can you do?" asked Jim Emerson.

Dobbs shook his head. "Not a thing," he said. "I'm completely helpless. Can't do anything but wait and see if her body throws it off. How old is she anyway?"

Emerson did some quick calculations. "Seventy-four," he said at length.

Dobbs shook his head again. "That isn't good," he said. "Someone that age doesn't have the resistance you or I would. Besides, she looks like she's had a pretty good dose. If I were you," he said as slowly and as carefully as possible, "I'd prepare for the worst."

"Oh, my God," shrieked Doreen.

"Where's my gun, Doreen?" Emerson asked angrily. "I'm gonna kill that fuckin' cow."

Dobbs looked at him in surprise, then shrugged without saying anything. People reacted in different ways to news of impending death, he knew, and there was no point in arguing with Emerson. He probably would regain his sense before he actually shot the poor dumb beast.

An hour later, Sara Emerson trembled violently for the last time. With a deep sigh and a grimace, her eyes flew open and stared unseeing at the ceiling for several seconds before rolling slowly upward.

Gently, Dobbs reached forward and pulled her eyelids closed. Without speaking further to the grieving couple, he slipped out of the wagon.

More social and less literary minded than Dobbs, Benoit spent most of the long evenings on the trail visiting among the emigrants. On occasion, usually when his conscience began to bother him about neglecting his family, Benoit abandoned his wagon-hopping and dug out his writing implements as well. While Dobbs was tending to Sara Emerson, Benoit, returning to the campsite and finding Dobbs absent, began a letter to his parents.

> 7 July 54
> Somewhere in Kansas

*Dear Mamman and Papa,*

*Greetings from your older son, who is communicating to you after one week into his Great Adventure. So far, the trip has been anything but adventurous but that is not to say that it is unpleasant. Although the routine is rather boring I have taken occasion during the day to visit with some of my travelling companions and I have to report that they are a diverse and interesting lot. Many of them, like you and Papa, come from across the Atlantic. While Papa was lucky enough to settle in a community where he could utilize both his native language and his training in the law, many of these newcomers have not fared nearly so well, finding themselves isolated linguistically and occupationally.*

*My favorite group is composed of three families of relatively recent immigrants from Germany. Heinrich and Johanna Mueller are travelling to Oregon with their two sons, Werner and Wilhelm, aged four and two*

*respectively. Heinrich was a shopkeeper before immi-
grating to New York three years ago. In the wagon
immediately behind theirs are Hans and Hildegard
Schmidt and their two children, Inge and Erich, two
happy, healthy-looking young people, who are also the
best English-speakers in the group. A jeweler, Hans has
been in New York for six years and still speaks hardly a
word of English. In the third wagon are Heinz and Else
Hartmann, another delightful young couple, with three
children: Emmi, Karl, and Agnes, who is still an infant.
Heinz had a small farm where he grew grapes for wine
before he was wiped out by a vine disease in '49.*

*Yesterday at noon, Hans, with his daughter as inter-
preter, invited me to share their main meal, which consisted of pork, shredded vegetables, and horseradish.
While Frau Schmidt's cooking cannot compare with
yours, Mamman, I have to confess that the meal was
quite good, probably better than I will eat again for a
long time. Herr Schmidt, who insists that I call him
Hans although he is almost as old as Papa, apologized
profusely because he could not offer me any German
beer to wash down the dinner.*

*They explained to me that all of them come from the
same general area near Frankfurt and met by chance in
a German club in Brooklyn, New York. They became
fast friends and decided to travel to Oregon together.
After talking to some Germans who had been there,
Heinz became convinced that the new territory was
prime land for growing grapes. Gottfried and Hans will
be his partners and together they plan to found what
they predict will one day be a famous winery . . .*

He paused, looking up as Dobbs approached the fire.
Reaching for the pot of coffee, he poured himself a fresh
cup and sat cross-legged on the ground, staring into the
embers.

"What the matter?" Benoit asked, sensing a problem. Although Dobbs sometimes proved taciturn he knew the surgeon well enough to read some of his moods.

In clipped, medical terms, Dobbs told him about the death of the old woman and how he had been powerless to stop it.

"Don't take it badly," Benoit suggested, "it wasn't your fault."

"Oh, I know that," replied Dobbs, "but sometimes I feel as if science has not come any farther than the days when we used to beat drums and scream at the heavens, figuring that would scare away the death demons."

Sighing, he tossed the remainder of his coffee onto the coals. "It isn't the same," he said quietly, "as having a soldier die on you when he's shot full of holes and blood is pouring out of him like water through a sieve. To me, as a surgeon, it's much harder to deal with disease. When I've got a broken body in front of me, I feel like I may be able to do something to save a life. In a situation like that, I can use my skills. But when some parasite attacks a person's insides and there's nothing I can do, it really gets to me."

Not knowing what to say, Benoit said nothing. When Dobbs gave no indication he wanted to discuss the matter further, Benoit picked up his pen and took up where he left off in his letter to his parents.

*"An interruption,"*
he wrote.

> *"Dobbs just returned from a wagon where he had been summoned to treat an emigrant woman suffering from a severe malady. Unfortunately, she died. Her name was Sara Emerson and she was seventy-four years old, a native of Columbus, Ohio. I didn't know her but she must have been brave. I can't imagine someone her age tossing away a whole lifetime and starting*

*an arduous journey through the wilderness simply to begin afresh. That attitude, which is surprising to me, is prevalent among the emigrants. I am constantly amazed by their spirit and their willingness to face all kinds of adversity in search of a dream. I hope when I get to be seventy-four, I still retain that spark. From what did she die, you are undoubtedly asking. The answer is something unbelievably mundane. She succumbed to a poisoning that resulted from her cow eating the wrong plant. Dobbs says the illness is not uncommon, the same thing killed the mother of Abraham Lincoln, a fairly well-known politician from Illinois.*

# 8

Pale Otter waggled the finger of her free hand within inches of the nose of the plump white dog that she and her husband, Roaring Thunder, had been raising since it was a pup, almost a year ago.

"You are completely undisciplined," she said angrily. "I have tried my best to teach you manners but you persist in acting like some wanton coyote, stealing any food within reach, even that which is meant for my husband and my children. I don't know where I went wrong with you," she continued. In the face of the tirade, the dog plopped on its stomach, put its head between its paws and stared up at Pale Otter with large, wet, brown eyes. "When you want, you can be the best of dogs. You never try to hide when it comes time for me to attach the travois and you don't try to run among the horses when we are moving camp. As a watchdog, you are superb; you do a marvelous job of protecting the lodge. But," she said, her voice getting higher, "you have a very bad heart. When you should be working, you are off chasing rabbits, taking the other dogs with you. This makes others in the band very mad at me. And then you make it worse by howling all night when everyone else is trying to sleep, and that makes the other wives, not to mention their husbands, even madder at me. You cause me much grief, which I could tolerate if only you weren't such a thief. You not only steal from the family that feeds you and cares for you, you steal from those in nearby lodges. Mountain Pine came to me this morning and said you had sneaked into her lodge and taken a great piece of fat that she was roasting in front of the fire for her children. It is bad enough that you steal from us—that I could probably forgive—but I am unable to accept the fact that you also steal from others because it makes my life very difficult. I have tried to make you behave better but all my efforts have failed. You are a bad dog, and you leave me no other choice!"

With her other hand, which she had hidden behind her back, Pale Otter hefted the heavy stone mallet and brought it down sharply on the dog's head, crushing its skull. "Now," she said sadly, "you will have to repay us for all the food you have stolen by becoming a meal yourself."

Grabbing the dead dog by its hind legs, she dragged it over to a fire that she had built. Calling her oldest daughter, a girl of about twelve, Pale Otter instructed her to grab the dog's front legs. With her lifting from the back, the two held the carcass over the fire until its hair had been singed off. After waiting a few minutes for it to cool, Pale Otter took the sharp knife she used to butcher buffalo and other game, and slit the dog up the middle, eviscerating the animal. She then chopped it into pieces and dumped them into a kettle, where water was starting to boil. When the meat was almost done, she added a basket of wild turnips and simmered them together while instructing her husband to gather his friends for an impromptu feast.

Fire-in-the-Hills belched contentedly and settled back
on the small pile of buffalo robes that Pale Otter had
carefully arranged for each of the guests.

"You seem to have recovered from your winter-long
illness," commented Jagged Blade. "I guess we'll have to
put up with your sarcasm for yet another season."

"Unfortunately for you, I think you're right," Fire-in-
the-Hills retorted with a smile, realizing that Jagged
Blade was trying to show friendship in his own dull,
clumsy manner. "Now that my cough has finally gone I
feel like a youth again. The only problem is I can't get
my arrow straight anymore. If I ever have occasion to
use it on a target, I don't think it will penetrate."

Roaring Thunder's daughter, who was helping her
mother collect the bowls, blushed and covered her face
with her hands.

"What you need," said Roaring Thunder, "is more
fresh meat. Pemmican and jerky are not meant to be
consumed after the snow has melted."

"How would you know about such things," Fire-in-
the-Hills shot back. "I don't see any young children
scampering around your lodge."

"Roaring Thunder's right about the fresh meat,"
added Badger. "We've been scrimping by on a few deer
and antelope but what we really need is some fresh buffalo."

"That's true," agreed Conquering Bear, slipping his
prized pipe out of its soft leather cover. Carefully packing it with *shongsasha*, he leaned forward for a firebrand.
"Now we have horses. The prairie is green so the herds
are on the move."

"I've been thinking the same thing," said Roaring
Thunder. "I'm ready to take a group of young warriors
and see if we can find a herd."

"If the white man hasn't chased them all too far to the west," Badger added somewhat bitterly.

"That *has* become a problem," said Scalptaker, puffing deeply on the pipe as it made its way around the group.

"There's only one way to find out," said Roaring Thunder. "We'll go see."

"Who do you plan to take with you?" asked Badger.

Roaring Thunder shrugged. "I haven't really thought about it, but I assume that White Crane would want to go, along with Lame Elk's son, Diving Beaver."

"Take my son, too," added Buffalo Heart. "Little Crow is getting old enough to begin seriously preparing for his life as a hunter and warrior."

"He would make a good addition to the group," agreed Roaring Thunder. "Tell him to be ready to go at dawn tomorrow." Turning to Badger, he looked with concern at his friend. "How is Running Antelope?" he asked.

"You mean 'Crooked Leg,'" Badger replied. "Physically, he's doing well. The wound is healing much better than anyone anticipated. But his spirit is poor. He mopes around all day and has little interest anymore in practicing with his bow and tomahawk. I worry that he will go into a decline and die like Eagle Claw."

"I remember that well," said Fire-in-the-Hills. "Eagle Claw was a promising young warrior: strong, brave, and blessed with good instincts. Then he became ill with a throat ailment and decided it was time for him to die. In just a few days, he went rapidly downhill and his father found his body in the forest. There was not a mark on him; he willed himself to die because he thought it was his time."

"Would it help Running . . ." Roaring Thunder began, then corrected himself. "Would it help *Crooked Leg* to join our scouting party?"

"It might," Badger said, "but I don't think he's well enough yet to withstand such a rigorous trip."

"Ummmmm," said Roaring Thunder. "That's too bad. He showed great bravery in facing that Kangi."

"He will recover," Badger said, then added solemnly. "Or he will die. It is up to *Wakan Tanka*."

As soon as the scouting party left, the Wazhazhas began making preparations for a *wani-sapa*, a community buffalo hunt that required a tremendous amount of organization and cooperation.

While the scouts were scouring the nearby plains for a suitable herd, the Nacas, a group of respected tribal members separate from the council, began preparing for their main function: inventorying the available meat supply, putting together an estimate of how much meat would be needed, and organizing down to the last detail the roles the various members of the band would play in the hunt. Even more than the war party, which was the important event in the life of a warrior and the determinant of status among the male members of the band, the *wani-sapa* was the single most important event in the lives of the Plains Indians because if it failed, the whole band could starve.

Since the event played such an important role in their lives, preparation for the *wani-sapa* was not a purely physical activity. While the scouts were gone, the band's most respected shamans, particularly those who specialized in the hunting ritual, the Buffalo Dreamers, isolated themselves and went through a series of sweat baths designed to encourage visions of a successful hunt. Once the Buffalo Dreamers were confident of their prognosticative ability, they organized a special dance asking *Wakan Tanka* to smile favorably upon the Wazhazhas' efforts.

A week after they left, Roaring Thunder and his scouts returned with good news: a sizable herd consisting of a large number of fat cows had been sighted to the southwest, a two-day march away.

With high spirits, the Wazhazhas collapsed their tipis and loaded them on travois to move closer to the herd and make it easier to complete the huge job of butchering the carcasses and preparing the hides once the hunt itself was over. Spread out in a wave that ran for a mile from one end to the other and was several hundred yards deep, the band rolled across the prairie to get in position. Horses dragged the heavy lodgepoles and the skins that made up the tipis' outer coverings, while personal possessions were loaded upon smaller travois pulled by dogs. Elderly and sick members of the band or those too young to withstand a sustained march rode in special basket-like devices that also were pulled by horses. Warriors, heavily armed and on the alert, rode the flanks to protect the group during a time when it would be especially vulnerable to enemy attack. Other warriors spread out from the larger group and travelled parallel to the line of march so they could sound an early warning if they happened across a party of Crow or Shoshoni who might be zeroing in for an attack.

Laughing and joking, yelling back and forth to each other like schoolchildren on a picnic, the group moved ponderously in the direction that Roaring Thunder had indicated. Two days later they found a quiet clearing on the banks of a clear-running stream and reestablished the camp. Within a couple of hours, it was as if they had never moved.

Even before the women had the tipis back up, Roaring Thunder and his scouts again rode off to make sure the herd had not deviated from its previous route. Within half a day, they galloped back, shouting joyously

that the herd had not wandered off and was a half-day's
ride away, moving steadily in the same direction.

Early the next morning, the hunters excitedly
mounted their horses and waited for approval from the
Nacas to formally begin the hunt. Although a few of the
hunters carried rifles and lances, most were armed only
with their bows and a quiver full of arrows, each
marked with the owner's particular symbol so they
could precisely determine later which hunter killed
which buffalo. This was important because the successful hunter got the choicest parts: the brains, the tongue,
the liver, the rump ribs, and the gristle around the nostrils. Each hunter had two horses. One was to ride until
they were within striking distance; the other, usually the
better trained of the two, was kept fresh in order to be
ready for the actual hunt. Each also strapped to his wrist
a rawhide band a sturdy whip to encourage the horses
when extra speed was needed.

Before setting off, Roaring Thunder gathered the
young men who were taking part in their first *wani-sapa*
and cautioned them about the dangers involved.

"Don't be fooled into thinking just because the buf-
faloes are big and clumsy-looking that they are stupid or
incapable of quick action," he warned. "Once you get
close enough to loose your arrow, the buffalo is going to
know you're there and he's going to try to attack your
horse. Don't panic and don't fire wildly at the animal.
Pick a fat cow or a young bull and get as close as you
can. Then aim for a spot just below the hump. Once you
have shot one animal, select another from the herd and
move quickly. Don't stop hunting until you hear my signal or until the herd is completely dispersed. And," he
said with emphasis, "don't approach a downed animal
until you're sure it's dead. I have seen too many good
hunters make that mistake, which usually proves fatal.
A man afoot is no match for a pain-crazed buffalo."

"Are we ready yet?" White Crane asked impatiently, trying to control the roan he was riding, one of the horses he had liberated from the Crows. His spare horse, the one he would ride into the herd, was the black gelding he had borrowed from Crooked Leg, who was still too weak to participate in the hunt.

Roaring Thunder shot him an angry glance. "No, White Crane," he said sharply. "I'll tell you when we're ready."

Turning his attention to the others, Roaring Thunder offered one further piece of advice. "Don't get so involved in the hunt that you forget to look where you're going. The prairie is cut by ravines and if you accidentally guide your horse into one you're going to be in considerable trouble. If by chance you do find yourself on the ground, try to find cover: a ravine, a boulder, even a dead buffalo. If you're trapped on foot in the middle of the herd you almost certainly will be trampled."

Fighting to control his own horse, which sensed the excitement and was anxious to get started, Roaring Thunder examined the group of youths, most of them between twelve and sixteen years old. "Any questions?" he asked.

"All right," Roaring Thunder said when none of them replied, "we had better go find the herd."


For the next three hours the hunters galloped after the buffalo. The women and members of the band who would not be hunting, including Crooked Leg who had to ride in a travois, followed at a slower pace. The plan was for them to set up a temporary butcher shop near the site where the hunt began so they could start preparing the meat for shipment back to the main camp, where final operations, including the start of the laborious hide-tanning process, would take place. Except for one old man who was feeling too feeble to make the trip—Fire-in-the-Hills's aged uncle, Rising Moon—the stream-side campsite would be abandoned for a day or so.

An hour before noon, under a cloudless blue sky, the hunters caught up with the buffalo, which were ambling steadily along on a southwesterly setting so true the leader might have been using a compass. The herd was of considerable size, a quarter of a mile across and stretching forward almost as far as the eye could see. Since the hunters approached from the downwind side, the buffalo, blessed with an amazingly acute sense of smell to compensate for notoriously poor eyesight, were not yet aware of the Wazhazhas' presence.

In places, the animals were bunched so closely together that White Crane was certain he could walk across the packed mass, stepping from one animal's back to the next. Toward the edges, the animals were more scattered and individual buffalo were easily distinguishable. Still feeling their springtime surge of lust, a few of the young bulls were fighting over cows, charging head-on at each other, creating a loud clap that was clearly audible to the hunters. A few, uninterested in the mating ritual, rolled furiously on the ground, setting up large clouds of dust. In addition to the clash of horns from the young males, a loud uneven roar arose from the herd as the plodding animals bellowed hoarsely to each other or themselves.

Calling the men to a halt, Roaring Thunder quickly selected a half dozen experienced hunters and directed them to make a wide circle around the herd and come at it from the front quarter. Once they made their move, the wind would be blowing their scent into the herd, which would spook and probably turn more to the north. At that time, the rest of the hunters would approach rapidly from the rear. As a result, there would be Wazhazhas on two sides of the herd and the buffalos would have no choice but to go forward.

Glancing at the sun, Roaring Thunder told the group that would be making the encircling movement to make haste. "We'll give you until noon to get in place," he said. "And then we'll begin our dash into the herd. Try to be in position," he barked, "because we'll be going then whether you're ready or not."

At precisely the designated time, although there was no sign that the other hunters had completed their maneuver, Roaring Thunder gave the order to start the hunt. "*Hoka he*," he yelled, digging his heels into the ribs of his fresh mount.

Following Roaring Thunder's lead, the three dozen hunters in his group let out a collective shout and eagerly sprang forward.

Just as they started, the other group of hunters popped out of a ravine on the other side of the group and simultaneously charged.

Suddenly coming alive to the danger, the buffalos, who had been moving leisurely across the grass-covered plain, broke madly behind their leaders, heading, as Roaring Thunder had predicted, toward the northwest.

For the next two hours, it was mass confusion. Although the hunters were screaming almost continuously, it was impossible to hear them over the noise of the pounding hooves of five hundred stampeding bison. Similarly, it was impossible to see more than a few feet because of the cloud of dust that enveloped both the hunters and the hunted. Although the hunt itself was a masterpiece of organization, once it began—once the hunters got among the herd—it was every man for himself.

At Roaring Thunder's signal, White Crane had been among the first to plunge among the running animals.

Peering through the dust, aiming at a dark form, he
found himself facing a half-grown calf, which was not to
be killed since precedent was to be given to adults, either
bulls or cows. Silently cursing his luck, he ignored the
young animal and urged the gelding to spurt past him
until he was alongside the calf's mother, a medium-sized
cow that was scrambling forward in panic, leaving her
offspring to fend for itself. As he got closer to the animal,
she turned her head slightly and eyed White Crane bale-
fully with a large, moist brown eye. Without slowing, the
cow hooked her head sharply to the right. If Crooked
Leg's gelding had not been well-trained and less dexter-
ous, it would have been impaled by the buffalo's horn,
which was sharp and wicked looking despite the fact
that it was half-buried in thick dark curls.

"Ah-hah," White Crane told the uncomprehending
animal, "you want to play games. Well, let's see which
of us is better at this sport." Loosening his grip on the
twisted-hair rope he was using as a halter, White Crane
used his knees to guide the gelding while he notched an
arrow. Leaning to his left until his steel arrow point was
less than three feet from the plunging cow, White Crane
drew back the string and let the missile fly. His eyes
opened wide in surprise when the arrow plunged into
the cow's side up to its feathers. Giving White Crane a
hateful glance, the cow's knees buckled and she tumbled heavily to the ground. Buffalos coming behind her
effortlessly swung around the fallen animal, concerned
only with their own rush for safety.

Grinning happily over his success, White Crane
urged the gelding forward and notched a new arrow.
Within seconds, he had zeroed in on a huge bull and
moved closer to repeat the process.

Concentrating intensely on his own efforts, White
Crane was only vaguely aware that the other
Wazhazhas were replicating his action. In an instant, the

band had been turned into an efficient killing machine
that soon left the prairie dotted with carcasses of slain
buffalo. Approach ... aim ... shoot. Approach ... aim
... shoot. It quickly became a pattern that repeated itself
again and again with only minor variations. On two
occasions, White Crane had to fire three arrows to down
his target. One particularly large bull absorbed five
arrows before it finally went down. Otherwise, White
Crane kept at his deadly task until his quiver was empty
and his arms were too tired to pull his bow. But by then,
the herd had spread across the plain until the animals
were separated by dozens of yards and it was no longer
practical to try to chase down individuals. By this time,
too, the gelding was heavily lathered and panting for
breath. Accepting the reality that the day's hunt was
over, White Crane wheeled the horse around and
headed back in the direction he had come. Slowing to a
trot, he approached the last animal he had killed, a
medium-sized cow with three arrows bristling from her
side. Halting the gelding, White Crane slipped off his
buffalo-skin saddle and dropped to the ground.

As soon as his moccasins touched the earth, he
thought his legs were going to give way. He had been
so caught up in the excitement of the hunt and he had
been using his legs so long to effectively control the
gelding, that the muscles rebelled under his full weight.
Grasping the horse's mane to brace himself, White
Crane waited a few moments to regain his land legs.
Fumbling for the water bag which he had thrown
across his shoulder he drank copiously, ignoring the
fact that the water, although cool when he had collected
it from the stream that morning, had grown hot and
tasted coppery.

When he was confident his muscles were under control, he staggered like a drunk the few yards to the
downed buffalo. Reaching for the knife that he had

belted securely around his waist, White Crane knelt heavily on top of the dead buffalo. Again, he had to pause to recover his strength. Chiding himself for his perceived weakness, White Crane plunged his knife into the buffalo's throat and sliced strongly across. Reaching into the wound, he grasped the tongue by the roots and sliced it free. Extracting it through the hole he had made, he dropped it into the small parfleche he had brought along specifically to collect the prized buffalo parts. Turning his attention to the cow's belly, he again plunged his knife into the carcass and pulled it strongly upward, toward the head. Making a deep, two-foot-long incision through the matted hair, White Crane reached into the body cavity and felt around until his fingers closed on what he knew was the animal's liver. Pulling and slicing, he freed the organ and yanked it from the beast's belly. Silently congratulating himself on his success, White Crane sliced off a large chunk and plopped it greedily into his mouth, ignoring the thick, warm blood that coursed down his chin and covered his hands. He was eating his second large chunk when Lame Elk rode up through the still-thick dust.

"You are well?" he asked without preamble.

"Of course I'm well," White Crane mumbled through a mouthful of raw liver. "Why shouldn't I be?"

"Diving Beaver did not listen to Roaring Thunder's instructions," Lame Elk said heavily.

Looking closely at the tall Wazhazha, White Crane noticed that his cheeks were lined with streaks where tears had etched a path through the dust. "What do you mean?" he asked carefully, afraid of what he was going to hear.

"My son is dead," Lame Elk said sorrowfully. "He apparently approached a bull he thought was dead but, in actuality, was only wounded."

White Crane stared at the man, waiting for him to continue.

"The buffalo was able to rise to its feet and charge. Then he collapsed and died on top of my son."

White Crane dropped his head in empathy. Knowing there was nothing he could say to ease Lame Elk's sorrow, he said nothing at all.

"I'm going to need some help to move the dead buffalo and recover Diving Beaver's body. I saw you through the cloud of dust. Will you come help?"

"Of course," White Crane replied.

"Despite all the warnings we hear about the inherent dangers in the hunt," Lame Elk said, speaking more to himself than to White Crane, "it never really sinks in until there is an actual death." Without waiting for a reply, Lame Elk turned his horse and headed back in the direction he had come, his shoulders dropping, his chin on his chest.

White Crane felt his excitement drain away. Disgusted with himself for enjoying the moment while his friend lay dead, he added what was left of the liver to the parfleche and returned his knife to its sheath. On legs that felt even more leaden than before, he returned to the gelding. It seemed as if it took all his remaining strength to heave himself onto the horse's back and slowly follow in the direction Lame Elk had gone.

Once the other Wazhazhas learned about Diving Beaver's death, it tempered the celebratory mood that followed the successful hunt. But being practical people, they could not immediately stop to mourn because there was too much work to be done.

Returning to the main group for the horses they had originally rode to find the herd, now somewhat rested, they swapped mounts and went back to the scene of the

kill for the preliminary butchering, taking as many
spare horses as they could find. The women and others
who had not participated in the hunt followed.

As with the hunt, the butchering was also highly
organized. Some members of the band were particularly
proficient at cutting up the carcasses and the others
made room for them when they approached a dead animal. The first thing they did, after feasting on the
tongue, liver, and pancreas, was remove the skin.

The intended use of the hide determined how it
would be removed. Cow hides were much preferred for
making tipi covers so they were removed intact. Once
the decision was made to use a particular hide for that
purpose, the animal was flipped on its back so the skinner could make the initial cuts on the underside of the
front legs, slicing inward toward the breast. The next
incision was made upward to the lip, then curved
around behind the nose and went upward again to a
point between the horns. Moving the knife back to the
starting place, the skinner moved downward, slicing
along the belly to the inside of the hind legs, then to the
tail. If this was done skillfully, the hide could then be
peeled back on each side and laid on the ground beside
the animal, which was then rolled onto its stomach.

If it was a bull and the hide was to be sewed to make
a robe, the skinner made a slice behind the nose and
went straight down the backbone to the tip of the tail. It
was then removed in two pieces rather than one because
it was easier to tan. When it was time to complete the
robe, after the tanning process, the two halves were
sewn back together and the seam covered with quill or
beadwork.

The carcass itself, once the prized organs were
removed, was cut into eight pieces to make it easier to
transport back to the main camp. This in itself was a
rather slow process because it took at least two horses to

carry the meat of a single buffalo. A cow might yield more than four hundred pounds of meat, which was too heavy a load for one horse, and a bull roughly twice that.

The Wazhazhas wasted no part of the animal, finding more than two hundred uses for its various parts. Besides the meat and organs, they cracked open the bones for the marrow and used the intestines to make sausage. Tanned hides that were not used for trade went to tipi covers, robes, and items of clothing ranging from mittens to moccasins. Raw hides were used for, among other things, shields, saddles, lariats, and snowshoes. The horns were fashioned into cups, spoons, ladles, and powder flasks. The bones were used for knives, arrow-heads, shovels, sled runners, and war clubs. The hair made good padding and, once braided, halters for their horses. The tail made a dandy fly brush or whip. Stomachs and bladders were used for water bags, cook-ing vessels (which then could be eaten as well), cups, and buckets. The sinew was used in bow making and for thread. The brains that were not eaten were used in the hide-tanning process. Even the droppings were put to good use as fuel when wood was not available.

After loading the buffalo meat and hides onto horses and travois, the Wazhazhas began the march back to their camp. Riding at the head of the procession was Lame Elk. Behind him was another horse pulling a travois on which rested Diving Beaver's body. Black Swan, Lame Elk's wife and Diving Beaver's mother, walked alongside the body.

Although it was late in the afternoon by the time the group finished the butchering, Scalptaker ordered them to return to the main camp. "I had a dream last night," he explained, "in which evil befell our village. I didn't want to mention it earlier because I didn't want to ruin the hunt. Securing enough food to feed our people is the paramount issue."

When they got within a hard hour's ride of the camp site, Scalptaker's dream seemed to come true. Topping one of the hills that roll across the land like swells on an ocean, Lame Elk brought his horse to an abrupt halt. In the distance he saw a thin plume of smoke rising straight up in the sky, which was rapidly darkening because of an approaching storm.

"Look at that!" he called loudly. His shout brought a handful of warriors rushing to his side.

"That must be the village," said Blizzard, straining to bring the image into sharper focus.

"We must go see what it is," added Badger.

"You're right," Blizzard quickly agreed. "Who else will go with us?"

If Scalptaker had not stepped in and used his authority, every Wazhazha warrior would have ridden off to investigate the smoke.

"Don't be rash," Scalptaker had reasoned. "It could be a trap to lure all our warriors away."

"I don't think it's a trap," Blizzard said harshly. "I think someone has set our village ablaze."

"That could very well be," argued Scalptaker. "But how many men does it take to start a fire in an unoccupied village?"

"It isn't unoccupied," Fire-in-the-Hills interjected. "My uncle, Rising Moon, is there."

"And he would be a big deterrent, wouldn't he?" Blizzard added sarcastically. "An old man too ill even to leave his lodge. Would he put up any fight against a war party?"

"You're right," Fire-in-the-Hills reluctantly agreed.

"We're wasting time," said Blizzard.

"Wait!" Scalptaker said forcefully. "If it was a raid we

have to assume it was the Crow. They are devious enough to fire the village and, knowing we would see the smoke and come running, have their main body of men wait until all our warriors dashed forward, then attack the women and children."

"He has a point," agreed Badger. "But we can't just stand here."

"Blizzard!" Scalptaker ordered. "Take some warriors and ride straight for the village. Badger! Take some more and follow them at a distance, spreading out as you go in case it's a trap." Turning he looked until he saw Spotted Bear. "Take a half dozen men," he said, pointing at him, "and ride to our left, keeping pace with the main group."

"Otter, where are you?" he called loudly.

"Here, Scalptaker," Otter answered, nudging his horse forward.

"You take a half dozen men and go to the right. Buffalo Heart!" he called.

"Yes," came the reply.

"Take a half dozen men and follow behind us to make sure no one sneaks up on our rear. Whoever is left will stay with the main group and be prepared to fight."

"I want to go with Blizzard," Fire-in-the-Hills said quickly.

"Don't make me laugh," Blizzard sneered.

"Just because I'm no longer in my prime and I sometimes take on the role of camp jester doesn't mean I've forgotten how to fight."

Blizzard laughed. "Listen to the rabbit."

Fire-in-the-Hills put his hand on his knife. "I'll show you how a rabbit fights when it has to," he said coldly, seemingly ready to pounce.

"Enough!" said Scalptaker. "We have enough to do without fighting each other. Take Fire-in-the-Hills with you," he ordered Blizzard. "He has the right. His uncle is in the village."

"All right," Blizzard agreed reluctantly. "Fire-in-the-Hills, Jagged Blade, Roaring Thunder, come with me. Jagged Blade, select six more and let's go." With a shout, he swung his buffalo-hide whip sharply across the flank of his horse and sprang forward. The others in his group fell quickly into line. Moving with less haste were Badger and his group that included White Crane.

Before he left, White Crane galloped over to the travois that contained Crooked Leg. "May I take the gelding?" he pleaded. "You let me use him on the hunt and I need his strength now. My horse is too exhausted."

"By all means," Crooked Leg replied tightly. "I just wish I could go with you."

"Next time," White Crane replied, vaulting off his horse and onto the gelding. "I'll count a coup for you," he added, racing to join the others.

## ~*9*~

Hildegard Schmidt hovered over Benoit like a mother bear, pushing food upon him until he thought he would explode.

*"Bröt, Herr Leutnant?"* she asked, waving a basket of fresh, hot bread under his nose. *"Honig? Noch etwas schwarzen Kaffee?"*

"No honey," he replied, helping himself to a slice of bread, "but yes on the coffee. As you well know," he added with a smile, "it's one of my weaknesses."

The matronly looking woman, sturdy and solid with a beam as broad as an ax handle, grinned in delight. Her eyes, the color of ice in a mountain stream, twinkled and almost disappeared in the folds of her cheeks when she smiled. Leaning forward, she emitted a stream of German that left Benoit looking baffled.

"She said," Inge Schmidt interpreted, "that she wished she had the facilities to fix you a proper breakfast: *Orangensaft . . . Spiegeleier mit Speck . . . Brötchen mit Käse . . . Apfelsinen-Marmelade . . .* "

"Sounds delicious," Benoit agreed. "What is it?"

"Aren't you ever going to learn German?" Inge said in mock annoyance. "You've been taking meals with us for almost three weeks and you've barely gotten beyond *Ja* and *Nein*."

"You think so, huh?" Benoit said. "Well, listen to this."

"*Frau Schmidt?*" he called loudly, causing Hildegard to turn abruptly. When she did, the hem of her long dress swirled across the campfire, picking up hot coals on the way.

"*Ach du Scheisse*," she exclaimed angrily, slapping at the places where the embers were burning through the material. Since the trip began, all her skirts had shortened by about three inches, the result of working around ground-level fires.

Benoit grinned. One of the things he really liked about the Germans was their forthrightness. With them you were never in doubt about where you stood; they said what they felt.

In another long burst, Hildegard apologized for her language, a statement that Benoit did not need to have translated.

"*Frau Schmidt*," he began haltingly, watching Inge out of the corner of his eye, "*das Essen . . . das Essen War . . .*" he fumbled until he found the words he was looking for: "*Das Essen War sehr gut.*"

Hildegard Schmidt smiled until her eyes were mere slits. Inge clapped her hands together in delight. "Very *good*, lieutenant. Very good indeed."

"Inge," he said seriously, "how many times have I asked you to call me Jean. I'm not that much older than you and it makes me feel self-conscious. Why can't you do it? Your brother doesn't seem to have any trouble in that regard."

"I sure don't," said a voice behind him. "As a proper German young'un I've been taught to do what

I'm told and if you tell me to call you 'Jean,' 'Jean' it will be."

"Don't be disrespectful," Hildegard said sternly in German.

"You see," Inge told Benoit with a wink, "I told you she understands English much better than she speaks it. *Vater*, too. They all do, all the ones who came over from the Old Country. They understand but they won't speak. It's only us kids that feel comfortable in both languages."

"I'm the same way," Benoit reminded her. "My brother, sister and I speak French around the house, but it's English everywhere else."

"What's on for today?" asked Erich, plopping on the blanket that had been laid on the ground near the fire, the wilderness substitute for a kitchen chair. In his hand was a thick slice of his mother's bread heaped with butter, compliments of the cow Hildegard had insisted on bringing along.

"Good news about that," said Benoit. "One of the scouts told me that by the time we make camp tonight we'll be in pronghorn country."

"Pronghorn!" Erich cried excitedly. "That *is* goddamn good news."

"Don't swear," Inge said reprovingly. "Next thing you know *Vater* and *Mutter* will be picking it up. And they do well enough on their own in German."

"Sorry," Erich said, looking totally unabashed.

"Ca' be gaanunt?" he mumbled through a mouthful of buttered bread.

"What?" Benoit said in confusion.

"Don't talk with your mouth full," Hildegard told him in German.

Erich swallowed. "Can . . . we . . . go for a hunt?"

"Oh." Benoit smiled. "Why didn't you say so? That was the second half of my surprise. I think the answer is an almost definite yes."

"Hooray!" Erich shrieked. "What made Old Man Stuart decide to let us have the time?"

"He doesn't confide in me," Benoit said, "but I guess he feels we need a break. We've been moving steadily without a stop and there are a lot of details that need taking care of. Besides, maybe he just has a hankering for fresh meat?"

"Hankering?" asked Hildegard. "*Was bedeutet dieses wort?*"

"'*Wunsch,*' mother," Inge said tiredly. "'*Verlangen.*'"

"*Ach so,*" Hildegard replied, turning back to her chores.

"Unless something comes up," Benoit told Erich, "this time tomorrow we'll be stalking a pronghorn."

Hildegard turned in their direction and opened her mouth to speak, but Erich beat her to it. "*Antilope, Mutter. Gergrilles Wild. Leber,*" he added, licking his lips. "*Herz. Nieren.*"

Benoit looked at Inge and raised an eyebrow. This was beyond his meager vocabulary.

"That's just my brother." She sighed. "Always letting his stomach rule his brain. All he ever thinks about is food."

Benoit nodded. *She thinks that's strange,* he thought, *wait until he discovers sex.*


"I'm beginning to believe," Benoit said to Dobbs that evening, "that all the talk we've heard about the hardships of the emigrants is just so much horseshit."

Before answering, Dobbs helped himself to another cup of coffee from the pot the two of them kept boiling over their small campfire. "You have a good reason for coming to that conclusion?" the surgeon asked with a smile.

"I've been looking back through my journal," Benoit

said, flipping the pages of the open book that rested on his knee. " *... good roads ... found good grass tonight ... Scouts bring in fresh meat; two deer, which we shared ... Made first river crossing; it was easier than I expected ... Land is getting dryer with fewer trees but still plenty of water ... Covered twenty-three miles today ...* There's nothing there that's particularly traumatic."

"So you think this is just a walk in the park?" Dobbs asked.

"From what we've seen so far, I'd say that was a pretty accurate description. Except for old lady Emerson's death, the only other thing we've had close to being a casualty was that abscessed tooth you had to yank. And that wasn't exactly major surgery."

"That's easy for you to say." Dobbs laughed. "It wasn't your tooth."

"True enough." Benoit smiled. "But you have to admit the trip has been almost pleasant. We haven't even seen any Indians except the tame variety that were all over Independence. Even the Germans are starting to wonder if the dangers haven't been exaggerated."

"They're good people," Dobbs said. "Makes me feel regretful that I don't belong to a real family."

"What they're doing takes guts. Can you imagine what it must be like to throw over everything you've ever done and take off for a new life? And this is the second time for them."

"It takes a special breed. I'll admit that."

"You think they're going to be able to make it? In Oregon, I mean."

Dobbs shrugged. "Who knows. Except for Heinz Hartmann none of them knows anything about farming."

"There's bound to be towns in Oregon, don't you think? Someplace where Heinrich and Hans can set up shop."

"If there aren't now, there will be soon, judging by the number of people flocking out there. If there's another gold strike, there'll be even more."

Benoit tapped the end of his quill pen to his chin and stared into the fire. "I figure there's going to be more with or without a gold strike. There's a fever afoot, thanks to Horace Greeley."

"I agree there's a fever," Dobbs said, "but Greeley played only a minor role."

"What do you mean? 'Go West Young Man' . . . "

"Greeley didn't write that," Dobbs said. "That's a popular misconception. The article commonly attributed to Greeley was actually written by John Soule for his newspaper, the *Terre Haute Express*."

"But Greeley . . . "

"Greeley just reprinted the article in his newspaper, the *New York Tribune*."

"No kidding," said Benoit, impressed. "How do you know that?"

Dobbs laughed. "I read a lot."

"What have you read about the Indians?"

"Which ones?"

"The ones we'll be facing."

Dobbs threw another branch on the fire and poked the coals until they flamed. "Depends on whether you're talking about good material or bad material. When I say 'good' I mean 'reputable,' as opposed to the dime-store novel crap. So far, there's been very little 'good' material published. The best I've seen has been *The Oregon Trail* by Francis Parkman. Another Harvard grad, I might add. I knew his uncle. He was a physician in Boston."

"What does he say about the Indians?"

"He deals mainly with the Sioux," Dobbs said, freshening his coffee. "He spent a year with 'em, then came back East and published his book. It came out about five

years ago. He didn't say much about the other tribes: the
Crow . . . the Cheyenne . . . the Pawnee . . . the Blackfeet
. . . the Shoshones, and so forth. What he did say,
though, was they're all damn good warriors and a right
bloodthirsty lot as well."

"Bloodthirsty, huh?"

"Well," Dobbs said, picking his words carefully.
"Maybe 'bloodthirsty' isn't entirely accurate. His
book—which is pretty much of a personal journal, by
the way, and not a scholarly text—describes the Indians
as very aggressive, warrior-oriented people almost constantly at war with each other. And it's a take-no-quar-
ter situation. They play for keeps. He figures it's only a
matter of time before that aggressiveness is directed at
us instead of their traditional enemies, which to members of every tribe means practically anyone that isn't a
member of that tribe. That'll probably happen when the
Indians finally begin to realize that the white man is a
threat to their way of life, that we're not just going to go
away."

"I take it you don't believe in Manifest Destiny?"

Dobbs looked sharply at Benoit. "It's not a matter of
believing in it. I'm certain it's going to happen; the
whites will people the West. Where we're sitting right
now conceivably one day could be a large city. The East
is becoming too crowded and there's too much pressure
for expansion. Unfortunately for the Indians, they happen to be in the way."

"I can't say I blame them for being angry about *that*,"
Benoit said.

"Me either," Dobbs replied. "But, like just about
everything else, it isn't black and white. Maybe," he
added with a chuckle, "I should say red and white.
Seriously, though, it's a complicated situation. One of
the most aggressive of the Western tribes is the Sioux,
and the headquarters, if you can call it that, of the Brulé

branch of the Sioux Nation happens to be smack dab where we're going. The irony is, the Sioux haven't always been there. They came from Minnesota, or around in there, and only moved west when the pressure on *them* to expand got too great. So they pushed out some other poor sonsabitches. Now, we're trying to push *them* out. I wonder if someone eventually is going to come along to try to push us out, too."

Benoit smiled. "That might be," he said, "but I can just about guarantee you it isn't going to be the French."

Dobbs laughed. "Thank God for that."

"I wonder why they haven't attacked more than they have," Benoit said, ignoring the jab. "The Sioux, not the French."

"I knew who you meant. But as I said, I think it's just a matter of time. As soon as the Sioux decide that we pose a serious threat to their existence, they're going to be on us like ticks on a dog. In a way, it's kind of scary. There are thousands of them out there and right now only a few hundred of us, not counting the ones just passing through like this group here. If they really wanted to, they could wipe out Fort Laramie without working up a sweat. They've got the manpower, the skill, the knowledge of the country, and the will to fight."

"Then why don't they?"

Dobbs shrugged. "Who knows. Maybe they don't feel we're worth the effort. Maybe they still hold us in awe. They could be intimidated by our firepower, but I don't think that's it. The real reason, if you want my opinion, is that they just can't get organized. They can't put together an effective force under a powerful leader."

"But their chiefs . . ." Benoit began before Dobbs raised his hand.

"See, that's where reasoning like yours falls apart. From everything I've read their chiefs don't really have any power. Chiefdom is a conceit of the white man. We have to have everything systematized. In the Army, there's a general, who gives orders to a colonel, who gives orders to a lieutenant colonel, who gives orders to a major and so on down the line. But the Indians—at least not a single tribe I've ever heard of—don't have any such concept. They have warriors aplenty, but no real leaders. There just isn't any provision for it in their culture."

"How strange."

Dobbs smiled. "You can say that because you've been conditioned differently. The Indians, according to everything I've read, live in a true democracy with no individual truly superior to another. At least in the sense that one can say, 'We're going to attack that wagon train tomorrow and everybody had better shape up.' The best a potential Indian leader can do is use his personal magnetism to get some other Indians to go along with him because they believe in him as a person, not in the concept that it is a good thing to have a leader. While there are occasional powerful and persuasive individuals, their power has never yet extended beyond their own small group."

"What you're saying is that this guy Conquering Bear, for example, who signed the Treaty of Fort Laramie . . . "

"Ah-ha," Dobbs interrupted. "You *have* been doing some reading."

Benoit was abashed. "Well, I'm not completely, totally fucking ignorant . . . "

"Sorry. "Dobbs smiled. "Go ahead."

"What you're saying is that although this Conquering Bear, to use an example, may in the eyes of some people . . . "

"Most of whom live in Washington . . . "

". . . be a Brulé leader, he doesn't really have any power at all."

"Exactly!" said Dobbs. "The Indians must be laughing their asses off, telling each other how stupid we are to entertain such a notion."

"Then that's good for us. The fact that they are virtually disorganized."

"Now you get the idea," said Dobbs. "If they *did* have a leader who had any intelligence at all he would see the seriousness of the threat we pose to their culture and we'd be fresh meat. We wouldn't stand a chance, not with the handful of troops we have out here. The problem is, sooner or later a smart Indian is going to come along who recognizes this, and then the shit is really going to fly."

"But that would mean all-out war. Don't they know what we did to Mexico?"

"No, they don't, as a matter of fact." The surgeon laughed. "And even if they did, I doubt they'd give a damn. They know they're superb warriors and that's all that matters to them. They have no idea what our potential strength is or how many people we have beyond the boundaries of their known world. Right now, they think we're just another tribe—and an inconsequential one at that. We're surviving mainly because they figure we're not worth messing with."

"That's a sobering thought."

"Yeah, but it's true. It also may be changing. There have been more conflicts lately and it's probably going to get worse before it gets better. I hope it doesn't come to war, but in my opinion, it's inevitable. We'll eventually win but it'll be a bloody fight. There's a chance," Dobbs said with a tight smile, "that you might even lose your hair before it's all over."

Involuntarily, Benoit patted his head. "I've wondered about that. What's the significance?"

"According to the scholars, it's a religious thing and not just an act of outright savagery. A scalp is important to an individual Indian's status; it's like a medal to us. But in the long run a medal is just a ribbon. On the other hand, a scalp, to an Indian, also is a symbol of the fallen warrior's spirit. There's a lot of ritual attached to collecting a scalp, much more than just having something to brag about."

"Like what?" Benoit asked, fascinated by the subject.

"There are special dances and ceremonies connected with scalptaking, certain rites that need to be performed. Not all the honor goes to the scalper; in many cases the scalpee is also remembered and cited for his valor. In some tribes," Dobbs added with emphasis, knowing it would catch Benoit's attention, "warriors who've taken a scalp are forbidden from having sex with their wives—or anyone else, I guess—for as long as six months."

"*Sacre merde!*" exclaimed Benoit. "I don't think I'd like that even a little bit."

Dobbs smiled. "I didn't think you would. Anyway, I have some books on the subject, including Parkman's, in my kit. You're welcome to borrow them once our stuff catches up with us."

Benoit showed no sign of having heard. "Six months," he mumbled disbelievingly. "Jesus Christ. Might as well cut it off."


Of the more or less permanent members of the wagon train crew, Benoit's favorite was the chief scout, Jim Ashby. A short, slim man somewhere between thirty and fifty, Ashby was the most Indian-looking white man Benoit had ever seen. His skin was the color of bark-stained creek water, thanks to years of exposure to the harsh western sun, and he wore his dark, shoulder-length hair bound into a tight braid which dangled down the center of his back. His clothing, which Benoit had never seen him change, consisted of moccasins, patched deerskin leggings, and shirt. One thing that had puzzled Benoit at first was Ashby's distinctive rolling gait, which made him look, when he sometimes walked ahead of his horse, like a sailor freshly ashore from a long voyage. When he mentioned this to Dobbs, the surgeon had smiled.

"Frostbite," he said.

"Frostbite?"

"Sure," said Dobbs. "Look at his right foot when he soaks his feet in hot water at the end of a long day. No toes to speak of at all. They simply froze and fell off."

"I'll be damned," Benoit commented, shaking his head in astonishment. "Guess I'm not in Louisiana anymore."

Ashby carried a .52 caliber Model 1819 Hall rifle whose rapid-fire capability made up for its lack of stopping power. "My intent is to keep the Injuns at a distance, not kill a buffalo at five hundred yards," he explained to Benoit one night, sitting around the campfire. "The savages might not think much of us as warriors but they sure as hell respect our rifles."

A fearsome-looking knife with a ten-inch blade sharp enough to shave with rode on his right hip, and stuck in his belt was a Cheyenne tomahawk. "Most goddamn won'erful weapon ever invented," Ashby contended. "Split a man's skull like an apple, or chop off an arm at the elbow easier'n cuttin' off a hen's head. I'll guarandamntee you, first time you see a redskin comin' at you with one of these in his hands, you'll flat shit your pants."

"If you like the Indians' weapons so much," Benoit retorted, feeling his manhood somehow had been challenged, "how come you don't carry a bow?"

Ashby looked at him and smiled. "'Cause they're too hard to replace," he said. "Only an Injun can make a

good bow and they mighn't be so anxious to sell one to
an *isan hanska* if they figured he was going to be usin' it
again 'em. But mark my words, it's one hell of a
weapon. Just wait'll you see one in action. 'Til then, I
wouldn't be too quick to make fun of 'em."

"*Isan hanska?*" Benoit asked, ready to change the subject. "That's a white man?"

"That's the Brulé word," Ashby confirmed.

Benoit was prepared to question him further, curious
about his experiences with the Plains Indians, when Alf
Stuart cut off the conversation.

"I swear," Stuart said. "You got more questions than
a six-year-old. Why'n't you hold 'em for a spell and let
me talk to Ashby about where we're goin' tomorrow?"

Recognizing he had been not so politely dismissed,
Benoit went back to his own fire, mumbling to himself.
"*Alf Stuart is a detestable son of a bitch,*" he swore. "Hope
I'm around to see him pulled down a peg."

That incident had occurred early in the trip, and as
the train rolled westward, Benoit got to know Ashby
better and rather quickly came to respect his knowledge
of the land and its inhabitants, a territory that could not
have been more different from what Benoit had known
than salt from pepper.

Whenever he felt he could persuade Ashby to suffer
his company and his questions without incurring the ire
of Alf Stuart—"Man's got a goddamn job to do," Stuart
often would say, "leave 'im be"—Benoit would accompany the scout on his excursions in advance of the train.
As often as not, whenever he could convince Dobbs to
loan him his horse while he rode on the wagon next to
Frau Schmidt or felt the need to stretch his legs, Erich
Schmidt also would tag along.

"Why do you put up with them two dumb greenhorns?" Stuart asked Ashby one night, sure that Benoit
was within earshot.

"Two reasons," Ashby had replied. "I sometimes kinda like the company. My life tends to be solitary and it's good ever' now and then to have someone to talk to. 'Sides, it ain't hurtin' nothin'. We ain't got to the point yet we havta worry about Injuns so it gets right dull ridin' by myself."

Stuart, knowing the scout was right, grunted. "See that it don' interfere," he said gruffly, shooting Benoit a hard look.

On the day after he told Erich they were on the edge of antelope country, the German youth and Benoit had ridden forward with Ashby after being careful to slip away while Stuart's attention was elsewhere.

Catching up with the scout a few miles in front of the train, Benoit rode directly up to the scout. "Mind if we join you?" he asked.

Ashby looked at Erich's eager face and remembered how enthusiastic he had been when he first came to the West after running away from his Illinois farm home at age twelve, tired of the nightly beatings vigorously administered by an alcoholic father. One hot August night he had waited in the barn and tossed a blanket over his father's head when he came through the door, planning to retrieve a jug of white lightning he had hidden under the hay. Before the man could free himself, Ashby hit him over the head with an ax handle, knocking him unconscious. As he lay on the ground, Ashby began kicking him in the ribs and kidneys. "This'uns for ma," he said, delivering a boot. "This'uns for Betty," he added, smiling when he heard the faint crack of a bone breaking. "This'uns for Little Jim. This'uns for Mary. And this'un," he said, turning his father on his back and stomping down with as much force as he could muster on his father's genitals, "is for me." Climbing on the old mule he had already saddled, the one his father would sorely miss when it came time to plow, Ashby rode off and never looked back.

"I reckon not," Ashby replied.

Thirty minutes later, surprising both Benoit and Erich, Ashby brought his horse to a quick stop. Slipping out of the saddle, he dropped into a squat, pointing to marks in the dust so faint that Benoit could barely see them.

"Pronghorn," he said simply. "Right on schedule. Jes' where I expected 'em to be."

Climbing back into the saddle, Ashby moved forward at a walk.

"Shouldn't we be hurrying?" Erich asked. "We don't want the antelope to get away."

Ashby looked at him in mild amusement. "Get away?" he said, not unkindly. "You figure we can catch up with a pronghorn?"

Erich blushed. "W-Well," he stammered. "I don't know. I mean, how else are you going to shoot one?"

"Boy," Ashby said, "we have to wait for them to come to us."

Benoit and Erich exchanged glances. Afraid to show their ignorance, neither was anxious to say anything.

"Prongs 're the goddamnest animals you ever seed," Ashby said after an appropriate pause. "Faster'n lightning."

"Faster than a good horse?" Erich asked.

Ashby laughed quietly. "Shit, boy. The horse ain't never been born could keep up with a pronghorn. Them little sucker's can run circles around the fastest horse alive. An' even if you could find an animal o' some sort that might be able to keep up, wouldn't do you no good 'cause pronghorns never run in a straight line. Like goddamn hummin' birds. Dartin' here, dartin' there. Jumpin', dodgin', weavin'. Gives a hunter the fits, they do."

"Then how do you hunt them?" Erich asked earnestly.

"Well," the scout drawled, enjoying his role as tutor. "There's several ways. I seen members of a wolf pack take turns running 'em until the prongs are exhausted. I seen Injuns hunt 'em from blinds they built near water holes. But me, I got my own method."

"What's that?" Erich asked quickly.

"I wait for 'em to come to me," Ashby said with a smile.

Erich looked at Benoit and raised his eyebrows. "Wait for 'em?" he asked.

"Yep," Ashby said, enjoying himself immensely. "You heard the sayin' about curiosity killin' the cat."

"O-Of course," Erich stammered.

"Well, it goes double true for prongs. Nosiest god-damn creatures God ever created. They simply can't *stand* not knowin' what's going on. The way I like to get 'em is to lure 'em within' shootin' distance."

"You mean you entice them to come within range?" asked Benoit.

"That's right. 'Course it helps you got somethin' to attract their attention. Like a piece of white cloth. You hang it on a stick or a bush and you wait for the prong to come close enough and you pop 'im. That's one way. But I got a favorite I'll show you in a bit."

Looking at Erich carefully, he asked, "You ever shoot a rifle?"

"He sure has," interjected Benoit. "I've been taking him out for target practice with my Sharps. He's damn good. Seems to have a natural talent for it."

"That's good to hear," Ashby said noncommittally. "Reckon you'll get the chance to show me soon enough."

Topping a small rise, they eased their horses down the other side and onto a plateau that ran as flat as a tabletop for as far as the eye could see. Several days before, they had moved out of the forests and begun a gradual ascent onto the high plains where the only trees were along the creek bottoms. Ashby shaded his eyes and scanned the horizon. "Ahhh," he said finally, pointing to the northwest. "See over yonder."

Benoit and Erich strained their eyes until they could pick out a group of black dots.

"Them's prongs," Ashby said confidently. "Now we just set up shop and see what happens. This is where you get the chance, boys, to test your patience and your marksmanship."

Dismounting, Ashby grabbed his rifle and spare ammunition and began walking in the direction of the herd, followed by Erich and Benoit. After several hundred yards, he found a level spot fairly devoid of brush and plopped down on his stomach, motioning to Benoit and Erich to do the same.

"What we do," he instructed, "is lie here and wait. Don't fire 'til I tell you because I know the range and I know how close I can get 'em to come. Who's gonna do the shootin'?"

"He is," Benoit said, handing his rifle to Erich. "I figure I'll have plenty of chances later."

Erich accepted the weapon eagerly, gently stroking the walnut stock.

"Okay," said Ashby. "Here's what we're gonna do. I'm gonna lie down and raise my right foot in the air like this," he said, bending his leg at the knee and waving his moccasin-clad foot in a small arc. "The prongs are gonna wonder what in hell that is and they're gonna come up to investigate. It may take 'em awhile," he cautioned. "They can be right spooky. But if they run off, they'll be back. Take my word for it. Remember, don't fire 'til I do."

For the next hour, the three lay prone in the dirt,

waiting for the pronghorns' curiosity to be piqued. Twice they approached, only to bolt and run away, flashing their white rumps in the sunshine. But each time, as Ashby predicted, they came back, venturing a little closer. On the third try, they cautiously edged forward and Ashby whispered so quietly that Erich was not sure he had heard him, "Get ready." Five minutes later, he whispered a little louder. "Now!" he said, squeezing his trigger. There was an explosion, a cloud of smoke, and a large buck near the front of the herd jumped straight up and dropped to the ground.

Erich, who had not been totally prepared, jerked at the trigger and pulled the rifle off target. The ball kicked up a cloud of dust between the feet of a doe, which made a jumping, spinning turn and in an instant was racing off across the plain. *"Verdammtnochmal!"* he swore.

"That's all right," Ashby said soothingly. "It happens to the best of us. You'll get another chance."

The scout unsheathed his knife as he walked up to the fallen animal, which he quickly eviscerated and threw over his horse's rump, behind the saddle. "We'll do it again tomorrow," he promised. "You'll get the hang of it."

The following day, Erich bagged a doe and the day after that, as the pronghorns became more numerous, two bucks. "This is great fun," he said excitedly to Benoit. "Before you know it I'll be a regular *Rothaut*."

"A what?"

"A redskin." He grinned.

# ~ 10 ~

Even before they got to the village, Fire-in-the-Hills knew it was going to be bad.

Cresting the last hill before riding down to the narrow valley where the Wazhazhas had pitched their camp, they could see that a half dozen tipis had burned to the ground and a half dozen others were in various stages of spoliation.

Using the clarity of mind that made him such a good warrior, Blizzard ordered the men to halt.

"Why are we stopping?" Fire-in-the-Hills demanded.

"Which is your uncle's lodge?" Blizzard asked coldly.

Fire-in-the-Hills looked at him, then looked at the village. "That one," he said after a few moments, pointing to a partially burned tipi on the edge of the encampment.

"That's what I thought," said Blizzard. "If that's the case, it's not going to do us any good to rush in. Whatever is going to happen to him probably already has."

Fire-in-the-Hills knew that Blizzard was right, but he still did not understand the hesitation. "But why are we waiting?" he asked again.

"Because," Blizzard explained calmly, "I don't want our horses to ruin whatever tracks may be there. We're not in any hurry now and we need to find out what happened while we can." He pointed to the southwest sky, where lightning was flashing in an almost black sky. "That's another reason," he said. "I want Roaring Thunder to go in alone and see what he can tell from the available tracks before the rain wipes them away."

Fire-in-the-Hills nodded impatiently but did not answer.

When he saw there was going to be no further argument, Blizzard motioned Roaring Thunder forward. "You're our best tracker," he said. "Go see what you can read. Then come back and tell us. We'll remain here and stop Badger and his group when they arrive."

Without replying, a grim-faced Roaring Thunder moved his horse down the hill at a trot, never taking his eyes from the fire-blackened ruins.

Twenty minutes later, he rode back up the hill to the group. "It was only two men," he said. "They must have been scouts or hunters and they stumbled across the village by accident. Seeing it was empty, they couldn't resist the temptation."

"What about Rising Moon?" Fire-in-the-Hills asked anxiously.

Roaring Thunder shook his head. "Dead," he said. "Scalped and mutilated."

"Mutilated!" Fire-in-the-Hills cried bitterly, not really surprised.

"It was messy," said Roaring Thunder. "They cut off his genitals and the index finger on his right hand. Apparently, judging by the amount of blood present, they did it while he was alive."

Fire-in-the-Hills accepted it grimly. "Any sign that he fought back?"

"No," Roaring Thunder said sadly. "He was a sick, old man, no match for two young braves. They probably caught him by surprise."

"Any idea who it was?" asked Blizzard.

Roaring Thunder nodded vigorously. "Kangi!" he spat.

"How do you know that?"

"They left their mark," Roaring Thunder said, pointing to a grove of trees near the northern end of the camp. "They stripped the bark from a cottonwood and left a sign carved in the trunk. It is a Crow sign."

"The sons of dogs," Fire-in-the-Hills said angrily. "They will pay for this. I promise before all of you that Rising Moon will be avenged."

None of the men responded; they knew he was right. They would feel the same if it had been their relative.

The rest of the Wazhazhas arrived with the first large raindrops. By then, Rising Moon's body had been removed from his tipi and wrapped in a robe. Working alone amid the lightning flashes, Fire-in-the-Hills had taken Rising Moon into his own lodge and lovingly prepared the body for the ceremony that would send him to the Land of Many Lodges, the place that the Brulé believed was the destination of most human spirits. Not every soul made it to heaven; to gain entrance, the spirit first had to be examined by an old woman called Hihankara, the Owl Maker. If the spirit did not have the proper tattoo marks on the forehead, wrist and chin, she would give it a huge push and it would fall back to earth, where it was destined to become a ghost and wander about forever. Even if the spirit passed Hihankara's inspection, it still had to be judged by Tate, the wind, and Skan, the sky. Once admitted, however, the spirit was free to join his other dead ancestors and friends, who lived for eternity in an Eden-like paradise where game was eternally plentiful and the weather was always mild.

When Scalptaker saw the destruction he winced visibly. What should have been a time of joy for the Wazhazhas had turned exceedingly solemn. There had been an exceptionally good hunt; the Wazhazhas had gathered enough meat to keep them well into the fall, when another hunt would be organized. But their good fortune was balanced with two untimely deaths: The young warrior-to-be, Diving Beaver, and the old man, Rising Moon. Plus their village had been desecrated by the villainous Kangi. The fact that the Wazhazhas would have done exactly the same thing to a Crow village under identical circumstances was mentioned by no one. Throughout the band, the only thought was of revenge.

Blizzard wanted to put together a war party and leave immediately to try to find the Crow, but Scalptaker quickly spoke out against the idea.

"We have too much to do first," he said. "We need everyone for the next few days to finish butchering the meat and helping to replace the destroyed lodges. Then we have to hold the *wacekiyapi*, the burial ceremonies for Diving Beaver and Rising Moon."

Blizzard's face darkened and he seemed on the verge of rebellion.

"You know," he said slowly, "you have no authority to stop me if I collect some warriors and we leave immediately."

"Of course I know that," Scalptaker replied crossly. "I can't order you not to go. But as a warrior you have obligations other than satisfying your blood lust. The first responsibility of every Wazhazha is to his band and at this time there are chores that need to be done before we can begin planning a move against the Crow. They

will still be there in the Moon When the Chokecherries
Are Red."

Then, because he understood the rage that was burning within him, Scalptaker told Blizzard: "Stay here and
discourage the warriors from acting precipitately. It is to
all our interests. Wait six days and then you can go. No
one, least of all me, is denying the need for revenge."

Grudgingly, Blizzard agreed, mainly because he
knew that Scalptaker was speaking wisely; that every
hand was needed at this crucial stage.

That night, as hail pelted down on the buffalo skin
lodges, making rat-a-tat-tat noises that caused the
infants to scream and the young children to shift
uncomfortably on their beds, impromptu wakes were
held for Diving Beaver and Rising Moon. These would
not take the place of the *wacekiyapi*, which stretched
over four days, but were temporary rites designed to
suffice until the butchering of the buffalo could be completed.

Both Rising Moon and Diving Beaver were dressed
in their most splendid finery and propped up inside
the lodges where the rites would be held, Diving
Beaver in his parents' tipi, Rising Moon in his
nephew's. Robes were spread on the ground for those
who had come to join in the mourning and, as they sat
silently in front of the fire, men in the front, women in
the rear, a pipe passed from hand to hand.
Occasionally a woman would come forward and throw
a large piece of buffalo fat onto the coals, causing the
fire to flare up and brightly illuminate the expression-
less faces. All the while, the storm roared about them
with lightning adding nature's surreal accompaniment
to the grief.

Two days later, when the butchering had passed the
critical stage and the Wazhazhas had more time, the
*wacekiyapi* officially began.

The bodies, which had been wrapped tightly in robes and bound like bundles, were set in the center of the group. Fire-in-the-Hills, as Rising Moon's closest surviving relative, ran slender, sharp-pointed pegs through the fleshy parts of his arms and legs as a demonstration of his grief. His wife, Short Woman, slashed her legs, creating a series of barberpole-like wounds. Lame Elk and Black Swan did the same for Diving Beaver. Afterward, Black Swan, who was inconsolable, took a tomahawk and chopped off the tips of her little fingers.

Lining up carefully in a predetermined order, first the men and then the women, the Wazhazhas walked in solemn procession around the camp, weeping, wailing, and chanting songs of grief. This procedure was repeated on each of the four days, at the end of which specially designated women picked up Diving Beaver's body and placed it on a travois. With Rattling Wind, Diving Beaver's older brother, leading Diving Beaver's horse, which had been painted with red blotches and covered with a robe, the procession moved into the cottonwoods along the stream where a burial scaffold had been prepared.

Once there, his two sisters and other female relatives, using buffalo-hair ropes, raised his body to the floor of the scaffold. To a long pole that marked the head of the platform, they hung Diving Beaver's shield and his bow.

Rattling Wind, hefting a heavy, ancient pistol he had borrowed from Scalptaker, made a brief speech, putting his hand on the horse's neck. "Brother," he said solemnly to the animal, "Diving Beaver thought much of you and now he is dead. He wants to take you with him, so go with him joyfully." Having said that, he put the pistol next to the horse's ear and pulled the trigger. The animal was dead before it hit the ground.

Leaning over the dead horse, Rattling Wind unsheathed his knife and cut off the horse's tail, which he handed up to one of Diving Beaver's sisters, who attached it to the pole alongside her late brother's weapons. After that, amid much crying and chanting, the group scattered thorn bushes around the base of the scaffold to discourage predators, then dispersed.

The ceremony for Rising Moon, who was virtually alone in the world except for his nephew and his wife, was much briefer. Instead of a scaffold, Rising Moon's body was buried in a shallow grave at the top of the hill overlooking the camp. Once the grave was filled, Fire-in-the-Hills and his friends rolled boulders onto the spot to keep it from being dug up by wolves.

After the *wacekiyapi* ceremony, Blizzard spread the word that he and Fire-in-the-Hills were going to try to find the Crow camp and any warriors who wished to join them were welcome. Not surprisingly, there was no shortage of volunteers; the problem for Fire-in-the-Hills and Blizzard was not recruiting enough men but in limiting the group to a manageable number. Fire-in-the-Hills, as the aggrieved party, called a feast at which he announced the names of those who would be participating in the raid. After selecting a little more than two dozen men, and explaining to the others that they were passed over because someone needed to stay behind to guard the camp in case the Crow returned with reinforcements, final preparations began.

More so than on the horse raid, because this time the warriors were out for scalps, not animals, there were religious rites and social amenities that needed to be observed before the group could set out. Shamans were asked to interpret their dreams and consult their deities. Some of the warriors initiated their own fasts and went off into the hills to see if they could commune with their personal muses. Two days later, the shamans reported that the signs were favorable. However, one warrior, Big Belly, removed himself from the group, explaining that he had a dream in which he was warned not to participate.

"We each have to listen to our own guardians," Fire-in-the-Hills said understandingly, appointing a replacement.

Among the braves who would comprise the war party, to no one's surprise, were Jagged Blade, Badger, Roaring Thunder, Buffalo Heart, and, of course, Blizzard. White Crane, because he had proved himself a promising warrior both in the horse raid and the buffalo hunt, also was selected. Crooked Leg had volunteered but Fire-in-the-Hills had politely turned him away, rightly pointing out that his wound was not yet sufficiently healed to stand up to the rigors he knew they would be facing.

After a brief period of fasting and meditation, the members began packing their kits. Into elk-hide parfleches went the warriors' war shirts, their best leggings, and bone breast plates. Two of the more experienced warriors — Grizzly-That-Growls and Bellowing Moose — were chiefs in an elite military society called Strong Hearts, which imposed a unique responsibility upon its members. Each Strong Heart owned a brilliantly decorated piece of elk hide about six feet long and two feet wide called a "no retreat" sash. In one end of the sash was a slit through which the owner inserted his head. The other end was attached to the ground with pegs. Once the sash was in place, it kept the owner from moving beyond a prescribed distance, which meant he could not run away in battle even if he wanted to. Also jammed inside the travelling kit were small buffalo horn containers of paint and small porcupine-tail brushes, which the men planned to use to apply their war decorations once battle was about to be joined. Those who owned them, took along their feathered war bonnets, which were carefully packed in rawhide cases, where they would stay until the time of the expected raid on the Crow village.

They also brought along buffalo bladders stuffed with pemmican and jerky for the time when they got into Crow territory and would not be able to build fires. Each man also had his own buffalo horn drinking cup and a wooden bowl.

Weapons were an individual choice. Every warrior carried a knife, a bow, and a goodly supply of arrows. A few of them brought their cumbersome flintlocks. Several had shields, which were more good luck charms than protective devices, and lances. Virtually every man also carried a tomahawk or war club. Fire-in-the-Hills was designated the *blotahunka* and the formal pipe carrier although several had brought along their own pipes as well. Each man also selected two horses, one he would ride on the search and a war horse he would not mount until it came time to go into battle. Once everything was ready the men mounted up and rode out in a northwesterly direction, toward Kangi territory. As they left, the women gathered along the route, chanting and wailing since there was a good chance at least some of them would not be returning.

Three days out of their village and still within Brulé territory, the group stumbled upon a small buffalo herd. Anxious to conserve the food they had brought along, Fire-in-the-Hills summoned White Crane to the head of the column.

"This is your chance to prove what a good hunter you really are," he told the youth. "We could use some fresh meat and I want you to work your way into the herd and kill a fat cow."

"Very well," White Crane said, bursting with pride that he had been chosen to perform the task. He was about to whip his horse forward when Fire-in-the-Hills stopped him. "Wait," he said, "there's one condition."

"A condition?" White Crane asked, puzzled.

"You can take only one arrow."

White Crane gulped. "One arrow?" he asked in surprise.

"Yes." Fire-in-the-Hills nodded. "If you're successful with a single arrow you will gain much respect among the men."

"And if I fail?"

"Then you will have to learn to live with the shame and find a way of overcoming it. The path to warriorhood isn't an easy one and if you want to get there you have to learn to take chances. Honors aren't given; they have to be earned."

"I understand," White Crane said, smiling to hide his apprehension. "In the meantime, you'd better tell the men to build a fire because when I come back I'll be loaded down with the choicest parts of the plumpest cow in the herd."

As the group watched from a forested hilltop, White Crane circled around the herd to make sure he was downwind, then infiltrated the group, zeroing in on a three-year-old cow that was grazing near the edge. Galloping forward, he came almost within arm's length of the animal before he loosed his arrow. At that close range, it hit with such force and buried itself so deeply that Fire-in-the-Hills could not see it go into the animal. Worried that White Crane had somehow missed, Fire-in-the-Hills's frown turned to a happy grin when he saw the cow take three steps forward before plunging nose first into the prairie, never moving a muscle after she fell.

Turning to Blizzard, Fire-in-the-Hills said smugly, "I knew he could do it."

Blizzard only grunted.

Digging his heels into his horse's flanks, Fire-in-the-Hills led the howling group down the hillside to help White Crane butcher the animal. They found him sitting arrogantly atop the cow's shoulder, a broad smile creasing his narrow face.

"Let's have soup," Badger suggested.

"Good idea," agreed Fire-in-the-Hills.

Carefully, they removed the cow's paunch and cleaned it out. Then they butchered the cow and distributed the meat for transportation. Jagged Blade remembered they had crossed a stream not long before, so they doubled back and set up camp along the bank. While some of the men built a fire and tossed in a double handful of stones to begin heating, another filled the buffalo paunch with water, and set aside pieces of liver, kidney, and tongue. When the stones were glowing red, they were collected with forked sticks and dropped into the paunch, which had been braced with pieces of cottonwood. Once the water began boiling, the meat was tossed inside.

As *blotahunka*, Fire-in-the-Hills was entitled to eat first, selecting a center section of the choicest part, the tongue. After the meat was finished, the men drank the broth and, to cap off the meal, ate the paunch as well.

Full and feeling lethargic, several of the men stretched out to sleep, only to be roused by Fire-in-the-Hills.

"We're too close to Crow territory to relax," he warned them. "A wandering group may have seen the smoke from the fire. It is better if we move on."

Despite some mild grumbling, the men remounted and pushed on for another three hours, until well after sunset, where they made a cold camp along a tumbling creek.

For more than two weeks, the group wandered through the forests searching vainly for the Crow village. Each day, Fire-in-the-Hills sent out scouts, who climbed to the tops of hills with buckskin head covers to hide their black hair, which would stand out like a signal against the dun-colored ground and green trees.

Each morning, well before dawn, the scouts returned saying they had not been able to locate the Crows who, like other nomadic Plains tribes, were almost constantly on the move during the summer, searching for buffalo, elk, deer, wild vegetables, and berries that were coming into season. Trying to find a village under such conditions was not unlike searching for a particular ant hill on a broad prairie.

Despite the bad news from his searchers, Fire-in-the-Hills remained optimistic. "Today we will find them," he said encouragingly each morning.

On the eighteenth day after they left their own camp, Roaring Thunder and Buffalo Heart returned bubbling with excitement.

"You've found the village?" Fire-in-the-Hills asked enthusiastically.

"No," Roaring Thunder said, shaking his head. "But we have found a party of six Crow braves, apparently out seeking fresh game."

"How far?" Fire-in-the-Hills asked eagerly.

"Just over the next hill."

"That means the village can't be far off," Blizzard added.

"Not necessarily," replied Fire-in-the-Hills. "In the summer, the hunting parties roam widely."

"Well," Blizzard said archly, "what do you want to do? As *blotahunka* your suggestion carries much weight."

Fire-in-the-Hills nodded, aware of his responsibility. "Let's discuss it," he said, reaching for the pipe case.

For two hours, the men argued about the course of action. Blizzard, Grizzly-That-Growls, Bellowing Moose,

Jagged Blade, and a few others wanted to make a wide circle around the hunting party and continue the search for the village itself. Another faction that included Roaring Thunder, Badger, Spotted Bear, and Fire-in-the-Hills was in favor of attacking.

"We may never find the village," argued Roaring Thunder, "especially if the group is on the move. I suggest we jump the hunting party and then convince one of the braves to tell us where the camp is."

"That makes sense," agreed Fire-in-the-Hills.

"But if we wipe out the hunting party, the villagers will wonder what happened to its men and be on the alert," argued Blizzard. "We have a good chance of being victorious if we attack an unprepared camp, but our group would be no match for a village full of warriors who are expecting us."

"That's a chance we have to take," said Fire-in-the-Hills. "At least we won't come away empty handed."

In the end, Fire-in-the-Hills proved persuasive. The men agreed, some reluctantly, to attack the hunting party.

"Leave someone alive," Fire-in-the-Hills cautioned. "We want to know where the village is."

An hour later, with the sun just starting to peek over the eastern mountains, the Wazhazha warriors encircled the Crow camp, whose leader, feeling safe deep in his tribe's own territory, had not posted any guards. At a signal from Fire-in-the-Hills, the Wazhazha pounced.

Grizzly-That-Growls picked off one Crow who had walked into the woods to relieve himself with a single arrow through the throat. Blizzard leaped upon the party's designated cook and crushed his skull with a powerful blow from his war club. Roaring Thunder stopped another as he was running for his horse, neatly impaling him with his lance. Bellowing Moose, who had been one of the warriors packing a rifle, shot another as he struggled to free himself from his sleeping robe, the large caliber ball, capable of stopping a charging bull, turning his head into a red pulp. Badger had another warrior on his back and was about to slit his throat when Fire-in-the-Hills ordered him to cease. "We need someone alive," he explained.

A few minutes later, White Crane and Jagged Blade emerged from the forest leading another Crow. "He thought he could slip away." Jagged Blade laughed. "It shows how stupid the Kangi are."

Fire-in-the-Hills motioned the men around him, telling them to bring the two prisoners. Using sign language and the few words of Crow that he knew, the *blotahunka* demanded that the men tell him where the village was located.

They looked at him defiantly. One, who wore feathers attesting to his prowess as a warrior, spat at Fire-in-the-Hills, hitting him squarely in the forehead with a large glob of yellow phlegm.

As Fire-in-the-Hills turned to find a leaf to remove the sputum, Spotted Bear came running up, babbling excitedly.

"What is it?" Fire-in-the-Hills demanded angrily, seething with rage at the Crow.

"Look what I found among their possessions," Spotted Bear said emotionally, handing Fire-in-the-Hills a deerskin parfleche.

Frowning, irritated that his questioning was being interrupted, Fire-in-the-Hills peered inside the container. As soon as he recognized what it was, he let loose a strong oath and glared at the captives so fiercely that White Crane worried he might have to be restrained.

"Look at this," Fire-in-the-Hills said coldly, having regained control. Reaching into the parfleche removed an item.

Crowding close to see what had so enraged the

*blotahunka*, White Crane gasped in recognition. It was a necklace constructed of alternating groups of blue and white beads strung along a strip of deerskin. Spaced at intervals of several inches around the necklace, eight in all, were dried human fingers. Also tied to the decoration were two small deerskin pouches. With trembling fingers, Fire-in-the-Hills opened one of the sacks. Inside, dried and shriveled, was a man's sexual apparatus, a penis and a pair of testicles.

Fire-in-the-Hills turned his head, afraid he was going to vomit. Only with an impressive exercise of will was he able to control himself.

Walking close to the man who had spat upon him, Fire-in-the-Hills waved the necklace. "Is this yours?" he asked in Siouan, knowing well that the Crow needed no translation.

The warrior did not deny it. Instead he threw back his shoulders and readied to spit again at Fire-in-the-Hills.

Blizzard, who had been watching in fascination, acted before the Crow could carry through. With a backhanded swipe of his war club, he struck the Crow across the face, smiling to himself when he heard the jaw bone shatter.

Fire-in-the-Hills, who had drawn his knife and was ready to stab the Crow, shot Blizzard a sharp glance, one that conveyed both gratitude and anger at his interference. Lifting his leg, he stomped hard on the fallen Crow's genitals, angry because the enemy was unconscious and unable to respond to his kick.

Struggling to gather himself, Fire-in-the-Hills turned to Spotted Bear. "Build up the fire," he said coldly. Turning to Jagged Blade, he commanded, "Cut some long branches."

While waiting for the Crow cooking fire to rekindle itself and grow into a respectable blaze, Fire-in-the-Hills questioned the other prisoner. Although he lacked the brazenness of the one with the broken jaw, he stoically clamped his teeth together and refused to speak.

"Very well," Fire-in-the-Hills said finally, turning to make sure the fire was going well. "If you won't talk you'll have to suffer the consequences. But before making a final decision, see what happens to your companion."

"Bring him here," he ordered Jagged Blade, pointing to the injured Crow, who had by now, with the aid of a container of stream water poured over his head, regained consciousness. Although his jaw hung loosely and he was unable to speak, his eyes continued to flash with hatred.

"I doubt if you understand me," Fire-in-the-Hills began, speaking in his own language, "but I want to tell you, before I kill you, that I hope you suffer much before you die and that your painful death, in some small way, brings peace to Rising Moon's spirit. After seeing that cursed necklace, which undoubtedly is yours, there is no doubt in my mind that you were the one who mutilated and killed my uncle. I hope what I am about to do to you helps avenge his passing."

While Jagged Blade and Roaring Thunder held the Crow erect, Fire-in-the-Hills draped the necklace around the Crow's neck. Then he drew his knife and calmly walked up to the enemy. Looking him in the eye, he grabbed a handful of his hair and jerked his head back. Without hesitation, he raised the knife and deftly removed the Crow's scalp.

Blood flowed in a river down the captive's face, across his shoulders and over his chest. But except for a grunt, he never uttered a sound. Still conscious and still standing under his own power, the Crow returned Fire-in-the-Hills's stare.

Motioning to his men to tighten their grips, Fire-in-the-Hills lifted the Crow's legs, one at a time, and neatly severed the tendons in the back of the man's ankles. Immediately, his legs collapsed, but Jagged Blade and Roaring Thunder held him erect. Grabbing first his right arm and then his left, Fire-in-the-Hills severed the tendons in his wrists. When he finished, the Crow was unable to stand or to push himself off the ground with his arms.

"Now throw him in the fire," Fire-in-the-Hills commanded. "And if he tries to roll out, push him back in with the poles."

It took the Crow fifteen minutes to die.

When he was no longer moving, Fire-in-the-Hills turned his attention to the other captive. Although his color had drained and his eyes showed deep fear, he remained defiant. Knowing he would be killed regardless of what he said, he continued to refuse to divulge the location of the village.

Disgusted at what he had found and feeling drained because of what he felt he had been required to do, Fire-in-the-Hills turned to Badger, who had captured the surviving Crow.

"Kill him however you see fit," he said, turning and walking into the woods, seeking a few minutes of solitude. Sitting on a boulder, his head between his legs, his stomach heaving, Fire-in-the-Hills heard the other Crow scream three times before silence again descended upon the campsite.

When Fire-in-the-Hills returned to the group he did not ask Badger what he had done to the captive. The fact that the Crow's bloody scalp now dangled from Badger's belt was mute testimony to his fate.

"Let's go," Fire-in-the-Hills said tiredly. "We've accomplished all we can here."

Two hours later, he called a halt beside a sylvan stream. "As far as I'm concerned," Fire-in-the-Hills said, "Rising Moon has been avenged. I see no further need to continue searching for the Crow village. We have six scalps and I found the man who killed my uncle. I'm ready to go back to camp."

Although he stuck by his decision, he was not surprised when Blizzard objected, insisting that the group keep looking for the main Crow camp.

After arguing the issue for most of the afternoon, the group split almost neatly in half. A dozen men, including Fire-in-the-Hills, Badger, and Spotted Bear, announced they were returning to their own camp. Sixteen others, including Blizzard, Grizzly-That-Growls, Bellowing Moose, Roaring Thunder, and Jagged Blade, elected to continue the search. White Crane, torn in his loyalties, decided to go with the group that now had Blizzard as the *blotahunka*.

"Fire-in-the-Hills may feel he is avenged," White Crane explained to Badger, "but I agree with Blizzard that the Crow must be taught a lesson they will not soon forget. I think we need to keep looking for their main camp."

Badger nodded understandably, remembering how hot his blood ran when he was a youth. But as he aged, his judgment had become more measured. He was and always would be a warrior, but the older he got the more he realized that he could not single-handedly kill every Wazhazha enemy that roamed the Plains. There was a time for killing, he acknowledged, and a time for rest and rejuvenation of the spirit. Also feeling depleted after the encounter with the Crow, Badger agreed with Fire-in-the-Hills that it was time to return; it was time to fast and commune with *Wakan Tanka* and purify himself with sweat baths. At the same time, he understood White Crane's eagerness for battle, it was what every Wazhazha male was bred for. Far be it from him, he told himself, to try to temper White Crane's enthusiasm.

When White Crane told him he was continuing with Blizzard, Badger simply nodded. "I will tell Crooked Leg about your feats of bravery," he said. "But," he added with a tight smile, "not so much that you won't be able to boast before the whole village when you return."

A week after the first pronghorn hunt, shortly after noon on the thirty-third day after leaving Independence, the wagon train pulled within sight of Fort Kearny, a fragile-looking collection of weathering buildings straddling the southern bank of the Platte River.

"This ain't the original fort, y'know," Jim Ashby explained to Benoit as the fort grew larger on the horizon. The two of them were riding a couple of miles ahead of the wagons, Ashby because it was his job and Benoit because he found he enjoyed the scout's company. "The 'riginal Kearny was four days east of here, on the Missouri."

"Why was it moved?" Benoit asked curiously.

"Too far from the Trail," Ashby said. "'Twas meant to protect emigrants but it were too far away. So the Army just shut that mother humper down and moved 'er over here. That was in '48, 'case you're as nosy as I reckon you are. Some people call this the New Fort Kearny, but that's mainly the ol' timers who remember the first 'un. Don't matter much, though, what they call it. The 'portant thing is it's a goddamn godsend when you been on the trail for five, six weeks. You can get a hot bath here, if you want. And a bottle of good whiskey, if that's your inclination. They might even still got ice and you can probably get a cold beer, too. I'm gettin' right old for it myself, but the boys're are lookin' forward to gettin' their ashes hauled."

"Oh, yeah?" Benoit responded with a laugh. "By what? A sheep?"

"Might's well be." Ashby laughed, leaning to the side to spit a stream of tobacco juice into the dust. "Injun whores. Operate right outside the fort in them scraggly tipis you can't see yet. Cheap, too. Might be able to get one for a handful of beads. 'Course," he added, emitting a high-pitched giggle, "you might get the pox, too. Take my advice," he said with a wink, "stick to the sheep."

Benoit gave him a disgusted look. "Thanks for the tip. Maybe I'll settle for the hot bath and a beer."

"If'n you do that," Ashby said, spurring his horse forward, "you ain't as dumb as Alf Stuart says you are."

"That sonuvabitch," Benoit mumbled. "One of these days he's going to need my help and I'll tell him to go piss up a flagpole."

Ashby chuckled. "He ain't as bad as he seems. Not that he's a 'good' man, mind you, but he knows what he's doing and he knows this country. He comes across right gruff because he doesn't know you yet. As far as he's concerned, you're just another dumbass Army officer out here to kill Injuns and win hisself a medal. Alf ain't one to accept people too quickly."

"If you ask me, he doesn't particularly care for anyone. He drives the people in the train mighty hard."

"That's because he's worried about the Injuns. He doesn't want to dawdle too much."

Benoit looked surprised. "That's strange," he said. "Lieutenant Dobbs and I were talking about that just the other day. We decided that Stuart was painting too rosy a picture about the possibility of a hostile attack, that there's something he isn't telling us."

"Well, it ain't a big secret," Ashby replied. "After we get past Kearny we'll be moving into Brulé territory and they've been a mite nervous lately. From what I hear, there's a lot of grumbling going on within the bands about what they should do about us."

"How's that?"

"Didn't you hear about the incident last summer at Fort Laramie?"

Benoit searched his memory. "Not that I recall. What happened?"

"'Twern't much, really, far as the Army is concerned. There was a group of Miniconjou . . . "

'Mini what?"

'Mini . . . con . . . jou," Ashby said slowly. "Another division of the Sioux, cousins to the Brulé. Anyway, they was camped near Fort Laramie, partyin' more'n a little I suspect, and one of 'em got a little lickered up. Tried to steal one of them ferry boats that go across the Platte in times of high water. God knows what he'd a done with it. One shot was fired; a soljer said it was at him but he weren't hit or nothing."

"That doesn't sound like something serious enough to get anyone riled up."

"I'm gettin' there," Ashby said crossly. "That weren't all."

"Sorry," Benoit apologized. "I get impatient."

"I noticed that. Anyways, the commander at the fort decided it was a serious threat to his authority and he had to step down on the savages right quick or there'd be more trouble."

"I'm beginning to get the picture."

Ashby nodded. "He sent one of his shavetail lieu-tenants—the type we call 'carpet knights' out here—into the camp, along with a few men, to arrest the Injun that was 'sposed to have taken the potshot at the soljer."

"'Carpet knight,'" Benoit chuckled. "I like that."

"Needless to say," Ashby continued, ignoring the interruption, "the Injun wasn't exactly anxious to spend some time in the Army hoosegow. So he refused to go quietly."

"Let me guess what happened," Benoit interjected. "They started shooting."

"Sure did. Before it was over, there were three Miniconjou dead, three wounded, and two were taken prisoner."

"Any Army casualties?"

"Nary a one."

"Hmmmm," Benoit said. "I guess that's why I didn't hear about it. It isn't news if no soldiers get hurt. Is that it?"

"Yep," Ashby nodded. "That's pretty much it. The Injuns was pretty mad and there was a lot of talk about some retaliatory raids but they was about to get their treaty annuities and they didn't want to make too much fuss. So, the wise men talked to the hotheads and they pretty well smoothed it over, at least on the surface."

"You say that like you don't believe it's ancient history," Benoit said.

"I know the Injuns," Ashby said. "An' I know they ain't forgot it, no matter what their chiefs say. I reckon they're just biding their time until they get the right opportunity."

"I don't know," Benoit said. "That was almost a year ago but there hasn't been any trouble since. Is that right?"

"Time don't mean nothin' to an Injun."

"Still . . ."

"The way I see it, the Injuns ain't ready yet to tackle the fort so if they want a white man to push on they'll get a wagon train. By the time the talkin' got done, it was almost winter and there weren't no more trains coming through. This 'uns one of the first of the new season. Might be a problem."

"And Alf Stuart agrees with that?"

"He sure does. Him and me think alike on that. He figures there's trouble brewing and he'd just as soon not get caught in the middle. Can't say I blame him for that."

"Me either," Benoit agreed. "But knowing that background makes some other things fall into place. In a way, it's kind of scary. There's not enough men on the train who know how to use their weapons to defend against a major attack."

"That's true," said Ashby, "but I reckon when an' if an attack comes it won't be a major one. More'n likely just a small band of Injuns out to make a point. But that's why, after we leave Kearny, I'll have to start earnin' my pay. Won't have much time for huntin' then. Or socializin'. Not that I don't enjoy our conversations."

"I understand," Benoit said. "And thanks for the information. After we leave Kearny I guess I ought to start sticking pretty close to the Schmidts. They might need my help."

"You've become right fond of them, haven't you?"

"Yeah, they're almost like family."

"Except for that good lookin' daughter," Ashby said with a bit of a leer. "Guess there's nothing familylike about that."

"She's just a kid," Benoit said hotly. "My little brother is older than she is."

Ashby gave him a studied look. "Whatever you say, lieutenant. But I think it would be a good idea to stay handy. You never quite know what them damn Injuns is gonna do."

"It isn't very impressive, is it?" Benoit said, rising in his saddle to get a somewhat elevated view of the collection of buildings that made up Fort Kearny.

"I've seen worse," replied Dobbs, adding, after a pause, "I guess."

Benoit smiled. "Couldn't have been much worse. A few wooden buildings that look as if they're going to blow over in a strong wind. A sutler's store complete with drunken Indians laying about. A parade ground ankle deep in dust . . . "

"The dust isn't too bad," said Dobbs. "I'll take it over the mud."

Benoit and Dobbs had decided to ride ahead; the wagon train would not arrive until late in the afternoon. But anxious to get their first glimpse of a real frontier post, they had told a distracted Alf Stuart they were going to push on a little faster so they could present their orders to the commanding officer.

"That's fine with me," Stuart had said, more worried about briefing the emigrants about the do's and don'ts of how to behave on their first stop at an Army garrison.

"Reckon by now you realize you've brought more junk than you need," Stuart was lecturing the Muellers when Benoit and Dobbs rode up. "You can sell what you don't want to some o' the hangers-on at the fort but you gotta know you ain't going to get what it's worth."

Inge Schmidt, who was acting as interpreter since Stuart's brand of English was hard to understand, even for an American, paused when the two officers approached. Nodding to Dobbs, she turned to Benoit and gave him a dazzling smile. "Hi, Jean," she said warmly.

Benoit nodded and waved to Stuart. "Don't let us interrupt you," he said.

"I was jus' tellin' these folks what they got to be careful of once they get to civ'lization."

Turning back to the Muellers he raised a stubby, weather-beaten finger. "Watch out for the soljers. Some of 'em ain't nothing but scum. Joined the Army to get outta goin' to prison or were too lazy to work at reg'lar jobs. I ain't sayin' all soljers are worthless," he said, glancing at Dobbs and Benoit, "but some of them 'nlisted men are just out 'n out thieves."

He paused while Inge translated, continuing when Heinrich and Johanna nodded solemnly at Inge's rapid-fire German.

"An' the Injuns is even worse. Them that hang around the fort ain't nothing but sticky-fingers. They'll flat steal anythin' that ain't nailed down, an' they'll take that, too, if they think they can get away with it. Them loungers is right skillful beggars, too. They'll come 'round to your wagon, struttin' an actin' mean, and demand you feed 'em. I'm tellin' you, you don' have to do that, but it might be easier if you gave 'em a little somethin'. Mostly it's show; they wan' to 'timidate you. But givin' 'em a cup o' coffee and a hard biscuit ain't gonna hurt you none and it might get 'em off your back. You un'erstan'?"

The Muellers nodded again when Inge finished translating.

Stuart figured he'd finished his lecture when Heinrich addressed him in German.

"How's that?" he asked, turning to Inge.

"He wants to know how long we're going to be at Fort Kearny and will he have time to complete some repairs on his wagon. He's worried about one of the wheels and he would like to find a blacksmith."

"If it ain't too major, it should be okay," Stuart

replied. "I reckon we'll be there two or three days. Long enough to take care o' stuff like that, get some washin' done, re-provision, and so forth. But lemme warn you, services and goods come dear. You gotta watch those traders, too. Be careful what you buy. One o' their fav'rit' tricks is to put iron filings in the coffee to make it weigh more. Another is to put hemlock in the cheese to give it a better color . . . "

"Hemlock?" asked Inge.

"A plant," Stuart explained. "Can be poisonous if'n too much is used but usually it's harmless. Trouble is, you can't be sure too much wasn't used."

"I believe we have sufficient supplies," Heinrich Mueller said in perfect English.

Stuart's eyebrows shot up. "Thought you didn' speak the lingo?" he said.

"He doesn't," Inge added with a smile. "That's a phrase I taught everyone in our group to say by rote. It kept the peddlers away in Independence."

"I'll be damned," Stuart replied, impressed.

Dobbs coughed. "We just wanted to tell you we're going on to the fort. We'll meet you there."

"Fine," Stuart said with a wave. "You red-tape soljers figure you can find it?"

Dobbs gave him a sour look. "We'll try our best."

Contrary to Stuart's doubts, the two officers had no difficulty. They could find the fort, but picking out the commanding officer's headquarters was more difficult; none of the buildings they saw looked like a proper command post. Finally, Dobbs stopped a private who was carrying a load of flour on a buckboard and asked directions.

"Cap'n Robinson, you mean, sir?" the soldier asked.

Dobbs shrugged. "Whoever is commanding."

"That would be Cap'n Robinson then," said the private, obviously a man that would have delighted Alf

Stuart as an example of the intellectual capabilities of the frontier Army's enlisted personnel.

Five minutes later they were standing at attention before the most roguish looking officer Dobbs had ever seen, including the battle weary veterans of the Mexican War.

Arnold Robinson, Captain, U.S. Army, was in his late thirties, a short, dark man, with heavy brows and a five o'clock shadow so dark that Dobbs doubted he had shaved at all that day. With his blue uniform shirt open at the collar and the sleeves rolled up to the elbow, Robinson looked as though he had just come back from a hard day's duty at the stable. As a matter of fact, Dobbs thought, his nose twitching, he smells like it as well. Instead of being seated, the preferred position of most deskbound C.O.'s, Robinson was standing behind a makeshift, lecternlike piece of furniture that was almost as wide as his desk.

"At ease, men," Robinson said in a whiskey-hoarse voice. "We don't stand much on formality around here."

Looking alternately from the papers they had presented him to the men standing before him, Robinson asked, "Dobbs?"

"Yes, sir," said Dobbs, straightening his shoulders.

"You a doc?"

"A surgeon, yes, sir," Dobbs replied.

"Well, I guess if you're a surgeon, you're qualified to take a look at my hemorrhoids. They give me fits. Some days I can't even use my chair, which explains this device that Private Harrelson cobbled together for me," he said, thumping the framework addition. "It's even worse when I try to sit a horse."

"I'd be happy to examine you, sir." Dobbs lied.

"Good," Robinson said with a nod. "I'll hold you to it."

Switching his attention to Benoit, he looked at the

papers in his fist. "Ben-oight?" he asked, his voice rising toward the end of the misinterpretation.

"Ben-*wah*, sir," said Benoit, rolling his eyes.

"Ben-*wah*, huh? How in hell you get 'wah' out of 'oit'?"

"It's French, sir."

"French? No shit? I thought you were an American, seeing as how you went to the Academy."

"My family's French, sir. I was born in this country."

"Good to hear it. I'd hate to think we're accepting frogs in one of our most prestigious institutions."

Folding the papers and handing them back to the men, Robinson seemed anxious to get rid of them.

"Well," he said briskly. "Thanks for coming in. Lieutenant, I'll expect you at oh-eight-hundred tomorrow for the medical exam. Enjoy yourselves while you're here, but I'd like to give you a piece of advice."

"Yes, sir?" said Dobbs.

"Stay away from the Injun whores."

Benoit and Dobbs suppressed smiles. "Yes, sir. I believe we can do that," said Dobbs.

They saluted and were preparing to leave when Robinson stopped them.

"Oh," he said. "One more thing."

Dobbs and Benoit stopped and turned.

"At seventeen hundred hours," he said, pulling a watch out of his shirt pocket, "exactly one hour and fifteen minutes from now, punishment will be administered on the parade ground. You might find it instructive."

"Punishment?" Benoit asked. "For what?"

"Desertion," Robinson said, sounding tired.

"Is that a major problem here, sir?" Dobbs asked.

"You bet your ass, lieutenant. Worst problem we've got next to fighting in the barracks during the winter when everybody's cooped up and suffering from cabin

fever. These Easterners come out here all fired up about
the *romance*," he said, stressing the word, "of the West
and they find they've been fed a lot of horseshit. There's
nothing romantic about frontier duty, as you're going to
find out soon enough."

Dobbs and Benoit exchanged glances.

"Not surprisingly, once reality sets in, they want the
hell out. Out of Fort Kearny. Out of the Army. So they
run off in the middle of the night. Or they go out on
patrol and don't come back. I've had entire squads disappear on me. It doesn't help when they hear exaggerated tales about gold in California and Oregon. Too
many of them figure they'd rather take their chances in
the gold fields than end up with an arrow in their backs
and their hair gone."

"Do you vigorously pursue them, sir?" asked Benoit.

"As well as I can, given the circumstances. I'm not
going to chase anyone all the way to California, but if I
think I've discovered them missing in time and they
might still be in the area, I send some men after them."

"Are you successful?"

Robinson shrugged. "Not usually. Sometimes we catch
them, sometimes we don't. I had a situation once where I
sent a squad out under a sergeant and every damn one of
*them* deserted too. But that was a couple of years ago
when we didn't have quite so many amenities here."

Amenities? Benoit thought. Jesus Christ! I'm glad I
never saw this place earlier. Aloud, he asked: "Who's
being punished today?"

"A couple of privates. A dumb Polack named
Jabbowski and a tough guy named Means, who absolutely, positively lives up to his name. He's been a
sergeant. Actually, he's had stripes at least twice.
Always gets busted for the same thing: fighting. He's
big and he's strong and he's got a killer streak. The men
call him 'Grizzly.'"

"What's the punishment, sir?" asked Dobbs.

"The usual," Robinson said nonchalantly. "Branding."

*"Branding?"* Benoit asked in surprise. "You mean with a hot iron? Like you would a horse?"

"Exactly," Robinson said, trying to hide a smile. "This is the West, lieutenant. It's a hard life out here. Drastic action is necessary, not only to control the men but to set an example for the Indians. They think we're a bunch of pushovers, that we don't know how to hand out discipline, much less fight. Besides, it's intended as a deterrent. Nobody wants to go around with a four-inch-tall capital 'd' on his butt for the rest of his life."

"I can't understand why not," Dobbs muttered under his breath.

"You say something, lieutenant?" Robinson asked sharply.

"I said," Dobbs added, meeting Robinson's stare, "That we'll be there, sir. It isn't every day you get to witness a spectacle like that."

Robinson nodded slowly. "It's completely within the regulations, lieutenant. The code gives us frontier commanders a lot of leeway."

"I'm sure it does, sir," Dobbs added. "I didn't mean to imply you were doing anything illegal."

"That's good, lieutenant. I'd hate to think one of you effete Army surgeons would presume to tell a veteran commander, *especially one who outranks him*, how to discipline his men."

"No, sir."

"Wait until you've been at Laramie a while. Then come back here and tell me you think I'm being harsh with my men."

"Yes, sir," Dobbs replied. "Are we dismissed?"

Robinson sighed. "Yes, lieutenant, you're dismissed. Both of you. Have a good trip to Laramie. And watch

your asses. The Indians can play rough. And don't forget my hemorrhoids. I sure as hell can't."


No one had bothered to tell Benoit and Dobbs before
they embarked for Fort Laramie but they were quickly
learning that five P.M. was the hottest part of the
Western day and early July was the hottest part of the
Western summer. All morning and afternoon the sun
beat down under virtually cloudless skies and by five
P.M., still some three hours before dusk in July, the heat
was almost unbearable. After dark, the desert tempera-
ture was prone to plummet, dropping as much as thirty
degrees, but the late afternoons were real killers. Both
Benoit and Dobbs were sure that Robinson's decision to
administer punishment at that hour was a carefully considered ploy: If the threat of being branded was not
enough to impress upon a soldier the risk he might be
taking in deciding to abandon his post, the fact that he
would have to face his punishment late on a July afternoon was a superfluous fillip. To make sure the men got
the point, they had to turn out in full uniform, which
meant long-sleeve wool shirts.

"I don't know about you," Benoit told Dobbs, "but if
I were a private and one of my messmates was thinking
about deserting I'd do everything I could, including
tying him to his bunk, to keep him from running. Just
the thought of having to form up at five P.M. to watch
him get punished would be a powerful factor in keeping
him on the post."

Since they were not part of the fort's contingent they
were exempt from following the prescribed order of
assembly. As far as Robinson was concerned, they
were civilians and they could station themselves wherever they wanted on the parade ground and did not
have to fall in with the other troops. As a result, they

picked a spot near the flagpole, which would be the
focus of activity. A few feet in front of the pole was a
fire ring, a circle about five feet in diameter, that was
filled with hot coals. From the blackened condition of
the rocks that formed the fire ring's walls, it appeared
that it was often used. Projecting out of the coals was a
metal bar about four feet long. The other end, the one
submerged in the coals, presumably was formed into
the letter "d."

Since Benoit and Dobbs planned to return to the
wagon train, which was camped on a large, flat expanse
about three miles away, both had their horses with
them, saddled and ready to ride. Unwilling to make the
animals suffer their weight unnecessarily in the heat,
both had dismounted and were standing next to their
steeds, reins in their hands.

Promptly at five P.M., initiated by a special bugle call,
the two prisoners were led from a nearby building that
Dobbs noted had bars on the windows and obviously
served as the stockade.

As the prisoners were marched across the parade
ground, Dobbs took special note of the one with blond
hair, apparently the man named Means. Although his
companion was no midget, Means dwarfed him.
Standing at least six-foot-five, he had shoulders like a
buffalo and wrists thick as a horse's foreleg. His uniform
shirt, although generously cut, threatened to rip under
the strain of the muscles that rippled across his chest
and biceps. Far from looking frightened, Means's lips
were twisted into a snarl and his black eyes flashed with
hatred.

"Thank God he's in chains," Dobbs whispered, pointing with his chin at the manacles that encircled the
man's wrists.

The men were led by three guards, a corporal who
was carrying a rifle and two unarmed privates. They

quick-timed directly to the fire ring, where they stopped, came to attention, and waited for a command from Robinson.

True to his earlier statement that he wasn't a stickler for formality, Robinson's order was curt: "Let the punishment commence," he said loudly.

At the captain's order, one of the privates, a skinny, mustachioed youth with pimples on his chin, marched to the fire ring. Producing a soot-blackened rag which he wrapped around the topmost end of the metal bar, he lifted the branding iron from the fire. The end with the "d" glowed redly, like the sun just before it plunges below the horizon.

The second private, a small, feral-looking man, walked straight to the smaller of the two men, the one Dobbs took to be Jabbowski. Adroitly, as if he had done it before, he unbuckled the prisoner's belt and pulled his pants down in one swift motion. On cue, the soldier with the branding iron pressed it against Jabbowski's bone-white right buttock.

As Benoit and Dobbs watched in fascination, a thin stream of smoke curled upward and a loud sizzling noise, like that of fat thrown onto a fire, was clearly audible. Overcoming his shock, Jabbowski threw back his head and let out a bloodcurdling scream.

Immediately, without waiting for further reaction, the guard who had undone Jabbowski's trousers moved close to Means, intending to go through the same scenario. But as soon as he got within reach, Means emitted an ear-numbing battle cry and grabbed the guard by the throat. In the blink of an eye, Means snapped the man's neck and threw his body against the guard with the rifle. Knocked off balance, the corporal stumbled. It was enough of an opening for the agile Means. Grabbing the rifle out of the man's hand, he hit him across the side of the head with the stock, sending him crashing to the ground.

"Nobody's going to brand me like I'm a fucking animal," Means screamed, bringing the rifle to his shoulder and pointing it directly at Robinson, thirty yards away. Before the captain could move, Means squeezed the trigger and Robinson tumbled backward, a .54-caliber hunk of lead in his side.

Means, moving quicker than Dobbs had thought possible, spun and ran straight at Benoit. "I want your horse," he screamed, raising the rifle like a club. Although Benoit was already fumbling with the flap on his sidearm, Means moved too fast. As Benoit lifted his left arm in defense, the prisoner brought the rifle around, striking Benoit on his left forearm. The bones cracked like a dry pine branch.

Benoit was sure he had never felt such pain. It shot up his arm and ran straight to his brain, causing his ears to ring and his eyes to water. Reflexively, he bent over and vomited on his boots. At the same time his body was rebelling, his mind was telling him to defend himself, that if he didn't take some action he was surely going to die. Using every last fragment of his willpower, he commanded himself to act when all he really wanted to do was curl up in a ball on the ground. Despite the fact that his left arm was dangling like a piece of spaghetti, Benoit used his good arm to try to draw his pistol. "Fuck you!" he told Means between clenched teeth, determined to bring his weapon to bear. Before he could get his pistol free, however, Means hit him again with the rifle. Fortunately for Benoit, the blow was partially deflected by the horse, which had spooked at the sudden activity and moved practically in front of Benoit, as if trying to shield him. The rifle still struck Benoit across the side with considerable force and Dobbs was certain that his friend had suffered several broken ribs as well.

While Means was concentrating on Benoit, Dobbs

had pulled his Walker. Nervously, he tried to level the four-pound pistol but his mind rebelled. I'm a physician, he thought. My duty is to save life, not take it. But he knew that if he didn't shoot Means, Benoit was as good as dead. He, too, probably. Bringing his muscles under control, he pointed his pistol directly at Means's chest and pulled the trigger. The explosion startled him momentarily, but he was nevertheless relieved to see a cloud of dust rise from Means's shirt near the top of his shoulder. While the wound would have felled most men, it simply spun Means around and sent him staggering backward for several yards. With a surprised look on his face, the prisoner quickly regained his balance. Letting out another angry yell, he raised the rifle and charged again at Benoit, drawing back the rifle for a third swing.

Dobbs raised his pistol a second time. By then, Benoit had his pistol out as well. When Means was only three feet away, Benoit and Dobbs fired simultaneously. Dobbs's .44-caliber slug struck Means in the chest, precisely in the center of his sternum. The slug from Benoit's Colt Dragoon connected just below Means's chin, ripping a large round hole in his throat and tearing away his Adam's apple. This time, Means did not rebound; he was dead before he knew what had hit him.

"Does it hurt?" Dobbs asked solicitously.

"Only when I breathe," Benoit replied. He tried to laugh at his own humor, but quickly convulsed in pain. "Goddamn," he wheezed once the spasm had passed. "I'd have to say that smarts."

"It could have been worse," Dobbs told him. "Much worse."

"Well, what's the prognosis?" Benoit asked weakly.

"Your arm was broken pretty badly, but it was a good clean break and unless it gets infected where the bones came through the skin, you'll eventually be okay. That forearm may be a little crooked, but you should still have full mobility."

"And the ribs?"

"That's the good news. Your horse probably saved your life. If Means had hit you full-force, your ribs probably would have shattered and punctured your lungs. God, that man was strong. As it is, I think you have only two cracked ribs and, while it's going to hurt like hell for awhile, they're going to heal before your arm."

"How long altogether?"

Dobbs shrugged. "Barring complications, your ribs will be okay in a few weeks. The arm will take longer."

"Can I travel? Can I go on to Fort Laramie with the train?"

"That's up to you. You won't be able to ride a horse for any period of time for at least a couple of weeks because of your ribs. After that, the big problem will be the arm. You'll definitely need someone to saddle your mount for quite awhile yet."

"You're encouraging."

"Well, it isn't all bad. I'm sure the Schmidts wouldn't mind having you along as a passenger until you can ride, which should be before we reach Fort Laramie."

"Well, what's the disadvantage of going on?"

"You're going to be uncomfortable as hell for a few days no matter how you travel."

Benoit thought about it for several minutes. "I think I'll go with the train," he said finally. "This place depresses me and nobody here is going to take care of me like you and Frau Schmidt."

"That's probably a wise decision. I wouldn't want to stay here either."

"Speaking of that, how's Captain Robinson?"

Dobbs shook his head. "He didn't make it. The bullet severed a major artery and he bled to death."

"That's too bad," said Benoit. "I guess he was an all-right officer. He had just been on the frontier too long."

"Look at it another way," said Dobbs.

"How's that?"

"He doesn't have to worry about his hemorrhoids any more."

## ⚡ 12 ⚡

Four days after Fire-in-the-Hills and the others left them deep in enemy territory, Blizzard and his group found the Kangi village. But the elation that initially accompanied the discovery was tempered by the fact that the situation was not what they had hoped. While Blizzard had counted on the village being virtually empty of warriors, who he had been sure would be out hunting since it was the middle of the prime meat-gathering season, the raiders instead were faced with a Crow camp overflowing with braves. Blizzard's scouts could see at a glance that the Crow, as had the Wazhazha a few weeks before, were fresh off a successful buffalo hunt and everyone in the village, from a child old enough to help scrape a hide to the old people fit only for gathering firewood, was working to get the meat ready for winter storage.

"It would be suicide for us to try to attack while all their warriors are there," said Bellowing Moose.

"I thought suicide was what the Strong Hearts were

all about," snapped Blizzard, who was angry because his plans for a raid had run into unexpected difficulty.

"Bravery doesn't equate with stupidity," Bellowing Moose shot back. "If you insist on attacking the village while all their warriors are there, you're going to do it without me."

"Calm down," interjected Roaring Thunder. "There's no sense fighting among ourselves. Maybe something can be salvaged from the situation after all."

"A raid isn't out of the question yet," argued Blizzard, unwilling to give up his scheme without a fight. "If we strike quickly, we could be in and out before the Kangi knew what hit them."

"There's not a chance of that," said Roaring Thunder. "They have a whole herd of fresh horses and they could run us down long before we could get back to friendly ground."

Blizzard looked thoughtful for a moment. "Fresh horses, eh? That's an idea. If you can't kill a buffalo you might have to settle for a pronghorn."

"You mean we could raid the horses again?" White Crane asked timidly, not sure if he would be put down for presuming to speak among the more experienced warriors.

"The bear cub lives," Grizzly-That-Growls snarled, glancing at White Crane. "Maybe he thinks he's qualified to join his betters."

"Leave him alone," said Jagged Blade. "He's performing well."

"Are you telling me what to do?"

"Anyone stupid enough to carry a no-retreat sash may indeed be stupid enough to pick a fight with me," Jagged Blade said, reaching for his knife.

"Enough!" Blizzard said firmly. "We're all tired and on edge. Let's smoke a pipe and let our tempers cool. We need to examine this situation rationally or we may as well go home now and admit to Fire-in-the-Hills and the others that we were all old women."

"That will be the day," grumbled Grizzly-That-Growls.

"I won't admit anything to Fire-in-the-Hills," added Bellowing Moose.

"We'd never live it down," agreed Roaring Thunder.

"Even the children would be laughing at us," said Jagged Blade.

"Then let's work out a plan of action," said Blizzard, packing the pipe with *shongsasha*.

After almost a full day of discussion and arguing, it was decided to do nothing right away. The group would find a comfortable, secure place to hole up for a few days to see what developed. Maybe the Crow warriors would become restless after several days and an opportunity would present itself.

Each day a different member of Blizzard's group was assigned to work himself close to the Crow village and spy on their activities, but not too close to risk discovery. If the Crow were to stumble upon their camp, reinforcements would be called in and the Wazhazha would never stand a chance since the Crow would outnumber them at least twelve to one.

"Our best opportunity," Blizzard explained on the second evening, "would be for a small group of Crow braves to leave on a horse raid. Then we can follow them and ambush them once they get away from the village."

That hope turned into reality two days later when Jagged Blade returned from a spying expedition and reported that a dozen or more Crow were making preparations to depart.

"On foot or on horseback?" Blizzard asked anxiously.

"On foot," Jagged Blade replied with a smile. "The perfect situation."

While the rest of the group hid deep within the forest, Roaring Thunder tracked the Crow warriors as they moved northwest, apparently heading for Blackfoot territory.

"Let's give them one more day to make sure they are well away from the village," Blizzard said, smiling to himself. "This goes to prove," he said, turning to White Crane, "that patience pays off."

Not sure how to respond, White Crane simply nodded.

It was at this juncture that Blizzard made a crucial mistake. He called his men together and they made a cold camp several hours behind the Crow raiding party, waiting for the opportunity to attack. What he failed to do was send a scout to watch the Crow village to see if there were other developments that he needed to know about. As a result, he was unaware that a second party of Crow departed several hours after the first, travelling in the same direction. While Blizzard's group tracked the first Crow party, a second group of Kangi had moved in behind them. Although unaware of the Wazhazhas' presence, the second group of Crow was close enough to the first to come running when they later heard the unmistakable sounds of fighting. Blizzard unknowingly had sandwiched his men between two enemy groups.

The initial attack went well. Roaring Thunder came galloping out of the trees, spearing one Crow so thoroughly that he nailed him to a tree with his lance. "That's for Rising Moon," he screamed triumphantly. Turning his horse, he returned to the fray and nearly decapitated a Crow with one sweep of his tomahawk.

Bellowing Moose jumped off his horse and, with a loud, long cry he had perfected to help him live up to his name, attacked a Crow on the ground with his knife. "See how it feels to fight against a warrior and not some old man who can't fight back," he grunted, slitting the Crow neatly from belly button to sternum.

White Crane was looking for a target when he saw a Crow dashing for the thick forest. Digging his heels into his pinto's sides, he quickly closed the gap and before the Crow could reach the safety of the trees White Crane leaned over and shot him with an arrow, much as he had done earlier with the buffalo cow. He watched in fascination as the arrow went almost completely through the Crow, entering between his shoulder blades and exiting over his right nipple. Never again, he told himself as he jumped off his horse to collect his scalp, will I doubt the power of my bow.

Jagged Blade, Grizzly-That-Growls, and Blizzard also took advantage of the surprise and killed or mortally wounded three Crow in the first minutes of the attack.

If the fighting had remained hand-to-hand and weapons had been confined to the traditional variety, things may have gone smoother for Blizzard and his men. But two of the Crow also were carrying rifles and they immediately opened fire. It was the gunfire that alerted the second group of Crow to the fight.

After the surprise wore off, the Crow showed they were all experienced warriors by quickly forming a line of defense and moving back into the trees where it would be harder for the mounted Brulé to maneuver. Standing side by side, they fought with determination and skill. One of the Crow riflemen shot Grizzly-That-Growls precisely between the eyes as the Brulé warrior recklessly charged the pocket of enemy braves, seemingly adding strength to Blizzard's comments about the suicidal tendencies of the Strong Hearts.

Red Deer, another Wazhazha warrior, was knocked off his horse by an arrow through his shoulder. As he scurried for cover, two Crow rushed forward and beat

him to death with their war clubs. Another Crow bow-
man loosed an arrow straight at Blizzard's heart and the
Brulé warrior would have been instantly killed if his
horse had not stumbled at exactly that same moment,
throwing him out of the missile's path.

Quickly realizing that the moment of surprise had
passed, Blizzard rallied his men with the intention of
gathering for a fresh attack. It was then that the second
group of Crow ran screaming out of the pines, charging
down upon the Wazhazhas' backs. This time, it was
Blizzard's turn to be surprised. Although he and his
men were mounted and all the Crow were afoot, the
advantage had definitely swung to the Kangi, who out-
numbered the Wazhazha two to one.

Faced with the possibility of being surrounded,
Blizzard recognized the futility of the situation and
ordered a hasty retreat. On their horses they quickly
outdistanced the Crow, but they continued to ride for
two hours before stopping to check their losses.

"We suffered much," Blizzard said angrily, mad at
himself for his tactical mistake in not keeping a spy at
the Crow camp and at the Crow for inflicting such
heavy damage against his men. In addition to Grizzly-
That-Growls and Red Deer, who were felled in the initial charge, two other Wazhazhas were missing and
presumed dead. Slowly, he went among the wounded
examining their injuries. Roaring Thunder had taken an
arrow in his thigh and, although he remained stone-
faced, it was obvious that he was in great pain. Leaning
Pine, a youth not much older than White Crane who
was on only his fourth raid, was bleeding badly from a
knife wound between his ribs. As Blizzard was examining the injury, the youth's eyes rolled back in his head
and he slipped from his horse. Seeing red froth bubbling
from the wound, which indicated that his lung had been
punctured, Blizzard clapped his hand over the hole. But

it was too late. Leaning Pine coughed wetly several times and died.

Two others had wounds that Blizzard considered serious enough to need treatment by a shaman and four had minor injuries. In the beginning there had been sixteen warriors in the group, but it was now down to eleven, including four who were badly wounded and three others who suffered from lesser injuries. Reluctantly, knowing his reputation would suffer mightily as a result of the botched raid, perhaps to the extent that it would be several seasons before men would be ready to follow him into battle again, Blizzard turned the bedraggled group toward home.

"Where do you think we will find our people?" White Crane quietly asked Roaring Thunder.

"At this time of the summer, they probably have moved east near the *isan hanska* lodge to await the presentation of the annuity," Roaring Thunder replied through gritted teeth. Although his wound, barring an infection, was not considered life threatening, it was extremely painful. It was not so bad as long as he was mounted and there was no weight on the leg, but once he slipped off his horse's back, his leg felt as if it had been stuck in a campfire.

"Do you think that's where we're headed?"

Roaring Thunder looked at the sun to get a rough estimate on the direction they were travelling. Since he didn't feel like talking, he simply grunted.

Sensing the mood of the men, White Crane slowed his horse until he was at the tail end of the procession. Then he slowed it still further until the others were a quarter of a mile ahead. They will be looking for someone to take their anger out on, he thought, and I don't want it to be me.

Three days after the incident at the Fort Kearny parade ground, the wagon train left the garrison heading almost due west, travelling along the southern bank of the north fork of the Platte River. Ever since the group had left Independence more than a month before, the emigrants had been anticipating striking the Platte because it would mark their path for much of their journey. Accustomed to the deep, crystalline streams of the East, they were at first taken aback by the Platte, which was the most unlikely river they had ever encountered. *Platte*, meaning "shallow" in French, could be navigated afoot in many spots, but it made up for a deficiency in depth in its breadth. When it was running full with snow melt and water from the spring rains, it spread its arms over a wide stretch of prairie land, frequently burgeoning out until it was more than a mile across.

"At last," Erich Schmidt shrieked when he and Jim Ashby first came upon the river. "The infamous Platte."

Vaulting out of his saddle, he ran to the muddy bank and threw himself down on his stomach. Sticking his head in the churning water, he took a large mouthful and almost immediately spat it out.

"*Ach du Scheisse*," he said, continuing to spit, "that tastes like dirt. Might as well have taken a bite out of the bank."

"Maybe that'll learn you to be more cautious about somethin' you don't know nothin' about." Ashby laughed. "If you want to take a drink out of the Platte, you'd best put it in a bucket and let it sit a spell until all the silt settles to the bottom."

"Is it always like this?" Erich asked, making a face.

"Pret' near. But right now it's still running high and it's got more prairie in it than usual. Come September, it'll calm down a bit."

Erich took off his hat, filled it with water, and held it

in his hands, waiting for the grit to sink. "Guess there's still some things I got to learn yet," he said with a grin.

Ashby laughed. "Shit, boy, you ain't even started good. The amount of stuff you don't know would cover the Plains six inches deep."

Ever since the pronghorn hunt before they arrived at Fort Kearny, Erich had tagged along after Ashby like a bright-eyed puppy, trying to imitate his every action. Although he was not one to take quickly to strangers, Ashby had grown fond of the youth because he reminded him so much of himself at that age. As a result, he not only tolerated Erich's almost daily presence, he welcomed it. In his mind's eye, he was the teacher and Erich was the bright, eager pupil. At times, the scout was amazed at how quickly the German boy caught on to things, like how to read tracks in the dust and how to predict a weather change simply by studying the clouds at sunset. Some things, such as a feel for where to find deer when the prairie seemed bare, were instinctual and Ashby was inwardly delighted when he could detect the bud of an outdoorsman's sensibility in the former city dweller. Although Ashby's duty required him to push hard from before sunup to after sundown, the scout noticed with relief that Erich had the stamina to keep up with him mile after dusty mile. He didn't complain when the rain soaked him through or the sun blistered his fair skin.

Importantly, too, he seemed to have what it took in the guts department, as evidenced by the time he jumped off his horse and stood between Ashby and a young buffalo bull. Ashby thought he had killed the animal and dismounted too soon, walking nonchalantly toward the motionless bison. Suddenly, it sprang up and charged, evidencing every intention of pounding the two-legged adversary into the clay.

Erich had calmly raised his rifle—Benoit's rifle to be
accurate—and shot the bull squarely between the
horns. Truly, the scout had told Benoit over a pot of
coffee around the campfire that night, if he had to
pick a protégé he could do worse than the Schmidt
boy.

Benoit had smiled at the news. Since leaving
Kearny three weeks before he had been a virtual
invalid, unable to saddle his own horse or sit the animal for more than a couple of hours at a stretch.
Although he could feel himself growing stronger
every day, thanks in large part to Frau Schmidt's cooking and Inge's devoted attention, he was still a long
way from being fully recovered. His ribs no longer
troubled him so much, but his arm was an almost constant source of irritation. Dobbs examined it almost
every day, searching anxiously for signs of the
dreaded gangrene. When the punctures healed without apparent difficulty, Dobbs breathed a sigh of
relief. Although Dobbs kept the arm tightly wrapped
to help insure a favorable mending of the bones, he
worried that he might not have set it properly and
Benoit would either have to go through life with a
deformed forearm or would have to submit to having
it rebroken and reset, options decidedly lacking in
appeal to both Dobbs and Benoit.

Even worse than the throbbing—which Benoit happily noted seemed to be diminishing daily—was the
itching. Sometimes, despite admonitions from Dobbs to
leave the wrapping alone, he was tempted to rip off the
covering and scratch to his heart's content.

"Must have gotten ants under it," he said to Dobbs,
waving it about in the hope of creating a little friction
that might relieve the torture.

"Be gentle with it," Dobbs said sharply. "Pretend it's
a woman."

"But it itches like crazy."

"One of life's little inconveniences."

"Goddamnit, *you* don't have *your* arm wrapped up like a macabre Christmas present."

"That's because I'm smart enough not to try to stop a man swinging a rifle with my arm. I used a pistol."

"Aw shit," Benoit swore, "a fat lot of sympathy I get from you." Stomping off into the darkness to sulk, he noticed the itching had stopped; Dobbs had taken his mind off of it and the sensation had passed.

What worried Benoit more than his wounds, however, was the mounting evidence that Inge looked upon him in a fashion that hardly would be described as brotherly. And he was surprised to find that he was hardly resisting. Once he was confined to the Schmidts' wagon he began to notice things about the German girl that he had not noted before, namely that she was quite pretty. Her hair, he confided to his journal, was as golden as the prairie at dawn, her eyes as blue as the Atlantic Ocean, and her skin as white as fresh cow's milk. What he also noticed, once he had to the time to observe her closely, was that she had a woman's body, something he did not suspect in a girl of only seventeen. In addition to her physical attributes, she had a quick mind and a finely honed sense of humor, which she had exhibited time and again.

On the second day out of Fort Kearny, while Benoit had still been almost totally immobile because of the tenderness in his ribs, he lay in the wagon when Inge crawled up to him with a wet cloth to mop his forehead.

"For a good man, a lot of bad things seem to happen to you," she said, smiling in spite of herself. "How do you say that in English?"

"'Accident-prone,'" Benoit suggested.

'"That sounds very stiff," she said. "We have a better term in German. We refer to someone like that as *'ein Pechvogel.'* It means someone who is unlucky in the physical sense."

"*Pechvogel*," Benoit repeated, the word sounding strange on his lips.

"It isn't a bad term," Inge assured him. "On the contrary, it can be quite affectionate. In fact, that's what I think I'll secretly call you from now on, *Pechvogel*."

Oh, great, Benoit thought. Just what I need: another goddamn nickname. Why can't people just call me by the name I was christened with?

One day when firewood was low Benoit was helping her collect buffalo chips, which burned quite readily, producing sufficient heat for cooking. Picking up one of the brown, pancake-flat patties, the thought occurred to Benoit that it was an opportunity to further Inge's education.

"Do you know what the French trappers call this?" he asked.

"No," she said innocently. "What do they call it?"

"*Bois de vache.* Literally, that means 'wood of the cow.' What do you call it?" he asked, expecting to hear an unpronounceable, polysyllabic German phrase.

Inge looked up and batted her blue eyes. "Buffalo shit."

The growing attraction that each felt for the other did not go unnoticed by the Schmidts. On more than one occasion, after Benoit, Erich, and Inge were asleep, Hildegard and Hans put their heads together as they lay on their makeshift bed under the wagon and discussed the budding romance.

"I don't think I like it," said Hans.

"Why not?" Hildegard asked in surprise. "He's a fine young man."

"But he's a soldier," Hans countered. "His job is to kill people."

"I don't think he would kill anyone who wasn't trying to kill him first," said Hildegard. "He has a kind heart. I can see it in his eyes."

"A lot you know. You didn't see him shoot that other soldier at Fort Kearny."

"Well, you didn't see it either. It was in self-defense. Lieutenant Dobbs said so, and so did Jean. Besides, if it had not been justified, he would have been arrested."

"They don't arrest an officer for killing an enlisted man."

"Maybe not at home," said Hildegard, "but they do in this country."

"He will be living out here in the middle of nowhere. This is not the kind of country for my Inge."

"Well, just where do you think *your Inge* is going to be living when we get to Oregon? That's not exactly Frankfurt, you know."

"That's different. At least it's green."

"What appeals to you may not appeal to Inge. I say if she's happy, I'm happy."

Hans grunted. "There's one other thing I don't like."

"What's that?" Hildegard asked with concern.

"He's a Frenchman."

Despite herself, Hildegard started giggling. The absurdity of the argument had proved too much. "Oh, Hans," she sighed. "You're like a child. You're impossible."

His feelings hurt, Hans struck back. "You talk too much. You're just like your mother, *eine Quasselstrippe*, a chatterbox. *Halt's Maul*. Be quiet and go to sleep."

Satisfied that he had the last word, he rolled over and in less than two minutes was snoring loudly.

Blizzard and his battle-weary force of warriors were plodding lethargically toward the spot where they presumed the Wazhazhas had moved, a favorite campsite about a half dozen miles east of Fort Laramie, when they encountered a group of a dozen Northern Cheyenne, who were travelling south. Since the Brulé and the Cheyenne were allies, the meeting was friendly.

"We have fresh meat if you'd like some," Brown Hawk, the leader of the Cheyenne, said hospitably. Sizing up the bedraggled warriors, he added: "You look as if you could use it."

That evening, feeling refreshed after their first full meal in four days, Blizzard explained to Brown Hawk what had happened to his party.

"It sounds as though you had incredibly bad medicine," the Cheyenne commiserated.

"I wish I could blame it all on that," said Blizzard. "Unfortunately, some in my party, and undoubtedly many other Wazhazhas as well, will say the misfortune is a result of my poor leadership."

"That's too bad," said Brown Hawk. "Things of that nature happen to the best of warriors. They can't be helped."

"I agree with you," added Blizzard. "But what happened is irreversible; it can't be changed. Now I will have to wait for a long time before I will get the opportunity to rehabilitate myself, to prove that I am still the Wazhazhas' best warrior."

Brown Hawk was silent for several minutes, puffing contentedly on the pipe he and Blizzard were sharing.

"What if I were to suggest to you," the Cheyenne said slowly, "a way that you might be able to recover some of your lost dignity, a way that you could still return to your camp in victory rather than defeat."

Blizzard studied the Cheyenne carefully. "Explain yourself," he demanded.

Brown Hawk revealed that he and his group had come south looking for Pawnee, who were their bitter enemies. They found three of the enemy tribe's hunters two days before, whom they killed and scalped. Now he and his group were heading home but before returning they wanted to satisfy their curiosity about the whites. He had heard, he said, of a steady stream of emigrants that were traversing the Plains on their way west. "The whites might be easier targets than even the Pawnee."

"But that's against the terms of the Treaty of the Long Meadows," Blizzard pointed out.

Brown Hawk laughed. "Did *you* sign the treaty?" he asked.

"No," admitted Blizzard.

"Neither did I," said Brown Hawk. "And since I didn't agree to it I see no reason to be bound to its provisions."

"That's a good point," Blizzard conceded.

"Join up with me and my men," Brown Hawk proposed. "I hear that the white man's riches are there for the taking if only someone is bold enough to reach."

Blizzard rubbed his chin. "I need to talk it over with my men," he said. "Some are seriously wounded and are eager to get back to their lodges."

"That's because they don't have the same concerns as you," said Brown Hawk.

"That's true," admitted Blizzard. "But let me discuss it with them."

The next evening, Blizzard again broke out his pipe and invited Brown Hawk to sit with him by the fire.

"Well?" asked Brown Hawk after the formalities had been dealt with.

"We have discussed it," said Blizzard. "Two of us— myself and a Strong Heart named Bellowing Moose— feel we have more to gain by joining your group than by going immediately back to our camp. We have agreed to put ourselves under your command. The others will continue on their journey."

"I think you've made a wise decision," said Brown Hawk. "The others will come to think so too when they hear of our success. Let them go. In the meantime, we have plans to discuss. I respect your reputation as a warrior and I value whatever you might have to say."

The train was only a two-day march from Fort Laramie when Heinrich Mueller's wagon broke down.

"I knew that blacksmith at Fort Kearny didn't know what he was doing," Heinrich complained bitterly in German. "I tried to tell him how to fix that wheel and he called me a dumb kraut and told me if I didn't like what he was doing to go somewhere else. As if that was an option."

"It's too late to worry about that now," said Heinz Hartmann. "Now we just have to figure out what we can do about it."

Alf Stuart had to be summoned from the front of the train and by the time he rode back to the Mueller wagon, he was in a foul mood.

"I can't hold up the group," he said bluntly. "We need t' keep movin'. We're smack dab in the middle of Brulé country and them people has been mighty nervous lately."

"Well, what do you suggest?" Heinrich asked as calmly as he could, using Inge as interpreter.

"Load your stuff on your friends' wagons and continue to Fort Laramie. Then you can get the blacksmith from there and come back with a squad of soldiers, fix the wagon an' bring it back to the fort."

"That wagon's all I have," Heinrich argued. "My friends don't have enough room for everything. If we leave it here, it will be stripped by the *Rothäute*. I'd bet my life on it."

"You're bettin' your life if you stay, too," Stuart said angrily. "'Cause the train is goin' on."

After discussing the matter briefly with Heinz and Hans Schmidt, it was agreed that they all would stay and try to patch up the wagon enough to get it into Fort Laramie. Three families would have a much better chance than one, Hans explained to Stuart through his daughter. They had come this far together and they did not intend to separate just because there was a little problem. "Besides," said Hans, "we haven't seen an Indian since we left Fort Kearny and that was almost a month ago."

'You poor dumb fuckers," Stuart grumbled. "You just don't un'nerstan' the dangers involved. I'm gonna take the train on into Fort Laramie and I'll send back some help when I get there."

"*Arschloch*," Heinrich muttered under his breath. "What an asshole."

As the wagon train was moving on, Jim Ashby rode up and pulled Benoit aside.

"You staying with 'em?" he asked.

"Of course," Benoit replied. "I'm not up to a two-day ride on a horse. Also, I might be able to help, or at least offer moral support."

Ashby studied the officer and decided there was no sense trying to talk him out of it. "You'd best be watchful," he said. "I cut some Injun sign this mornin' so I know they're roaming around out here somewhere."

"Any reason to think they might be hostile?" asked Benoit.

Ashby shook his head. "Nope. Jus' instinct. I tole you before I ain't real happy with the talk I been hearin' about the Brulé, but I got no evidence to back it up. You know," he added, "I'd stay with you if'n I could. But the boss man says go and I gotta go."

"I understand," said Benoit. "Don't worry about us, we'll be all right. As soon as we get that wheel fixed, we'll be right behind you."

"I inten' to have a talk with Erich too," said Ashby. "I want to tell him some things to look out for. I'm gonna leave my rifle with 'im, though, just in case."

"We have mine," Benoit protested, "and Heinrich has an old trade gun with plenty of powder."

"That's all you got?" Ashby asked, surprised.

"I think so. It doesn't much matter though, since none of the Germans, except for Erich, knows how to use a weapon anyway."

Ashby spat a long stream of tobacco juice. "I'm gonna' have another talk with Stuart. He can spare a couple o' his men for a short spell, jus' to make sure you're not in danger."

"Well," said Benoit. "Dobbs wanted to stay too but I told him that was ridiculous. He's a physician, not a rifleman. I doubt if he's ever even fired a rifle."

"That makes sense," Ashby agreed. "But it wouldn' hurt to have a few experienced Plainsmen to help stand guard. In the meantime, make a circle out of those wagons and get the livestock in the center. Jus' in case."

An hour later three of Stuart's men came galloping into the camp. "Mr. Stuart tole us to stay with you a spell," said Andy Matthewson, the spokesman for the trio.

"Fine with me," said Benoit. "Climb down and have some coffee. Frau Schmidt just baked some fresh bread."

# ~ *13* ~

"Hand me the hammer, Heinz," Heinrich said, wiping the sweat from his forehead. "Now grab right here. Hold it tight, otherwise it's going to slip. All right. You ready?"

"Ready. Swing away."

With three quick, solid blows, Heinrich secured the metal rim to the newly repaired wheel. "Well, that does it," he said, breathing heavily. "Now let's see if it works. Hans," he called, "come give us a hand."

Together, they wrestled the wheel onto the axle and got it secured. "You ready to try it?" asked Hans, red-faced from the exertion.

"May as well," said Heinrich. "We have to know if it's going to support the load."

Heinrich grabbed the reins and cautiously urged the team forward. Slowly the wagon inched ahead, then gathered speed.

"Not too fast!" yelled Heinz. "You don't want to ruin everything now."

"All right," Heinrich said, easing back. "Slow, slow," he whispered to the oxen. "We have to take it easy."

As Heinz and Hans held their breath, the wagon moved slowly and unsteadily down the well-travelled path.

"It's working! It's working!" Heinrich hollered joyfully. "I'm going to keep moving. You load up and follow me. You won't have any trouble catching up."

"*Gott sei Dank*," Heinz said in heartfelt sincerity, wiping the grease from his hand on a rag made from one of his wife's old skirts, no longer fit to wear because of the damage the campfires had inflicted on the hem.

For the rest of the day, the trio of wagons plodded steadily westward in the direction taken by the other members of the wagon train eight hours earlier. Although their progress was slow, Heinrich was optimistic. "We may yet rejoin the others before they reach Fort Laramie," he said hopefully to his wife, Johanna.

That night they stopped near a grove of cottonwoods that grew thickly along the Platte. The river, still running swiftly, had dropped considerably since they first turned along its banks almost a month earlier. For the next six months, until it was fed again by water from the melting snow, the river would continue to diminish in size until it was little more than a trickle.

Shortly after dawn the next morning, the three wagons, still lumbering clumsily along but making steady progress nonetheless, continued westward. Shortly before noon they stopped near another cottonwood grove. While the men continued to tinker with the troublesome wheel, the women put together the day's main meal.

"One of the bad things about this trip," said Heinz, "is I find myself losing track of time. What day is it anyway?"

"I figure it's Monday," said Heinrich.

"But what date?"

"Let me think a second. Must be the fourteenth of August. I checked the calendar at Fort Kearny and my calculations were correct."

"*Hallo, alle miteinander!*" Hildegard called loudly. "*Das Essen ist Fertig!*"

"Food's on," whooped Erich, putting aside the cleaning patches and oil he had been using on Benoit's Sharps rifle. "And I'm hungry enough to eat a whole buffalo all by myself."

"This is almost like a picnic," said Heinrich, helping himself to a heaping mound of fried potatoes the women were serving chow-hall style from a communal kitchen. "What more could one wish for? This is heaven: *Bratkartoffeln, Schinken, Brötchen mit Käse und Kaffee.*"

"A good cold lager would really hit the spot," added Hans.

"And," Hildegard added dreamily, "so would a nice chocolate layer cake filled with cream and cherries and flavored with cherry brandy."

"To be realistic," said the literal-minded Heinrich, "you know what would really be good would be a fresh venison roast."

"Venison." Hans laughed. "We haven't seen a deer for days and days."

"No," Erich said brightly, "but I saw a small herd of pronghorn off to the west just before we stopped."

"Ahhh," Heinrich sighed. "An antelope steak would do nicely."

"And some fresh berries, too," Inge added enthusiastically. "No cherries but I think I saw some blackberries along the bank when I filled the water casks earlier. It's no more than an hour back down the trail. While you *Älteren* are taking your afternoon nap we youngsters can collect the prizes. Erich will bag us a pronghorn and Jean and I will collect the berries."

"You know," Hans commented, lighting up one of his few remaining cigars, "I think I like travelling by ourselves better than with the whole group."

"Wait a minute," said Benoit. "We can't split up like that. This is not the place to start acting as though we're on an outing in the park."

"Don't be such a spoilsport," Inge said, digging her elbow into his ribs. "We're not going that far, just back a few miles. We can be back here in a flash. Besides, I think Old Man Stuart has been exaggerating the dangers. We haven't seen a *Rothaut*, friendly or otherwise, in ages."

"When you don't see 'em is when you got to start worrying about 'em," interjected Matthewson, who along with Stuart's other men, Brunelli and Fitzgerald, had been sitting silently during the exchange, mainly because much of the conversation was in German.

"That's why you're here," Inge said. "To protect us. You can stay here and keep guard while we collect the provisions for a feast. Doesn't a nice broiled antelope rump sound good to you? Topped off with some berries and fresh cream."

Matthewson grinned, obviously entranced with the idea.

"Besides," Erich added, "don't the *Rothäute* always attack at dawn? This sure as hell isn't dawn. And where would they come from anyway?" With a sweep of his arm he encompassed the horizon. "Out here you can see for at least fifty miles and there aren't any trees to hide behind. Do you see any hostile forces approaching?"

"I think it's a bad idea," said Benoit.

"We're not in the Army," Heinrich Mueller said stubbornly. "You can't tell us what to do."

Benoit knew the German was right; the Army had no authority over the emigrants and even if it did, it didn't apply to him since his orders said only that he was to *accompany* the train as far as Fort Laramie; his papers gave him no command responsibility.

"You're right," he said grudgingly. "But I still don't think it's a wise thing to do."

"Don't be an old spoilsport," Inge said with a pout. "If you're afraid to leave the other *men* for a few minutes, I'll go by myself."

Benoit reddened, knowing he was being goaded into something that ran contrary to his better judgment. At the same time, he knew he didn't have much choice. "You know I can't let you do that," Benoit said angrily to Inge.

"Then I'll take Mr. Matthewson with me. I know he'd be delighted to go, wouldn't you, Mr. Matthewson?"

The muleskinner's eyes lit up. The last woman he'd had was one of the Indian whores at Fort Kearny, and he couldn't remember the last time he'd bedded a white woman, much less a young blonde white woman.

"It'd be my pleasure," he said with a leer.

"All right, all right," Benoit said, caving in. "I'll go with you. But if we don't find those berries within two miles we're turning around and coming back. Agreed?"

"*Ja, ja, ja,*" Inge said eagerly. "Don't just sit there on your *Arsch*. Let's get going. We're wasting time."

"I'll be heading west," said Erich, "which is the way we're going to be going anyway. If I don't find those pronghorn in an hour I'll come back empty-handed. Is that all right?"

"Perfect," said Benoit. "Remember, though, no more than an hour. Absolutely, under no circumstances, stay longer than that."

"Agreed," Erich said with a smile. "May I use your rifle or do you plan to shoot those berries?"

Benoit sighed. When the Schmidts joined forces they presented a formidable team. "Take the Sharps. I don't guess you're going to bag many pronghorns with an ax."

Erich laughed. "Hell," he said, "maybe I can even get two."

"I can't believe these *isan hanskas* are so dumb," Blizzard whispered to Brown Hawk. "They walk around like they haven't a care in the world and they set up camp without posting guards or even sending out scouts to make sure there are no enemies nearby."

"It's a good thing they didn't," Brown Hawk whispered back, "or they surely would have discovered us. We've been following them since yesterday afternoon and they have no idea we're here."

Using the deep arroyos that cut randomly through the Plains, the raiding party had been travelling south of but roughly parallel to the Germans' path for almost a full day, never being spotted because they kept to the gullies and out of the emigrants' line of sight.

"What magnificent good fortune," muttered Bellowing Moose, whose eyes sparkled with the prospect of the forthcoming clash.

"Have you ever fought a white man before?" asked Brown Hawk.

"Never," admitted Blizzard. "But I assume they bleed and die just like everyone else."

"I think we should attack now," said Brown Hawk, "while they are relaxed. My best scout, Long Nose, says even the men who apparently are supposed to serve as guards are asleep, full of the big meal they've just finished."

"I think that's a good idea," Blizzard agreed. "When they stopped last night they gathered their wagons in a circle, which makes them harder to attack. But now they're in single file and vulnerable. Apparently they think nothing can happen to them as long as the sun is shining."

"Better for us." Brown Hawk grinned.

"What about the three who rode off?" asked Bellowing Moose.

"The soldier with the injured arm and the woman went east, maybe to look for wild vegetables," said Blizzard. "I would guess the boy is off hunting."

"That's fine for us," said Brown Hawk. "Two less guns we have to worry about."

"It's too bad about the young woman," said Black Bull, another of Brown Hawk's warriors. "She would have brought four or five horses from the Assiniboin."

"There are the others," Bellowing Moose pointed out. "Those children will be valuable."

"Let's get just a little closer before we show ourselves," said Brown Hawk. "I want to keep the advantage of surprise as long as we can."

As quietly as possible, he dismounted and removed his containers of war paint from the parfleche he had slung across his shoulder. The rest of the group, including Blizzard and Bellowing Moose, followed suit. Twenty minutes later, they remounted, readying their weapons. Blizzard removed his shield from its buckskin case and slowly swung his war club over his head, loosening his shoulder muscles.

"Are you ready?" he asked, turning to Bellowing Moose.

The Strong Heart replied with a broad grin. "A white scalp is going to look nice hanging from my lance."


"Oh, look," Inge gushed, pointing to the berries that were growing in wild profusion along the bank. "More berries than we'll ever be able to pick."

Adroitly slipping out of the saddle, she jumped to the ground and grabbed the flour sack she had slung over the pommel before they left the camp.

"Come and help me," she urged Benoit. "Even one arm," she said teasingly, "is better than nothing."

Looking nervously over his shoulder, straining to see the grove where the wagons were pulled into the shade, Benoit joined her and began filling the sack with blackberries. "We have to hurry," he said. "We've come farther than we should have."

"Don't worry so much," she teased him. "What could possibly happen in the middle of the day? Mr. Matthewson and the others are keeping watch."

"I'll *bet* they are," Benoit replied with heavy sarcasm. "After that meal, I'll bet they're sound asleep under the closest tree."

"But my father won't be asleep," Inge said. "He always uses the midday break to write in his diary."

"I hope so," Benoit said, sounding not at all relieved.

"Nothing's going to happen," Inge said, trying to reassure him. "I've never seen such a peaceful-looking place."

Erich was scanning the horizon, looking for the herd of pronghorns he had seen earlier, when he spotted the cloud of dust approaching from the west. What the hell? he asked himself, checking to make sure the Sharps was ready to fire. He was preparing to turn and race back to the wagons when he recognized the horse of one of the four riders approaching. It was Jim Ashby's.

As the group got closer, Erich saw that there were three soldiers riding with the scout. One was Lieutenant Dobbs; with him were two enlisted men he had never seen before.

Ten minutes later, Ashby reined his horse to a halt where Erich sat, patiently waiting.

"What's wrong?" the youth asked immediately.

"Maybe nothing," Ashby drawled. "But first tell me what the hell you're doing out here. Where's the rest of the group?"

"Over by those cottonwoods," Erich said, pointing to the grove, which was only a thin line of green in the distance.

"What'd you go off an leave 'em for?" Ashby asked in some irritation. "Didn't I tell you to stick together?"

"They decided they wanted some pronghorn steak," Erich said, unable to understand Ashby's irritation. "I thought I'd try to get one for dinner tomorrow."

"So you jus' rode off?"

"Why not?" Erich asked. "Everything's fine. Herr Mueller got his wheel fixed and we've been travelling since yesterday. Slow, but steady. Haven't seen anyone or anything since the train pulled out."

"Where's Lieutenant Benoit?" asked Dobbs.

"He and my sister went back a couple of miles," he said, pointing to the east. "They went to pick some berries. Everybody else is taking the usual midday nap."

"Pickin' berries. Huntin' pronghorn. Taking a nap. You think you're in the middle of Pennsafucki'vania or somethin?" Ashby asked. "Ain't I been able to learn you nothin', boy? Don' you realize this is fuckin' Injun territory?"

Erich blushed and dipped his head in embarrassment. "W-Well, shit, Mr. Ashby," he stammered "Everything seems peaceful enough."

"Where's Stuart's men?" Ashby asked sharply.

"They're supposed to be standing guard," Erich said. "But I guess, to be honest, they're probably taking a little snooze, too. What shouldn't they be? Ain't nothing happening. What are you doing here anyway? And who are these other soldiers?"

"They're from Fort Laramie," Dobbs said.

"They're part of a patrol we ran across this morning,"

added Ashby. "They were out lookin' for a couple of deserters. They tole us they run across a group of about a dozen Injuns yestidy. They didn' really like the way they looked but the redskins wern't doin' nothin' wrong so there weren't anythin' they could do. 'Twern't any of their bidness anyways. Least that's what they felt 'til I explained how we had some stragglers. The sergeant reckoned as how he could spare two men to come along with me an Dobbs here to make sure you was all right."

"We couldn't be better," Erich said. "It's been quieter than a Sunday in church."

"That's good to . . ." Ashby began when the unmistakable sound of small arms fire resounded across the Plains.

"God*damnit!*" he said angrily. "Peaceful my ass. Let's go, men!" he said, digging his spurs into his horse's flanks. "We may be up to our ass in Injuns."


Benoit had his right hand full of blackberries when he heard the shot. Inge, who had popped a few into her mouth, had a thin stream of dark juice trickling down her chin.

"*Sacre merde!*" Benoit exclaimed. "I *knew* we shouldn't have left the group. Let's go," he said, vaulting into his saddle as quickly as he could with his injured arm.

Inge looked up, alarmed.

"Come *on*," Benoit said irritably. "Get on your horse. We've got to get back."

Dropping the almost-full flour sack, Inge struggled to get into her saddle, cursing her skirts in fluent German.

"Stay behind me," Benoit yelled over his shoulder as he pointed his horse toward the camp. "But not too far behind me."

Long Nose, moving only a few inches at a time, crept noiselessly through the underbrush that grew thickly along the southern bank of the Platte. Peeping cautiously around a thick cottonwood, he saw Matthewson sitting on the ground with his back against a trunk. His mouth was open and he was snoring gently.

Smiling to himself, Long Nose allowed himself another five minutes to circle around behind the sleeping guard and approach him from the rear. With one swift motion, he grabbed Matthewson's hair and yanked his head upward. The guard's eyes flew open in surprise. He tried to yell, but it was too late. Long Nose swiped his knife across Matthewson's exposed throat, cutting so deeply that he almost decapitated his victim. Matthewson's scream ended in a gurgle. Without ever letting loose of Matthewson's hair, Long Nose deftly took his scalp and jammed it into his belt, feeling the dead man's blood trickle warmly down his thigh.

At the same time Long Nose was slicing Matthewson's throat, Antelope Skin was levelling his bow at Brunelli. There was a barely audible twang and the arrow flew forward, entering the side of Brunelli's head just above his right ear with a dull thud. Stuart's second muleskinner also died without making a sound.

Unaware that his companions had been murdered, the third guard, Fitzgerald, was awakened by the need to empty his bladder. Rising to his feet, he made his way sleepily into the nearby brush, almost stepping on Fat Goose, who had been quietly and slowly approaching. Bunching his powerful legs beneath him, Fat Goose leaped at the white man, his tomahawk raised above his head. Before the weapon struck home, splitting Fizgerald's head like a ripe melon, the guard managed a truncated, startled scream.

"What was that?" Hans said loudly, tossing aside the thick journal in which he had been writing. "Heinz! Heinrich!" he screamed. "Something is happening!"

Heinz rolled out from under the wagon where he had been taking his nap and pushed himself to his feet. As if in response to his action, Brown Hawk and his raiding party, whooping their traditional war cries, came galloping out of an arroyo only fifty yards away and quickly closed the distance.

Heinz scrambled into his wagon and pawed for his rifle. Grabbing the weapon, he turned toward the rapidly approaching Indians, fumbling with the firing mechanism. Before he could lift it to his shoulder, three arrows slammed into his chest. Knocked backward by the impact, Heinz, already dead, toppled on top of his wife, Else, who had been startled out of a deep sleep. She took one look at his copiously bleeding body and started screaming hysterically.

Heinrich, who had been making love to Johanna inside their wagon, rolled off his wife and fumbled for his pistol, which he kept in a small chest under the spare bedding. Seizing the bulky weapon, he fired off a panicky round, missing Fat Goose by three feet. While he tried to steady the weapon for a second shot, Fat Goose levelled the rifle he had taken from Fitzgerald and fired. The large caliber ball hit Heinrich on the point of his chin and travelled upward, blowing off the back of his head and splattering the screaming Johanna with blood and brain matter. Leaping into the wagon, Fat Goose grabbed Johanna by the throat and pinned her to the floor. Raising his knife, he plunged it into her chest just beneath her left breast. Since he had never seen a blonde before, Fat Goose paused to marvel at her waist-length hair, amazed at its color and fineness. He was removing her scalp when a shot from one of the soldiers slammed into his left kidney and threw him forward, on top of the woman he had just killed.

The Mueller and Hartmann children, who had been napping in a group under the Schmidts' wagon when they were awakened by the Indian charge, began yelling and running in several directions. Laughing as if it were all great sport, Brown Hawk's men scooped them up.

Eight-year-old Emmi Hartmann, the only one old enough to put up any kind of resistance, dug her nails into the eyes of her captor, a heavy-set brave named Short Hair. Grunting in pain, he grabbed the young girl in a bear hug. With a massive heave, he snapped her back, then angrily tossed her body to the ground.

Bellowing Moose dug his heels into his horse's side and made straight for the Schmidts' wagon, trying to cut off Hans, who was sprinting across the dusty ground. He caught the German in midstride, smashing the back of his head with his war club. Dropping quickly to the fallen German's side, he was removing Hans's scalp when Hildegard jumped out of the wagon and ran at him, waving a large knife she used for butchering game. Spinning to face the new threat, Bellowing Moose had only half turned when Hildegard stabbed him, exerting such force that the long, thin blade went entirely though the Strong Heart's neck, severing his left carotid artery and sending blood spurting two feet into the air, as if from a fountain. With a grunt, Bellowing Moose grabbed for the blade but his fingers had no strength. He died with a surprised look on his face, cursing his fate at being killed by a woman.

Horrified at what she had done, Hildegard was standing petrified, her hand to her mouth, when a Cheyenne arrow whacked into the back of her left calf, its head nicking the tibia as it passed through the muscle, severing the arteries, and emerged out the other side. Shocked by the force of the blow and the sudden pain, Hildegard staggered sideways for three feet before collapsing to the ground.

Long Nose, who had run toward the wagons after killing and scalping Matthewson, smiled when he saw three-year-old Karl Hartmann running aimlessly around the clearing, screaming for his mother. Effortlessly, he grabbed the crying boy and was searching for his horse when he saw Hildegard stagger and fall with the arrow in her leg. Dropping Karl, he sprinted toward the woman, intending to kill her with his war club, when he suddenly jerked upright and pitched forward, an Ashby bullet in his back.

Realizing they could not reach the wagons in time to stop the raiders, the group of soldiers, along with Ashby and Erich, had dropped to the ground several hundred yards away and were firing at the Indians with their rifles.

Erich put his sights on Fat Goose, whom he could see through the open end of the Mueller wagon. Imagining the Indian was a pronghorn, Erich took careful aim and squeezed the trigger. "I got him! I got him!" he yelled excitedly when Fat Goose toppled.

Ashby aimed his Hall at Long Nose, grinning in pleasure when he saw his shot strike home. Reloading with amazing dexterity, he settled his sight on Brown Hawk and fired, smiling when his .52-caliber ball hit the Indian in the left hand, blowing away most of his middle and index fingers.

"Oh, God! Oh, God! Oh God," Benoit muttered over and over to himself as he pushed his horse as fast as it would go toward the wagon camp. He was barely within sight of the group of wagons, that loomed like ghosts through the cloud of dust that encircled the encampment, when he heard Inge's startled cry.

Looking over his shoulder, he saw her horse pitch forward, tossing her over its head.

Wheeling his own horse around, Benoit galloped to where Inge lay in a crumpled heap. Almost falling to the ground in his haste to dismount, he ran to the fallen girl and turned her on her back.

"Where are you hit?" he asked anxiously?"

Slowly, her eyes came into focus. "Goddamn prairie dog hole," she mumbled.

Benoit exhaled in relief; he feared she had been shot. "Can you move your arms and legs?" he asked.

Inge sat up and shook her head. "My legs work; I think I'm okay."

"Try standing up," he said, pulling her to her feet.

She teetered briefly and Benoit thought she might swoon.

"It's all right," she said, letting go of his shoulder. "I'm just a little dizzy. Where's my horse?"

The animal was several feet away, emitting a sharp, keening noise and trying to hobble on three legs.

Sizing up the situation in a glance, Benoit drew his pistol and moved rapidly toward the horse. Grabbing the reins, he held on tightly as he put the barrel up against the horse's ear. "It's more humane this way," he told Inge as he pulled the trigger.

"Oh, no," she said, tears streaming down her cheeks. "My poor horse."

Ignoring her, Benoit grabbed the reins of his own horse and climbed awkwardly in the saddle. "I have to get to the camp," he told Inge. "I'll come back to get you as soon as I can. In the meantime you stay here." Without waiting for a reply, he spurred his mount toward the German wagons.

Riding straight into the Indians' midst, Benoit waited until he was alongside one of the warriors before leveling his pistol and firing at almost point-blank range. His bullet struck Antelope Skin at the back of his neck, just above the line of his shoulders. Flinging his arms into the air, the Cheyenne pitched from his horse and hit the ground with a loud thud, already dead.

Turning his horse, Benoit spotted Blizzard in the rear of the Hartmann wagon. The Wazhazha had Else pinned to the floor of the Conestoga and was about to bring his tomahawk crashing down onto her forehead when Benoit fired. The bullet ripped through the wagon's plank side and tore into Blizzard's thigh. Although much of the force of the slug was deadened as it passed through the wagon wall, the impact was still sufficiently strong to send Blizzard reeling. As he lay on his back struggling to regain his footing, Benoit leaped out of his saddle into the wagon and grabbed Blizzard around the throat with his good hand. Since he had only one arm, Benoit was no match for the powerful Blizzard. With a massive heave of his shoulders, the Wazhazha easily broke Benoit's hold and propelled the soldier backward.

Struggling to regain his balance, Benoit stumbled. When his right shin struck the top of the wagon's rear gate, he lurched forward and flew into open space. Reflexively, he stuck out his arms to try to break his fall, forgetting his injured arm. When the heel of his left hand hit the ground, Benoit could hear his arm snap anew. He felt a second jolt of pain, following closely on the first, when his left shoulder slammed into the ground. An array of brilliant colors and bright lights flashed before his eyes just before he lost consciousness.

Grunting in satisfaction, Blizzard was ready to leap on Benoit's chest and slit his throat, when Brown Hawk galloped between them. "It's time to go," the Cheyenne screamed.

Looking down, Blizzard saw that Brown Hawk was grasping the spurting stumps of the fingers on right hand, trying valiantly to stop the bleeding.

"Soldiers are coming," Brown Hawk yelled. "Get your horse and follow me."

Looking regretfully at the unconscious Benoit, Blizzard was torn between the desire to follow the other raiders and finish off the soldier.

Brown Hawk settled the issue by inserting himself and his horse between the two men. "You'll have the chance to kill other soldiers," he said, "but you have to stay alive to do it. Let's go."

Realizing the Cheyenne spoke wisely, Blizzard fought back the urge to spill more blood and swung on his horse's back, grimacing at the pain in his leg.

Whooping as loudly as when they charged, the raiders escaped across the Platte, carrying the two Mueller children, four-year-old Werner and two-year-old Wilhelm, with them. By the time the soldiers arrived in the camp ninety seconds later, the raiders had a good head start, riding furiously to the north.

After checking Benoit to make sure he was still breathing and had not been shot or stabbed, Dobbs hurried to the German victims. All three men—Heinz, Heinrich, and Hans—the girl, Emmi, and Johanna Mueller, were obviously beyond help. It took the surgeon several minutes to calm the hysterical Else Hartmann, only to learn that the blood with which she was covered was her husband's and she herself was unhurt. Picking up the dazed and frightened Karl, Dobbs ran his hands quickly over the boy's small body, sighing in relief when he found only minor cuts and scrapes. Handing the child to his mother, now calmer but still sobbing loudly, Dobbs turned to Hildegard.

Despite the arrow that had pierced her calf, Hildegard had been pulling herself along the ground toward the Hartmanns' wagon, trying to get to Heinz's rifle, when her son rode in with Ashby and the soldiers. By the time Dobbs hurried to her side, Erich had levered her into a sitting position with her back against one of the wagon wheels and they were carrying on an animated conversation in rapid-fire German. Biting back tears of pain, Hildegard pointed to the arrow, which had entered on the outside rear of her left calf and protruded four inches out the other side. Telling her she should thank her Teutonic God that it was not worse, Dobbs bent to examine the wound.

"*Das tut weh*," she said through clenched teeth.

Dobbs looked at Erich and raised his eyebrows.

"She says it hurts," the youth translated.

"I'm sure it does," Dobbs mumbled with a grim smile. "Tell her," the surgeon said carefully, "this is going to hurt her even more but it will be over quickly."

As the youth repeated the words, Hildegard threw back her shoulders and grabbed tightly to her son's hands.

Grabbing the arrow at the feather end, he broke off the shaft as close to her leg as possible. Then, taking a deep breath, he yanked forcefully on the forward end of the arrow, pulling the shaft through the calf muscle and out the exit side. Hildegard let out a small scream and fainted.

"Don't worry," Dobbs told Erich when he saw the look of alarm in his eyes. "She'll come around in a minute. It was just the shock."

While Dobbs tended to the Germans, Ashby and the soldiers examined the Indians.

"Don't expect any trouble from this one," said Corporal Sean Flannery, kicking the body of Bellowing Moose, which was sprawled in a large pool of blood that was seeping rapidly into the dry ground.

Ashby walked almost casually over to the fallen Long Nose, who was lying on his stomach. There was a hole a half-inch in diameter just to the right of his spine about midway up his back. Flipping the Cheyenne over with his toe, Ashby recoiled at the sight. The bullet had made a relatively small entrance wound but where it came out on his right side there was a crater large enough for the scout to insert his fist. Remarkably, Long Nose was still breathing. Looking down, Ashby saw the bloody scalp that was still tucked into Long Nose's waistband. Gently removing the hunk of hair that had once covered the top of Matthewson's head, Ashby put the point of his knife against Long Nose's chest just below the sternum. "I guess you deserve this as much as anyone," he said, pushing the blade home.

Private Hawkins, the second Fort Laramie soldier who had been detailed to accompany Dobbs and Ashby, followed a trail of bright red blood that led into the trees A wiry, feral-looking man nicknamed "Spider," Hawkins followed the tracks cautiously, unsure what he was going to find at the end. A few yards into the brush, he came upon the grievously wounded Fat Goose, who had managed to climb down from the Mueller wagon and was trying to crawl away. When Hawkins found him, Fat Goose was on his hands and knees, blood flowing heavily from the wound in his lower left side. Hawkins watched the Indian for several seconds, then walked up to him and kicked him in the ribs, knocking him on his back. Fat Goose, obviously in considerable pain, glared up at Hawkins and tried to rise. With his right hand, he reached for his knife. Grinning, Hawkins raised his pistol, aimed it at Fat Goose's face and pulled the trigger.

"What the hell is that?" Dobbs yelled, reaching for his sidearm.

"Nothing to be disturbed about," Hawkins yelled back from the trees. "I found a wounded Injun and he tried to attack me. But I got him first."

Hurrying to Benoit, Dobbs found him pale but conscious.

Although he had worked himself into a sitting position, Benoit was bent at the waist, cradling his injured arm.

"I broke the son of a bitch agai," he said through gritted teeth. "I heard it."

Gently lifting the injured arm, Dobbs gave it a careful inspection. "If you keep making such accurate diagnoses," he said, trying to raise his friend's spirits, "I'll have to recommend you for an honorary M.D."

"What's the damage?" Benoit said, staring hard at Dobbs. "Among the others, I mean."

Dobbs shook his head sadly. The camp site was the worst scene of carnage he had seen since Buena Vista. In a way it was more shocking than what he had experienced as a battlefield surgeon because this time the victims were civilians, not soldiers whose job was to kill or be killed. Fighting back his rage at the senseless slaughter, Dobbs told Benoit there were eight dead whites: Stuart's three men, the three German men, Johanna Mueller, and the Hartmann girl, Emmi. The survivors among those who had been in the camp at the time of the attack, in addition to Else, were her son, Karl, her infant daughter, Agnes, who had been sleeping in a cradle inside the wagon and escaped discovery, and Hildegard Schmidt. And then there were the two missing children, whose fate was unknown. In a matter of minutes, Dobbs explained, the Indians had inflicted better than fifty percent casualties. If Benoit and the others had not arrived precisely when they did, the whole camp would have been wiped out.

Suddenly, Dobbs realized that Inge was missing.

"Where's Inge?" he asked Benoit with concern. "Was she with you?"

"She's okay," Benoit said. "Her horse stepped in a prairie dog hole and broke its leg. I had to shoot it. I told her to stay there and I'd come get her. But I doubt if she did."

"You're damn right I didn't," said an angry, red-faced Inge who materialized at Dobbs's shoulder. "You shouldn't have gone off and left me. I had to run all the way here. Are you all right?"

"I'm fine," he said. "Just my arm again. You'd better go to your mother."

"Oh, sweet Jesus," sobbed Inge. "Where is she?"

"She's going to be all right," Dobbs added hurriedly. "She's over there against the wagon."

"Thank God," Inge said, running to join Erich at her mother's side.

Seeing her daughter, Hildegard held out her arms. "Your father is dead," she cried as she enveloped the girl. "Killed by the redskins."

"What about you?" Inge asked anxiously.

"She has an arrow wound in her leg," said Dobbs, who had joined them. "I've seen much worse."

"And you?" she asked, turning to Erich.

"I'm fine," he said. "I wasn't here when the attack occurred."

"Where's *Vater*?" she asked soberly.

Erich pointed with his chin toward a blanket-covered form a dozen yards away.


Late that afternoon, three hours before sunset, Dobbs officiated at a brief, impromptu ceremony. After the eleven bodies, including those of the three Indians, were laid in hastily dug graves along the river bank, Inge read a solemn passage from a German-language Bible and Dobbs delivered a brief eulogy.

As soon as the ceremony was over, he anxiously

ordered everyone to pack up and be prepared to move
out as quickly as possible. "For all we know, the Indians
may be coming back with reinforcements," he said.

At first, the soldiers had wanted to go after the
Indians, but Dobbs had quickly squelched that suggestion. "There are too many of them," he said.

The soldiers also had rebelled briefly at Dobbs's
order to bury Bellowing Moose, Long Nose, and Fat
Goose along with the slain Germans, but Dobbs had
commanded them into silence. Since he was a lieutenant and they were only enlisted men, they did as he
said.

Hildegard Schmidt was made as comfortable as possible and laid on a makeshift bed inside her wagon,
which was driven by Corporal Flannery.

Benoit, who flitted in and out of consciousness, was
put on a pallet in the Hartmann wagon, along with Else
Hartmann and her two surviving children, Karl and the
baby, Agnes. It was driven by Private Hawkins.

Before leaving the fateful site, the Muellers' pitifully
few personal possessions were loaded into the
Schmidts' vehicle and the wagon, which had been
the cause of the Germans falling behind the rest of the
wagon train, was set afire.

Although in pain, Hildegard Schmidt was lucid
and conversed volubly with her two children as the
small group limped westward. Despite the loss of her
husband and her friends, she remained optimistic,
continually reminding Inge and Erich that the worst
was over and things were going to get better. When
Inge tearfully told her mother she must be delirious
because she was not fully comprehending the full
scope of the disaster, Hildegard abruptly shushed
her.

"*Du machst Dir über alles Gedanken,*" she said, bringing a small smile to Inge's lips.

"What did she say?" Dobbs asked curiously.

"It's what she used to tell me when I was a small girl," said Inge. "She said that I always worry too much."

# ~14~

It was Jim Ashby who finally broke the silence.

For two days the small group had been intent on a single goal: reaching Fort Laramie without additional problems. It was a solemn procession, each of its grief-stricken members trying to cope with the disaster in his own way. It was late in the morning on the third day, almost time for a planned noontime stop to take on needed if not particularly welcome sustenance, before Ashby broached the subject.

"You gonna report what I done to Cap'n Granger?" Ashby asked.

"I've been thinking about that," Dobbs replied slowly, knowing at once that the scout was referring to the murder of Long Nose.

"An'?"

Dobbs sighed. "The way I figure it, you know a hell of a lot more about the West than I do. I've known you awhile now and I don't think you're a murderer, at least not in the Back East sense of the word. I saw things happen in

Mexico that I'll never repeat to anyone. I figure until I've been around long enough to understand how things operate I don't have the right to pass judgment. As far as I'm concerned, all the Indians who died were killed in the skirmish."

"That goes for the one that Hawkins kilt too?"

Dobbs nodded. "Hawkins claimed it was self-defense. If I bring it up to the captain, hinting that I consider otherwise, it will be his word against mine. But he'll have the advantage because he was there and I wasn't."

"But you're an officer."

"That's true, but Captain Granger doesn't know me from a fence post. Hawkins is one of his men. I'm not anxious to go into this new post and build a reputation as a troublemaker. Besides, the Indian's initial wound was mortal. He would have been dead in another hour anyway."

"I see your point," Ashby said slowly.

Anxious to change the subject, Dobbs asked Ashby which band of Indians he thought was responsible for the attack.

Ashby shrugged. "Hard to tell. One of the dead 'uns was a Brulé, the other two was Cheyenne."

"Is that unusual?" Dobbs asked.

"Not nec'essarily," said Ashby. "The two tribes are friendly, real bunghole buddies. I knew they sometimes joined forces to go after the Pawnee, but I never heard of 'em going after an emigrant train before."

"What about the children?" Dobbs asked. "You think they killed them?"

Ashby shook his head. "Likely not. Children make good captives. Them redskins is allatime stealin' each others' kids and women. Take 'em back to their lodges and try to make 'em their own. From what I hear, sometimes it works and sometimes it don't. Since these kids are so young, I reckon it's got a good chance o' takin'. The way I figure, in five years those German kids'll think they're Cheyenne. 'Course," he chuckled, "they may have a hell of a time explaining their blond hair and blue eyes."

"You think we can get them back?" Dobbs asked.

"*Us*? Me and you?"

"No." Dobbs smiled. "I meant the Army."

"Oh," Ashby said, looking relieved. "Maybe they could if they had a full division o' troops with nuthin' else to do. Fact is, them Injuns is probbly halfway to Canada by now. Might even *be* in Canada by the time we get to Laramie. You think Cap'n Granger is gonna strip the post o' troops to send 'em off lookin' for two little emigrant kids? 'Specially when he starts to thinkin' this might just be the start of real trouble with the Injuns and the fort itself might be in danger of being overrun?"

"You think it is?" Dobbs asked. "The start of real trouble, that is?"

Ashby shook his head. "How 'n hell would I know? I ain't on no Injun council. But," he added in a more con-ciliatory tone, "I don' think so. I think them bucks jus' got a cockamamie idea to see what it was like to kill a few white people, which seems reasonable since they been killing each other since hist'ry began. I don' think anybody oughta read into that attack more'n what's there."

For several minutes, the two men rode in silence. Then Ashby spoke up. "How about Lieutenant Benoit? He gonna be all right?"

"Oh, yes," Dobbs answered promptly. "Physically, he's not in bad shape. He broke that left arm again and suffered some serious ligament damage to his left shoul-der. For the next few weeks he's not even going to be able to ride a horse, but he's going to recover."

"Then what's bothering you about him?"

"I'm not sure what the commander of Fort Laramie is going to do."

"Whatcha mean?"

"Captain Granger may figure that Lieutenant Benoit shouldn't have left the emigrant camp; that it was his duty to stay there and protect them. He could bring him up on charges."

"Shit," Ashby said, spitting. "What he done weren't neglectful. He had no reason to think the Germans was in any danger. An' he left some men in charge."

"I agree," Dobbs said. "And I'll tell that to Captain Granger, too. I'm just pointing out that he might have a different view. But," he added, "there's nothing we can do about it until we get to Fort Laramie. I've got other things to worry about right now."

"Like what?" Ashby asked. "Them Injuns ain't coming back. I can guarantee you that. What else you got bothering you?"

Dobbs looked at the scout, trying to determine if he should take him into his confidence or if what he was about to say was a breach of medical ethics. He decided it was not. "I'm worried about Frau Schmidt," he said finally.

"Mrs. Schmidt? Outside that arrow hole in her leg she seems to be all right. An' that ain't really a major wound."

"You're right," said Dobbs. "Normally it wouldn't be. But I don't like the looks of it. It's already beginning to fester."

"Ummm," Ashby said thoughtfully. "That's possible."

"I was *very* careful about keeping it clean," Dobbs said, sounding offended.

"May a had nothin' to do with your treatment, doc," Ashby added with a smile. "Sometimes them Injuns poison the tips of their arrows. Dip 'em in shit."

"Human excrement?" Dobbs asked in surprise.

"If you say so." Ashby smiled. "To me, it's shit. But it can cause some real serious problems."

"I'll say it could," said a grim-faced Dobbs. "That's precisely what I didn't want to hear."


By the time Blizzard got back to the Brulé camp, his leg was swollen grotesquely. The fact that the bullet had struck the side of the wagon before hitting him had indeed been fortunate since the wooden planking took most of the punch out of the round. Still, it had penetrated deeply enough into his thigh muscle to cause him problems, even though he had dug it out himself.

Before allowing himself to be treated by the Wazhazhas' most successful shaman, Blizzard insisted on speaking to the council. He wanted to tell the story of what happened in his own words before they heard it from someone else; there were few secrets on the Plains despite the lack of a sophisticated communications system.

Since the group already knew about Brown Hawk and his men thanks to the other warriors who had returned, Blizzard picked up the tale at that point.

Sitting on a buffalo robe that his wife, Trembling Pine, had only recently finished tanning, Blizzard kept his injured leg straight out in front of him, covering it with an old piece of deerskin that was impervious to bloodstains.

In a calm, even voice, pausing occasionally for a sip of water from a drinking bladder Trembling Pine had left at his side, Blizzard related how he and Brown Hawk had conceived and carried out the raid. Looking directly at Roaring Thunder, who had been Bellowing Moose's cousin, he told how the Strong Heart had died.

Roaring Thunder clamped his jaws shut, but said nothing.

"It was well planned and well executed," he said. "No one could have predicted the appearance of the soldiers. If they had not shown up, we would have collected many scalps and brought much honor to the Wazhazhas."

"Instead," said Conquering Bear, seemingly unable to restrain himself, "Bellowing Moose's wife is a widow and his children have no father."

"Those are the fortunes of war." Blizzard shrugged. "It wasn't my fault he got killed."

"Even worse than that," interjected Fire-in-the-Hills, "you have angered the *isan hanska*. What you did was stupid. Stupid, unnecessary and . . . "

"Let him finish," Scalptaker said sternly. "After he is done we will have plenty of time to discuss the consequences of this action."

Fire-in-the-Hills glared at Blizzard but said nothing more.

"After the soldiers arrived," Blizzard continued, almost as if he had not been interrupted, "we rode to the north, travelling all night to make sure we weren't being followed. Brown Hawk was unable to stanch the bleeding in his hand and he died soon after moonrise. The next morning, after a brief rest, we continued heading north, way past the point when I should have turned west to come here. I didn't want to take the chance that the soldiers might be coming behind us and have my tracks lead them to this camp."

"It was the only smart thing you did," Fire-in-the-Hills mumbled under his breath.

"On the afternoon of the second day," Blizzard continued, ignoring the remark, "we finally realized that no one was behind us, so we went our separate ways. It has taken me another full day to get here."

"And the children?" asked Conquering Bear. "They could present real problems for us."

Blizzard shrugged. "One of the Cheyenne, Steel Knife, said he planned to take them into his lodge since he and his wife have no children."

"Does he know that he is going to have to take them much farther north than the place where the Cheyenne usually summer?" asked Fire-in-the-Hills. "Almost certainly the *isan hanska* will be looking for them."

"He knows," Blizzard said tiredly.

"Is that all?" asked Scalptaker. "Have you finished?"

"I have."

"What Blizzard has done . . ." began Fire-in-the-Hills.

"The consequences of this . . ." started Badger.

"The Treaty of the Long Meadows . . ." said Conquering Bear.

"Silence!" commanded Scalptaker. "All of you will have a chance to talk. But do so one at a time. I agree that this is a very serious matter with a strong potential for danger to the Wazhazhas, but we're not going to get anywhere if everyone tries to talk at the same time. Let's move orderly around the circle, beginning with Conquering Bear."

"According to the treaty . . ." Conquering Bear started to say.

"Wait," said Scalptaker, holding up a wrinkled hand. "This is going to take a long time. Before we begin, let's smoke a pipe and give ourselves time to collect our thoughts. We don't want to be too hasty in our comments."

Although each of the men was anxious to voice his thoughts, they followed Scalptaker's suggestion, sitting silently and smoking, preparing their arguments.

"Pretty, ain't it?" Ashby asked.

"God, yes," agreed Dobbs.

The small convoy had reached Fort Laramie late on
the third day. Typical of August, the day had begun hot
and dry but in the afternoon a thunderstorm struck,
bringing with it lightning-punctured clouds as thick and
dark as ink, a wind that could blow a child off his feet,
and rain that came down like it was being poured from
a bucket. But by the time the small group reached the
series of low cliffs bordering the valley in which the garrison was located, the storm had moved on to the east,
leaving behind a wall of air so fresh, clear, and crisp that
it felt like autumn.

From their vantage point, Dobbs and Ashby looked
out on the valley and beyond, to the rolling mounds so
dark with pines and juniper that they were called the
Black Hills. A little farther in the distance was a huge,
round-topped mountain that still glistened with snow. It
was the tallest formation Dobbs had seen since he left
Mexico and for several minutes he stared at it intently,
as if memorizing its shape and location.

"Laramie Peak," said Ashby, noting Dobbs's interest.

"And that?" Dobbs asked, pointing to a river that
flowed in from the west, a clear, cool-looking stream
that could not have contrasted more sharply with the
murky Platte.

"Laramie River," said Ashby.

"What's a 'Laramie'?" Dobbs asked, figuring it was a
word derived from one of the Indian languages.

"A Frog." Ashby smiled.

"A frog?" Dobbs asked in surprise. "You mean an
amphibian?"

Ashby looked puzzled.

"One of those green things that hops? You know,
those things that go brrrrp, brrrrp."

"No." Ashby laughed. "Frog as in Frenchman.
Actually, a Canadian. Way I hear it, lots of things
around these parts are named after a trapper named,"

he paused, trying and failing to give it the French pronunciation, "Jacques La Ramee."

"Interesting," Dobbs said. "You ever meet him?"

"La Ramee? Hell no, he died long before I ever got out here. Believe he was kilt by the 'hos."

"Who?" Dobbs asked.

"The 'hos," Ashby repeated. "The Arapahos. They live south of here now. Got pushed out by the Sioux."

"So a man comes out looking for plunder, gets killed by the aborigines, and immediately people start naming things after him?"

"Guess so." Ashby smiled. "Mount Ashby don't sound half bad but I ain't anxious to get scalped to win the honor."

"The fort's named after him, too, I guess."

"Reckon so. But it ain't a lot to be proud of."

Compared to the countryside, Fort Laramie was a dreary sight. Looking down on it from their slightly elevated position, Ashby pointed out its main features.

"That's the 'riginal part," he said, gesturing toward a crumbling, adobe-walled square near the Laramie River. "Began as a trading post in '34. First called Fort William, then Fort John. Then the gov'ment bought it 'bout five years ago, when the emigrant traffic started gettin' hot and heavy."

"What made the government want it?" Dobbs interrupted.

"Location," said Ashby. "This place is plumb on the easiest east-west trail 'tween the states and Oregon. Also sits smack on the major north-south trail. Off thataway, he said, pointing to the south, "is Santa Fe."

"And that way?" asked Dobbs, pointing to the north.

Ashby shrugged. "Canada. Wilderness. Buncha Injuns. Nothin' worth worryin' 'bout 'cept it's a popular trail."

"So the Army wasn't impressed with the original

structure?" Dobbs asked, steering the conversation back to Fort Laramie.

"Nope," agreed Ashby. "That's why they built 'em one from scratch."

Unlike the original post, the Army's Fort Laramie had no walls and no guard towers. "Doesn't look much like I envisioned a Western fort would be," said Dobbs.

"That's what most Backeasters say," Ashby said. "But I guess it serves its purpose. Over there," he pointed, "is the enlisted men's barracks an' there's the officer's quarters," he said, singling out a white two-story wooden building. "They call it Old Bedlam."

"That's a strange name," said Dobbs. "Do you know why?"

"Nope," said Ashby. "But over there's the bakery, there's the smithy, there's the wagon maker's shop, and there's the sutler's store. You can figure out where the parade ground is and the stables. And over there," he pointed to the northwest, "is the wagon train. Stuart must be gettin' itchy to leave."

As they were absorbing the sight, the clear notes of a bugle wafted up to them. Dobbs cocked his head. "Stable call," he said matter of factly.

"What's that mean?" asked Ashby.

Dobbs grinned. "It means it's four-thirty. Guess we'd better get down there and report to the C.O. so he doesn't chew our asses for keeping him working late."

Captain Samson "Sam" Granger was a lot younger than Dobbs had expected him to be. A short, spare man with a luxuriant, jet black moustache that seemed to cover half his face, Granger had graduated from West Point only five years before. Like the rest of his classmates, he probably would still be a lieutenant except for one thing: He had been the officer sent to the Miniconjou camp just outside the fort the previous summer to arrest the warrior thought to have taken a pot shot at the soldier operating the Platte River ferry. It had been Granger's decision to open fire on the Indians.

While the memory of the act still sparked considerable anger among the bands of the Teton Sioux, there had been some members of Congress who viewed the incident as a prime example of Army heroics. Granger's hometown Representative, a longtime but ineffective lawmaker expert only at feeding from the public trough, spearheaded a campaign to get the then-lieutenant promoted on the spot—jumped ahead of dozens of his fellow officers at a time when promotions of any sort were rare—in recognition for his "bravery" against the "savages."

Since the pro-Westward expansion faction in the House needed a *cause célèbre* to keep the movement alive in the public eye, pressure was exerted on the Department of the Army to give Granger his two gold bars despite considerable opposition at a high level, including that of Secretary of War Jefferson Davis. In the end, though, Granger got not only his promotion but the job of commanding one of the most important garrisons on the Frontier. As more emigrants headed west and the possibility of serious conflict between the Indians and the whites grew dramatically more likely, Fort Laramie's position became increasingly significant and the responsibility of its commander, virtually overnight, increased multifold.

Granger, who impressed Dobbs as an overly self-important young officer more worried about the impression he was making on others than about fulfilling his responsibilities as commanding officer, greeted Dobbs and Benoit, who was mobile but still shaky on his feet, seated behind his desk in his tiny office. When Benoit and Dobbs began telling him about the Indian attack on the German camp, Granger held up his hand. "Dinner's in ten minutes," he said, pulling out his watch. "I want all the men to hear your report so we may as well wait until they've eaten. We'll have to use the dining room anyway since that's the largest assembly room. Get your horses taken care of, get washed, eat, and then I'll take your report."

Granger was rising to his feet, a sign of dismissal, when Dobbs spoke up.

"Sir!" he said, sharper than he intended.

Granger frowned at him. "Yes, lieutenant?" he said, stressing the word.

"I have a wounded woman who needs immediate medical attention. Since I'm the first physician to be attached to Fort Laramie I don't imagine you have a surgery."

Granger ran his fingers through his moustache. "No," he said. "I hadn't thought of that. Tell you what, though. There's an empty room in the enlisted men's barracks. We've been using it to store tack. I'll have a couple of privates clean it out for you and you can use that temporarily."

"Can you have them do it now, sir?" Dobbs asked.

"Now?" Granger asked in surprise. "You mean right this minute?"

"Yes, sir." Dobbs nodded. "I wouldn't be in a hurry except I'm really worried about this woman. I suspect the arrow that wounded her was poisoned and I'm afraid I'm not going to be able to stop the infection."

"What does that mean? You think she's going to die on us?"

"No, sir. I mean, I hope not. But I might have to perform surgery."

"Surgery? What type of surgery?"

"I may have to amputate her leg. Which means I will need someplace to work."

"Amputate her leg? Now?"

Dobbs nodded. "Yes, sir. If gangrene is setting in I can't afford to wait. I haven't examined her for several hours but the last time I looked I wasn't at all happy with the situation."

Granger sighed. "Why me, Lord?" he muttered under his breath. "All right," he said to Dobbs in a resigned tone. "I'll put a couple of men on it right away. And why don't you go and examine her now and include that in your report. I'll call the assembly for 1830 hours. Can you make that?"

"Yes, sir," said Dobbs.

Turning to Benoit, Granger gave him a long look. "You're awful quiet, lieutenant. Something bothering you?"

"No, sir," Benoit said weakly. "It's just been a long trip, sir."

"He's broken the same arm twice in the last four weeks, sir," Dobbs interrupted. "The last time just three days ago."

"That's no excuse," Granger said unsympathetically. "You have to be tough to survive on the frontier, Benoit . . . "

"That's Ben-wah, sir," Benoit interrupted.

"Oh, French, eh? Good. You speak the language?"

"Yes, sir. Both my parents are French. I grew up in New Orleans."

"*Very* good. We still have a lot of French trappers out here and I can't understand a goddamn word they're saying most of the time. Some of the Indians speak some French, too, thanks to the trappers. The language will come in handy."

He paused. "Where was I? Oh yes. Tough. You have to be tough to survive out here. Be at the 1830 assembly. Both of you. I want to hear what happened with the savages."


As Dobbs had feared, Frau Schmidt's wound had worsened. When he unwrapped the bandage to examine it, a strong odor assaulted him.

"What *is* that?" asked Inge. "It smells like a cat crawled under the house and died."

Focusing on the wound, Dobbs ignored her. Without touching the area around the wound, the surgeon studied the area carefully. A greenish white pus was coming out of the holes created by the arrow and a red line that looked like a streak of Brulé warpaint extended up Hildegard's leg for several inches.

"That line wasn't there this morning. Did you notice it when you changed the bandage?" he asked Inge.

Inge peered over his shoulder. "The red mark?"

"Yes."

"Yes, I saw it early this afternoon. But it wasn't so long. It only went up this far," she said, holding her thumb and forefinger about two inches apart.

Gently Dobbs touched Hildegard's swollen calf. Before he could ask her if it hurt, she let out a cry. He shook his head and sighed.

"Come with me," he told Inge, grabbing her by her elbow and leading her outside.

The parade ground was deserted. The only soldiers visible were guards posted at strategic intervals around the post.

"Where is everybody?" Inge asked, curious.

"Eating dinner," Dobbs replied distractedly. "Where's Erich?"

"He went out to the wagon train. Frau Hartmann asked him to take her over there. It seems she is intent on continuing the journey to Oregon. She says she and her husband have friends there, some Germans who migrated two years ago. She feels they will take care of her and her children. Or at least help."

It was not a problem Dobbs wanted to deal with at the moment, so he let it drop.

"Inge," he said solemnly, "I'm worried about your mother's wound. I think gangrene is developing."

"Oh my God," she said, biting on her knuckle. "I thought you said the wound wasn't serious."

"The wound itself isn't," Dobbs explained. "Or it shouldn't have been. I think the arrow had been dipped in poison. In any case, an infection has set in, an infection I don't think I'm going to be able to stop. I think I'm going to have to amputate her leg."

"Oh, sweet Jesus! Her leg! What happens if you don't?"

Dobbs shrugged. "Then she'll die. The infection will go to her heart. You saw that red line? That's the infection. It's heading straight up her body."

"Are you *sure*?"

"About ninety percent. I'll know more in a couple of hours."

"That quick?"

"It doesn't take long."

"How much would you have to amputate?"

"If I do it tonight, I'd take the leg at the knee."

"You think that will stop it?"

"I hope so." Noticing the look of despair on the young woman's face, he corrected himself. "Although nothing is for sure in medicine, I'm almost positive that will be sufficient."

"I need to talk to Erich."

"Of course you do," said Dobbs. "Your mother, too. You can't keep her in the dark. Look," he said, trying to sound encouraging. "I have to go to an officer's meeting. Jean and I have to present a report on the attack. I expect that will take a couple of hours. After the meeting, I'll come back and check on your mother. If the infection is worse, I'd like to amputate right away. The sooner the better. Can you get word to Erich and have him here? I want both of you to agree to this before I do anything."

"I'll find him," Inge said, throwing back her shoulders. "He likes you and respects you. We all do. I don't think there will be a problem. But—," she hesitated, "—I have a question."

"Fire away."

"Have you ever done this before? Amputate a leg, I mean."

Dobbs's face sagged. "Lots of times," he said. "In the war."

"Did they all live afterward?"

Dobbs shook his head. "No," he said. "I can't lie to you. Not all of them survived. *But*," he added forcefully, "the ones who didn't were in much worse shape than your mother. Gangrene was much more pronounced. Your mother's relatively young and she's healthy. The infection is bad but not *that* bad. If it continues to progress and I don't amputate, I can just about guarantee you that she will be dead in three days."

Inge nodded. "I'm going to make *Mutter* comfortable. Then I'm going to find Erich. We'll be here when you get back." She turned and started going inside, then stopped.

"Oh," she said. "I just thought of something. There's nothing wrong with Jean, is there? I mean, is he all right? No infection?"

Dobbs smiled. "Jean is fine. I'm sure he'll want to be here, too."

Dobbs had brought in half a dozen lanterns and had them scattered about the windowless room. The more light, he figured, the better. In a corner, giving off an uncomfortable amount of heat, was a brazier filled with glowing goals, in the middle of which rested two broad-bladed axes, already red from the heat.

The bed on which Hildegard had been placed when they first arrived had been pushed outside to make room for a table borrowed from the enlisted men's mess. Dobbs would need a solid, sturdy surface. Several sheets were draped over the table and Hildegard had been laid on top of them. Erich and Inge, one on each side, were holding her in a semi-sitting position.

"Just a little more, *Mutter*," Inge urged, holding out a cup of dark brown liquid, whiskey that Dobbs had requisitioned from the sutler because his own supplies had not yet arrived.

"I'm already drunk, daughter," Hildegard replied in German. "How much do you expect a lady to be able to hold? Do you want me to make a fool of myself?"

Inge smiled in spite of the circumstances. "Just a little more, *Mutter*. Until you can't feel this," she added, touching her finger to the tip of her mother's nose.

"Feel what?" Hildegard asked, her words slurred.

"Maybe she's had enough," said Erich.

"It's impossible for her to have enough," Inge said sharply. "Not as long as she's conscious."

"I think I'm ready," Dobbs said quietly. Leaning forward, he asked. "And you, Frau Schmidt? Are you ready?"

"She said she has faith in you," Inge translated. "She wants you to hurry and get it done with."

"All right," said Dobbs, checking his surgeon's tools. "I want you three," he said, nodding at Inge, Erich, and Benoit, "to leave the room and send in the soldiers."

"*No!*" Inge said emphatically. "I want to stay."

"Me, too," echoed Erich.

Dobbs shook his head. "Please don't give me any trouble. This room is too small and I absolutely need those soldiers."

"He's right," said Benoit. "There's nothing we can do here right now. It's better if we wait outside."

Reluctantly, Inge and Erich left the room, along with Benoit. Taking their places were three brawny enlisted men, the huskiest Dobbs could find when he asked for volunteers.

"You need to be here," he told one of the men, pointing to a spot near Hildegard's right shoulder. "And you here," he told a second one. "Did one of you bring the implement?"

A dark-haired private, the youngest of the three men, nodded and handed Dobbs a block of wood about the size of a bar of soap he had gotten from the carpenter. Dobbs took it and leaned forward. "Frau Schmidt? Take this in your mouth. I want you to bite on it as hard as you can."

Nodding in comprehension, she opened her mouth.

"And you," Dobbs said to the third man. "When I call for the ax I want you to be ready to hand it to me. Understood?"

The man nodded.

"All right," Dobbs said, taking a deep breath. "Ready?"

"Ready," they replied simultaneously.

It was over in a matter of moments. First, Dobbs made a surgical incision through the flesh and muscle. Then, as quickly as he could, he sawed through the bone. Finally, using the red-hot axe, he cauterized the wound to prevent further infection and stop the bleeding.

"It went well," he told Inge and Erich, both of whom were as white as snow.

"Thank God." Inge sighed. "Can we see her?"

"You can, but she's unconscious. I hope she'll sleep for awhile."

"Will she recover?" asked Erich.

Dobbs nodded. "It all will depend on whether I stopped the infection in time, but I think I did. I think she's going to be fine."

Inexplicably, Inge started giggling.

"What's so funny?" Erich asked, surprised at his sister's behavior.

"I . . . I . . ." she said, struggling to control her emotions. "I was just thinking of what *Mutter* said when I told her that Lieutenant Dobbs was going to remove her leg."

"What is that?" Erich asked.

"Remember when we were young?" Inge said, "and we used to make fun of old Herr Schweickhard.?Remember what we used to call him?"

Erich smiled. "Oh, yes. I remember now. We called him '*Holzbein*.'"

"And remember how we thought *Mutter* never knew about that?"

"Yes," said Erich.

"Well, when I told her what was going to happen, do you know what she said?"

"No," Erich said. "What?"

"She said, '*Ich bin ein altes Holzbein*.'"

Inge and Erich doubled over laughing.

Baffled, Dobbs and Benoit looked at each other.

"What's so funny?" Benoit asked.

"It's what *Mutter* said," Inge explained, wiping tears from her cheeks. "When she found out about the operation."

"Well, what did she say?" Benoit asked. "In English."

"She said," Inge began, starting to laugh anew, "'I'll be an old 'wooden leg.'"

Benoit and Dobbs looked at each other again as Erich and Inge once more doubled over.

Benoit shrugged. "It must lose something in the translation."

## ~~~≈~~~ *15* ~~~≈~~~

"Tell me," Benoit said, filling Dobbs's coffee cup and setting the pot between them on the scarred wooden table, "how's Frau Schmidt?"

"Doing as well as can be expected," Dobbs said.

Tentatively sipping the proffered coffee, he grimaced. "Jesus, Jean, aren't you *ever* going to run out of chicory?"

"I hope not," Benoit replied with a smile. "I brought enough to last a year and by then I hope to get a new supply."

"This stuff is going to kill you, you know. And that's a professional opinion."

"What a way to go."

"As to be expected," Dobbs continued, "she's in consid erable pain but that should start easing off in a few days. Otherwise, I'm very happy with her progress. There's no extraneous bleeding and the stump seems to be healing well. More importantly, there's no sign of renewed infection. I think we caught the problem just in time."

"You did well, Jace. If I ever have to have a limb sawed off, I want you to do it."

"That isn't funny, Jean. But speaking of limbs, how are you doing? Any problems with your arm or shoulder?"

"Not really," said Benoit. "It still itches like hell under the bandage and I can't sleep on that side, but outside of that I find it more an inconvenience than anything else. When will I be able to sit a horse again?"

"You're progressing faster than I hoped. Maybe next week for short periods, but no patrols for at least a month. If I hadn't been there the second time you broke it, you might have lost that arm. You been out to the train?"

"Yes," Benoit said. "Granger made a wagon available to me. He wasn't very happy about it but he's so short-handed I think he wants to put me to work no matter what."

"Did you see Stuart?"

"Yeah. Ashby, too. Ashby really hopped on Stuart for going off and leaving those Germans. Told him those deaths were on his conscience."

"No kidding? I'll bet Stuart didn't take that very kindly."

"You can bet your ass he didn't." Benoit smiled. "Told Ashby it was his show and if he didn't like the way it was being run he could fucking well leave."

"So what happened?" Dobbs asked in surprise.

"Ashby told him if that was going to be his attitude, he could cram it up his butt. Said he figured he'd hang around here for awhile, maybe make some money doing some hunting for the fort. Seems Granger likes fresh meat."

"Does that mean Stuart is ready to pull out?"

"Yeah. Says he's worried now about snow catching them before they can get to Oregon. He's also getting some pressure from the travellers. They aren't too happy about paying Fort Laramie prices for things: sixty cents for a loaf of bread they could buy for ten cents back in Missouri. Vinegar, two dollars a gallon, and coffee a couple of bucks a pound." He paused, then added, "And that's without chicory."

Dobbs whistled. "That's pretty steep."

"Sure is, but they really shouldn't expect much better. It's a seller's market out here in the middle of nowhere."

"Is Frau Hartmann still determined to go on?"

"Yes. She talked to Erich about driving her wagon out there for her but he begged off. Said he'd rather stay here and work with Ashby. So I negotiated with one of the Irish kids to give her a hand. She won't be able to pay him much but it will be one less mouth his family will have to feed. By the way, I have good news about Inge and her mother."

Dobbs raised his eyebrows. "So?"

"So I had a little chat with Granger. Asked him what plans he had for handling the reinforcements everyone knows are on the way. You know, did he have provisions for kitchen help, laundresses, and so forth."

"He already has a laundress."

"Yes, one lazy old woman. I suggested to him that he would be much happier if he knew that the facility was being run by two industrious, hard-working Germans. He seemed to like the idea. Said he wanted to wait until he saw how Hildegard progressed before making a final decision but at least he didn't say no right off."

"Speaking of decisions, did he talk to you? About what happened on the trail, I mean."

Benoit shook his head. "Not really. Said he had a lot on his mind right now and he wanted to think about it for a few days. He knows I'm not going anywhere so there's no hurry."

Both men fell silent, drinking their coffee.

"What do you think of him?" Benoit asked. "Granger, I mean."

Dobbs considered carefully before replying. "I think basically he's not a bad type. I've seen a lot worse officers in my time, some that I felt never should have been allowed to wear the uniform. Granger doesn't fall into that category. But he's out of his class as commander out here. He doesn't have the experience or the temperament to be a commanding officer; he's too young and inexperienced. His Congressman didn't do him any favors. If I were Granger I'd go back east and shoot that sonuvabitch."

Benoit chuckled. "I don't have your experience but I feel much the same way. I'm not impressed with his indecisiveness. I think he needs some seasoning."

"I haven't had a chance to ask you," said Dobbs, "but you knew Lieutenant Grattan at the Academy, didn't you?"

Benoit's mouth turned down. "Yeah Johnny Grattan was third year when I was a plebe. We never got along very well."

"Oh," Dobbs said, surprised. "Why not?"

Benoit shrugged. "Different backgrounds, I guess. Johnny's Irish through and through. A bit of a braggart and a bully in my book. I was friends with another plebe, Don Davis, from Georgia. For some reason Johnny took a dislike to him. Used to badger him all the time."

"So what happened?"

"One day Davis had enough. Told Johnny to get off his back. Suggested the two meet behind the armory one night man-to-man, none of that upper classman-plebe crap. Johnny agreed. Davis stomped him into the ground. Johnny had to tell his dorm commander that he fell down the stairs in the dark, his face was so busted up."

"Did that solve the problem?"

"It should have, but it didn't. Johnny only increased his hounding. Finally, Don said screw it and went back to Savannah. Last I heard, he went into his father's business."

"That's too bad; it's not an uplifting story. From what you say, then, Grattan isn't the humble or forgiving type?"

Benoit laughed. "Hardly. He grew up in Vermont and, no offense, New Englanders aren't known for their warmth, compassion, and sociability. He thinks the secret to a successful Army career is being tough on the men under his command. Maybe he'll learn . . ." he began, only to be interrupted by the bugle call. "Well, there it is," said Benoit. "First call for tattoo. I'll tell you one thing about being out here in all this clean air."

"What's that?"

"Makes me sleepy as hell." Benoit laughed. "Guess my days as a carouser are finally over."

"That's better than me," said Dobbs, rising to return to his own monklike quarters. "I never had any."


Atmospheric conditions on the Plains were such that sound could travel a long way. Sometimes at night or early in the morning, when the wind was right, the Wazhazhas could hear the Fort Laramie bugler from their camp along the Platte. But on this night, no one in the band was paying much attention; there was a more important issue that had monopolized debate since Blizzard returned. Ever since then, the band had been divided about what action to take, if any, in the wake of the attack on the Germans. Essentially, there were three separate schools of thought.

One group, with Badger as its main spokesman, held

that nothing should be done, that Blizzard had been acting within his rights as an individual. Badger insisted
that the Wazhazhas, as well as members of every other
Plains tribe, had enemies. It was the way the world
worked. Given the fact that enemies were everywhere, it
was not unreasonable to expect violence from time to
time. Therefore, in the ever-changing scheme of things,
whites had simply become another enemy tribe.
Blizzard would certainly not be censored for fighting the
Crow or the Pawnee, Badger argued, so he should not
be blamed for attacking the Whites. After all, he said, it
was not as if the *isan hanska* were allies, like the
Cheyenne.

Another faction, led by Fire-in-the-Hills, held that
Blizzard was at fault not necessarily for attacking the
Whites but for being thoughtless enough not to consider the possible consequences it might hold for the
Wazhazhas. The attack had not been motivated by
revenge or to seize horses, which were worthy traditional incentives, but was a purely selfish act designed
only to enhance Blizzard's own self-esteem. If this had
been against the Crow, it would have been acceptable
because everyone knew that the Crow deserved it. But
the Wazhazhas were supposed to be at peace with the
Whites and Blizzard's action threatened to alter that
situation. If the Wazhazhas wanted to add the *isan
hanska* to the enemy's list that was one thing, but it
should have been a decision by the council and not by
Blizzard acting alone. Furthermore, Fire-in-the-Hills
argued, Blizzard should have sought support from his
own band, not the Cheyenne even if the two tribes
were friendly. By acting as he did Blizzard revealed a
major defect in judgment that deserved to be punished.

The third group, with Conquering Bear as its advo-
cate, contended that the only issue the Wazhazhas

should be concerned with was the fact that Blizzard's
action was a blatant violation of the Treaty of the Long
Meadows. As the one who signed that pact as the representative of all the Sioux, Conquering Bear felt qualified to interpret its provisions, and the primary one
guaranteed the emigrants protection from attack.
While the *isan hanska* might wink at intertribal squab-
bling, they would certainly call the Wazhazhas to
account for Whites who were only travelling through
the country. In view of that, Conquering Bear suggested that he go to the fort and try to negotiate a
peaceful settlement. Otherwise, the annuity would be
in jeopardy.

"All you worry about is the annuity," Blizzard had
said bitterly. "Are a few trinkets so important to you
that you would forfeit the rights of your people?"

"You're hardly in a position to talk about 'the people,'" Conquering Bear countered. "You certainly
weren't thinking about the Wazhazhas' welfare when
you joined forces with Brown Hawk."

"I am a warrior," Blizzard said sharply. "Not an old
man who spends his days sitting in the sunshine thinking up new ways of ingratiating himself to the people
who are driving off the buffalo and threatening to make
us change our ways."

"He has a very good point," agreed Badger. "The
Whites are not our friends no matter what they tell us or
how they try to bribe us."

"That's not the issue," said Fire-in-the-Hills. "The
issue is whether Blizzard overstepped his bounds by
acting alone."

Scalptaker coughed deeply, a signal that he had
something to say.

"We've been discussing this for three days now," the
old man said, sounding tired, "and we haven't gotten
any closer to a resolution. So far, we've been presuming

that we know what the white man's posture is going to be. Before we make a decision on our position, I think we need to know how the white man stands."

"That makes sense," conceded Fire-in-the-Hills.

"I agree that's a wise opinion," Badger said.

Conquering Bear nodded. "Since I'm the one that the Whites seem to recognize as the official spokesman, I feel it is my duty to meet with the white chief and feel him out on the issue."

"Does anyone have any objections to that?" asked Scalptaker.

When no one offered any argument, Scalptaker said he would send an emissary to the fort to arrange a meeting.

"Are you ready, Mr. Auguste?" Granger asked, staring down the table where the interpreter perched next to Conquering Bear, who sat stiffly in the straight-backed chair, looking neither at the blue-clad men who lined the walls of the room nor at the man who would be translating his words.

"I'm ready, Cap'n," Auguste confirmed, rubbing his whiskey-reddened nose.

"Before hearing from Chief Conquering Bear I would like to make a statement," Granger said. "Mr. Auguste, you will please translate as accurately as possible not only exactly what I say but what I imply as well. Understood?"

"Yes, Cap'n."

"Very well," Granger said, clearing his throat. "Chief Conquering Bear, I want you to know that I am very—make that *extremely*—displeased with the events that have been reported to me by the survivors among the party that was so viciously attacked four days ago in their camp along the Platte River. I have been told that a group of Indians, including at least one member of your band, initiated the cowardly, craven assault that resulted in the deaths of eight innocent civilians, including a woman and an eight-year-old girl. These people did nothing to provoke that onslaught. Instead, they were travelling peace-fully along the road that had been declared a safe haven in a pact negotiated not far from this very spot not quite three short years ago, a pact which you your-self signed and swore to uphold . . . "

"Can you slow down just a bit, Cap'n?" Auguste asked, "I'm having a little trouble with your two-dollar words."

Granger stared coldly at the interpreter, nervously drumming his fingers on the bare pine tabletop. When Auguste quit speaking and turned toward him, Granger resumed.

"From all appearances, Chief Conquering Bear, this was a wanton act of cold-blooded murder. Not only were eight innocent people killed, two young children barely off their mother's teat were abducted and carried away to God-knows-where to serve some sinister pur-pose known only to you and your kind. It is my convic-tion that this is an act that must be punished. Discipline must be both swift and severe because assaults of this nature cannot and shall not be permitted. I have agreed to council with you before taking retaliatory action because of the high respect I have for you and your peo-ple. If you can convince me that this was not an action condoned by the Sioux, but rather was the misguided exploit of a single deranged individual and a few of his similarly misdirected followers, I will not hold the Sioux Nation responsible. Otherwise, I will have to assume that the Sioux have no interest in abiding by the terms of the agreement that was so delicately fashioned on this very ground."

Nodding at Auguste, Granger added, "Please tell the chief he may reply when you have finished translating my declaration."

Conquering Bear sat silently for several minutes after Auguste concluded, composing his reply.

"The White chief," he began, speaking slowly and distinctly to make sure that Auguste understood every word, "has every right to be angry about what has occurred. The Wazhazhas would be equally disturbed if the situation were reversed. However," he said, "let me remind the White chief that we did not seek retaliation last year when a party of soldiers, led by the man who now demands retribution, killed three of our Miniconjou brothers, wounded three others, and took away two, much as the two children were captured, never to be returned."

Granger's face grew increasingly red as Auguste translated Conquering Bear's words. For a moment, Dobbs feared the captain was going to leap across the table and try to throttle the Brulé.

When he saw he was not going to be interrupted, Conquering Bear continued.

"As to the recent occurrence, I would like to tell the White chief what I know."

Grander nodded. "Please do," he said tightly.

"The assault," Conquering Bear said, "was the idea of a hot-headed warrior from the Northern Cheyenne, a group that lives far to the north and found itself in this vicinity almost by accident."

"Why were they here?" Granger asked.

"They were having some mischief with the Pawnee," Conquering Bear replied, "and were on their way back to their own land when they encountered a party of Wazhazha warriors returning from a skirmish with the Crow."

"That seems to fit," Granger mumbled, more to himself than Conquering Bear.

"The leader of the Cheyenne group," Conquering Bear said, "was a warrior named Brown Hawk. His blood was running hot as a result of his clash with the Pawnee and he thought it would be good sport . . . "

"Good sport?" Granger asked incredulously. "Is that exactly what he said, Mr. Auguste?"

Auguste conferred at length with Conquering Bear. "What he meant to say," Auguste said, "was that Brown Hawk found it 'militarily challenging' to test his skills against the Whites."

"That's not much better," Granger groused, "but it's within the context. Please ask him to go on."

"Brown Hawk said he planned to attack the Whites since he was curious about what type of resistance they would offer . . . "

Granger's jaw tightened, but he did not interrupt.

". . . he asked our warriors if they would like to join him. Only two agreed to do so. One of them, Bellowing Moose, was killed in the raid, stabbed to death, I understand, by a *woman*."

Granger suppressed a smile. Good for Frau Schmidt, he thought.

"The other, a warrior named Blizzard, was wounded. I would like to emphasize that Blizzard is not responsible for any of the deaths, all the victims were slain by members of the Brown Hawk group."

"Will Conquering Bear help us find this Brown Hawk and bring him to justice?" Granger asked.

"Brown Hawk is dead," said Conquering Bear. "He died of his wounds soon after the assault."

"And the others? Will Conquering Bear help us bring them to justice and recover the children?"

"I am a Brulé," Conquering Bear replied proudly. "I cannot speak for the Cheyenne. But I will use whatever influence I have to try to negotiate a settlement. It is important that I do this because I don't want the White chief to think the Brulé condone such action. We are a peace-seeking people and we intend to stand by the promises we made in the Treaty of the Long Meadows."

"What about your warrior that participated in the attack? Will you turn him over to me?"

Conquering Bear knew that question was eventually going to be asked and he had pre-formed his response.

"My people feel that this is an issue that has moved out of the military realm since it involves interpretation of the treaty," the Brulé said carefully, watching Auguste intensely as he translated. "As such, it is only proper that retribution be discussed on the political rather than military level. It would be better," he suggested, "if the issue were to be brought before the man who represents the Great White Chief."

"You mean you want to wait and discuss this with the Indian Agent and not with me?" Granger asked, his face purpling.

"Yes," Conquering Bear replied evenly. "Precisely for the reason that a treaty is a political document, not a military one. Among the Brulé, the warriors do not make the policy, they only enforce it."

"It's out of the question," Granger said angrily. "We're going to settle this right here and right now. We're not going to wait for any mealy-mouthed government namby-pamby to come in here and make decisions relating to the *murder* of eight people who were under my protection and the *kidnapping* of two toddlers. I simply will not allow it. My question to you, right now, is will you surrender this warrior, what was his name, Blizzard? Will you turn him over to my men so he can be punished for his crime?"

"His crime," Conquering Bear said smoothly, "was bad judgment. But I have no authority to order him to surrender."

"What do you mean?" asked Granger. "Aren't you the chief?"

Conquering Bear sighed. These *isan hanska* simply do not understand, he thought. Aloud he said: "Blizzard is a Brulé warrior and not under my jurisdiction. I cannot order him about any more than you can command," pointing at the interpreter, "Mr. Auguste. I *will* talk to Blizzard to see if I can persuade him it is in his best interest to go with you, but I cannot make any promises."

Granger pondered the offer, his knee pumping nervously beneath the table. "I need to discuss this with my sub-chiefs," he said after a few minutes of thought. "I will let you know our decision."

"Your thoughts, gentlemen?" Granger asked after Conquering Bear had departed.

"I think he has a point," said Zack Adamson, a lanky second lieutenant who had been at Fort Laramie only four months. "I mean, it makes sense. If the attack was carried out by the Cheyenne, you can't hold the Brulé responsible."

"But two Brulé warriors also were involved," argued John Grattan, also a second lieutenant and also a relative newcomer to the post. "You can't just let these guys get away with *murder*, for Christ's sake."

"Conquering Bear said his warrior didn't kill anyone," Granger pointed out.

"That's a bunch of bullshit, Sam," Grattan said, pounding a fist on the table. "You should have told that fucker . . . "

"You're being impertinent, lieutenant," Granger said icily. "I am *Captain* Granger and, as your commanding officer, you don't have any goddamn right to second-guess my tactics. If I wanted your opinion I would have asked for it. Is that clear?"

"Yes, sir," Grattan said, blushing until his cheeks were as red as the thatch of hair that grew profusely everywhere on his body: his head, his chest, his arms, and his hands. "Sorry, sir. I didn't mean to speak out of turn."

"As I see it, we have two things to do here," Granger said. "First, we need to develop a plan to see what we can do about the Cheyenne. Where they camp is way to hell and gone and I simply don't have enough troops to send a detachment up there right now, what with the need to police the trail, track down deserters, and start getting the fort ready for winter. Once the reinforcements get here, that will be another story. Second—and this is actually the more important issue — we have to do something about that Brulé warrior. I *know*," he said, turning to Adamson, "that he wasn't the instigator in the attack but we can't just let him go and ignore the fact that he was one of the participants. It makes us look soft in the Indians' eyes. Besides that, just wait until the word of what happens gets back to Washington and the Congress starts screaming for retaliation."

"Exactly my point, sir," Grattan said excitedly. "We have to let them know we mean business, that we're not a bunch of goddamn *girls.*"

Benoit opened his mouth to speak, but Dobbs jabbed him in the ribs.

"Best keep out of this, Jean," he whispered. "We're too new here to be considered part of the group. They don't want your opinion and anything you say likely will come back to haunt you."

Benoit looked for a second if he was going to ignore the advice. Then he whispered back, "You're right, Jace. It's just that I hate to see that goddamn Johnny Grattan bully the captain."

Dobbs shrugged. "That's the captain's problem. It's going to be interesting to see how he handles it."

"You have a powerful argument, lieutenant,"

Granger told Grattan. "You notice how the savage referred to the lesson I taught him last summer. That seems to have gotten his attention."

"That it did, sir." Grattan smiled. "Maybe it's time to repeat the instruction."

"What about the Indian agent?" asked Adamson. "That old Indian seemed pretty savvy about the politics involved here."

"What's your point, lieutenant?"

"I mean, sir," Adamson said hurriedly, "that perhaps it would be better to consult with the agent before we take any action. If we go ahead on our own, he's certainly going to tell his boss that we deliberately bypassed him."

"That's tough shit," said Grattan. "We're the ones responsible for keeping the peace out here. All the goddamn agents do is come out here and give presents to the redskins, kissing their asses and telling them how great they are."

"Grattan's right about that," said Granger. "The agent isn't going to do anything to Blizzard. He'll pat him on the head and increase the Brulés' annuity for being so honest about the incident."

"Why don't you let me take care of it, sir?" Grattan said.

"How do you mean, lieutenant?"

"Give me ten men and a couple of light artillery pieces and I can handle all the goddamn redskins west of the Missouri."

Benoit leaned forward and seemed about to speak. Dobbs jabbed him a second time. "Jean!" he whispered urgently.

Granger permitted himself a small smile. "Specifically, what do you propose, Grattan?"

The lieutenant jumped at the opening. "Let me take a party of men to the Brulé camp, sir. We can arrest this

Blizzard, bring him back here, and hold him until the agent arrives. Then you and him can discuss what should be done."

Granger twirled the ends of his moustache. "Sounds like a reasonable plan to me. You don't think you'd have any opposition in the camp?"

Grattan grinned broadly. "I'd *welcome* it, sir, but I don't think I would. You put the fear of God in those savages last summer and now we have a chance to reinforce that position. I think we've been given a golden opportunity to show these people we can be tough. And I think we'd be crazy not to take advantage of it."

"How many men you think they have in that camp?"

Grattan shrugged. "It doesn't matter, sir. How many did they have last summer when you went in? You didn't let that stop you, did you? These people may be good at killing buffalo and each other, but it's going to be a different story when they come up against the U.S. Army."

"You really think you could do it, huh?"

"Absolutely, sir. I'd relish the chance."

"Okay," Granger said, sounding relieved that he had come to a decision, "here's what we'll do. Right now, I have a hundred men on the post, minus those that are out cutting wood or looking for deserters. You take roughly a third, say thirty men including yourself, and go get Blizzard. Understood?"

"Yes, *sir*," Grattan said eagerly. "How do I pick the men and when do I leave?"

"Ask for volunteers. You shouldn't have any problem there. And go tomorrow. No sense letting this thing sit. Oh, and one more thing. Take Auguste with you."

"That drunk?" asked Grattan.

Granger nodded. "Drunk or not, he's all we've got. You'll need somebody who talks the lingo only if it's to find out where Blizzard is."

As if it were an afterthought, Granger turned to

Dobbs and Benoit, making no apology for leaving them out of the discussion. "Either of you have anything to add?" he asked abruptly.

Benoit, after heeding Dobbs's admonitions to remain silent, was surprised when the surgeon spoke up.

"You think you'll need me along, sir?" Dobbs asked. "In case there are any casualties."

"If there are any casualties they won't be ours," Grattan interjected. "I don't need him, sir. He's probably better off staying here and treating that old woman and the men that're having problems with their bowels."

Dobbs bit his tongue. "It's up to you, captain," he said tightly.

Granger smiled slightly. "It's Grattan's show. If he says he doesn't need you, I guess he doesn't."

"Yes, sir," Dobbs replied, adding: "One more thing, sir."

Granger looked at him curiously. "Yes, lieutenant."

"Jim Ashby, the scout."

"Yes, I know who Ashby is."

"Well, sir," said Dobbs, "he told me this morning that he had been down near the Sioux camp yesterday while he was out looking for deer."

"So?"

"He says there's an awful lot of them down there, not just Brulé but Oglala and Miniconjou, too."

"How many?" Granger asked, sounding disinterested.

"Ashby said six hundred lodges. That didn't mean anything to me so I asked him to clarify. He said that worked out to more than four thousand Indians."

Granger nodded.

"Plus," Dobbs continued, "Ashby said if you have four thousand Indians you have to figure that about twelve hundred of them are warriors. I just thought Lieutenant Grattan might want to know that."

Grattan laughed. "As if I give a shit. They can have every Indian in the territory down there for all I care. I'm going to get that Blizzard and bring him back."

Granger turned to Dobbs and smiled. "There you have it, lieutenant. Here's a man who knows his duty and is anxious to perform it. Now let's get to work. We have other things to do."

## ~16~

"Excuse me, sir," Hawkins said, adroitly blocking Grattan's path.

"What is it, private?" Grattan said crossly. "I'm in somewhat of a hurry."

"I know that, sir. That's why I wanted to talk to you. I understand you're going to be looking for volunteers to go to the Injun camp and arrest one of the redskins."

"How in hell did you know that?" Grattan asked, surprised.

"The post grapevine, sir." Hawkins smiled. "There ain't no secrets here."

"As a matter of fact, I was getting ready to address the men at formation, as soon as I have a little talk with the ordnance sergeant. It happens that I *am* going to be asking for volunteers and I assume you're interested. Why do you want to go? It's not going to get you out of latrine duty."

"I know that, sir. It's just that I don't have much use for them redskins and if there's a possibility there might be a little action, I'd truly love the opportunity to kill me another savage."

"*Another?*" asked Grattan.

"Yes, sir. It was me that kilt one of them Injuns wounded in the raid on the German emigrants." Lowering his voice he said conspiratorially: "I took me one of his ears, but Lieutenant Dobbs don't know about it. Would you like to see it, sir? I plan to make me a necklace."

Grattan smiled. "No, private, I don't want to see it. But I like your attitude. We need men who think like you out here on the frontier. You don't, by chance, know anything about operating a howitzer, do you?"

Hawkins beamed. "Yes, sir, as a matter of fact, I do. I was with an artillery company for a spell in Mexico."

"Excellent, Private . . . what is it?"

"Hawkins, sir."

"Very good, Hawkins. We'll be leaving about mid-afternoon."

"Does that mean I can go?"

"If you operate one of the howitzers."

"Yes, *sir,*" Hawkins said, saluting smartly.


Dobbs and Benoit stood in front of Old Bedlam and watched the expedition set out: Grattan and the interpreter, Lucien Auguste, on horseback, followed by a mule-powered wagon carrying two small artillery pieces: a twelve-pounder and a mountain howitzer. Several soldiers were riding on the wagon and the others were marching in loose formation, their rifles slung over their shoulders.

"There goes my transportation," Benoit chuckled. "Guess I'm really homebound now."

"I count twenty-seven privates, a sergeant, and a corporal, plus Grattan," Dobbs said.

"Thirty men against more than a thousand Sioux

warriors," Benoit said. "Doesn't sound like very good odds to me. That's probably why they're carrying the howitzer."

"Good luck to them then," said Dobbs. "Those twelve-pounders are next to useless. They can fire two shells a minute but they're about as accurate as a man tossing rocks. I guess they hope the noise alone will cause the Sioux to keel over with heart attacks."

"How far is the camp?"

"According to Ashby, only about six miles. It's, let's see," he said, pulling out his watch, "half past two now. So they should be there about four-thirty or five at the latest."

"You think they're going to run into trouble?" Benoit asked.

"I'd be willing to bet on it," said Dobbs. "Those Sioux aren't a bunch of fort loafers. They're veteran warriors."

"You think we could persuade Granger to call them back while he still has time?"

"Don't even think about it. It would be a waste of breath and you'd only make him angry. He's happy that he finally made a decision and he wouldn't back down on it now if you put a pistol to his head."

"Look at that!" Benoit said, pointing at Auguste. The interpreter had a quart bottle of whiskey in his hand. As they watched, Auguste tipped the bottle back and drank deeply. Noticing them watching, he grinned foolishly and raised the bottle in a toast. "If I'm going to die today I may as well die drunk."

Dobbs shook his head sadly. "Dumb sonuvabitch. I hope for Grattan's sake he doesn't need a lot of interpreting done."

The troops, laughing and joking, occasionally breaking into snippets of a bawdy Army song, cleared the fort perimeter, marched across a foot bridge that spanned the Platte, and disappeared around a bend.

"They seem happy enough about their assignment," said Benoit.

"They think they're going on a picnic," Dobbs said. "God help them."

About halfway to the Sioux camp site was a trading post operated by the American Fur Company called Gratiot's. Grattan stopped the troops there for a last-minute briefing.

"Okay, men," Grattan said, trying unsuccessfully to hide his excitement. "Here's what we're going to do. When we get to the Brulé camp we're going to ask that a warrior named Blizzard be handed over to us. From what I hear, he's a mean bastard who was part of the raiding party that killed the Germans a few days ago."

"Sir . . ." said Taylor, a husky corporal from Ohio.

"Wait until I'm finished, corporal," Grattan said sharply. "Then you can ask questions."

"Yes, sir."

"What we're going to do is *demand* that he be surrendered. If the old man, Chief Conquering Bear, refuses, then we're going to take him. If anybody tries to stop you, shoot him. All right? Now are there any questions?"

While Grattan was talking to the soldiers, Auguste occupied himself by haranguing the Sioux who had come to the trading post to pick up provisions. As the Indians watched impassively, Auguste raced his horse back and forth, in a style the Sioux commonly use before battle, whooping and yelling insults. "You are a bunch of old women," he screamed drunkenly in their language. "We're going to be eating your livers tonight."

"What's he doing?" asked a private named Hansen, pointing at Auguste.

"Just acting like the drunk he is," Grattan said with a disgusted look on his face.

"How are we going to deploy?" asked Taylor.

"Good question, corporal." Drawing his saber, Grattan began making lines in the dust. "Here's where we are right now. Here's another trading post run by a Canuk named Boudreau. About a half mile from Boudreau's, right here," he said, carving a semicircular mark, "is the Brulé camp. Now, let's say this is Conquering Bear's lodge. He's the one we're going to talk to first. I want a half dozen riflemen," looking up, he pointed at the men, "you two and those four over there, to form a line here. I want another half dozen—you men over there—to be here. The rest of you, except for the ones operating the artillery, I want here. Speaking of artillery," he said looking around, "who's on the mountain howitzer?"

"I am, sir," said a skinny private named Johanson.

"Okay, private. When we get to the camp and if it appears we're going to have to use force I want to operate that weapon myself. You take my horse and stand by. Is that clear?"

"Yes, sir."

"And I want Private Hawkins on the twelve-pounder. Any more questions."

When there were none, Grattan smiled. "Okay. Load your weapons but don't cap until I give the order. And if it comes to fighting there are only two people who will be giving orders: me and Sergeant Duffy, who will be second in command. Nobody else. Now let's get moving."

As they left the trading post, Auguste galloped up to the wagon and tossed the men a bottle of whiskey. "I got some more from the trader," he said loudly. "You men have a drink on me."

Grattan gave him a hard look but did not object.

"Is it all right, sir?" asked Duffy.

"Yes, sergeant, but just a swig. I don't want any drunken riflemen standing behind me."

The Wazhazhas knew the soldiers were coming long before they arrived. One of the Oglalas at the trading post had galloped ahead of the column and spread the word, first among his own band, which was ensconced at the westernmost end of the semicircular encampment. From there, the news spread rapidly to the Brulé, who were camped in the center, and finally to the Miniconjou, who occupied the easternmost end of the site.

"Come on," White Crane urged, sticking his head inside Crooked Leg's tipi. "The soldiers are coming."

Crooked Leg reached for his bow and a quiver of arrows, sticking his tomahawk in his belt. "You think they're really going to try to arrest Blizzard?"

"You can't tell about the White soldiers," replied White Crane. "But if they do, they're going to be in for a surprise. This isn't going to be a repeat of what happened with the Miniconjou last year. Hurry up, will you?" he said impatiently. "I don't want to miss this."

Crooked Leg smiled. "Don't be in such a hurry, old friend. Nothing is going to happen right away. There will be talking first. Did you get our horses, just in case?"

"Yes," confirmed White Crane, "the pinto and the black gelding are picketed behind the brushwood, just over that little rise. If we need them, I'll run get them and bring your gelding back here. That way you won't have to strain your leg."

"Don't worry about my leg," Crooked Leg said angrily. "I wish everyone would just try to forget about it and quit treating me like a cripple."

"Don't be that way," White Crane said, offended. "I was only trying to help."

"I know," Crooked Leg apologized. "Let's go take a look at the soldiers."

"Ata!" Summer Rain said breathlessly, scrambling into the lodge she shared with her husband, Badger. "Did you hear the news?"

"What news?" asked Badger, who had just returned from a hunt and was restringing his bow.

"The soldiers are coming."

"Then I guess Conquering Bear didn't do as well at the negotiating table as he thought," he said, apparently unfazed. "Did you hear how many?"

"Bull Bison, the Oglala, says there are thirty-one, including that detestable man they use as an interpreter?"

"You mean Cut Face." Badger smiled. "The one who drinks so much?"

"Yes," Summer Rain said, making a face. "He's the one. And he has a bottle with him today, too, according to Bull Bison."

"What else did Bull Bison say?"

"He said Cut Face is acting in a warlike fashion, insulting and taunting our people."

"That sounds like him. Are the soldiers on horseback or afoot?"

Summer Rain paused, trying to recall everything Bull Bison had said. "Most of them are on foot," she said brightly, "but some are in the wagon with the big guns."

"Big guns?" Badger asked, surprised.

"Yes," she said, remembering Bull Bison's words. "Two of them. Big shiny ones, one bigger than the other."

"I saw them fired once at a celebration at the fort. They make a lot of noise. It's like being inside a thunderstorm."

"The council members are gathering at Conquering Bear's lodge," said Summer Rain. "Are you going?"

"Of course, I'm going, Ina. I want to see if Conquering Bear can talk his way out of this."

Roaring Thunder, Jagged Blade, Buffalo Heart, Scalptaker, Fire-in-the-Hills, and Blizzard were already there when Badger arrived. Bending over and climbing through the entranceway, Badger smiled to himself at the scene in front of him. Conquering Bear had unwrapped his prized pipe but no one was showing any interest in the instrument. Instead, they were sitting knee-to-knee, cramped in the small space, their heads together, talking rapidly and gesturing.

"I don't care what you indicated to the soldier chief," Blizzard said. "I'm not going to surrender. If I let the White soldiers take me away, they will throw me in a small room without windows, where I can't even see the sky, and leave me to die, if they don't torture me to death first."

"The Indian agent wouldn't let that happen," argued Conquering Bear.

"The Indian agent isn't here," Blizzard said. "The White soldiers are."

"You can't fight them," said Scalptaker. "You can barely stand on that leg."

"I can fight," Blizzard said determinedly. "Wait and see. I am a warrior, not a woman. If it comes to it, I will die like a Wazhazha and I will take as many enemies with me as I can."

"If it comes to a fight, Blizzard will not be alone," Roaring Thunder said solemnly.

"I will stand by him," said Jagged Blade.

"As will I," said Buffalo Heart.

"As much as Blizzard and I disagree on most things I think he's right on this," said Badger. "The Minniconjou acted like cowards against the soldiers last year and I don't think we want to follow in their footsteps. I know I don't. I will stand by Blizzard as well."

"Blizzard acted foolishly in deciding to join the Cheyenne in the raid against the emigrants," said Fire-in-the-Hills. "But what is done, is done. You can't recall an arrow in flight. The attack was carried out by the Cheyenne and if the White soldiers are looking for someone to arrest, they should go to the Cheyenne camp. They think because Blizzard is closer, it will be easier for them. They're foolish, too. They're not listening when we try to tell them they cannot have their way with us, that we can only be driven so far. If they attempt to use force to arrest Blizzard, it will be too much. Every Oglala, Miniconjou, and Brulé in this camp will rise up against them."

"That would be in direct violation of the Treaty of the Long Meadows," argued Conquering Bear.

"And what about them coming to arrest Blizzard?" asked Roaring Thunder. "There is nothing in the treaty that provides for that."

"Roaring Thunder is right," said Scalptaker, speaking for the first time. "This time the white soldiers threaten to go too far."

"I will not take up my bow or my lance against the White soldiers!" Conquering Bear said, throwing back his shoulders.

"Then you will be the only one," Blizzard said in disgust. "We have talked enough. I'm going to my lodge. If they want me, they can come get me. But I promise you that more than one of them is going to die."

"Blizzard is right," said Roaring Thunder, who rose and followed him out.

One by one, the others departed as well, leaving Conquering Bear sitting alone with his pipe in his hands.

"We've come to arrest Blizzard," Grattan told Conquering Bear through Auguste.

"I thought the soldier chief was going to wait for the agent to arrive before taking any action," Conquering Bear said.

"We're not stupid," Grattan replied. "Where do you think Blizzard would be by the time the agent arrived? Away with his friends the Cheyenne, I suspect."

"He will not go anywhere. He is not a coward who runs away in the night."

"He was coward enough to attack a group of helpless emigrants, wasn't he?" Grattan asked, not knowing that his words were embellished by Auguste, who was involved in a feud with the Brulé over two of his horses that were missing.

"As I explained to the soldier chief, I don't have the authority to order Blizzard to surrender," Conquering Bear said.

"Well, who *does* have that authority?" Grattan asked angrily. "I guess you're just another old man who talks incessantly and is afraid of shadows."

Conquering Bear had absorbed as many insults as he felt he could handle. Crossing his arms across his chest, he stared at the red-haired lieutenant.

"You're a soldier," he said evenly, "and you claim to be brave. If you want Blizzard go get him. His lodge is over there."

Nodding in satisfaction, Grattan returned to where the artillery pieces had been set up.

"Are they sighted in?" he asked.

"Yes, sir," said Hawkins.

"Have all the men capped their rifles?" asked Grattan.

"Yes, sir," replied Sergeant Duffy.

"Very good, sergeant. You take three men and go to Blizzard's lodge," he said, pointing out the tipi, "and put him in chains. I'm going to stay here and operate the mountain howitzer if it's necessary."

"Yes, sir," said Duffy, signalling to Corporal Taylor and two privates. "You men," he bellowed, "come with me. We're going to get ourselves an Injun."

Granger and the three lieutenants remaining at Fort Laramie—Dobbs, Benoit, and Adamson—were sitting down to dinner in Old Bedlam when they heard the roar.

"Thunder," muttered Adamson. "That's unusual. We've already had our storm for the day."

"Thunder my ass," shouted Dobbs, jumping up. "That's artillery."

The men ran outside to the east side of the building, staring in the direction the troops had gone three hours earlier.

"Listen," Dobbs said, cocking his head. Although there was no more booming of artillery, they could faintly hear the patter of small arms fire.

*"Sacre merde!"* cursed Benoit. "I guess they got themselves in trouble after all."

"Small arms!" said Adamson, awakening to the implications of the distant rattle. "Let's go," he yelled, racing for the stable.

"Hold it, lieutenant!" Granger yelled. "Where in hell do you think you're going?"

Adamson skidded to a stop. "Well, I guess to see if they need some help, sir," he said with a puzzled look.

"That's just great, lieutenant," Granger said sarcastically. "I guess you think we ought to just go off and leave the fort open to whoever might happen to walk in."

"I . . . I . . . I never thought of that, sir," Adamson mumbled in embarrassment.

"That's okay, Adamson. You're still wet behind the ears. But get over to the barracks and tell the bugler to sound assembly. Then get your ass over to ordnance and see that every man on the post is issued a weapon and plenty of ammunition. I'm assuming that Grattan can handle anything that comes his way, but just in case some of the Indians decide this might be a good time to collect a few Army scalps, we want to be ready. Get moving."

Turning to Dobbs, he asked, "Can you fire a rifle?"

"Yes, sir."

"Good," said Granger. "And you, lieutenant. Are you going to be any good at all?"

"I may be a bit stove up, sir, but I can handle a sidearm and maybe a rifle, too, if I have a surface to brace it on," Benoit answered.

"Okay," Granger said, "let's get cracking." Quickly he gave orders to Dobbs and Benoit, telling them which platoons they would command and what positions they should be prepared to defend. "And don't forget," he told Benoit, "send a man out to alert the wood choppers. Have them get their asses back here as fast as they can."


"God, I could sure use a little sleep," Benoit said to Dobbs the next morning as dawn broke clear and bright, making the Platte look like a ribbon of silver winding through the peaceful valley. "We've been at the ready for almost twelve hours and we still don't know anything."

"At the risk of sounding like a pessimist, I would expect the news at this stage is not going to be welcome," said Dobbs.

"Isn't it a good sign that things have been pretty quiet? After that first flurry there's been only sporadic rifle fire."

"If it were okay," said Dobbs, "Grattan and his men

would be back by now. Or he would at least have sent a runner. If you want to know what I think, I think their gooses are cooked. What puzzles me is that the Indians haven't attacked."

"Good morning, Jean, Jace," a soft voice said behind them.

"Well, hello Inge," said Benoit. "You're up awfully early."

"What do you mean *up*? You think you're the only ones who have been up all night?"

"Is your mother all right?" Dobbs asked anxiously. "Do you need me?"

"*Mutter* is fine. She was curious about all the activity and I thought she'd never get to sleep. When I told her we might be attacked by Indians, she wanted me to move her out to the parade ground and give her a rifle."

"No kidding?" Benoit laughed. "I take it that means she feels better."

"She says her leg hurts like hell but she isn't going to let that stop her. She's already wanting to know when she can be fitted for a wooden one. But what's the situation? Is there still danger of an attack?"

Benoit shrugged. "We don't know any more than we did last evening."

"What about Erich? *Mutter* keeps asking about him."

"I wouldn't worry," said Dobbs. "He's out hunting with Ashby. They were heading west, looking for buffalo, when they left yesterday just before the soldiers. They were going in the opposite direction so I doubt seriously if they're in any danger. I wish I could be as optimistic about the men. I don't think they're going to be coming back."

"Oh my God," Inge said. "You think they've all been killed?"

"There are more than four thousand Indians out there . . ." Dobbs began.

"Rider coming!" yelled one of the sentries from his position on the eastern edge of the fort's defensive line.

"Tell the captain," said Dobbs. "I'll go see who it is."


"Slow down, Mr. Boudreau," Granger said, shoving a glass of whiskey in front of the visibly shaken trader. "Otherwise I can't understand you." Looking over his shoulder he called to Benoit. "Come over here, lieutenant, and interpret for me."

"He speaks Canadian French, not Louisiana French," said Benoit, "but I can catch the drift. You want me to ask him what happened?"

"You're goddamn right I want you to ask him what happened," Granger said, sounding disgusted. "You think I want to know how much he's charging for a rasher of bacon?"

"Sorry, sir," said Benoit. "My brain is tired."

"Well, get your tongue in action anyway, lieutenant."

"It was horrible," Benoit translated. "They are dead. All of them. Dead and cut to pieces, like butchered animals. They never stood a chance."

"Tell him to back up," said Granger, refilling the trader's glass. "Tell him to take his time and explain in detail the events as he knows them."

"Yes, sir," said Benoit, speaking to Boudreau in French.

"I tried to tell the lieutenant to get rid of that loudmouth Auguste," Boudreau began. "He was drunk and insulting the Indians. I tried to tell this to the lieutenant but he wouldn't listen. I told him, 'Lieutenant, do you see how many lodges there are?' and he told me, 'I don't care; with thirty men I can whip all the Indians in the West.' Before they left my store I heard him tell the soldiers, 'Men, I don't think there's going to be a fight, but I hope to God there is.' Auguste made things worse; he

was not a good man for that job. They had not been
gone long when Conquering Bear sent a messenger to
my store to ask me to come act as the translator but it
was too late. As I was saddling my horse, I heard gun-
shots."

"So what did you do then?" asked Granger.

"I climbed up on my roof," said Boudreau. "From my
store to the Brulé camp is less than half a mile and I
could see clearly. Lieutenant Grattan was standing at
one cannon and there was a soldier at another. As I
watched, they fired both weapons but they weren't
sighted properly and they only blew off the tops of a
few lodgepoles. After the soldiers fired the cannon, the
Indians swarmed like bees out of their lodges and over-
ran the wagon, bringing the lieutenant to the ground
almost immediately. Some of the other soldiers formed a
group and tried to retreat, firing as they went. It was an
impossible task. Indians charged out of the cottonwoods
on their ponies and they worked their way behind the
group of soldiers. Within minutes they were surrounded and after that they never had a chance. It was
all over in just a few minutes."

"Were they all killed?" asked Granger.

"No," Boudreau replied. "One man survived the
attack by hiding in a clump of brushwood, but he was
badly wounded. An Indian with whom I am friends
brought him to my store and I put him in my bed.
Unfortunately, he died during the night without ever
regaining consciousness. I can't believe how quickly it
happened."

"In that case, why haven't you come to tell us before
now?" Granger asked sharply.

"Do you think I didn't want to tell you?" Boudreau
asked angrily. "But I couldn't. After the massacre, many
of the Indians came to my store demanding that I give
them 'presents.' I think they wanted me to say no so

they would have an excuse to kill me, too. But I gave them everything they asked for and now my storeroom is empty. They stayed all night, drinking my whiskey and eating my food."

"Where are the Indians now?" asked Granger.

Boudreau waved his arm. "Gone," he said. "Most of them. By dawn, most of the lodges had been struck and they were leaving, travelling toward the northwest."

"The whole camp gone?" Granger asked in mild disbelief. "Six hundred lodges?"

"It doesn't take them long, captain. But not all of them left. There are still some hotheads who are gathering other warriors about them. The Indians friendly to me said they are talking about attacking the fort. They say you do not have enough men to stop them if they make a big attack."

"Too true," Granger muttered.

"Do you know how many casualties there were among the Indians?" Dobbs asked.

Boudreau shook his head. "From what I was told afterwards there were several wounded. Among them was Chief Conquering Bear. I understand he was gravely hurt."

Granger sighed. "Thank you, Mr. Boudreau. You've been a tremendous help. Can you make it back to your trading post all right?"

"Certainly," the trader said, wearily rising to his feet. "They won't harm me. They look upon me as a friend."

Boudreau had no sooner ridden out of sight when Dobbs approached Granger.

"Captain," he said, "I'd like to take a few men and recover the bodies."

"I've thought of that," Granger said heavily.

"Well?"

Granger stared at the surgeon. "Absolutely not!"

Dobbs stared at him in disbelief. "You can't mean

that, captain? You can't just let those men rot in the sun.
That's unheard of. Even during the war we promptly
recovered the bodies. Those men deserve a decent
burial."

"It isn't what they deserve, lieutenant. It's what has
to be done. You heard Boudreau. The Indians may even
now be grouping for an attack. I'm not going to let you
go out there until we're sure the fort is safe. I have too
few men to risk losing you and your party, too."

"I protest, captain . . . "

"Protest all you want, lieutenant, but you've heard
my decision. Now get back to your post. We need to be
ready. Let the men sleep in two-hour shifts but there is
to be no stand-down. Not until we're sure the danger is
over."

*22 August 1854*
*Fort Laramie*

*Dear Mamman and Papa,*

*So much has happened in the last few weeks that it is
difficult for me to explain it coherently. But let me
begin by assuring you that I am well and healthy, "fat
and sassy," my insolent sister probably would say. I
had an accident in which I broke my arm; I guess it
doesn't always happen to schoolboys but sometimes to
grown men as well. In any case, the limb is mending
rapidly thanks to the excellent treatment I am receiving
at the hands of my friend, Lieutenant Dobbs. If that is
the worst that ever happens to me as a soldier, I will be
lucky indeed.*

*By now you may have heard of the incident in which
several of my fellow soldiers were killed in a fight with
the Sioux. I imagine it will be a prominent item in* Le
Machacebe *and probably will be blown entirely out of
proportion. In actuality, something that you probably
never will know by reading the local newspapers, it was*

*all very sad. So unnecessary and so preventable. As a
result of this unfortunate incident, my commander,
Captain Granger, is almost certain to lose his job. We
are expecting to hear any day now that he is being
transferred back East, as we in the West refer to the
United States. Because of the incident, we also are
expecting a rapid influx of reinforcements. Since the
size of the post will increase dramatically our new commander probably will hold the rank of major, as befits
an officer with so much responsibility. I am still a
"brevet lieutenant" and I may be that for the rest of my
career if I don't quit stumbling over my own big feet.*

*On a personal note, I find myself becoming very
fond of the daughter of one of the emigrant couples I
mentioned to you in my last epistle. Her name is Inge
and although she is only seventeen she is quite mature
for her age. And quite beautiful, too, I may add. By the
way, Mamman, how old were you when you married
Papa? Not that I think of marriage. God forbid. I only
mention that to put the age situation in perspective.*

*Sadly, too, several of the Germans which I men-
tioned before also have been victims of a terrible fate.
Eight of them, including Inge's father, were killed in an
Indian attack shortly before we reached Fort Laramie.
Her mother was wounded in the leg, which had to be
amputated after it turned gangrenous. She is making
excellent progress, however, and her spirits are so good
you would hardly believe it possible. As a result of their
tribulations, Inge, her mother, and her brother, Erich,
have decided to remain at Fort Laramie, at least temporarily, instead of pressing on to Oregon. It is a terrible thing to confess, but I have to admit I have profited
by their misfortune because I can continue to enjoy
their company.*

*The messenger leaves in the morning for Fort
Leavenworth with the mail, so I will close this for now*

since I am anxious that you receive it as quickly as possible. I will bring you more details (Marion would call it "gossip") in the next report. Please do not worry about me and give everyone a hug and a kiss.

Your Loving Son,
t-Jean

**KEN ENGLADE** is a bestselling author of fiction and nonfiction whose books include *Hoffa*, *To Hatred Turned*, and *Beyond Reason*, which was nominated for an Edgar Award in 1991. He lives in Corrales, New Mexico.

# For Fans of the Traditional Western:

## Critical Acclaim for Douglas C. Jones:

### Elkhorn Tavern
The Civil War swept through the border states of Missouri and Arkansas, and the hill people of the Ozarks quickly chose sides. But it would take guts, decency, and more to weather the furious winter of '62 and ride out the storm into the sudden spring that followed.

### Gone the Dreams and Dancing
Jones's thrilling narrative of a proud and powerful peoples' surrender to the white man's world captures the pain and triumph of a difficult but inevitable journey, while weaving an engaging tale of majesty, surrender, and acceptance.

### Season of Yellow Leaf
A ten-year-old girl is captured on a South Plains raid in the 1830s. Reared by the Comanche tribe, she survives the pain of losing her world and becomes a unique witness to a vanishing way of life.